walking green flag

A NOVEL

CAMELLIA BOOK FOUR

MARIE VEILLON

HOMEGROWN PUBLISHING LLC

This is a work of fiction. Names, characters, places, and incidents either are the product of the author's imagination or are used fictitiously. Any resemblance to actual persons, living or dead, events, or locales is entirely coincidental.

The author is in no way affiliated with 4-H or FFA. Use of these organizations are done fictitiously for the purpose of the story, not with the intent to gain anything or profit from them.

First Edition February 2026

ISBN 978-1-967217-02-1 (ebook)

ISBN 978-1-967217-03-8 (paperback)

ISBN 978-1-967217-04-5 (hardcover)

Cover design by Cindy Ras (@cindyras_draws)

Editing by Kaitlin Ford

marievwrites.com

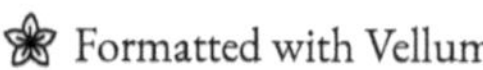 Formatted with Vellum

author's note

This novel could be categorized as a "minty rom-com" or a closed-door romance with the door cracked open. It incorporates Christian themes, especially Catholic views on prayer, marriage and family, discernment, and chastity.

This book also includes heavy innuendo and discussions of sex, chastity, fertility awareness, and natural family planning, as well as some semi-steamy and fade-to-black love scenes, implied nudity, crude humor, and mild language; however, there are no sexually explicit scenes or detailed descriptions of "spice." If it were a movie, it would probably be rated PG-13.

Additionally, please be aware of the following content and depictions, which may be controversial or triggering for some readers: women's health, specifically endometriosis and infertility; allergic reactions and anaphylaxis; epilepsy and seizures; and divorce. It is my intent to treat these topics with the sensitivity they deserve, and I promise to deliver a HEA in the end.

On a lighter note, the writing style of this book purposefully reflects some of the grammatical and syntactical quirks more common to those who speak and think in a Cajun accent. In other words, it sounds weird on purpose.

Love is patient; love is kind; love is not envious or boastful or arrogant or rude. It does not insist on its own way; it is not irritable or resentful; it does not rejoice in wrongdoing, but rejoices in the truth. It bears all things, believes all things, hopes all things, endures all things.

Love never ends.

1 COR. 13:4-8, NRSVCE

*For everyone who has ever felt like
they are either too much or not enough,
let Him love you, anyway.*

walking green flag

ONE YEAR AGO

ROWAN

"IS, UM, EVERYTHING OKAY?" I ask hesitantly after my date growls.

She rolls her eyes, her fingers moving furiously over her phone screen. "Okay, sorry," she replies, her tone shifting as soon as she turns the phone face down. "You were saying?"

"Actually, you were telling me about your tattoo ..."

"Oh, right." Loren smiles shyly, and despite my reservations about letting my best friend set me up with his little sister, I can't help thinking she's a pretty girl. There's definitely a family resemblance, but it's not as weird as I thought it would be.

"It's from *The Lord of the Rings*, the Leaf of Lór—shit, sorry," she curses quietly when her phone buzzes again. "Just ... ignore that, please."

I take it back—this date *has* been relatively awkward, but it has less to do with Loren being Landry's sister than it does with her being Blake the Snake's ex.

Within minutes of our arrival, the designer suit-clad, former frat boy had sauntered over to subvert his claim over Loren under the guise of a polite introduction. I recognized the infamously promiscuous Bourgeois bro from Landry's rants over the years, especially the accusations of Blake and his brother, JD, robbing Landry of his dad's attention both on and off the football field. And based on the way Loren squirmed uncomfortably in her chair as Blake hinted about their ongoing physical relationship and openly flirted with her in front of me, I imagine she's too busy worrying I'll rat her out to her overprotective older brother to care whether I actually like her.

"So, yeah," she says, helping herself to another French fry from my plate. "What were we talking about?"

I force a polite smile. "The series you loved enough to honor with a tattoo?"

She rubs her palm over the little green leaf on her ankle, her expression coy. "Landry mentioned you're a pretty devout Catholic, so I get the feeling you could teach me a thing or two about classical literature and allegory."

"You don't grow up as a homeschooled Catholic and not study Tolkien," I say with a shrug, though I can't help thinking my religious background isn't exactly a turn on for Loren, especially if she's been collecting tattoos and getting romantically involved with guys like Blake.

"So, what's your favorite Easter egg? Wait, let me guess ..." She leans onto her elbows and taps a finger over her lips, and I force myself to look away before my subconscious gets any funny ideas. "Lembas bread and the Eucharist? No, you're a 'Gandalf the White as the Resurrected Jesus' kind of guy, aren't you?"

"Those are good ones, but I have a special appreciation for the obscure, like Lady Galadriel gifting the fellowship with cloaks in the same way the Blessed Virgin Mary conferred the brown scapular to St. Simon Stock, and all the times Aragorn acts as a priest and mimics the sacraments."

"Hmm," she hums, leaning back to size me up. "Landry forgot to mention you had a knack for dirty talk."

I blink a few times before I realize she's kidding. "He did say we should go out because, and I quote, 'she's almost as nerdy as you.' "

Loren snorts out a laugh. "Funny, he told me the same thing."

But the true motivation behind Landry's setup is clear now. He didn't send me on this date with his sister because he thinks we're a perfect match or because he trusts me. Landry doesn't see me as a threat at all, because he knows I'm not capable of the things guys like him and Blake Bourgeois do on the regular.

What he didn't account for, however, is Loren entertaining the kind of men who are only interested in her for one thing. And even if she hadn't been so easily distracted tonight, it's only a matter of time before she picks up on my strict celibacy policy and gives me the "you're too nice" speech.

I glance up when I hear a throat clearing.

"I hope you've saved room for dessert," our waiter cuts in to say. "Compliments of your, um, *very close friend*." He sets a chocolate-heavy dish onto the table as he gestures toward Blake, who's watching us carefully with a smug grin.

"Oh my gosh, is this ... *ugh*, peanut butter? My favorite," Loren gushes, practically moaning at the sight of it. But her reaction isn't what has me on high alert.

"Wait," I blurt out, scooting my chair back instinctively. "Did you say peanut butter?"

Loren pouts. "Okay, hear me out, though. I know it seems weird to accept a gift from another man, but I think he'd actually get off on us sending it back. So we might as well enjoy it, right? In fact, let's make him watch while we—"

"No!" I practically yell, and she winces at my stern tone. "I'm allergic. Like, *severely* allergic," I explain, holding my hands up. Her shoulders droop, and I instantly feel guilty. "But, I mean, if you really want to enjoy your dessert, I can ..." I hitch a thumb over my shoulder, and her frown grows deeper.

"I'm so sorry. I had no idea," she says quickly before adding, "Thanks, anyway," for the waiter.

"Maybe you could box it up for the lady?" I ask as I hand him my credit card.

"Yes, sir. Of course," he replies deferentially before he scurries away.

Loren's expression lightens. "You didn't have to do that."

I let out a sigh. "It'd be a sin to let it go to waste, don't you think?"

That fondness in her gaze grows more sympathetic, and I can almost guess what she's thinking before she speaks again. "You're entirely too nice. You know that, right?"

There it is.

I grit my teeth and hope it looks like a smile, because that's about all I have the energy for at this point. "Thanks. Would you excuse me for a second, though? I'm going to hit the men's room before I get back on the road."

"Yeah, that's probably smart, since you've got, like, a two-hour drive home," she mumbles as I stand.

And I don't need to glance back to know she's replying to Blake's texts before I can even round the corner.

***

CLAIRE

"Uh ... ma'am? Are you okay?"

An alarm goes off in my head once it registers with me—the voice coming from the other side of the bathroom stall door is entirely too deep for my current surroundings.

I clench my core muscles, but it's too late. I'm already mid-pee and mid-cry. I have no choice but to let go and finish my business. I cringe as the trickling tapers off and clear the emotion from my throat.

"I'm fine, thanks," I call out awkwardly once I'm done.

"Okay, then," the stranger with very masculine feet replies.

"May I ask why you're asking?" I venture.

He shifts, pointing the toes of his shoes in a different direction before turning back toward the stall. "Because you just ran into the men's restroom looking very upset ... and very much like a lady."

"Who you callin' a lady?" I force out, imitating his low timbre.

Those dress shoes shuffle around again before he answers. "The person who just sat to use the toilet, I suppose."

His humor catches me off guard, and I barely manage to hold in an inappropriately loud laugh. "Actually, I'm hovering. See how much you know."

"I beg your pardon, sir. That's what I get for assuming," he replies, stifling a laugh of his own.

But I dampen the mood with a whimper as soon as I make the mistake of looking down. Even though I knew what I'd find, I'm still devastated by it.

"Are you sure you're okay?" my bathroom buddy asks after I'm unable to hold back a quiet sob, his voice much gentler this time.

"I don't suppose you have a tampon on you?"

"Ah, no, I'm sorry. But hang on, and I'll see what I can do."

He almost sounds more disappointed that he doesn't have what I need than bothered by the word "tampon." I furrow my brow when I see his feet moving.

"I was just kidding, you know. You don't—"

"No, really. I'll be right back. Okay?"

"Okay," I concede, my voice barely above a whisper.

His footsteps on the tiled floor and a squeaky hinge from the swinging door usher in the silence, and my frustrated growl echoes across the empty bathroom.

I'll give this guy two minutes before I default to using the old rolled-up toilet paper trick until I get home. Then again, Jeremy won't want to leave until he's done with his dinner, regardless of how I'm feeling.

The door creaks open again, my spirits lifting when I think it's my knight in shining armor returning to save me from bleeding out. But my shoulders sag as soon as a pair of cowboy boots drifts past my stall. Normally, I wouldn't be able to stop myself from cracking a joke in a situation this embarrassing and awkward. But I guess I'm feeling a little more vulnerable than usual tonight, because I instinctively lift my feet and keep silent as the intruder makes use of the urinal.

I'm concentrating so hard on hiding from the man who just

flushed and didn't wash his hands that I almost miss the return of my new favorite brown dress shoes. Relief washes over me when he raps a knuckle lightly over the door, and I lower my feet as he wordlessly reaches under the partition with his offering.

I bite my lip and stifle a smile as I take the tampon, even though my crush can't see me.

Okay, so I'm a married woman, and I would never go after another man. But that doesn't mean I can't appreciate a gentleman when I find him. Especially since I can't text my own husband to come to my rescue or even expect him to console me after learning that another month has passed and I am not, in fact, pregnant.

"Thank you," I whisper once it sounds like we're alone again.

"Glad to be of service, ma'am. Or do you prefer *sir*?"

I simper at the walls of my bathroom stall. "Did you steal this from your wife or something?"

"My date. But don't worry, she's too busy watching her ex from across the restaurant to ask why I'm tending to mystery women in the restroom."

"Oof. Sounds like we're both having a rough night," I reply, genuinely sorry that a man this nice seems to have gotten stuck with a crappy date. "For what it's worth, she's missing out."

He chuckles softly. "What about you? Date gone wrong?"

"I wish," I say on a sigh. "It's even worse. I married a guy who couldn't care less that I'm in here crying because ... Well, it doesn't matter. It is what it is."

My stranger clears his throat. "This might be an overstep, but I'm actually an OB-GYN, so I'm obligated to recommend you see your doctor if you're experiencing problems. That's what we're here for, you know?"

I smile. That's probably why he wasn't freaked out by my unfortunate menstruation situation. "Thanks. Know any good fertility doctors?"

He clicks his tongue. "Around here? Afraid not. I have heard good things about a new midwife in this area, though. She uses hormone screening and fertility awareness tracking to identify the root of the problem, so she can treat the cause and not just the symptoms."

"Oh. You're not from here?"

"Baton Rouge."

"I'd be willing to drive to see a specialist if they were worth it," I say.

"I do work with a fertility specialist, but I can't recommend him because … I don't agree with all of his practices," he says after hesitating for a second.

My brow lifts. "Good to know."

We're both quiet for a while before he speaks again. "Well, I'm sure you'd like your privacy now. Is there anything else I can do before I get back to my date?"

"No, I'm fine, thank you," I reply, a little sad he's leaving.

"Should I hang around and guard the door for you?"

I wonder for a second if he might be stalling, and it makes me smile to pretend he'd rather talk to me through a bathroom stall than return to the woman waiting at his table.

"Nah, I'm good. Tell your date I appreciate the tampon, but I'm gonna need her to quit acting like one."

I hear him choke on a laugh. "Tell your husband he's not doing his job well enough. And make sure he understands the critique applies to *all* of his husbandly duties."

This time a loud cackle bubbles up from my chest. "Yeah. I will."

And I watch his feet as he lingers for a second longer before walking out the door.

claire

"SO SORRY TO HEAR ABOUT your divorce, my baby," my great-aunt Verna leans in to whisper, patting my hand softly. "But good riddance. I know it's a terrible thing to say, but—Wait, are we talkin' shit on him yet?"

Half of my mouth lifts in a smile. "Yep. Let 'er rip."

"Thank God you never had kids with that asshole."

"Thanks, *Tante*." I know she means well, but it hurts all the same. And since she's one of my favorites, mostly because we both lack a filter, I try to take her consolation as the show of love and support she intended.

"What are you going to do now that you're single and on the prowl, my Claire Bear?" she asks as she takes a sip of the Bloody Mary a waiter has just placed down in front of her. "Mm, thank ya, *bébé*," she drawls and winks at him. Despite being born and raised here in the Acadiana area, she's developed one of those "Nawlins Dahlin' " accents after living in the Crescent City for decades. It's another reason she sticks out like a sore thumb now that she's returned to be closer to the rest of our family.

I shrug and take a sip of my own drink, a salty margarita, but it doesn't go down all that well. I've never been a huge fan of alcohol, anyway.

"I don't know. You lookin' for a roommate?" I bump her shoulder playfully and smile again so she knows I'm joking.

"Oh, hush, child. Although your mama and I would both love to have you close by, we both know you're meant for country living. You're too much for these city boys to handle."

"Are you referring to the boys I'd be teaching or the ones I'd be dating?" I pose, cocking an eyebrow.

"Both," she clarifies with a tilt of her chin. "They wouldn't be able to keep up with you in the classroom or the—"

"I'm only worried about the classroom for now."

"What you need is to get back on that horse." She wags her finger at me, making her bracelets clink together.

"I don't know. Maybe I'm just not meant for married life ... or kids."

Verna reaches over to smack the side of my thigh, and I wince. "No ma'am, none of that pouting. We don't sit around and *bouder*, hmm?"

She tips her head to look me in the eyes, wordlessly conveying her empathy. Her partner of over four decades, Reggie, passed away about five years ago. She'd followed him to New Orleans after they met in college, and they'd always seemed so happy together, even though they'd never actually gotten married or had children.

It took me years to understand why she moved away, especially when everyone loved Reggie so much. But I figure they simply wanted to evade the endless commentary on their decision to "shack up" and the constant questions about having babies.

"No, we don't," I say, offering her another sad smile.

"Your Reg is out there, somewhere, waiting for you. Don't stop looking until you find his handsome ass." My smile widens, and she sniffs and pulls me in to kiss my cheek, leaving me with an imprint of her bright red lipstick and floral perfume.

I always thought I took after Verna, and I'd basically followed in her footsteps when I'd chased my ex-husband to the small town of Camellia. But maybe my great-aunt had also felt like an outsider in her own family, despite their love and tolerance. Maybe it was the same for her as it is for me—too difficult to face her parents when she'd already second-guessed most of her decisions.

Unlike me, however, my *Tante* Verna is the type of woman that won't stay down, even with a gaping hole in her heart. I wish I were strong enough to crawl back to my family with my tail between my legs. But I'm not sure I can withstand my parents' disapproval of my life choices or that look on my mom's face when I inevitably say the wrong thing or laugh too loud in front of company. Better to stay where I am and take it in small doses.

"Can I ask you something?" I venture.

She waves off my trepidation. "Anything, my girl."

"Why didn't you and *N'oncle* Reg have any kids?"

I barely catch the flicker of pain in her eyes. "We only meant to put it off for a while," she begins, her voice laced with regret. "But by the time we'd done enough traveling and working and everything else you think is more important when you're young, I couldn't get pregnant. We talked about adopting, but they only wanted to give kids to married couples back then."

"And you didn't want to get married."

"I didn't. He did," she admits. "Can't even remember why I wouldn't do it anymore, though."

"Well, I'm sorry. You would have made the best parents," I offer, and I mean it.

She pats my thigh again. "Reg would have been a great daddy. But it wasn't in the cards for us, I guess. Or maybe we were too stubborn to recognize the opportunity before it passed."

I bite my lip and look away, my eyes stinging. "Yeah. Um, I think I've gotta visit the little girls' room. Be back in a minute."

She nods knowingly and lets me go. I keep my head down as I pass the rest of my extended family on my way out of the small yet lavish hotel ballroom hosting my great-grandparents' sixtieth anniversary party, no doubt chosen by my mother, then I dart into the lobby restroom to dry my tears.

I take a second to scrutinize my reflection in the brightly lit mirror. My fitted cocktail dress, blown-out hair, and full face of makeup were enough to shock my family tonight, as if they forgot it was even possible for me to wear anything else besides the button-down work shirts, steel-toed boots, and canvas carpenter pants I'm relegated to for my work as an agricultural sciences teacher—another one of my choices they never quite understood. My mother was at least hoping I'd have worn something modest enough to cover my tattoo sleeve, if the frown she failed to disguise upon my arrival was any indication. But I think I clean up nice, when I make the effort. And this party was worth the effort, especially since I knew I'd be fielding questions and mock concern after finally owning up to my change in marital status. I sure as shit wasn't going to show up alone *and* frumpy.

After one more dab at the lipstick stain on my cheek, I venture out and zero in on the hotel bar in the corner of the lobby. I'm not ready to face my family again. And I'm tired of talking about my failed marriage. But as soon as I take the first step toward the bar, a solid shoulder bumps mine, causing me to stumble backward.

"Oof, watch it," I grumble ungraciously, trying to right myself on the heels I don't wear often enough according to my mom.

"I'm so sorry, ma'am," a deep voice returns before a pair of firm hands grips my arms on both sides. "Are you okay?"

I look up to find a pair of crystal blue eyes gazing into mine. "Fine," I retort, taking a step back and extricating myself from the man's grasp. Though I immediately regret it once I realize he's absolutely gorgeous.

"Please excuse me, I'm ... not feeling well." He swallows hard, and I watch his chest rise and fall, as if he's struggling to breathe.

My brow furrows as I study him. He doesn't appear to be drunk; if anything, he's a little too tightly wound for that. He staggers backward to brace himself against the wall while he removes his suit jacket and lets it fall to the floor.

"Do you need help?" I ask carefully as he loosens his bowtie.

He clears his throat uncomfortably and nods after a second. "I think I might," he croaks, crossing himself as if he's sending up a prayer.

"Okay, what can I do?"

"Use ... this ... please," he wheezes between increasingly shallow breaths. One of his hands delves into his pocket while he takes mine with the other and slaps an EpiPen into my palm.

"Right, yeah, okay," I mumble when he pokes himself in the leg, miming an injection and prompting my memory, and I'm suddenly grateful our school nurse insisted on training me for this type of emergency.

I skim the directions on the pen. It's similar enough to the devices I've seen before, so I flick off the bright blue safety cap.

"Ready?" I ask.

His nodding grows more frantic as I kneel and cup one of my hands around his inner thigh, preparing to jam the syringe into his muscles. And what muscles they are. I can feel his hamstrings flexing through the fabric of his dress pants.

Focus, Claire. Sure, the man is sexy, but he's also dying.

Cringing, I force myself to stab his leg. The stranger barely flinches as his hands fly up to my shoulders, steadying himself and struggling to slow his breathing as I count to ten. He's still hyperventilating after I remove the needle, so I do my best to support both of us until his gasps and gulps start to sound more like measured inhales and exhales.

My eyes dart around when I realize we've garnered an audience. I can only imagine the assumptions they might be making, especially if they missed the part about me being down here to administer an injection. *Tante* Verna will certainly have a field day once she hears about me groping a stranger in the lobby.

"Thank you," the man rasps after a minute and moves his hands to scoop me up to a standing position.

"Yeah, no worries," I reply once I'm back on my feet, ignoring the way my skin tingles where his hands linger on my skin.

"I'm glad I bumped into you. Believe it or not, you may have just saved a life."

claire

THE STRANGER SMIRKS and takes the empty EpiPen case from me, and I can't help but simper back.

He might be the most handsome man I've ever seen, aside from his flushed cheeks and the dark purple splotches crawling up his neck. I mean, I'm not usually into the combo of light hair and eyes or the clean-cut look, but it's working for this guy. There's also something vaguely familiar about him, but I can't put my finger on it.

Is it his face? Or his voice? I'd have sworn we'd met before if he weren't acting like he didn't know me, reaching up to scratch his jaw absently while he waits for my reply.

"Are you always so willing to risk your life for a free meal?" I ask coyly.

He lets out a short laugh as he bends to pick up his jacket, his shoulders flexing with the movement.

"Not intentionally, but there's apparently a hidden peanut allergen in the jambalaya," he says, tilting his head toward the ballroom across the hall from my grandparents' celebration. He's a guest at a charity banquet for a local crisis pregnancy center, according to the sign outside the door, which means he probably paid a hefty price for that meal.

"And you'd think my instincts would have told me to stay inside, since I was surrounded by doctors. But for some reason, I went with the classic panic-and-run tactic when my throat started closing up. Thank God you were here," he continues, holding out his right hand. "I'm Rowan, by the way."

"Claire," I return, sliding my hand into his. He shakes it gently but doesn't let it go.

"This could be the epinephrine talking, but," he pauses to gulp, his nerves giving him a boyish charm I never thought I'd be into until now, "can I buy you a coffee or something? As a thank you."

"Oh. Um, well ... I ..." I turn to glance in the direction of my family. "I'm actually supposed to be at an anniversary party."

"Right. That's probably why you're ..." He takes a step back and gestures over me with his left hand. His ring finger is bare, and unlike mine, absent of the indentations or tan lines that would suggest he wore a wedding band before. "I mean, why you look so lovely. I should let you get back to your husband."

My lips quirk at his awkward demeanor. "My great-grandparents are actually the guests of honor. Sixty years," I explain. "But don't you need to get back to your own party?"

"Eh, I doubt anyone will miss me," he says with a self-deprecating shrug.

"Not even your date?"

His dimpled smile grows wider, and I think he might be blushing and not just red from the hives now. "No date. What about you?"

I shake my head. "It's actually just me and *Tante* Verna at the singles table."

"Well, we can't leave sweet Aunt Verna all alone, can we?" he replies adorably, scratching his neck again.

"Wait a second." Leaning in closer to get a better look, I tip his chin up and find a line of raised welts forming. "Aren't you supposed to go to the emergency room after using that EpiPen?" I ask, ignoring the strange urge to press my lips to his neck. Maybe it's because he smells so good—good enough to eat.

And I haven't had a nice meal in a while ...

"Ah, that's not necessary," he replies after a second, his voice hitching.

"Are you sure?" I drop his chin, but I don't move away as I allow my eyes to meet his. "You still sound like you're having trouble breathing."

His tongue darts out to wet his lips, drawing my gaze down to his mouth as he fumbles to speak again. "It's probably just a side effect of the medicine. Then again, it could also be the beautiful woman touching me."

I stifle a grin. "And the hives are completely unrelated?"

He coughs lightly. "Hives? What hives?"

My hormones get the best of me for a second, and I graze a fingertip down his neck, eliciting a shaky exhale from him.

"What, these old things? Nah, that's nothing," he says before he growls in defeat and reaches up to scratch, making me laugh.

"You should at least let one of your doctor friends check you out," I suggest, though I can't keep a flirty quality from seeping back into my tone.

"I'm fine, really, just a little itchy," he tells me, rubbing his palm over his chest now. "It's not my first time."

"Oh, so you've already popped your EpiPen cherry?" I lift an eyebrow and watch his face grow visibly darker again.

"I'm also a doctor," he offers shyly, dodging my question. "Just not the kind that usually treats anaphylaxis or dermatitis."

"That explains why you're too stubborn to go to the ER, but not why you're here alone," I muse, crossing my arms. "I'll play along, though. Are you some kind of surgeon with crazy work hours? Or maybe you've spent the past year on a charity mission in a third-world country?"

His lips twitch. "I may have used the second one as an excuse before, but I'm an OB-GYN—a maternal-fetal medicine specialist. While my hours aren't all that bad, sometimes I travel to work at different clinics and hospitals."

"Hmm. And you're straight?"

He snorts and pushes his collar aside to scratch at his shoulder, and I notice a brown cord hidden beneath his shirt. "I'm *very* fond of women. You could even say I have a healthier appreciation for the female body and all its inner workings than most."

An unexpected giggle bubbles out of me, but I'm unsure whether it was triggered by the sight of his collarbone or his witty comeback. Either way, he's sexy enough to turn me into a simpering teenager, and I can't remember that happening to me since ... Well, ever.

"And how do I know you weren't faking an allergic reaction just to hit on the first woman willing to help you?" I take another step closer, but his posture straightens and his throat bobs as if he's intimidated.

"I think the hives have ruled that out. But if you're asking me whether I'd purposefully eat a peanut just to get you to put your hands on me again, I'm afraid my answer is going to sound lamer than you think," he says, though he doesn't deliver the line as confidently as he could.

Could he really be this shy and wholesome? There's no way anyone this fine would still be available and not a total creep, right? Not to mention, he's a doctor—a specialist, no less. What's the catch? Where are all the red flags?

"So did you ask me out for coffee because you want to get to know me or because you think you have a shot at getting me back onto my knees before the end of the night?" I venture, lifting my chin daringly. He chokes, to my equal surprise and delight.

"I'm ... sorry," he rasps between coughs, holding a finger up until he collects himself. "Maybe ... maybe I should have let you call that ambulance for me."

I laugh softly, pleased with the way I'm affecting him until his demeanor seems to shift.

"I didn't mean any disrespect. I just wanted to say thank you," he takes a step back and adds once he catches his breath.

So the flirtier I get, the more he pulls away? This guy is a walking freaking paradox. Or maybe I'm just flattering myself by thinking he's as attracted to me as I am to him. Maybe he's simply grateful for my help, and I'm reading too far into this after being out of the dating game for so long.

Or maybe I'm just too much for a nice guy like him.

"Sorry," I say after a while. "A single woman can't be too careful these days, you know."

"No apology necessary," he replies with a less genuine smile. "I should probably try to find some antihistamines and get myself home before it's too late, anyway. Thanks again for your help."

"Right. Well, good luck with those hives," I mutter, unable to disguise the wobble in my voice after he shuts me down. I spin on my heels to go, but he reaches out and grabs my arm.

"Claire, wait," he says, turning me back to face him. "I'm sorry."

"For what?" I ask, shrugging out of his grasp.

"I'm not actually sure," he admits, cringing. "Look, I don't know what I'm doing right now, and I don't usually ask women out on the spot like this. But," he pauses for a deep breath, "I don't think it's the EpiPen making my heart race."

I feel my lips tugging up into a smile, against my better judgment. "So that's what you're going with? I make your heart race?"

He groans and runs a hand over his face. "I swear I'm not a creep. It's just ... I've never panicked during the whole anaphylaxis thing before, but I was already feeling sorry for myself tonight, and I think I'd genuinely started to worry I might die alone. Then you stopped to help me, and now all I can think about is how beautiful and funny you are and that I'd be crazy to let you go without at least taking a shot."

I narrow my eyes as I study him. He seems sincere. And the longer I stare at him, the more I sense something so familiar about him, something that makes me feel like I can trust what he's saying.

Either way, he's the handsome and witty one, while I'm the sad, lonely loser. Let's face it—I'd be an idiot to turn him down.

"So you *are* asking me out ... but just to talk?"

He smiles and scrubs the back of his neck. "Only if *Tante* Verna wouldn't mind sparing you a little longer."

"And you're sure you don't need to go to the hospital?"

He drops his hand. "I'm totally fine."

I pull out my phone and flick to a ride-share app, then punch in our information before I address him again. "All right, we can hang out for a bit, since you probably need someone to keep an eye on you and make sure your symptoms don't get any worse. I've got a room upstairs—" I click my tongue when his brow shoots up. "Don't get too excited. That wasn't an invitation. But there's a twenty-four-hour pharmacy a couple blocks down, so after we raid the hydrocortisone aisle, you can walk me back here ... to the lobby."

"Thank God, because I *really* need that itch cream," he says on an exhale before he returns to scratching behind his ear, making me laugh again.

"And, speaking of Aunt Verna, you'll have to come with me to check in with her first. You know, in case they need someone to identify you later," I add.

"Look at me. You can't really think I'm dangerous?" he asks with a smirk.

"Oh, honey, we both know I'd eat you alive," I retort, fluffing my hair over my shoulder. Although, after having wrapped my hands around Rowan's surprisingly thick hams earlier, I'm not as sure of that as I sound.

"Ah, so I'm the victim in this scenario," he says, his tone more playful.

My only answer is a shrug, and he grins and gestures for me to lead the way. He follows at a respectful distance as I weave through the ballroom toward the table where my mom is seated alongside my great-aunt and great-grandmother, the three of them making up the matriarchy of our family after my maternal grandmother passed away when I was a baby. Their eyes widen when we approach.

"Well, now I see what's been taking you so long in the powder room," Aunt Verna declares. My great-grandmother Daphne smiles and elbows her gently, while my mom presses her lips together in a hard line.

"I ran into a friend," I say, fibbing slightly. "This is Rowan. He's a doctor."

My great-grandmother coos, obviously impressed, and I introduce her first.

"Happy anniversary. Sixty years is quite the accomplishment," Rowan declares, making her smile again. "And you must be the famous *Tante* Verna," he says when my aunt reaches out to take his hand for longer than appropriate.

"You bet your adorable ass I am," Verna replies before glaring at me and adding, "Nice work, cowgirl."

My mom rolls her eyes, though I can't tell whether her disapproval stems from our eccentric aunt or the fact that I'm toting around a man who isn't my husband. "Hi, I'm Claire's mom, and apparently the only one of us with manners," she offers after a moment of awkward silence.

Rowan chuckles good-naturedly. "It's a pleasure to meet all of you. I hope you don't mind if I borrow Claire for a bit. I'm, uh, kind of having a rough night, and she's offered to doctor me up." He gestures to the rash covering his face and neck.

"Food allergy," I volunteer when they all look confused. "We're going out for antihistamines. Don't wait up."

I grab Rowan's hand and drag him out to the lobby, snorting to myself when my Aunt Verna calls out, "Go get 'em, Claire Bear!"

rowan

"CLAIRE LEBLANC?"

"That's me," confirms the gorgeous brunette who saved my life a few minutes ago as she directs me toward a small SUV in front of the hotel. "For a few more days at least," she adds to herself.

"I thought we were walking to the pharmacy?"

She ignores my question and ushers me toward the back seat, though I instinctively stand by and wait for her to duck in first. She rolls her eyes, but I catch the way one corner of her mouth turns up before I shut the car door and walk around to join her on the other side.

"Is this an actual emergency? You're not sick, are you?" the driver inquires after introducing herself as Tiana. I narrow my eyes at the destination set on the GPS screen as I buckle my seat belt.

"I told you I was fine." The protest comes harsher than I intend, and I clear my throat self-consciously.

"And I obviously don't believe you," Claire replies before turning to Tiana. "Don't worry, no one's contagious. It's a food-allergy situation, and I'm forcing this *tête dur* to get checked out for my peace of mind."

Maybe I am being stubborn. While that injection seems to have successfully alleviated my most life-threatening symptoms, anaphylaxis and hives aren't the only complications I've experienced in my prior peanut confrontations. And I'd definitely prefer to mitigate the risk of any gastrointestinal side effects tonight.

"Okay, so I'm not fine," I admit reluctantly. "But a dose of Benadryl and some hydrocortisone cream would have—"

"I can hear your tummy rumbling from here, Rowan. Do you really want my first impression of you to include dermatitis *and* diarrhea?"

Tiana snorts, and I groan and let my head fall back when my stomach gurgles loudly. At this rate, I really am going to die alone, even if it's not tonight. I say a quick prayer under my breath that my gut at least holds out a while longer.

"Hey," Claire continues in a more soothing tone. "I'm not trying to make you feel bad. But I can't let you suffer for the sake of your pride."

"My pride took enough of a hit when I realized you're only hanging out with me so you can make sure I get medical assistance."

She surprises me by reaching over to interlace her fingers with mine and offering me a rueful smile. "Maybe this isn't about you. Maybe I'm just too thirsty to let a trip to the ER ruin the vibe with a cute doctor."

I'm not sure how I feel about the way she keeps reasserting herself, since most of my prior dating experience has been shaped by more traditional gender roles. Still, my stomach dips as she stares me down, and I don't think it's the peanut oil from that jambalaya stirring up the butterflies now.

"Cute? Is that what you call it when a guy's gut troubles flare up in the middle of his attempts to get closer to a woman, especially when she's clearly out of his league?" I ask, unable to hold back a smile. I'm not usually this forward either, but there's something about her that seems to bring it out of me.

"No, but I thought it was more flattering than 'refreshingly honest and inadvertently hot,' " she replies smoothly, lifting her shoulder in a shrug. My gaze follows the movement down a bright collage of twisting vines and colorful flowers, and an appreciative growl rumbles through my chest without my permission.

I can't remember thinking much of tattoos before, but I'm mesmerized by hers. The way the delicate lines wrap around her toned arm might be one of the sexiest things I've ever seen, and I can't help wondering whether there's a story behind the artwork or if she's hiding more of it beneath her dress.

Another involuntary growl escapes, this one originating from my stomach, but I suppose I deserve it after those last few improper thoughts. Claire stifles a giggle as I shift uncomfortably in my seat.

"You can't possibly think this is attractive," I say, gesturing over the red rash covering my chest.

"For the record, I'd probably have gone with you no matter what, even if you'd have called my bluff on that joke about getting me back onto my knees," she leans in to whisper near my ear, and my breath hitches when I realize this is where the fairy tale ends.

Because gorgeous and witty as she may be, Claire is obviously not the kind of woman I'm looking for. And I definitely can't give her what she wants.

I try to disguise my embarrassment by scratching at my jaw, grateful when the car rolls to a stop.

"As much as I regret not being able to witness the rest of this as it unfolds, we have reached your destination," Tiana announces. "Good luck with your shitty situation, and please remember to leave a positive review."

Claire chuckles at our driver as she gathers her things.

"Listen, you don't have to stay with me," I turn to tell her. "I know we joked about it, but you deserve better than an evening in a hospital waiting room. Besides, *Tante* Verna would never forgive me if I subjected you to this."

But I'm afraid I've already let things go too far. She frowns, looking disappointed when I brush over her suggestive offer once again.

"I can't just leave you here, though," she says quietly.

"My brother and his wife live a few minutes away. In fact, he's a doctor, too. I can get him to pick me up later." I don't admit that Cyprien's a podiatrist, but Claire doesn't need to know that right now.

"Oh, well. I guess I thought ..." She looks away, her eyelashes fluttering as if she's actually hurt by my dismissal.

"Bruh," Tiana groans from the front seat. "You can't really be this dumb, can you?"

My head rears back in surprise. "I'm ... sorry?"

"Don't leave my girl hanging," Tiana continues, "especially after she was willing to overlook your tummy issues and take you to the hospital."

My jaw lowers. "But I didn't mean to—"

"Lead me on?" Claire interrupts and finishes for me. "So you didn't mean it when you said you'd do anything for the chance to talk to me a little longer?"

I swallow hard. "No, it was the truth, but ... I'm not ... I can't ..."

Tiana clicks her tongue and looks up to direct her advice at Claire through the rearview mirror. "I get it now. Poor baby's embarrassed. He's probably afraid of letting you down later if things don't go well in there, you know?" She cringes and whispers the last part, reinforcing the suggestive nature of her comment.

Claire glances back at me with a furrowed brow and waits for me to respond.

"Technically, epinephrine *is* a vasoconstrictor, which means it's more than likely restricting the blood flow to some of my ... vital parts," I explain awkwardly. "But that's not exactly what I'm worried about."

"You're afraid of getting the bubble guts in front of me, then?" Claire offers and presses her lips together in an effort to keep herself from laughing, but it doesn't work. She tilts her head back and cackles, and it's so contagious that Tiana and I join in.

Gah, she's beautiful, I catch myself thinking as I stare at her. I've never heard a girl this pretty talk the way she does, but it's surprisingly not a turn off. In fact, I might actually like that she speaks her mind so freely. It kind of reminds me of the way my mom and sisters interact, though Claire's language is a little more colorful.

It takes an amused glare from her to bring me back from my thoughts.

"The looming threat of gastrointestinal distress is another valid concern, yes," I concede after a while.

"Stop worrying," Claire tells me with a reassuring grin. "I won't hold any of your bodily functions against you. Besides, we've come too far for you to let me off the hook now."

I let out a measured exhale, my heart quickening at the idea of having her by my side for the rest of the night, even if it's spent in the emergency room. So what if she's more worldly and experienced than the women I usually date? That doesn't mean I can't enjoy her company for a few more hours. Now that I think about it, it'd be pretty judgmental of me to write her off because she might be into casual hookups or simply because she has a crude sense of humor in comparison with the women I've dated in the past. And it's not likely we'll find ourselves in a place of temptation with the aforementioned symptoms I'm experiencing, so there's no point in stressing over having to explain my stringent moral code.

"Only if you're sure you don't mind the lack of romantic ambiance," I say, softening my expression, and she shrugs.

"I'm not really into the romance thing, anyway," she replies.

My smile widens when Tiana lets out a short squeal, and I go around and get Claire's door, stopping to slip Tiana a few twenties from my wallet.

"Don't charge her card if you can help it," I ask our driver, and she nods approvingly.

"Good luck, you two," she calls out from her window. "I'll be on standby to give you a ride back later."

Tiana drives away, and I lead Claire on through the emergency room entrance before stopping at the triage desk to check in. Once I reassure the intake nurse that epinephrine seems to have done its job and I'm only here as a precaution, I'm directed to have a seat in the waiting area.

Claire settles next to me on a bench, running her palms over her arms. "Are you cold?" I ask, instinctively looking for my jacket.

"A little, but this is what I get for wearing my hoochie dress," she says with a laugh, taking the opportunity to scoot closer and press her side into mine when I reach up to scratch my neck.

My brow lifts as she makes herself comfortable. "Well, I'd give you my jacket, but I don't seem to have it."

"Tiana just messaged me. You left it in her car," she replies matter-of-factly, tugging my arm and forcing me to wrap it around her.

"Right. I guess I was distracted," I mumble and force my eyes away from the clear view of her cleavage. But I'm just as unnerved at the sight of her hand sliding casually over my knee.

"Do you ever work at this hospital?" she asks, glancing up at me.

"Uh, not really. I mean, I did a rotation here years ago, but that's all," I flounder through what should have been a simple answer.

She hums. "Where do you work now?"

"At a big women's and children's clinic on the edge of town," I reply, though I can't seem to remember the name.

"With Dr. Rozas?" she asks, referring to the infertility specialist in the practice who's equally famous for pressuring his patients into IVF treatments and for his IVF success rate.

"Yeah." Now I'm wondering about her history with an infertility specialist.

"I thought you seemed familiar. I've only seen him once, but I'm guessing your portrait's hanging on the wall with the rest of the doctors there?"

I nod. "It is."

"You mentioned traveling for work earlier," she presses on.

"I'm going to start seeing patients at some smaller, more rural clinics. I want to make specialized care more accessible. I hate that my high-risk patients have to go so far when they're already under so much stress, you know?"

Her expression softens. "That's thoughtful of you."

I open my mouth to downplay her compliment, but another loud gut gurgle interrupts me. "Ah, sorry. Excuse me for a second," I say quietly and scoot away from her, and I hear her snickering behind me when I scurry over to the bathroom.

rowan

"WELL, THAT WAS QUICK," Claire declares when I return, and my cheeks heat.

"Thanks, I guess."

Lucky for me, it was a single-user restroom, and my stomach was only crying wolf. Still, I'd turned on the faucet to muffle the sound as I conducted my business, just in case.

"I kind of expected you to camp out for a while. Did you just go in there to fart or something?"

I shrug and glance around the waiting room, grateful to find it empty. "I figured I'd spare you, since this is our first date."

"And they say chivalry is dead," she replies, miming a swoon, and my awkward smile grows more genuine.

The door swings open then, and a middle-aged woman in scrubs squints down at a chart. "Atha—Atta—"

"Athanasius?" I offer, raising my hand and smiling apologetically.

"If you say so, shug," she replies.

"I thought your name was Rowan?" Claire whispers harshly.

"My parents named some of their kids after the more obscure saints, so it's easier to go by my middle name," I explain quickly.

The nurse keeps her feet planted when we reach the door. "I'm sorry, baby, but only family is allowed past this point."

"Oh, but she's my ..." I glance back at Claire, debating whether it's worth lying to keep her at my side. Maybe it's best if she doesn't bear witness to the rest of this, anyway.

Claire clears her throat. "Fiancée. He proposed at Christmas, but my rock's getting resized," she says, waving her ringless left hand as she clasps mine with the other.

"Congratulations, then," the nurse says with a conspiratorial wink and ushers us through the next set of doors.

Guilt settles in my stomach as I force a smile in return, but the warmth from Claire's fingers intertwining with mine is a nice distraction. And I'm suddenly glad she's insisted on accompanying me.

"I'm Mrs. Ethel, and I'll be taking care of you this evening," the nurse tells me as she leads us back to a curtained partition. She pats a narrow cot. "Have a seat right here, *cher*, and tell me what's been goin' on."

"I think I ate something that triggered my peanut allergy. Luckily, I found a beautiful woman willing to administer my EpiPen just before my throat closed up," I explain, careful to avoid lying. "And I told her I was fine, but she insisted I come in to get checked out. She's such a worrier, that one." I whisper the last part as an aside to Mrs. Ethel, who chuckles as she clamps a pulsometer over my fingertip, and Claire clicks her tongue in annoyance.

"Sooner you learn she's always right, the better," Mrs. Ethel remarks and straps a cuff around my arm next. "Ooh, chile!" she exclaims, making me flinch. "Your pulse is through the roof."

I sigh. "I've noticed."

"That epinephrine will do it to you every time," she muses as she slips on a pair of reading glasses and begins jotting down my vitals.

I lift one shoulder in a shrug. "EpiPen aside, I'm afraid my heart rate hasn't been right since I met her," I admit, tilting my head in Claire's direction and making the nurse laugh again.

"*Cher pitié.* You better watch this one, shug," Mrs. Ethel tells Claire, her voice filled with amusement.

"Yeah. I've got my work cut out for me," Claire replies, shooting me a sultry look and making my heart quicken again.

"Pretty sure I'm the one in trouble," I mumble to myself.

Mrs. Ethel hums in approval. "All right, I just need to update your medical history, baby. Full address, phone number, and date of birth?" I confirm the details for her while Claire sits silently.

"Marital status, single, but not for long. Religion?"

"Roman Catholic," I reply quickly.

"Occupation?"

"Medical doctor." That one earns me another appreciative hum.

"Any other allergies besides peanuts?"

"No, ma'am." I shake my head as I continue answering her follow-up questions.

"Do you drink alcohol? Smoke?"

"No, ma'am."

"Are you sexually active?"

An audible gulp is the only sound I'm able to make.

The nurse pauses to glance up over her glasses when I don't answer immediately, her eyes darting back and forth between Claire and me while I reach up to scratch the back of my neck.

"Should we run an STI panel while you're here?"

"No need—I mean, no, thank you," I choke out after the silence stretches too long. Mrs. Ethel cocks an eyebrow and scribbles over her clipboard, and I stifle a whimper.

"I assume you're wanting to change your emergency contact. You have a Dr. Reed listed here, but we can replace his info with your fiancée's."

I cough lightly. "Oh, actually, you can just leave my, um, my brother-in-law's number on there." I can't help but cringe inwardly at Landry's new title.

Mrs. Ethel furrows her brow at me. "You sure?"

"I'm a teacher. I'm not always allowed to have my phone on me during class," Claire chimes in, to my relief. "Dr. Reed knows how to get in touch with me in case of an emergency."

"All right, then," Mrs. Ethel confirms, removing her reading glasses. "Lucky for you, it's been a quiet evening, and our best attending physician just started his shift. So he'll be coming through any minute now."

"Thank you," I mumble before Claire and I are left alone in our curtained quarters.

"Well, this is turning out to be pretty efficient," Claire muses. "I don't think I've ever gotten to know someone so quickly. I might take all of my dates here from now on."

"Feels a little one-sided, though. I shouldn't be the only one having to answer all the questions," I grumble after she mentions other dates.

"You know what I do for a living now, don't you?"

The corners of my lips turn up at that. "So you really are a teacher?"

She nods.

"You must like kids," I venture.

"I do," she says with a wistful sigh. "You?"

"Yeah," I agree. "I'm definitely looking forward to having a family one day."

"I could see that for you," she agrees, and I detect a hint of sadness in her tone.

"Do you ... want a family?"

She lifts a shoulder. "I used to. But things didn't pan out," she says quietly. "My ex and I never had any kids," she adds when she notices my curious stare.

"Oh, I'm sorry."

She shrugs again. "It is what it is, you know."

"How long were you together?" I ask carefully.

She sucks in a deep breath. "Just over ten years, but we were only married for the last few."

My heart skips a beat when she mentions being married. "And you split up ... recently?"

"It's been a while. We had to be separated for at least six months before we could get a divorce," she explains, her voice sounding smaller than it has all night. And even though my brain automatically counts her being divorced as another point against our compatibility, I'm more consumed by an unexpected surge of possessiveness and the need to protect her from anyone or anything that could hurt her again.

The monitor beeps when my pulse spikes, but I'm grateful when she ignores it and forces a more cheerful tone. "Have you ever been married?"

"No, but I'd like to be," I tell her with a smile.

"Earlier, you said you'd been feeling sorry for yourself because you were alone. Is it because you've gone through a recent breakup, too?"

I scrunch up my nose in embarrassment when I realize how pathetic I must sound. "No, not really. Actually, it's kind of a long story."

"I've got time," she assures me, tucking her legs beneath her.

"I honestly don't even know where to start," I say with a soft laugh. I hand her the thin blanket from the foot of the bed when I notice her arms are lined with goosebumps again. She accepts it gratefully, and I'm also thankful for a temporary reprieve from the temptation to check her out.

"The guy on your emergency contact list, your brother-in-law, is he the doctor-brother you mentioned before?" she prompts me.

"Ah, no. But he's kind of the main character, ironically enough."

She glares at me. "Go on."

I hesitate for another second before deciding I might as well trust her with this, too. "He was my college roommate and my closest friend, and I recently found out that he and my baby sister kind of eloped in secret."

Her brow shoots up. "The plot thickens."

"Yeah. Don't get me wrong, I'm really happy for them. But it feels pretty crappy knowing that my two favorite people hid their marriage from me, especially since they weren't even supposed to be romantically involved."

"Oh, wow," she breathes. "That is shitty."

I sigh. "I come from a large family, and even though there's a pretty decent age gap between my youngest sister and me, we were particularly close. And my friend, well, he's a great guy, but he's not always the easiest to get along with. He's also been adamantly anti-marriage until this."

"And since you've had to be responsible for each of them in a way, it felt like a betrayal when they went behind your back," she says for me.

"Yeah, a little," I reply, the weight of that guilt and resentment I've been carrying around for the past month or so dissipating. "I know they both still care about me and that they didn't mean to hurt me, but ..."

"They did," she confirms.

I nod and reach up to scratch my neck again. "It doesn't help that I'm officially the last of my nine siblings left unmarried."

She blanches. "And it's no fun riding solo over the holidays, especially when everyone else is paired up."

"Right. I'd actually just gotten a text from him about the big church ceremony they're planning when I sat down for that dinner tonight. He wants me to be his best man, of course."

"So you were already in your feelings when that allergic reaction knocked you on your ass? Oh, Rowan," she laments.

"There's more," I say on another long exhale.

"More?" she asks, her eyes wide.

I cringe. I'm probably not doing myself any favors by admitting the rest of this, but I'm too far in to stop now.

"A while back, that same friend tried setting me up with *his* sister, but it turned out she was only using me as a distraction. She didn't want him to find out that she'd been seeing this douchey frat boy he'd hated since they were kids. But the guy had the nerve to show up at the restaurant and ruin our date. I mean, they're happily married and everything now, but I found out later that he'd already gotten her pregnant by the time she went out with me."

She gasps. "No."

"Yep," I affirm. "Wanna take a wild guess *how* I found out?"

"No," she whimpers. "Tell me you weren't her doctor?"

I lift my hands in defeat, and she leans back in her chair to cackle so loudly that it echoes throughout the room.

"Oh, man. This is the best *and* the worst at the same time," she says once she catches her breath. "Congratulations, you've managed to one up my divorcée debut at a sixtieth anniversary celebration."

"Glad I could brighten up your night," I say, smirking at her. And I mean it.

"You'll be fine, though. I mean, look at you," she reassures me with a playful eye roll.

I twist my lips to the side. "I don't know. I haven't had the best luck in the dating department. Need I remind you of my current situation?"

"Yeah, all that trouble for another catch-and-release." She gestures over herself with a self-deprecating laugh.

That makes me frown, mostly because I was already thinking it. "I meant the part about you having to take care of me."

Claire shrugs me off. "This has been fun, and you're adorable," she says, waving a hand in front of me this time, "But from what I can tell, I'm not what you're looking for."

"What makes you say that?"

Her expression hardens, and she swallows hard before she replies. "You want a wife and a family, but I'm not exactly in the right head-space for anything like that."

"Because of your divorce?" I ask, unable to hide my disappointment.

"Yeah. But also because of me." She looks away as she says it, prompting another rush of protective instincts.

"Do you want to talk about it? We've still got time."

She forces a smile. "Nah. I'm not that emotionally deep," she says mockingly, but I can tell it's not the whole truth. And now I'm dying to know what's really bothering her.

"I don't believe that for a second," I reply, and she avoids my gaze as she shakes her head. "Especially since you seemed so disappointed about not having kids before," I continue, pausing to gauge her reaction. I watch as her eyelashes flutter and the corners of her mouth turn down. "Sounds like you at least wanted a family at some point."

Her chest rises and falls in a deep exhale, and she fidgets under the blanket. "Yeah. Maybe I did. But it wasn't ... We couldn't."

Before I can respond, a hand yanks the curtains back, and the doctor steps in. "Hey, what's up, guys? I'm Dr. Theriot. What seems to be—"

The doctor breaks off mid-introduction to slip my chart beneath his arm and reaches out to shake my hand. "Rowan? Well, I'll be damned."

"Hey, Jalen," I reply and take his hand, grateful to see a familiar face despite his untimely interruption.

"Dude, it's been a minute. What brings you and your lovely friend by tonight?" he asks with a smile, turning to acknowledge Claire with a nod. "Or is this one of your many sisters?"

I cough lightly as I tilt my head to show him the rash on my neck. "I had to use my EpiPen after accidentally triggering my peanut allergy, and," I pause and glance at Claire, "my *date* insisted we stop by. But I'm fine, really."

He ignores my tone as he leans in to examine me.

"How's your throat? Any swelling?" he inquires once he's done checking my vitals.

"Not since the epinephrine injection."

Jalen drapes his stethoscope over his shoulders and hums as he studies my chart. "Heart rate's pretty elevated."

I clear my throat. "That's, uh, coincidental."

He seems confused, so I nod my head to gesture in Claire's direction.

"Ah, I see. We haven't been properly introduced, though. I'm Jalen," he says, offering a hand.

"Claire. I'm the *date*." She grins and brings the blanket down for a handshake, and his brow lifts when she exposes her body in that tight-fitting dress.

"Dr. Theriot and I went to medical school together," I explain to Claire, unable to hide my displeasure after Jalen's perusal of her and a subsequent congratulatory nod for me.

"How'd you get them to let her back here, anyway?" he asks me, and there's a stab of guilt in my gut.

"The nurse thinks we're engaged," I admit begrudgingly.

Jalen glances back and forth between Claire and me. "But you're not?"

"No, we're not. But we *are* here together," I remind him, and he grins once she tugs her hand free.

"You guys been seeing each other long?" he continues, directing his question at her this time.

"Long enough," I retort.

Claire's eyes dart over to me, her expression amused. "Long enough to be responsible for jamming an EpiPen into his thigh, but not enough to become his emergency contact."

Jalen chuckles, and I roll my eyes, remembering how he'd built up a reputation for flirting with practically every female we'd interact with during school, patients included.

"That's too bad," he drawls. "How else am I going to accidentally stumble across your number now?"

My jaw snaps shut, and I fight the urge to reach out and grab him by the collar. I don't know where it's coming from, since I've never been the jealous type before. It must be those protective instincts again, I reassure myself. It's probably just a natural reaction to watching an unsuspecting woman get hit on.

"I'm just messing with you, bro," Jalen says, turning to me with a cocky smirk plastered across his face. Then he lifts his left hand to brandish a silicone wedding band, and I barely manage to ignore the little voice in the back of my head telling me to aim my fist at his smile.

"Congratulations," I grind out.

"Thanks, man. You should see my wife," he says, bouncing his eyebrows suggestively. "She's a total smoke show, too. We should all go out for a drink sometime. We'll get you a chocolate milk," he adds the last part lowly and nudges me playfully with his elbow when I glower back at him.

"This guy's still the life of the party, I see," he directs at Claire when he doesn't get a verbal response from me.

"How do you think I met him?" she replies smoothly.

"Well, he didn't graduate first in our class by accident," Jalen says with a chuckle. "By the way, how's your buddy Reed doing? You guys still in touch?"

I accidentally let out a growl while Claire snickers in the corner. "Sore subject, Doc," she whispers. Jalen cocks an eyebrow at me.

"He just married one of my sisters," I mutter, and he lets out a low whistle.

"Damn, and I would have put my money on you getting hitched before any of us."

"No kidding," I deadpan.

"So, any other symptoms to report?" Jalen asks cheerfully, returning to my chart as if he hasn't been making my life miserable for the past few minutes.

"I'm fine," I say through my teeth.

"Oh, babe, shouldn't you tell him about your *tummy trouble*?" Claire volunteers, mouthing the last part and gesturing over her stomach.

Jalen's grin widens. "Experiencing a little bit of the bubbly gut, are we?"

I blow out a breath, wishing I'd never stepped out of Tiana's car. "Tummy's all better now."

"Must have been that toot he let out in the waiting room," Claire tells Jalen, and he snorts.

I shoot her a pointed glare, but the way she's biting her lip to keep herself from laughing distracts me from my irritation. By the time she starts giggling, I can't help but join her.

"All right, my man," Jalen begins after a while. "I'd hate to keep you in here any longer than necessary, since you've obviously got a party to get back to, but there's always the slight risk of a biphasic reaction. You'll need to be under close observation for the next few hours. Got anyone willing to spend the whole night tending to your needs?" he poses, winking at Claire.

She lifts her hand in a mock salute, and I gulp.

"Great. Let's get you hooked up with a dose of diphenhydramine and a script for some hydrocortisone cream," he continues, pulling out a prescription pad. "Need a refill for your EpiPen?"

"Uh, yeah, thanks," I say faintly.

"Get this filled on your way home, and make sure you apply that cream as soon as possible. He can take another dose of Benadryl if he's still itchy, but I want you to call me directly and bring him back in if any of his other symptoms worsen. I'll leave my personal phone number on his discharge paperwork," he explains to Claire, his tone more serious.

"Thanks, Doc," she replies and takes the prescription from him.

"It was a pleasure to meet you, Claire. Take care of my boy, would you? He's one of the good ones," Jalen says conspiratorially.

Claire aims a sultry look my way, and my stomach dips. "He's in good hands."

"Rowan, great to see you, bro. Behave yourself." Jalen clasps a hand on my shoulder and lifts his brow in a smug "you can thank me later" gesture, then he disappears through the curtains before I can say another word.

"Well, he was nice," Claire remarks.

"I guess he was," I reply absently, just as Mrs. Ethel returns with a tiny cup of pink liquid.

"One shot of the pink drink, courtesy of your friend, Dr. Theriot," she says with a wink. "But he said the next round is on you, since he expects an open bar at your wedding."

rowan

"SO, HOW ABOUT THAT COFFEE?" I ask Claire when we make it back to the waiting room.

She bites her lip. "Guess I could use the caffeine boost, since it looks like I'll be up all night."

I clear my throat and try to ignore the fluttering in my stomach as I direct her toward the hospital cafeteria. My heart quickens when I guide her around the corners with my hand over the small of her back, and she glances up at me with a coy smile while the machine groans and releases a trickle of coffee into a cheap paper cup. I gesture toward the sugar packets and creamer cups, but she shakes her head.

"It's no Starbucks," I admit, bringing our cups over to an empty table.

"Community Coffee's better, anyway. But all that matters right now is that it's hot." She shivers as soon as her hands wrap around the cup.

"I'm sorry you're so cold," I tell her. "I promise I'll get you that jacket as soon as Tiana picks us up."

"And you said this wouldn't be romantic?" she poses with a smirk before leaning over to blow on her coffee, giving me an exemplary view.

I blink lazily at the sight of her pursed lips and her shapely figure, her sun-kissed skin a beautiful contrast to the deep plum of her dress and the hair cascading over her shoulders a near-perfect match to the coffee in her cup. I know I should look away, that it's wrong to objectify her like this, but I can't stop myself from indulging. Her eyes drift up to mine, catching me in the act, and my pulse throbs in my ears as I wait for her to call me out. Instead, she holds my gaze as she straightens and takes a sip, the lipstick stain she leaves on the rim making me wish I were that paper cup. And I'm starting to worry she's actually capable of giving me a cardiac arrhythmia or a neural disruption.

"How are you feeling, Benadryl Boy?" she rasps after a while.

"Warm," I say without thinking. "And a little tingly."

She laughs, and so do I.

"You'd better get some of that coffee in you before the pink drink takes over. Otherwise, I'll be forced to track down this Dr. Reed and have him take you home instead."

"I'd much rather a bedtime story from you," I mumble and take an obedient sip, sighing when the caffeine works its way through my system. She watches me carefully, looking amused.

I've never been much of a drinker, and I've certainly never done drugs, but this blend of medication and Claire's attention is giving me the best buzz I've ever had.

Then again, maybe that's her phone vibrating on the table.

"Tiana's here," she announces, and we chug the rest of the coffee and make our way outside, this time with Claire leading me by the hand.

"So, how's it going?" Tiana intones as soon as I lower myself into the back seat.

"Warm and tingly," Claire answers for us, and I squint an eye when Tiana squeals too loudly.

I find my jacket from earlier and drape it over Claire's shoulders. She looks really, really pretty when she says thank you.

The car lurches forward while Claire and Tiana start chatting, their voices mingling in a way that makes it hard for me to follow. I glance down and notice Claire's palm resting in the space between us, and I cover it with my own.

"I like holding your hand," I whisper, and she turns to smirk at me while Tiana keeps talking. She flips her hand over beneath mine and interlaces our fingers. It makes me smile.

"Looks like I'll have to drop you off a few blocks away from that pharmacy," Tiana announces after a while, her voice sounding clearer than it had a few minutes ago.

"Are you okay to walk?" Claire turns to ask me, squeezing my hand.

I blink at her. "Yeah, I'm fine."

"You sure? You're looking a little glossy-eyed," she muses.

I straighten and tug my hand free, realizing I can add "being a lightweight" to my list of emasculating moments tonight. "I'm good. The coffee helped."

"Wait, is that it?" Tiana protests as Claire and I step out of the back seat.

"What do you mean?" I ask.

"She saves your life and spends the past couple hours by your side in the ER, you've got sparks flying between all the whispering and the handholding and the gazing, and you still haven't kissed her yet? What are you waiting for?"

Claire snorts, and I realize I'm frowning. "To be fair, this isn't exactly a real date," I grumble defensively.

"Dude, this whole situation is one big rom-com meet-cute!" Tiana cries out. "Just kiss her already!"

"She doesn't want me to kiss her now, not while I'm covered in hives and hospital germs," I argue, turning my eyes back to Claire's. But the way her shoulders sag and she bites her lip as she looks away seems to disprove my claim. "Right?" I add low enough so that only Claire hears.

She shrugs and crosses her arms over her middle before she looks up at me. "I don't want to be kissed by someone who doesn't want to kiss me, that's for shit sure."

"But I—I never said … I didn't mean …" I trail off as I consider my next move. *Do* I want to kiss Claire?

My gaze zeroes in on her mouth and roams over her barely parted lips, and a very telling surge of heat courses through me. The diphenhydramine may have gotten the best of me for a minute, but I certainly don't need to worry about the long-term side effects of those vasoconstrictors around her.

Okay, so I definitely *want* to kiss Claire, but that doesn't mean I *should* kiss her. Because I shouldn't be kissing any woman unless there's real potential for us in the future, and Claire is most likely a dead end.

Then again, procreation is a pretty vital function of marriage, at least for me, and it's not like I haven't used kissing to vet my dates for compatibility in the past.

I clear my throat, considering the possibilities with the woman in front of me. She may not be a great candidate on paper, but she's already garnering a better physical reaction from me than my last few dates, maybe even better than anyone I can remember. And since kissing the others helped me determine we weren't well-suited, I should probably kiss Claire, too, even if only to make absolutely certain I can rule her out.

I take a step closer and reach for her arm before I attempt to speak again. "Then, would it be okay—"

"Not if that's how you're asking," Claire interrupts me to declare with her chin lifted tauntingly. "In fact, I think I'm pretty transparent most of the time. So I'm gonna go ahead and say you shouldn't have to ask at all."

My heart quickens again, but I think it's a fight-or-flight response this time. Because she's right—what a lame approach to the woman I'm practically dying to kiss, especially after she's been so open and honest about her feelings. And while my default move in this situation has always been flight, I think I want to stick it out and fight this time, for her.

Before I know it, my feet are moving of their own volition and taking her up on that dare. My arms are next, dragging her body flush with mine as I close my eyes and let my instincts take over completely.

Her hands fist into my shirt when I tip my head down to whisper beside her ear. "Fair enough. As much as I'd like to kiss you right now, you deserve to be kissed by a man who doesn't have to question whether he's earned it. And I don't think I've done enough to earn a kiss from you just yet."

The first thing I see when I open my eyes is her pulse thrumming beneath her skin, and she lets out a breathless sound as I graze my lips over the spot.

"Yeah. I should make you work for it," she rasps, contradicting herself with the way she bends her neck to give me more room.

I swallow hard, practically salivating over her suggestion. Have I ever wondered what a woman tastes like before? Have I ever been this desperate to kiss anyone, much less a stranger?

My tongue involuntarily darts out to wet my lips, answering the question for me.

"You should," I confirm, my voice deep and gravelly, and I brush my nose over her skin this time. She doesn't smell like the artificial and overly floral perfumes I'm used to. Instead, her woodsy, smoky scent clouds my brain and somehow elicits a growl from my chest.

Who am I right now?

What is she doing to me? How is she so easily dismantling decades of practiced self-control? I watch her teeth sink into her bottom lip, and I grip her arms tightly, afraid I might combust.

"Are you even the kind of guy who kisses on the first date?" she whispers, the reminder knocking me back into reality.

I cringe and let out a quiet groan before dropping my forehead to her shoulder. "Don't make me answer that," I mumble, and she huffs out a laugh.

"*Ugh*, fine! Take it slow, then," Tiana calls out mockingly. "But one of you better find me on Instagram later and give me an update. You owe it to me!"

I lift my head to find her pointing a finger at me. "Hey, I'm doing my best here, but I'm still working with a slight disadvantage," I say and raise my hands in surrender.

Claire's laugh grows bigger, and I beam at her as I absorb another scolding from Tiana. Eventually, our driver bids us a good night, leaving Claire and me alone on the sidewalk.

"Shall we?" I ask, gesturing in the direction of the pharmacy, and she nods before we begin walking in silence.

"Hold on, my feet are killing me," she groans after the first few steps and pulls us to a stop, using my arm for leverage as she slips off her shoes.

"You're not going barefooted out here?"

"I don't have much choice, do I?"

"I'll carry you," I tell her, my stomach dipping at the prospect of her wrapping her arms around my neck while I lift her.

She frowns, obviously not finding the idea as exciting as I do. "No way. You'll drop me."

"I'm fine, I swear. But if it makes you feel better, you can ride on my back," I offer.

"Have you seen how tight this dress is?" She opens my jacket to reveal her curves, and I gladly accept the invitation to peruse her body again.

"Oh, I'm well aware," I reply, my eyes glued to her thighs. She scoffs, but I can tell she takes it as a compliment.

"Fine. I guess the jacket will shield me," she concedes after a while, and I turn and crouch down for her to hop onto my back. Her first attempt is unsuccessful, and we both giggle when she slides down unceremoniously.

"I'll have to hike my dress up over my ass. And I opted for a thong tonight, so you'd better keep looking straight ahead if you don't want to get flashed," she jokes before she tries again, this time hooking her legs around my waist and draping her arms over my shoulders. My stomach practically bottoms out at that mental image, and I barely manage to catch my grip just above her knees.

"Good?" I ask as I stand and adjust our position, trying to ignore the warmth from her body pressing against mine.

"Yep," she confirms. She settles in, holding her purse with one hand and dangling her shoes over my chest with the other. Then she wiggles and kicks her feet out as she adds a "giddy up," making me chuckle.

I begin our trek to the pharmacy a couple blocks ahead, and she wordlessly reaches out to press the button when I stop at a crosswalk. I take a second to acknowledge how comfortable this feels, how well we seem to fit together when we have no business even hanging out right now. I guess I've never thought of a piggyback ride as a form of physical intimacy, but there's definitely an affectionate undercurrent to it, even if it's not overtly sexual. Although, I'd be lying if I said my hands weren't having the time of their lives right about now.

She squirms behind me when my thumbs stroke the soft skin of her thighs. "Getting a little handsy there, Doc," she whispers beside my ear.

"Sorry," I mumble.

"Don't be," she replies, shifting her things to one hand and reaching up to run her fingers through the hair at the base of my neck. I struggle to hide the way it makes me shiver.

"I bet you're just dying right now, aren't you? Have you ever wanted anything more?" she poses, her tone deep and heavy with desire.

My mouth runs too dry for me to respond, but she goes on. "It's been so long since anyone's satisfied that urge, since you've felt that sweet release ..."

"Yes," I rasp before I can stop myself.

"I can take the edge off for you, Rowan." She rakes her nails over my scalp again, laughing seductively when I whimper. Then she brushes the tip of her fingernail over one of the raised welts on my neck.

"Aren't you going to beg me to scratch that itch?" she asks, barely getting through the question without breaking character.

A loud groan escapes, which draws a cackle out of her. "You're killing me," I protest, and she obliges by scratching the rest of my hives, laughing again when I wiggle my shoulders and let out an exaggerated exhale. Suffering has never been more fun, and that's a bold statement coming from an overly scrupulous Catholic.

"You can set me down," she directs me once we reach the pharmacy's sliding doors, and I pause to pluck the high heels she's been holding.

"What are you—"

"Hang on tighter."

I pull her right leg in and slip the shoe back onto her foot. Sensing a change in her breathing, I decide to give her a taste of her own medicine and take my time with the other side, watching a trail of goosebumps line her skin before loosening my grip on her calf. And the idea that I might affect her anywhere near the same way she does me might be the most thrilling thing I've ever experienced.

She clears her throat and mumbles a thank you, and I dare to slide my hands back up her thighs under the guise of helping her down, still high off our exchange.

"I think it'll be easier if you just let go of me," she says quietly.

"Sorry," I murmur, my cheeks reddening again as I try not to think about all the parts of her brushing against my back. But the moment is lost to a loud rip when she hops down onto her feet.

"Well, shit," Claire curses. I turn to find her opening my jacket and inspecting a new slit up the side of her dress. We both cringe when the seam continues splitting all the way up to the armhole, leaving her hip completely bare save for a thin strip of dark lace. "I knew I should have worn the damned shape wear," she adds, struggling to reunite the two sides of her dress and inadvertently exposing more of her soft curves.

I cough, unable to look away. It's not like I haven't seen a woman's body before. Getting up close and personal with the female anatomy is literally a job requirement for me. Less so now that I'm a MFM specialist, but still. Catching a glimpse of a butt cheek shouldn't be enough to evoke the kind thoughts I'm having right now, and seeing this much of Claire's skin shouldn't make me feel more like a pervy teenager than the mature, professional I am, much less the respectful, chaste Christian I strive to be.

"Uh, maybe button the coat?" I offer, my voice cracking.

She nods and gives it a try. "Better?" she asks once she turns around and shows me her backside again.

I blink, every cell in my body taking notice of the fact that she's wrapped up in *my* jacket. "I think you're ... fine," I choke out after a while, drowning in my own testosterone. Before long I'll be forced to reclaim that coat in order to hide some body parts of my own.

"Great. You done checking out my ass or do you need another minute?" she asks, smirking when she cranes her neck to peer back at me.

I squeeze my eyes shut and scratch my chest. "Sorry."

"I'd be more offended if you hadn't looked," she says with a chuckle and turns to saunter in through the automatic doors, leaving me feeling dazed all over again.

rowan

CLAIRE WASTES no time in leading me to the pharmacist's counter in the back. As soon as I turn in my prescription and insurance card, she grabs my hand and hauls me down the aisle housing the allergy medications.

"Dr. Jalen recommended one-percent strength. What do you think?" she asks, scanning the shelves for hydrocortisone cream.

"One percent sounds good." I should probably offer more input, since I'm an actual doctor with my very own prescription pad and all, but I can't seem to focus on anything with her palm pressed to mine.

It's got to be the Benadryl fog, I reassure myself as an elderly man walks by. We trade polite nods before Claire lets go of my hand and bends to reach the bottom shelf. I panic when I imagine her hem riding up and instinctively step forward to block the old man's view.

"Whatcha doin' back there?" she asks as she slowly rises to her feet, sounding amused.

"Oh, um, I'm just ..." My nostrils flare as I fight the urge to look down, but she turns her head so that her hazel eyes meet mine.

"Collecting your payment after that piggyback ride?" she asks, her dark lashes fanning her cheeks, and my palms hover near her hips.

Okay, it can't just be the allergy meds, because this is the first time I've ever considered participating in an act of public indecency. In fact, I have to ball my hands into fists to avoid gripping her possessively. She cocks an eyebrow and arches her back slightly, and I gasp when she pushes into me, a plethora of obscene thoughts flooding my mind, many of which I've never even imagined were possible until this moment.

Half of my brain is screaming, *Abort!*

Unfortunately, it's drowned out by the more persuasive half claiming, *Mine.*

"Rowan," she whispers my name with a pained expression, and a low growl resonates from my chest. I relinquish my self-control and lean down to meet her lips when a loud throat clearing makes us both wince.

I jump back, scrunching my nose at the sound of more fabric ripping, and Claire spins around quickly, hiding her bare backside against the shelving. The same gray-haired man from a minute ago chuckles to himself and walks on in the opposite direction just before a mother and a young boy pass by. She shoots us a disapproving glare and hurries the kid along, and I let out a loud exhale once they clear the aisle, though I'm not sure whether I'm more disappointed or relieved by the interruption.

"I'm sorry," I begin. "That was totally ..."

Claire's whimper distracts me as she inspects her tattered clothes again. The jacket's hem must have caught on my belt buckle, causing the tear when we broke apart. And naturally, the seam that's currently unravelling falls on the same side as the rip in her dress.

"You've got to be kidding me," she says just before another one of her loud cackles bubbles up from her chest, and I can't help but join her. We're both delirious within seconds, laughing so loud that we lower ourselves to the floor to stop from falling over, triggering another wardrobe malfunction and a complementary fit of giggles.

"What are we going to do now?" I ask, gasping for air.

She sighs. "I guess I'll be needing your drawers."

"My what?"

"Your boxers," she clarifies as if the answer should be more obvious. "You're wearing underwear, aren't you?"

I nod and blink back at her in confusion, my brain still misfiring.

"Who am I kidding? Of course you are," she mumbles to herself as she shifts to show me the damage. Between the jacket and the dress, she's practically naked from the armpit down on one side, her dainty underwear notwithstanding. "I'll need something else to wear if I want to make it back to the hotel without literally freezing my ass off."

I frown, still staring at her bare hip. "Maybe we can flip the jacket around?"

"Nah, I'm pretty sure it wasn't long enough to cover everything even before it ripped. My undercarriage was already catching a suspicious amount of cool breeze on the ride here."

"But ... but you can't wear *my* underwear," I argue awkwardly.

She stifles a smile. "Why not? Are you embarrassed to show me your tighty-whities?" Then she cups her hand around her mouth and adds, "You didn't leave behind any evidence after your unfortunate tummy situation, did you?"

"They're boxer briefs," I reply more defensively. "And I'm pretty sure they're relatively clean, considering. But you barely even know me."

She shrugs. "I'll keep my panties on underneath if it makes you feel better, but the fact that I was just privy to your entire medical history makes that a moot point. I'd know if you had any booty cooties by now, unless that's why you turned down Nurse Ethel's offer to run that STI panel."

Another unexpected laugh escapes before I can help it. "Booty cooties?"

She smirks. "Crotch crickets, dirty deed receipts, freaky freebies? I imagine you've heard of sexually transmitted diseases in your line of work."

"No cooties," I confirm, ignoring the way my cheeks heat. "But my boxers are definitely going to be too big for you."

"You know what they say about men who wear big undies, don't you?" she replies, quirking an eyebrow. I roll my eyes and shake my head, and she continues. "I'll make them work. Get to stripping." She slaps me on the thigh and gestures to the restroom sign a few aisles down.

Reluctantly, I rise to my feet and shuffle off, leaving her snickering to herself on the floor before I duck into the men's restroom to remove my underwear. Maybe if I hurry, I won't have time to wrap my mind around the idea of Claire's soft, sexy curves being nestled within my underpants. Tripping over my pants leg and nearly falling serves as a decent distraction from the improper thoughts, but only for a second. The feeling of my dress slacks against my skin makes me cringe as I pull up on the zipper. Claire was right before—easy breezy isn't my style. Plus, I could really use the extra layer of support in my current predicament.

Claire grins up at me when I return, and I take it she's expecting me to carry her around again when I see her shoes resting on the floor beside her. Still, I can't help smiling and blushing when I retrieve the boxer briefs from my pocket.

"My lady," I say, holding out my offering and bowing.

She chortles as she takes the underwear, and I worry for a second that was too corny. "If this doesn't entitle you to a kiss, I don't know what will," she muses as she slides her bare feet into the shorts.

"Wait, aren't you going to change in the bathroom?" I whisper harshly when she rises to her feet, ignoring her flirty reply.

"What for? Everyone in this aisle has already seen my goodies by now," she replies nonchalantly and drags the waistband up over her hips. She tugs at her dress, and I force myself to look away and take a moment to scratch at my neck again.

"All right. I'm piggyback ready," she declares, modeling the shorts.

I pretend I'm concerned with finding a pack of generic diphenhydramine to avoid glancing in her direction and risking my body's reaction to the sight of her in my underwear. "Um, would you mind if we applied some of that cream before we go, at least around my neck? I'm getting pretty uncomfortable."

"Yeah, sure," she says distantly, taking a box from my hands and opening it up.

I nod gratefully before turning and crouching down, and she

spreads some of the hydrocortisone cream over my skin. In a small twist of good luck, she has to move the cord of my scapular off to the side before rubbing in the medicine, and it serves as both a distraction from her touch and a wake-up call for my conscience.

"Better take another dose of Benadryl while you're at it," she tells me as she opens up the bottle and hands me another shot of pink liquid.

Once we're done, she gathers our things and hops into place on my back. I wait for her to crack another joke or dig her heels into me as if I were a horse, but she's quiet on the ride to retrieve the EpiPen prescription from the pharmacist and then to the self-checkout. I reach up, and she hands over the cream without a word. She doesn't even reply to my strained apology for brushing against her thighs in the process of digging my wallet out of my pocket, and when I glance up at the security camera, I find her looking disappointed.

"Anything else?" I venture before I complete our transaction, gesturing toward the candy shelf. She sees me watching her through the monitor and shakes her head.

"I'm fine, thanks," she says with a soft smile. But it's obvious I've done something to hurt her feelings in the last couple of minutes.

"Claire?"

"Hmm?"

I scoff, annoyed with the delay after trying to communicate through the screen, and turn to set her down on the small checkout counter. "What's wrong?"

She shakes her head again, but the way she's blinking back the moisture in her eyes gives her away.

"Hey, what's going on?" I continue, leaning in closer and planting my hands on either side of her.

"I'm fine," she repeats with a sniffle. "I'm just ... silly."

My brow furrows in concern, and I think I'd do anything to keep her from looking this sad ever again. "Tell me."

She turns her eyes down. "I guess I thought you wanted ..." Her shoulders rise and fall in a dejected shrug before she looks up and forces another fake smile. "Never mind."

It takes another second for me to understand what she means. She's upset because she gave me another opening a minute ago, and I blew right past it in the name of stifling my inappropriate thoughts.

I swallow hard. "You're not silly."

"Seriously? Look at me right now," she says, gesturing over the current state of her outfit. Her smile grows more genuine as she continues. "I'm sitting here, dressed like a homeless person, *boudering* in the middle of the CVS because you don't want …"

She trails off when I use my knuckle to lift her chin. "You look amazing in my boxers. And I've never wanted to kiss anyone more than I want to kiss you right now," I blurt out, to my own astonishment.

Her eyelids grow heavy as she licks her lips and hooks a finger in my belt loop, and I take it as an open invitation to bring my mouth down to hers. But my heart rate skyrockets so quickly that I'm afraid I might lose consciousness, and I have to pause less than an inch away from her as I struggle to catch my breath.

She whimpers as she waits for me to close in that last bit of space, and the sound of it nearly does me in. With a sharp inhale, I slip my hand around her neck and pull her in to meet me, my own boldness taking me by surprise again. My doubt is short-lived, though. As soon as my nerve endings catch up to what's happening, I'm a goner.

Claire parts her lips for me, drawing my tongue into her mouth and making me groan. She tastes even better than I imagined. My fingers twist into her hair, and my free hand moves around to cup her lower back, bracing her as I press my body into hers. The contact sends a jolt of pleasure through me. It's all so overwhelming, the combination of heat and need forming something new, something delicious and addicting, unlike anything I've ever experienced before.

I may have kissed my share of women in my search for *the one*, but I've never felt so ravenous and greedy at the same time, not even in the confines of my more serious relationships. I've also never been compelled to make out on the self-checkout counter before, but I'm going to chalk that up to the medicine-induced brain fog.

Then Claire scoots closer and moans into my mouth, and I

couldn't care less what makes this so different, only that I don't want it to end. It's too bad a loud beep resounds from behind her a second later, making us both flinch.

We pull apart reluctantly, and she winces again when the register chimes and politely reminds us to bag the last scanned item. I glance over to find a small box sitting on the glass.

"What in the ..." I mumble, turning the unfamiliar package over in my hands.

Claire snorts. "The better question is *how* did a box of condoms get here?"

My stomach hits the floor just before the box does. She giggles when I fumble to pick it up, and I hope she blames the awkwardness on my nerves in general and not on the fact that I've never had a use for condoms before.

I clear my throat, and my head feels thick as I watch her pluck the box from my hands and deposit it within the bag. Then she twists around to add the other items to our haul.

"You're paying, right, Doc?" she asks, casting a flirty smirk my way. It takes me a few seconds to catch up, and I scramble to get my credit card out of my wallet. I complete the transaction in a daze, turning to hoist Claire onto my back again. She drops her shoes into the plastic bag before she crosses her arms over my chest, and I choke back a laugh at the irony of her dangling a box of condoms in front of me like a carrot on a stick.

The old man from earlier catches my eye as I begin tracking toward the door, and he shoots me a conspiratorial wink. I force a smile, but I'm honestly more annoyed than grateful.

There's a reason I've never had sex before, and it's not because I couldn't find anyone willing to sleep with me. I've been purposefully saving that level of intimacy for one person, because once I give myself away, I don't plan on holding anything back. If she wants my body, she's also going to have to accept my soul, my unconditional love, my flaws, my past, my hopes and dreams, and my fertility. It's one of the main reasons waiting until marriage has always been such a big deal to me—not simply because of the religious implications or the morality of it all, but because it's the most logical way to combat any self-serving tendencies within a relationship.

I bite my lip and tighten my hold on Claire's thighs as I trudge on, my mind still reeling from that kiss. For the first time in my life, I could see myself being somewhat amendable to the rules. I mean, it's not like I'm going to throw out everything I've ever stood for to sleep with a virtual stranger, even if she were willing, but ...

I'm not.

I'm not, I tell myself more sternly.

But if this were the start of something real, if Claire and I were to begin dating after tonight, I can't imagine how difficult it would be to regulate this kind of attraction. Seeing her all the time, listening to her sexy banter—the temptation would be downright unbearable.

I just wish I understood the purpose of all this. Where am I meant to go from here? How is meeting someone like her supposed to change me for the better or help me grow as a person? Or is this simply an exercise in self-regulation and an opportunity to harden my resolve to remain chaste?

Well, my resolve is rock hard at the moment.

I huff, scolding myself for the crude thoughts, and the answer becomes obvious. Claire may have literally saved me tonight, but I'm certain I'm the one who's meant to have a positive influence on her. Since I'm apparently the more morally conscious of the two of us, it must be up to me to introduce her to a better lifestyle, one in which she doesn't feel the need to throw herself at a man she barely knows to earn his love.

Claire sighs and rests her chin on my shoulder, and I frown once I realize I'm basing that conclusion on some pretty hefty assumptions. Judging her this way feels like the worst thing I've done tonight—and I've been on a roll. Suddenly, I'm more disgusted with myself over these thoughts than the impure ones I've been harboring for the past couple of hours.

She shifts uncomfortably behind me after a while. "Hey, you feeling all right?" she asks.

"Yeah," I fib, forcing a smile. "Maybe just a little drowsy."

"You don't have to carry me, you know," she says quickly.

"But then who's gonna reach the rest of my back hives?" My smile grows more genuine when she laughs and scratches at the splotchy skin beneath my collar, and I think maybe I'm just meant to enjoy her company for a while. Maybe this night with Claire is simply a reprieve from a lifetime of loneliness.

I march on toward the hotel, resolving to exercise the self-restraint I know I possess and savor her attention while I can.

claire

"CAN I bring you up to your room?" Rowan asks, and I'm grateful for the blast of warm air as we enter the hotel's main lobby. "So I can make sure you get there safely, I mean," he adds quickly.

"Yes, but you don't have to carry me all the way there," I remind him.

"I don't mind," he says again as we approach the elevator. Truthfully, I don't mind having his hands on my thighs, either. I tell him which buttons to press, and we fill the silence of the elevator ride with all of the sexual tension.

"Well, um, thanks again," Rowan begins as he sets me down onto my feet, and I use an app on my phone to unlock the door to my room. "I guess I should—"

I roll my eyes before I grab his sleeve and tug him forward. "Stop being so awkward and get in here, you big baby. I promise I won't bite."

But he digs his heels into the carpet and stays planted in the hallway, looking forlorn. "I don't know if that's a good idea," he says after a while.

"And I think you're going to be in a bind if you don't let me rub some more of that hydrocortisone cream on your neck."

He stops in the middle of scratching his shoulder and sighs as he drops his protest. I steer him toward the large king-sized bed, then I shove him down, forcing him to sit on the mattress.

"Now, start stripping," I demand again, and he looks up at me in a panic, his eyes as round as saucers. "You might as well take off your shirt and let me apply it to all the places you won't be able to reach yourself, like you said before," I clarify.

He gulps and nods before he complies, and I turn to retrieve the pharmacy bag.

"Claire?" he begins over the quiet rustle of his clothing.

My breath catches when I bring my attention back to him. "Holy shit, Rowan," I gasp, allowing my gaze to run over the hard lines of his body as he peels away the sleeves of his white button down. His lean build is deceiving, but I should have guessed he'd be this hot after practically copping a feel during that injection. "You're not one of those CrossFit obsessed guys, are you?"

"I'm a runner." He acknowledges my compliment with a frown, and I duck behind him to hide my shame. I screw up my face, scolding myself as I return to the bag. My cheeks heat when I pick up the box of condoms first and have to swap it out for the tube of hydrocortisone cream.

"Claire?" Rowan calls again.

"Hmm?" I squeak.

"Um, don't you want to change first?"

I glance down at myself, having forgotten that I'm wearing more of his clothes than my own. "Oh, yeah. I imagine you'll be wanting your drawers back before you go," I say and let out a tired exhale, since I can't seem to stop bringing up the man's body or his underwear. Could I be any more desperate?

"That would be nice," he replies evenly.

"Right. I'll just ..." I hike my thumb over my shoulder before remembering he can't see me. Still annoyed with myself, I grab my overnight bag and scamper off to the bathroom.

A disheveled, hot mess of a woman greets me in the mirror, and I click my tongue in disgust as I turn to inspect the various rips and tears in my clothes. After peeling away each tattered layer, I fold

Rowan's underpants and jacket, leaving them in a neat stack on the counter.

But all I find in my bag is a silky, white camisole set. I run my fingers over the black lace lining the matching shorts, unable to decide whether my choice of pajamas was lucky or unfortunate at this point. I shrug and redress myself, stopping to touch up the lipstick Rowan must have smeared when he kissed the living daylights out of me earlier. Heat flashes through me at the memory of our surprisingly intense public make-out session. I've never felt anything like that before. Hell, just thinking about his hands moving over me while his mouth explores mine has me breathing raggedly and pressing my thighs together.

I mean, if that's what a first kiss with Rowan is like, I can't imagine what he'd be like in bed ...

Who am I kidding? That's all I've been thinking about for the past few hours.

I bite my lip, reminding myself that he's still on the other side of this door. And I've already managed to get him into my bed and out of his shirt and boxers. All that's left to do is capture a bit of the tension that's been brewing all evening and light a spark under it, which shouldn't be too difficult, if our last kiss was any indication.

I finish freshening up, lamenting over the fact that these pajamas leave so little to the imagination. I should probably be too embarrassed to walk out like this, with my body practically broadcasting my thoughts for Rowan to see.

Then again, who cares if he thinks I'm coming on too strong? The worst that could happen is that he freaks out over my sexy PJs and storms out of my hotel room, and I never have to face him again.

My shoulders droop, because a large part of me hates that idea. Even worse, my chest aches at the thought of this being the only night I ever get with Rowan. He might very well be the sweetest, most adorable man I've ever met, as well as the sexiest, and I kind of want to cling to him forever, like one of those annoying chin hairs that always seem to grow back overnight. But I can't get caught up in my feelings, not when I'm still dealing with my divorce and all the mistakes I made leading up to it. Fair is fair, and I can't ask him to help me pick up the pieces of what I'm responsible for breaking.

So that's it. I'm going to go out there and lay my cards down, convince him I'm just as chill and nonchalant about the idea of a one-night stand as I'd like to be, and let him decide what he wants. And whatever happens, I won't allow myself to be disappointed or ashamed when it's all over, because I could do so much worse than a man like Rowan.

I take a fortifying breath before I poke my head out and find him lying back on my bed, staring up at the ceiling with his arm crooked behind his head. It's such a sexy sight that I have to talk myself out of running out and jumping on top of him.

"So, don't laugh, but I didn't expect I'd be wearing these pajamas in front of anyone tonight," I warn him.

He turns and furrows his brow. "I'm sure ..."

But he leaves the words hanging once I step out from behind the bathroom door. He sits up, his gaze devouring me for a few seconds before he turns away and clears his throat.

"Sorry," I say softly as I approach. "I know it's a little skimpy, but it's all I brought."

"You, uh ... I mean, they're ..." I smirk when he pauses his rambling to shake his head. "Don't worry about me. I'll be on my way out soon," he finally manages.

Well, that settles that.

"Right," I say and press my lips together, desperately trying to stop my chin from trembling as I find the medicine and squirt some of the cream onto my fingertips. "My hands might be a little cold," I warn him, and he reaches up to remove that brown cord before I begin at the base of his neck. He winces and shivers as I continue working, and I notice his breathing quickening again.

"What kind of necklace is that?" I ask.

"It's, um ... it's a scapular," he says, still tripping over his words. "Some Catholics wear them as a devotional."

"A devotional?"

"It's sort of like a penance, since it's made of scratchy felt," he explains, holding up one of the square pieces to show me the embroidered outline of a woman. "It also serves as a reminder to pray throughout the day and to imitate the Blessed Mother in everything we do, all rolled into one." He leans over to place it reverently on the side table.

"Hmm. I guess I can see the utility of something like that," I tell him and push gently on his shoulder, signaling for him to turn around.

My eyes are trained on my hands as I begin applying cream to his chest and collarbone, but I can see his shoulders rising and falling with every strained breath. His pulse throbs in his neck, and I can't stop myself from dragging my fingers up and pressing them to the spot. He closes his eyes, and I watch his throat contract as he swallows.

"Claire?" he rasps, and I draw my hand back when the vibration from his voice reaches my fingertips.

"Yeah?"

"I think I may have waited too long," he says before he opens his eyes and looks up at me, his mouth only inches away now.

"For what?" I want him to kiss me so badly that it's taking everything I have not to straddle his waist and press my lips to his.

"It feels like my Benadryl buzz is back." He blinks lazily, and I see the heaviness in his face now. "I was okay for a while with all the epinephrine and caffeine, but that second dose has me feeling a little … funny."

"Funny?"

He nods, his eyes refocusing on my mouth. "Yeah. Silly."

"Then you probably shouldn't risk driving home in your condition," I tell him.

He nods again. "Think our girl Tiana's still on duty?"

"Just … stay here," I offer, sliding my hands over his shoulders. "I did promise to keep an eye on you."

"I could call the front desk and ask them for my own room," he mumbles.

"That sounds like a waste of a good buzz to me."

His mouth curls into a one-sided smirk, and I don't think I've ever wanted a man as badly as I want him right now. "I suppose I don't have to rush off right away."

"At least stay long enough for me to make sure that cream is helping." I arch my back a little and hope my skimpy pajamas are working to my advantage.

He hums, drinking me in. "And what if it takes all night?"

"I know something we can do to entertain ourselves," I murmur before I give up and hitch my leg over his hip. Rowan doesn't hesitate to curl his hands around my back and draw me in closer, reassuring me that he is in fact into this.

"Do you have any idea how sexy you are? How tempting?" he blurts out, his eyes running over me and his voice sounding deeper than before, and my stomach dips. This isn't the same guy I saved in the hotel lobby. Between the allergy cocktail and my shameless advances, his inhibitions have obviously been lowered.

"I could ask you the same thing," I reply, clasping my hands behind his neck. It's too bad that cortisone cream has left his skin a little sticky, or I'd already have my mouth on him. But I don't have to lament for long, because his hand cups the back of my head and pulls me in.

His kisses are slow and heated this time, a little less frantic than before, but no less intense. He groans when I shift my position in his lap and begin fumbling with his belt buckle. But he surprises me by pulling away.

"I'm sorry, this isn't me. I don't usually talk like this, or act like this, for that matter," Rowan says, squeezing his eyes closed and shaking his head.

"It's okay. I like this guy—*a lot*," I reassure him with an overeager nod.

"I've never done this before, though," he confesses, still breathing heavily.

"Neither have I." He looks confused, so I continue. "I mean, I've been with the same man for most of my life, so I haven't really had the opportunity to hook up with a stranger. In fact, you're the first person I've kissed besides my ex in as long as I can remember."

He continues staring at me as his hand moves up to cradle my cheek, and it's surprisingly tender. "I'm afraid I might let you down."

I frown. "Are you still worried about some of those other side effects?"

He cringes. "It feels like everything's back in working order, but there's no guarantee—"

"Rowan, it's just sex," I cut him off, softening my expression. "It's awkward and messy, even in the best of circumstances. And while I'm not exactly thrilled at the prospect of undressing in front of you, especially now that I've seen you without a shirt, I'm not expecting everything to be perfect."

That adorable smirk forms on his lips again. "For the record, I find that idea pretty thrilling ... maybe even a little too exciting," he admits as he squirms beneath me.

"Oh," I say, finally understanding, and honestly somewhat flattered by his concern. "Would it help if we slowed things down and waited for your buzz to pass?"

"Yes, please," he says, relief washing over his face.

"We have all night, right?" I reassure him with another kiss.

He holds me there for a minute before he breaks the kiss, his smile lingering. "As long as the vasoconstrictors don't let me down, anyway."

"How about a little more coffee, just in case?" I propose, and he chuckles softly when I actually get up to use the Keurig machine on the dresser.

"It's not just my physical performance I'm worried about, though," he adds after a while. "I know you said it's just sex, but it's still going to mean something to me."

I shake my head, thinking back on the misguided pep talk I'd given myself in the bathroom. Because despite having only known him for a few hours, this already sounds like such a *Rowan* thing to say.

"Is this supposed to be your version of dirty talk?" I ask tauntingly as the last drizzle fills the cup.

He huffs and reaches up to scratch at his neck. "It's probably as close as it gets. Even if I had the vocabulary for that kind of talk, I couldn't bring myself to use it with you."

"Why not?" I ask carefully, joining him on the bed and handing him the cup. "I'm not easily breakable."

"You still deserve better. I may not know you that well, but I think you're much more sensitive than you let on."

My stomach tightens as I watch him take a sip. "What does that have to do with sex?"

"Claire," he begins, setting the cup down beside us and taking my hand in his, "whatever it is that ends up happening between us, I only want it to make you feel good and adored ... and desired. And I'd rather do that by telling you about how you already fill up every corner of my mind, that I can't help how desperate I am to get closer to you, that I've never been with anyone more beautiful before you, and I doubt I ever will again."

I draw in a shaky breath, unsure whether it's his touch or the earnest look in his eyes as he delivers those affirmations causing the warmth that blooms inside me. Good gracious, this man is something altogether different. I'm beginning to worry that a night with him might be riskier than I thought, because he's nearly altered my brain chemistry, and we haven't even gotten undressed yet.

"Who *are* you?" I ask after I find my voice.

He shrugs, looking shy again. "I'm a little old-fashioned, I know. Much too vanilla for a woman as sexy and confident as you."

I scoff. "And you're sure you're not just some weirdo looking for the girlfriend experience? You don't have any strange kinks or stalker tendencies, do you?"

"I do have this one fantasy about finding my soulmate in the most unlikely circumstances," he reassures me, stifling a smile. "But it's all relatively wholesome, I promise."

"Fine," I concede with a groan and a playful eye roll, secretly relieved by his witty reply now that the caffeine seems to have brought him back to life. "We can be soulmates or whatever, but just for tonight." I'm not sure whether I slip in that reminder of our expiration date for him or for myself, but I figure it can't hurt.

His grin widens, and I watch his muscles flexing as he turns to adjust the bedding behind us. Then he leans back, offering his shoulder as a pillow. I sigh inwardly and snuggle in closer to him, half-expecting him to turn and kiss me again. Instead, he leans down to press his lips to my forehead. I guess he wasn't kidding about wanting to take it slow.

I glance up at him as I slide my palm over his chest, and he lets out a pained exhale as he stares down at me. "Rowan?"

"Yeah?"

"I'm sorry for coming off the way I did just now. I don't think there's anything wrong with you, for the record. I'm just not used to this," I say softly. "But it's nice being adored."

"Thanks, I guess," he replies with a laugh, but it seems forced.

"You're different, but in all the best ways," I add.

His chest expands, and I tilt my head to look up at him when he opens his mouth. But he stops and seemingly thinks better of it, probably because he's afraid I'm still judging him for being so honest and emotionally vulnerable. Guilt settles in my stomach as he smiles down at me and finally speaks again.

"And you really are more sensitive than you let on, aren't you?"

rowan

"SO TELL ME MORE ABOUT YOURSELF," I say as I drag my fingertip down Claire's bare arm, finally getting to trace the outlines of her vibrant tattoos.

She sighs as she nestles into my side. We fit together so perfectly that it makes my chest ache.

"What do you wanna know?" she asks, and I shrug, accidentally jostling her head in the process and making us both laugh.

"Is there a special meaning behind your tattoos?"

"Besides annoying my mom, not really. I just like pretty things," she replies.

I hum, taking in her answer. "Okay. What grade do you teach?"

"I'm a high school ag teacher and welding instructor."

"Really?" I can't help but smile at that. "Does that mean you wrangle a bunch of animals all day?"

"The preferred term is 'adolescent boy.' But there isn't much I haven't seen," she replies dryly. "Or smelled. And it's probably why I have such an appreciation for your bathroom manners."

I chuckle, imagining her asserting her authority over a bunch of students. "I bet you handle those kids just fine, though."

"I manage all right." Her lips quirk, like she's trying not to brag even though she's proud of herself. It's unbelievably sexy, and I force myself to continue my line of questioning before I give in to the temptation to roll over and kiss her again. Not that I don't want to know everything there is to know about her, because that urge is just as strong as the more primitive ones I'm feeling right now, some for the first time in my life. But I have to manage myself better than ever if I want to survive this night.

"Do you enjoy teaching?" I ask, watching her expression change.

Her sigh sounds more like a tired exhale this time. "Most of the time."

"Hmm. What did you always want to do?"

She tilts her head to peer up at me. "What makes you think I wanted to do something else?"

"Answer my question first."

She narrows her eyes and studies me before she gives in. "I wanted to be a vet."

"Because you love animals?"

She nods. "But I got engaged midway through college, and we agreed I should forgo grad school for a job with better hours in case we ever had kids."

"Makes sense," I say.

"Except there were no babies, so I traded in one dream to lose both, I guess. At least I still get to work with kids this way. And I have my dogs to dote on for now. Frankie and Oscar are so spoiled and needy that you'd mistake them for a couple of toddlers."

I feel a twinge in my chest, and I stop to take her hand and bring it up to my mouth. "Frankie and Oscar are lucky to have you. And I'm sorry. I think you'd be an amazing mom," I tell her as I press a kiss to her knuckles.

She huffs. "Thanks, but God or the stork or whoever's in charge must see it differently."

My instinct is to correct her, but a theological debate wouldn't be helpful at the moment. Still, it saddens me to hear that Claire has not only been carrying so many crosses between her infertility and failed marriage but also a lack of faith. I understand her resentment, at least to an extent. I just wish there was a way to show her that trusting in

God's plans can actually lighten that burden. I can't imagine how she's been getting by without the option to offer up her suffering for a greater purpose.

"No, I don't think that's it. Life is just unfair sometimes, and it's even harder when we don't get an explanation for why things happen the way they do. We never really know what's in store for us. But it's not too late for you to try again with the right person." This time I drag my hand up to lift her chin so that I can kiss her again, and my heart skips a beat when she lets me. "Don't give up on your dreams yet. As your soulmate, I have a special sense about these things," I remind her between kisses.

Her expression softens and she smiles back at me. "No, really. Who *are* you?"

It's not the first time she's asked me that question tonight.

"Whoever I am, I'm thinking you must be pretty into it, since I'm also the stranger you brought back to your room despite the medical emergency and the embarrassingly bad lines," I volunteer. "Or maybe I'm just the best kisser you've ever had, since you don't seem to mind the coffee breath."

As soon as I say it, I realize it's much too bold, especially since I'm attempting to brush right over the fact that I'm still a virgin. I can't risk giving her a reason to overanalyze my hesitation to take her up on her offer and fill in the blanks on her own. But Claire also seems to bring out this confident, flirty side of me—a side I've never tapped into before.

It's not like I don't flirt at all, just not to this extent, and certainly not with a woman I barely know. I've always been careful not to make any claims I wasn't sure I could back up. But the thrill I get every time Claire doubles down with an even sexier reply is downright addicting. I'm afraid I can't help myself anymore.

She bites her lip coyly, and my stomach dips with her confirmation. "I'm not sure that's a fair claim. You haven't had much competition in a while," she admits.

"Neither have you, but that's not stopping me from saying it. The truth is the truth."

She clicks her tongue, but it only draws my attention back to her mouth. "You also believe in soulmates, so your version of the truth is somewhat questionable."

I bring my lips down to hers, and she melts into my kiss. We're both out of breath again by the time I force myself to pull away.

"The truth is no one's ever made my heart go crazy the way you do. Not even close," I rasp. I still don't know whether it's Claire or the adrenaline, but I'm certain it's at least a little bit of both.

She squirms and tries to downplay her reaction with another eye roll, making a grin spread across my face. "Seriously, *how* are you still single? What's your deal?"

"I don't usually pursue a woman if I don't see it going anywhere," I begin more timidly. "And I guess I haven't found anyone worth pursuing for very long."

"Oh, come the hell on. That's a cop out. You've got to have at least one red flag, something that scares the keepers away. And the severe peanut allergy doesn't count."

"I've actually been told that one was a deal breaker before," I point out, and she rolls her eyes as she props herself up on one of her elbows and stares expectantly at me.

"Fine, if you really want to know, according to the women I've dated before, I'm too ... *nice*," I say, cringing.

"You can't be serious," she deadpans.

I look away in embarrassment. "That's the explanation I've been given over the years, anyway."

"Well, sure, but they probably didn't mean it the way you're thinking."

"Okay, then tell me what it means." I turn on my side and mirror her pose, trying not to let my eyes stray from her face. Her current position highlights her curves in all the best ways, especially in those pajamas, and I can't risk a distraction when she's about to give me the secret to fixing my love life.

"Women want to be wanted. We need to be needed. We desire *desire*. We love chivalry, but we also need to know that we drive you absolutely wild." I shake my head, and she sighs before she continues.

"You're sweet and romantic, and you're eager to please the women you date, but only from a respectable distance. You're not making demands of them or pursuing them in a way that makes them feel like you can't live without them."

I furrow my brow. "Am I supposed to be a jerk, then? Should I forget to hold the door open and make her pay for her own meal? Act clingy and jealous or flirt with other women in front of her?"

"Of course not, but you can't leave room for any doubts, either. You've gotta tell her she makes your heart race and that she's the most beautiful woman you've ever beheld," she says in a mocking voice. But the way her eyelashes flutter when she looks at me again tells me she's not kidding.

Is this really it? The one time I loosen the reins and let my hormones speak for me is the time I get it right?

"You like that stuff, and you're actually admitting it?" I ask carefully.

"Dude, you've been practically melting my panties off all night," she replies with a smirk.

"Really?" I cock an eyebrow.

"Yes, really," she says, shoving me in the chest. "The combination of sincerity and yearning with that smile and those eyes ... not to mention all this." She gestures over my body before she hums appreciatively and shakes her head. "Forget *nice*, Rowan. You are a dangerous man."

"Am I?" I know my cheesy grin is giving me away now, but I've never been *dangerous* before.

"I think you know you are," she replies, reaching out to scrape a fingernail lightly down my chest and making me shiver. She smiles once she sees what she's done and repeats the move, watching for my reaction as she trails down past my navel this time.

"And I think you're the one who's dangerous," I hear myself saying, my voice taking on a deeper tone. My breathing quickens as I debate whether to shut out my conscience completely and just go with it for once. I know I'm playing with fire, but I may never get this opportunity again.

She shoots me a smug look after her gaze follows her fingertip up and down, because while my brain and my heart may be preoccupied, my body still has some ideas of its own. It's pretty obvious what I want right now—physically, at least. Emotionally ... I still don't know if I'll recover from this experience. Because even though I know this is wrong, I wasn't prepared for how amazing all of it would feel in the moment.

Kissing Claire, holding her and touching her like this ... It's all so different, and I can't even imagine what the rest of it might be like. Waiting until my wedding night has always been the plan, along with the assumption that my bride and I would both be relatively inexperienced and would need to work around the awkwardness. But I'm certain Claire knows *exactly* what she's doing. She'd probably be very accommodating, too, attributing the incompetency to my medicated state.

There's also the fact that I've never connected so well with anyone else, regardless of how long we've known one another. Maybe I didn't expect to find the cure for my loneliness in the arms of a stranger, but I'm already hooked on this intimacy stuff.

Now that I think about it, I might even resent denying myself this for the past few decades. I still believe in waiting for the right person at the right time and being rewarded with a blissful sex life, but what if I never get married? What if Claire *is* the right person, but we never make it past tonight? What if I end up spending my whole life alone and miss out on my only chance at a taste of heaven on earth?

I stare down at the breathtakingly beautiful woman before me, allowing myself the full weight of my desire for the first time in my life. There will be consequences later, I'm sure. But I don't think I give a damn about anything else right now.

I swallow hard before cupping my hand around her jaw and pulling her in for a kiss. She responds enthusiastically, letting out a soft moan before scooting in to press her body against mine. And my lingering doubts about the moral implications of all this are suppressed by the promise of her affection and warmth of her embrace.

My fingers slide around her neck and entangle themselves in her hair. I move to shift my position before I realize a couple of her locks are tangled around my middle finger, accidentally yanking her head back. She hums and pulls away to shoot me a wide grin.

"Didn't take you for a hair-puller, Doc. But I don't hate it," she says in that low, seductive voice.

I blink down at her, realizing I'm in way over my head again. This is the part when I'm supposed to confess my lack of experience or at least mention my celibate lifestyle. But I can't bring myself to risk ruining the moment. And even though I've always reassured myself that any woman who'd judge me for sticking to my beliefs didn't deserve me, I feel like I've held on to the truth for too long to spring it on Claire now and expect her to take it in stride.

Her smile softens after I'm quiet for a while. "You're not worried about hurting me, are you?"

"I-I don't ... I mean, we don't need to ..."

"Rowan, I'm far from an innocent virgin. I don't mind if you want to get a little rough," she tells me, wrapping her hand around my forearm and tugging so that her head jerks back again, squeezing the air from my lungs in the process. "And I trust you."

"No, um, I don't think that's my thing," I reply hoarsely and extricate my fingers from her hair. "Except maybe the part about earning your trust."

"What do you like, then?"

She sounds sincerely interested in my answer, and although I should probably reply with something along the lines of "I have no idea what I like in bed because I've never gotten the chance to find out," I don't think she'd care. Because, in spite of the way this night has consisted of one embarrassing and awkward debacle after another, Claire likes me. She practically knows everything else about me, and she still *wants* me. And that makes me want to place my trust in her, just like she trusts me.

I let out a more measured exhale as I muster up the courage to brush a knuckle down her arm. "You already know what I like."

"The soulmate experience?" she asks carefully, and I realize she's giving me an opportunity to help mitigate my learning curve.

I nod and slip my hands down to her hips, drawing her closer. "And I want to hear from you," I continue, scraping my palms over her thighs. My mouth turns up in a smirk as I allow my fingertips to venture beneath her silky shorts.

"Talk me through it, tell me what you need, and maybe give me a little positive reinforcement when I'm on the right track." She whimpers at my touch. "Yeah, that works," I declare breathily as I go in for another kiss.

"I want us to take our time, not just like we have all night, but all the nights after this one," I mumble against her lips before leaning back to gauge her expression. Her eyelids look heavy, and she tips her chin up to follow me, as if she doesn't want me to stop kissing her.

"I think you like that, too, though," I pose, my confidence growing. "You don't mind that I want to drag this out, to take turns worshipping your body and listening to you talk for the next few hours, do you?"

She sucks in a shaky breath and hitches her leg over my hip, confirming my suspicions. "I knew you were more dangerous than you let on," she murmurs, and I can't help the smile that spreads across my face.

claire

IS it actually possible to die from excessive yearning? Or dehydration?

That's it—I'm literally dying of thirst, but the sexy kind.

Don't get me wrong, I could lie here and talk to Rowan all night, especially when it involves this much skin-to-skin contact. I don't know if I'd ever get tired of kissing the man, and we've already proven my body responds extremely well to his touch. And, although I've always thought of myself as having a high sex drive, Rowan seems to be every bit as into it as I am. Yet, he's still stalling for whatever reason.

We haven't encountered any issues, despite all the medication he's taken over the course of the evening, so I can only assume he's worried about his stamina. But after he exercised enough self-restraint to stop me in the middle of an activity he claimed to enjoy *too much*, I don't see any cause for concern.

"You know what could be fun?" he poses, running a fingertip down my back.

I cross my hands over his bare chest so I can rest my chin and peer up at him. "Letting me finish what I started?" I guess.

His brow rises, and his face instantly flushes. "Oh, ah, yeah, that was ... definitely fun," he mumbles awkwardly, and I frown. "But I meant, fun for *you*."

"I didn't hate it," I reply coyly, and his throat works as he swallows hard.

"I really want to know what you like, though," he says, his voice strained.

I smirk at him. "Are you asking me whether I have a fantasy you might be able to fulfill?"

"Maybe," he says, stirring another ripple of desire within me.

I wouldn't normally share something like this, but I think his cheesiness might be contagious. And it's not like we're going to see one another again after tonight, anyway.

"Okay, promise you won't laugh?" I bite my lip and wait for him to nod before I go on. "I kind of think barns are sexy."

"Barns? Like, with the sheep and the hay and the ...."

"Shit?" I supply.

"Yeah," he confirms, regarding me strangely.

"To be fair, it's the hardworking man in the barn I find intriguing," I say sarcastically.

"So you have a thing for cowboys?" He cocks an eyebrow.

"Not exactly," I say, blushing.

"Farmers?"

I sigh. "I use to wish the country boy of my dreams would sweep me off my feet, buy me a piece of land, and build me a big old barn. And then I'd thank him by christening it, if you know what I mean."

A devious grin takes over his face, and he reaches down to stroke my lower back. "If you were my wife, I'd build you a barn, Claire Bear. A big one, with a loft full of hay to roll around in together. I'd even put a bed up there, if that's what you wanted."

I bite back a whimper, squirming and trying to keep my hips from seeking out his. But I'm wasting away. It's not fair that he keeps making himself more desirable, while I'm struggling to survive long enough to see him quench the fire he's been stoking.

"You keep mentioning a wife and a family," I begin, pausing to exhale and release some of the tension building up inside me again. "And earlier you said you only date women if you see things going somewhere ..."

"Is this a proposal?" he replies, his lip quirking as he tries to keep a straight face.

"It's a warning, because I don't think I'll bother with marriage ever again." My stomach tightens as I say it aloud, as if even my body knows how sad that makes me.

"I'm sorry to hear that," he says, sounding genuinely regretful. "Don't you think you might change your mind if you found the right person ... at the right time?"

I shake my head. "I'm not under the impression that I'm completely blameless. I contributed to the downfall of my marriage, too, and I don't think it would be fair of me to ask anyone else to take a risk on me again."

He swallows hard. "Do you mind if I ask what happened?"

"You still haven't answered my question," I remind him quietly, trying to postpone the part when I confess what a crappy wife I've been.

"Yes, I've never wanted anything more than to get married and start a family," he says, reaching out to brush a stray piece of hair away from my eyes. "Well, I take that back. I think I've been introduced to a whole new level of *wanting* as of tonight." He smirks as he adds the last part, and I feel the effects of it deep down within my core.

"Rowan," I object, but he only blinks down at me, waiting for me to continue. No man has ever looked at me the way this one does, and a small part of me wonders how I ever settled for a Jeremy when there were Rowans out there in the world, just waiting to stroke my back and gaze at me adoringly while I unload a lifetime of emotional trauma.

"Do you know what I want most right now?" he ventures, and my lady parts instantly take note, hoping to get called out by name.

"What's that?" I barely manage.

"For you to know that you can tell me anything," he replies, eliciting another sigh from me. Looks like I'm really going to have to pay the toll to get a ride on this ferry.

"I guess you could say that's what ultimately came between us, wanting different things," I begin after a while.

"Like what?"

"Like, I wanted to have a baby so badly that I was willing to try anything, and he wanted me to be satisfied with the life we had, mostly because we'd always done everything his way."

And even though it's already more than I've voiced aloud to anyone else before, Rowan looks so captivated by my story that the words continue tumbling out of me.

"He got tired of hearing me beg him to run tests and consider fertility treatments. He said I'd lost sight of the point of our marriage, but I couldn't understand why he didn't want to share something so important with me. I grew more and more resentful every time he refused to give me this one thing, the thing I wanted most. He wouldn't even consider adoption. He refused to argue with me about any of it, and eventually, he just started ignoring me altogether," I explain. "But the baby stuff wasn't the problem in itself. It was past time we acknowledged that we were both unhappy. We'd gotten together so young and grown apart over the years, and I think he'd fallen out of love with me a long time ago. Maybe he never really loved me in the first place."

"And you still loved him?" Rowan asks, his tone laced with concern and empathy.

"I cared about him and our marriage, but he was right. I'd become so obsessed with getting pregnant that I drove him away. Maybe I wouldn't have been so desperate for a baby if he hadn't always poured himself into his career. And maybe I didn't love him as much as I thought I did, anyway, since I made him feel like he wasn't enough," I explain, lifting one shoulder in a shrug. "In hindsight, I think we'd both become lonely. But the girlfriend he had lined up as soon as I agreed to our separation must have solved that problem for him, especially since she came pre-equipped with a bonus kid."

"I'm sorry," he says again as he reaches out to swipe at a tear on my cheek.

I've always been too embarrassed to cry in front of anyone, not only because it's another thing that makes me too much for most people to handle, but it doesn't fit in with my tough-as-nails persona.

But Rowan doesn't seem bothered by my emotional side. I don't think he minds that I cry too easily and laugh too loudly or that I don't have much of a filter, and he makes me feel like I don't need to pretend I'm so indestructible, at least not for him. I guess it's too bad my husband couldn't manage to do what this stranger has within a few hours of meeting me, or maybe I'd still be married.

My body rises and falls with Rowan's breathing, and I instinctively lean down and press a kiss to his chest. "Thank you," I whisper, though I'm not sure what I'm grateful for. Maybe he's given me the push I needed to open up and let those feelings out, or maybe it's the safe space he's provided. Either way, I've never felt more seen than I do right now. Not pitied, chastised, or ashamed—simply acknowledged and understood.

"Thank you for trusting me with that," he says softly. "I won't pretend to know the first thing about marriage, but I'm certain you've been harder on yourself than you deserve. And I can't imagine anyone stupid enough to take your love for granted."

I huff. "Says the man I've been practically throwing myself at all night."

He furrows his brow before he rises to sit and pulls me up to straddle his lap. Then he curls a finger beneath my chin and lifts my face to gaze into my eyes.

"My hesitation to spend the night with you is all my problem. I'm the one lacking the confidence for that kind of intimacy, especially with someone as beautiful and funny and sexy as you are."

I gulp. "Or maybe I've been coming off as so desperate that you feel sorry for me."

"Have you already forgotten the part when we met because you had to jam an EpiPen into my leg? Or the imminent threat of gastrointestinal distress and erectile dysfunction ever since?" he asks incredulously. "Do you really think I'm still here because *I* feel sorry for *you*?"

I giggle, grateful for his reassurance. "You are pretty dorky for someone so hot, although they do say the sexiest people have the worst tummy troubles."

He tries to force a serious look, but the corners of his mouth are still turned up. "Then I guess I am dangerous after all."

I stare at him, squinting my eyes. "Are you wearing contacts?"

"Yes," he answers hesitantly.

"Do you always wear them?"

He shrugs. "They're dailies, so I usually trade them out for my glasses before bed."

"I knew it!" I fire back. "You're even hotter and nerdier when you wear your slutty little glasses, aren't you?"

He tilts his head back to laugh. "I've never been under the impression that my nerdiness is hot or that my glasses are slutty, but—"

"What do they look like?" I demand. "Are they square, round, big, small, plastic or wire?"

"Uh, they're just plain glasses. Round, medium-sized, wire-rimmed ..."

"Slutty!" I declare with a grin, and he smiles back as he shifts his position beneath me and moves his hands down to grip my hips.

"I don't think they're particularly promiscuous, but maybe you'd like to see them sometime so you can decide for yourself?" he asks, his thumbs rubbing circles over my skin and making me shiver.

"Rowan," I breathe his name, fighting the near instant effects of his touch. "I can't ..." But I have to stop and bite my lip to keep myself from moaning when he uses his hands to steer my hips.

"I don't care about your divorce," he rasps. "I just want ... you."

I squeeze my eyes closed and shake my head. "That's not what we agreed to."

"Claire, tell me you feel this? I'm not crazy. We're meant for more than one night, aren't we?" I want to agree with every fiber of my being, especially after he begins kissing my neck, but I can't bring myself to do it.

"I'm sorry. I'm not ready for the kind of relationship you want, and I don't know if I ever will be," I choke out.

He groans, but he keeps going. "How am I supposed to function without you after this? I'll never find anyone who tastes as good as you do," he says, stopping to drag his tongue over the sensitive skin below my ear. "Or who sounds as sexy as you do," he adds when I let out a quiet moan. "Who makes me feel this good, or who makes my pulse speed up the way you do."

He backs away just long enough to bring my hand down to his left pec, where his heart thumps violently within his chest. "Please, don't break my heart," he begs breathlessly.

"You don't understand. I can't give you what you want," I reply, my voice trembling.

"I won't push you for anything serious until you're ready," he continues, ignoring my protest. "But I have to see you again."

I shake my head and lean in to kiss him before he makes me cry again. But he pulls away after a while.

"We can take it slow and keep it casual for now. All I'm asking for is the chance to make you feel wanted and needed and desired. I'll even wear my slutty little glasses to bed for you," he offers with a coy smile. "I'll take some extra allergy meds and eat a peanut butter sand-wich if I have to."

I heave out a sigh, because all of that sounds absolutely amazing, apart from giving him another allergic reaction. "I would choose you if I could. But I can't," I repeat, my voice cracking as I reach up to stroke his cheek. The short growth over his jaw scrapes my palm, making him even sexier. "You deserve more, and this is all I can give you for now."

"For now?"

I whimper when I realize I've given him false hope again. "Rowan, I'm a complete mess. What more do you want from me? I still have to finalize my divorce, and—"

"Wait, what?" He rears back and drops his hands abruptly. "Your divorce isn't final yet?"

"I mean, my marriage has long been over, and we've been living apart for over six months. Not to mention, he practically moved straight into his new girlfriend's house—"

"But you're still married." The words come out with a growl, and I barely hold back a flinch when I see his jaw ticking.

"All that's left to do is show up to the hearing this Tuesday and get the judge's signature. But, yes, technically, I am still legally married for the next seventy-two hours or so," I admit quietly, gathering the blankets around me to cover myself.

He frowns and nods solemnly. "Thank you for being so upfront and honest with me."

I narrow my eyes at him. "Are you being sarcastic right now?"

"I'm not sure," he breathes. He may be looking at me, but his gaze is distant now. "I'm sorry. I … I have to go."

He rolls out of bed and begins gathering his clothes from around the room, and I clutch the duvet tightly to my chest.

"Wait, I'm sorry. I really didn't think—"

"Thank you for taking care of me earlier and for the, um," he pauses to clear his throat as he slips his scapular necklace over his head, "the company, I guess."

My eyes sting as I watch him redress. "It's not like I purposefully lied about my divorce. And you and I aren't having an affair or anything, all right?"

He finishes buttoning his shirt and finally glances back at me. "Were you married in church?"

I shake my head. "We didn't even have a real wedding. I barely managed to drag him to the courthouse."

He lets out a relieved exhale before he turns to slip on his shoes. "Still, you made vows, even if he never intended to uphold his," he reminds me, and my chest feels tight.

"I guess this makes it easier for you to forget all about me then," I mumble once my sense of self-preservation finally kicks in.

"I don't think that's possible. You'll never understand what you took from me tonight."

He practically knocks the wind out of me with that blow. "Wow. Is this all part of that gratitude you felt after I saved your life?"

He cringes. "I'm sorry. I am grateful for your help, and I wish you the best. But I can't stay here."

"Where are you going?" I ask, not even bothering to hide the desperation in my voice. Because even though he's shattering that sense of safety I felt earlier, I can't help but worry about his well-being. And I probably deserve this, if I'm being honest with myself.

"Home," he replies, as if I should have known the answer.

"Okay, but how?" I wrap the sheet around myself and follow him to the door.

"I'm okay to drive, I promise," he says, softening his tone. Then he reaches out to pull me in and places a kiss over my forehead. "Goodbye, Claire," he whispers before he lets me go and slips out the door.

claire

"TOO BAD YOU didn't want alimony," my lawyer, Blake, grumbles under his breath before pasting on a fake smile and shaking hands with my ex-husband's attorney. "Jameson, always a pleasure," he drawls, and I snicker quietly when he turns to me and whispers, "and a pain in the ass."

Jeremy glances my way, and I offer him a counterfeit smile that rivals Blake's before we take off in opposite directions. I clear the emotion from my throat, not because I'm sad to watch the man I thought I'd spend the rest of my life with walk away for good, but simply because my best effort wasn't enough.

"Why do you hate that guy so much, anyway?" I ask, trying to lighten the mood. "I mean, he's obviously a tool, but …"

Blake smirks as he leads me through the courthouse. "But Ryan Jameson is no worse than I am, right?"

"Oh, is this where I'm supposed to say you're not like all the other lawyers?" I quip, and he snorts.

"He's Ethan Robin's biological father."

"*Ohhh*," I reply, thinking back to the custody battle Blake had helped his brother win just over a year ago. Of course my ex would hire the douchebag who refused to claim his own kid until there was something in it for him.

"Yeah. It's always personal with Ryan," Blake mumbles. There's a twinge in my chest, a reminder that I'm alone today, without any family or real friends willing to go to bat for me or even hold a grudge on my behalf.

"Wish I'd known earlier, before I left all that pettiness on the table," I say, making Blake laugh again. He probably thinks I'm kidding, but I'm not. Ethan's a great kid, one of my favorite students, and I enjoy working with his foster father, JD.

"Can I walk you to your car?" he asks as he opens the door for me.

"I'm fine," I tell him. "But thanks again for everything. You've made it all relatively painless."

He shakes the hand I offer, but he doesn't linger. "I'm sorry about the circumstances, but I'm glad I could help," he reassures me, flashing me one of his perfect smiles before he pulls his phone from his pocket.

There's no denying he's a handsome man. The former playboy might have topped my list for a rebound fling, had he not settled down with another one of my coworkers a few months back. Blake and Loren had stunned everyone by plunging headfirst into marriage and family life, not long after JD and Tenley had done the same when they eloped and secured custody of Ethan. Wonderful as that may be, the loss of Camellia's two most eligible bachelors has left the local dating pool as dry as a desert wasteland.

Apart from the proposition I'd received a while back from one of Jeremy's coworkers, my prospects look pretty bleak. Not that I'm all that eager to risk another belly flop after the events of last weekend.

My eyes catch the glint off Blake's wedding band when his thumb swipes across a lock screen photo of Loren and their twin baby girls. His smile kicks up on one side as he reads a text message, and that hollow feeling in my chest returns.

"You know, I can't help thinking you and Lo should be friends," he says, gesturing to his phone. "You've got the same sense of humor."

"Didn't think we had much in common," I reply quietly, trying not to give myself away.

"You'd be surprised," he reaffirms. "I'd better get back to work, though. Jada will let you know when all your paperwork is ready. In the meantime, you're officially a free woman."

I huff out an awkward laugh. "Yeah, thanks. Guess I've got some prowling to do."

"Take it easy on them, Claire."

He grins and goes back inside, leaving me amble over to my powder blue 1970s Ford Bronco. At least I managed to finish the restoration before downgrading to a single-salary household.

While I'm not usually one to fish for an invitation, I pause to send a text to my closest work friend, mostly because I can't bring myself to go home just yet. I'm mostly okay with living alone, but the arrival of Aunt Flo always seems to knock me down. And with my period due any day now, I'd rather not chance a pity party tonight.

CLAIRE

Hey, how's it going?

DAISY

Great! I was actually just about to text you. Loren's coming over to finalize some of the wedding plans, and I was hoping you could join us! ☺

Lovely.

Wedding planning doesn't top my list of ideal activities for today, but I can't exactly back out of the offer now. I reply that I'm on my way, attributing Daisy's oversight to her naivety. She's not usually this insensitive, but I doubt she's had much experience with divorce or even marriage, despite already having a legal husband of convenience.

Now that she and Landry Reed have decided to tie the knot for real, they're preparing for another ceremony to validate their union in the eyes of the Catholic church. From what I'm told, their marriage has to be blessed in order to consummate it, a concept I haven't been able to wrap my mind around.

But maybe I'm too jaded after giving myself to the same man for so many years and never noticing a difference. Married or unmarried, in or out of love, it was just sex. Sometimes it was fun, sometimes it felt more like a chore, but it's always been an essential part of a relationship. In my experience, men prefer to have their physical needs met without the hassle of emotional intimacy, and they certainly weren't willing to wait until marriage.

"I know you said it's just sex, but it's still going to mean something to me."

I bite my lip as I'm hit with another unfortunate flashback from this past weekend, but I can't even begin to deal with *that* right now. No, I refuse to let myself think about the kind of man I let slip through my fingers or whether things might have gone differently had my divorce been finalized a week earlier.

I sniff once and square my shoulders, stuffing my emotional wreckage back inside its box and resealing the airtight lid before I drive over to Daisy's place. It's a good thing, too, since her sister-in-law's minivan is parked in the driveway when I arrive.

"Okay, so we'll have a garden party motif for the bridal shower, and then we transition to the bachelorette party theme, 'Daisy Gets Her Garden Watered,' " Loren announces proudly as I walk inside.

I stifle a laugh and watch as Daisy's cheeks pinken, thinking my super-conservative friend will shoot down the idea.

"I love it!" Daisy says with an excited squeal, and her seizure response dog and I both raise an eyebrow in surprise.

I'd expect a little spice from Loren, since she isn't shy about her propensity for romance novels. Not to mention, she *is* married to Blake. But sweet, wholesome Daisy is another story. The woman's sewing her own wedding dress for crying out loud.

"What do you think, Claire?" Daisy asks, yanking a needle through the pile of white linen in her lap. Her recently acquired SRD, Juniper, settles at the foot of the sofa, watching dutifully.

"Sounds like fun," I fib. "Just let me know how I can help."

"Don't worry, my sister and I will plan everything. All you have to do is show up," Loren reassures us, barely casting a glance my way.

I nod and force a smile, wishing I'd gone straight home after all.

I look around for a distraction and pick up a framed family photo on the side table. A middle-aged man and woman huddle together, grinning widely as they pose among their nine adult children, judging from the resemblance. My gaze automatically zeroes in on Daisy's angelic smile. But my heart begins racing as soon as I recognize the blue-eyed, blond-haired hottie with his arm slung loosely over her shoulders, especially once I spot the brown cord peeking out from beneath his collar.

"So I'll be with Rowan?"

My head pops up when Loren speaks the name already caught in my throat.

"Who?" I blurt out like a belligerent owl.

Daisy glances my way, her brow furrowed. "My brother, Rowan? He's Landry's best man. They were roommates throughout college and medical school. You probably haven't met him yet."

My pulse throbs in my ears, and I blink down at the photo as I'm hit with one realization after another.

Holy shit ...

Did I really have a failed one-night stand with Daisy's brother?

No, it couldn't be the same Rowan, right? I mean, what are the chances?

Besides, my Rowan wasn't a LaFleur. He was a ...

Now that I think about it, I'm not sure I got his last name. Despite everything else I learned about Rowan during the ER visit, the only surname I remember is that of his emergency contact.

"Dr. Reed ... my college roommate and my closest friend ... he and my baby sister kind of eloped in secret ... the big church ceremony they're planning ... he wants me to be his best man, of course ..."

I curse under my breath as more of the pieces fall into place.

"That's actually how I ended up here, in Camellia," Daisy continues when she sees the confusion etched on my face. "Rowan's an MFM specialist, and he looked after Lo when she was pregnant with the twins. She mentioned needing a substitute teacher while she was on maternity leave, and he introduced us. Then I moved into her old house, and so did Landry, and the rest is history."

She grins at me, but I'm too busy panicking to return the favor. Having to live with Rowan's rejection is enough, especially after I was stupid enough to let down my walls for him. The last thing I need is Daisy and Loren finding out about the whole ordeal.

"Didn't ... didn't you go out with him before, Loren?" I venture, setting the picture down on the table and praying the others haven't noticed my reaction.

"Yeah, once, right before Blake and I got together," Loren replies, shrugging. "But we'll be fine to pose for a few pictures together at the wedding."

I accidentally let out a squeak. Scratch that earlier thought, because actually having to confront Rowan in front of everyone is the worst form of humiliation I can imagine.

"I'll just have to remember to avoid the peanut butter that day," Loren adds to herself, and my stomach practically hits the floor. Then her brows lift, as if she's just had an amazing idea. "Isn't Dr. Athanasius still available? Claire, you'll be back on the market soon, won't you?"

This time I stifle a whimper, and Daisy looks distressed.

"Oh, no," she says on a gasp, taking a step toward me. "It was today, wasn't it? Oh, Claire, I'm such a terrible friend. I didn't even ask you how your hearing went!"

"Nah, it was fine," I say too quickly, bumping into the table and tipping over the photo. I catch another glimpse of Rowan and Daisy together when it takes a couple of tries to get the frame to stay propped up, and my stomach turns.

"Yeah, just glad it's over. And thanks for letting me borrow your husband, Loren. I told him I might as well keep him on retainer for my next divorce."

"Sure," Loren says, narrowing her eyes at me, and my face heats.

"You know, if you want to talk about it, Lo and I both—"

"I'm good, Daze. Seriously," I reassure her. "In fact, I've gotta run. I, um, I forgot to let my dogs out before I came over."

"Oh, okay then." The disappointment in her big, green eyes immediately triggers my guilty conscience, *but I just can't ... not today.*

I know I owe Rowan an apology, but I'll never work up the

courage to face him again while I'm busy struggling to put on a good front for Daisy.

"I'll see you later. Or text me if you end up needing help with the wedding plans after all," I say as I back out of the door without waiting for a goodbye from either of them.

And I break the seal on that box as soon as I'm back inside my Bronco, letting out an exhale that sounds more like the beginnings of a sob.

rowan

MY EYES BEGIN WATERING against my will as I watch my baby sister trek down the aisle in a white linen dress, a crown of flowers adorning the veil on her head. But I'm not surprised. I always knew I'd cry the day I watched my favorite sibling get married.

What I didn't expect, however, was a view from this side of the altar. If anyone had told me six months ago that I'd be serving as the best man at her wedding to Landry Reed, I'd have laughed and asked for a sobriety check. Never would I have imagined the grumpy pessimist falling so hard that he'd marry a cheerful ray of sunshine like Daisy not once but *twice* within the same year. And even more unlikely than the two of them ending up together is the sound of Landry's quiet sniffles beside me.

I turn to glare at him incredulously while he swipes at his cheeks and flashes Daisy a sheepish smile. "You all right, Lan?" I whisper.

He clears his throat but keeps his eyes glued on Daisy as she beams back at him. "Never been better."

As if this whole scene isn't already weird enough, I glance over to find Loren watching her brother's open adoration of the bride with equal parts pride and amusement, and I realize I probably shouldn't look so surprised by Landry's affection, as uncharacteristic as it seems. I am supposed to know him better than his own family, after all.

I force a smile for Daisy as she reaches the end of the aisle, and she pauses to direct her seizure response dog to join the matron of honor. Our dad turns to embrace Daisy before pulling Landry in for a hug, one that lasts much, much longer than I would have guessed my friend would ever allow. Dad shoots me a wink when he backs away from Landry and places Daisy's hand within his, and I stifle a huff when Landry brings her knuckles up to his lips.

"Why are you crying, you big baby?" I hear Daisy whisper, reaching out blindly to hand her bouquet off to Loren before tossing her long hair over her shoulder.

"Because my heart has never felt so full, Blondie," he replies matter-of-factly.

I guess I've always assumed Landry was capable of this depth of unconditional love, but it's still surreal to hear him express it so freely. He surprises me again by leaning in to add something that leaves Daisy blushing and simpering back at him while he attempts to flatten his silly grin into a hard line. Even Juniper snorts at their over-the-top display this time, and I realize a second too late that I'm still wearing my uncertainty on my face. As happy as I am for both of them—and I honestly couldn't be more thrilled—I'm not sure I'm cool with watching my best friend whisper a non-church-appropriate proposition into my baby sister's ear, at least not yet.

If I'm being honest, though, most of my objections are just a reflection of my jealousy. Because I want this so badly—love and marriage and romantic companionship. Yet, here I am, the last of the LaFleurs ... always a groomsman, never a groom.

Sighing, I take a second to wallow in my loneliness before I garner a sympathetic look from Loren. I fidget uncomfortably as I rearrange my expression again, and she flashes me a polite smile in return. But it only reminds me of our epic failure of a blind date last year, which makes me feel even worse.

I turn away, my gaze catching on a familiar face in the pews. An audible gasp escapes my lips when I lock eyes with the one woman I never thought I'd see again, in the last place I thought I'd ever see her.

Claire smirks and lifts her brow in recognition, and I swallow hard and tug at the collar of my shirt before I manage a halfhearted smile in return.

What the heck is *she* doing here?

It's not that I haven't been secretly hoping to run into her again. And she looks just as beautiful and sexy as ever—that much I can tell from across the church. The problem is that we're *in* church, and I don't usually have this much trouble not thinking of anyone as sexy here.

My pulse quickens as I recall the night we spent together a few weeks ago, when I bent my self-imposed vow to remain celibate until marriage as far as I could without actually breaking it—with a married woman, no less. And while I may not have been fully culpable for that last bit, since I wasn't aware that her divorce wouldn't be finalized for a few more days, I'm still at fault for jumping into bed with someone I barely knew, ready and willing to surrender to my lust and take another soul down with me.

Maybe I'm being overly scrupulous by refusing to forgive myself for what I've done. But I'm supposed to be overwrought with guilt after breaking the rules and cutting myself off from God's grace. Yet, most of my remorse stems from simply hurting Claire.

No matter how many times I replay the events of that night in my mind, my biggest regret remains leaving her in tears, especially after everything she'd confided in me. It's also a reminder that I'm a hypocrite, because I know I'd still give in to temptation if I could do it all over again, except I wouldn't have the strength to walk out on her the second time around.

I blow out a careful exhale, suppressing the surge of emotions courtesy of Claire's presence, and I notice Loren eying me curiously. I force another fake smile and do my best to focus on the rest of the Convalidation ceremony, but I'm a total mess now that I know Claire could be watching. I end up fumbling Daisy's ring as I hand it over to Landry, then dropping it again and having to chase it down after it rolls away from the altar.

Great. I've managed to garner the attention of the entire congregation now, because the way my family looked at me as if I had two heads when I skipped Holy Communion earlier wasn't enough. I couldn't bring myself to go up, though, despite having already confessed my sins. I know my imperfect contrition is sufficient, but I can't help feeling like I don't deserve absolution this time, not with everything that's been swimming around in my head lately.

I'm practically crawling out of my own skin by the time we're reintroduced to "Dr. and Mrs. Reed." I've got to get out of this church before everyone sees the sweat stains forming under my armpits. Even Juniper senses my agitation, moving closer to Daisy and glaring at me with distrust. We finally get the signal to start the recessional, and Loren struggles to keep up when I nearly drag her down the aisle.

"Hey, you okay?" she stretches up to whisper as we reach the atrium.

"Yeah, I'm fine," I reassure Loren, though my voice cracks the second I spot Claire again. Someone tries to usher us back inside for pictures, but I pause to watch as Claire makes her way out to the parking lot, stopping to chat with Tenley, my new coworker, and her husband, JD. Daisy mentioned before that he was the assistant principal of their school, so it tracks that Claire would know him.

Because Claire must teach here, in Camellia, which means she and Daisy are coworkers. That's why she's here, at my sister's wedding. Because *they're friends*. I think Daisy's even mentioned her before, but I've been too stupid to put it all together.

Shit.

The entire bridal party turns to glare at me in shock when I inadvertently let the curse fly.

"Rowan?" Daisy's concern is certainly warranted this time. I rarely use that kind of language, and I'm still *in* church.

"Sorry," I mumble awkwardly. "I was just ... thinking out loud. Sorry."

Landry eyes me suspiciously before turning back to face the camera, and I let out another loud exhale before I follow suit. It's going to be a long night.

rowan

"CAREFUL THERE, DOC," Blake drawls as he winks at Loren and gathers a second baby at his side. "My wife had a peanut butter and pickle sandwich earlier, and I hear you've got a pretty severe allergy."

I snort out a laugh, but I still hesitate to take Loren's hand when the wedding party is called up for a dance. "Thanks for the warning. I'll be sure to keep my distance," I reply, doing my best to sound witty and totally not as intimidated as I actually feel.

"Ignore him," Loren tells me, rolling her eyes as she grabs me by the elbow. "He knows you're a gentleman. And even if you weren't, his arms are too full to defend my honor, anyway."

"Come on, Agnes. We all know I do some of my best work with my hands full." Blake grins at her as their twins squirm against his chest. "Look what I made last time."

From what I can tell, they're one of those couples who don't mind making everyone around them uncomfortable with their public arguments and borderline inappropriate banter. Except their threats always sound more like shameless flirting, especially with Blake undressing her with his eyes as he delivers his comebacks.

Loren hauls me onto the dance floor as she calls out, "Whatever you say, Daddy," over her shoulder, and I laugh through a groan.

Man, do I want this. Well, maybe not *this* exactly. I could certainly deal without the crude undertone. The memory of Claire's sexy smirk as she delivers a suggestive line flashes through my mind, stirring enough butterflies within me to immediately disprove that theory. I shake my head as I attempt to refocus.

"Sorry about that," Loren says with a contradictory smile. "We're weird. I know."

"This whole situation is still a bit weird," I retort as we shift into a platonic waltz.

"Oh, it's downright awkward. It's a good thing you're so cool."

"Yeah, sure." I know she intended it as a compliment, but I can't help that I'm getting tired of being Mr. Nice Guy.

"Wanna make it even weirder?" she poses with a bit too much excitement, and my brow lifts. "Let me set you up. Word on the street is you'll be spending more time in Camellia, and I work with a few cute, single teachers. A couple of them are here tonight."

I chuckle softly in relief. "I appreciate the offer, but I'm fine."

She frowns. "Are my friends not good enough for you?"

"Of course they are," I reply too quickly.

"I know what you must think of me, Rowan," she says quietly as we continue swaying.

My stomach dips in panic. "I don't think anything—"

"Oh, stop," she interrupts me, but she's smiling. "You may have told me you wanted kids, but we both know you're relieved after dodging this hyper-fertile bullet."

I tilt my head to the side and attempt to match her playful tone. "Do I seem relieved? I was going for gracious."

"And this is why things never would've worked out between us. You're entirely too sweet, even when you have every right to be a jerk."

I force a smile. I know she means well, but it's a little embarrassing to get this speech from a woman I've already dated, especially after divulging how desperately I want a family shortly before said date was crashed by the guy with whom she'd already started a family of her own.

Loren's grin grows wider as she leans over to catch a glimpse of our siblings dancing together. "Then again, who would have thought that combination of salty and sweet would balance out this well?" she asks, nodding her head in Daisy and Landry's direction.

"No kidding," I agree, my expression softening.

She sighs wistfully as she watches them. "It may not be obvious to everyone else, but we both know he needed her even more than she needed him." I nod, and she continues. "After everything he's been through, he deserves to be loved by someone as good and kind as Daisy. But I'm just as grateful to you and the rest of your family for picking up our slack over the years."

"Landry is one of the best people I've ever known. He's been a loyal friend, and I'm honored to call him my brother now," I tell her after swallowing down the unexpected emotion in my throat.

Loren's brows draw together in a way that makes me self-conscious. "You really are perfect, aren't you? You're definitely too emotionally mature to go to waste. Are you sure I can't set you up?"

My cheeks flush, and I force myself to look away, my gaze landing on Claire as she walks into the reception hall. "I'm far from perfect. Trust me."

"Even better," Loren replies. "Most women prefer their men morally gray."

I let out a huff, thinking back to Claire labeling me as a *dangerous man*. "So I've been told."

"Maybe you are just like the rest of them, then," Loren muses, nodding her head in Claire's direction when she catches me staring. "I get it, though. She's hot, and she's a total badass, but I'm pretty sure she's just gone through a divorce."

"Yeah, but she's—I mean—I don't ..." I stutter as my heart speeds up. If Loren or anyone else here were to find out about Claire and me, they might jump to conclusions and think we'd been having an actual affair. A knowing smile creeps across Loren's face, making it even harder to regulate my breathing.

"But you don't need me to tell you anything about Claire LeBlanc —or rather, Claire *Bergeron*. You already know her, don't you?"

I gulp and force a shrug. "Sort of."

Loren studies me carefully. "Do you ... *know* her, know her?"

I shake my head too quickly, dancing around another lie.

"Has Daisy introduced you?"

"This has nothing to do with my sister," I blurt out defensively.

"Hmm. And I didn't think she'd be your type, but ..." She bounces her eyebrows suggestively, ignoring my tone.

"Neither did I," I mumble to myself, and her grin widens when she catches it.

"Wait, is this like the time I went out with my brother's best friend because I was in denial about being so into the guy I wasn't supposed to be into?"

I swallow hard again. "Remind me, was that before or after your hands-free project?" I add my most charming smile at the end.

"We both know I was already knocked up by then. And don't think you're distracting me from drawing all kinds of inappropriate conclusions about you and Claire."

I cringe. "Let's just say this situation keeps getting stranger by the second."

"Does that mean you've been working on a secret project of your own in ag class?" Her eyes sparkle with excitement.

"Ah, I think you've lost me now," I fib in another poor attempt to create a diversion.

She gasps. "Oh my gosh, does Daisy even know her work bestie's been fitting your pipes?"

I choke and mumble something incoherent, but I'm afraid my train of thought derailed the moment Loren referred to Claire as my sister's *bestie*.

"Look at you, Doctor Athanasius," she continues, shimmying her shoulders, "I wasn't sure you had it in you, but maybe you *are* a bad boy."

My face feels like it's on fire now. The song finally comes to an end, and I mutter a polite thank you before darting off to the men's room to splash cold water on my cheeks.

I'm so busy searching the room for Claire as soon as I emerge that I bump someone's shoulder.

"Oh, sorry, ma'am," I say once I hear heels clicking against the floor. I reach out to offer a hand, but she manages to steady herself without my help. And I suck in a sharp breath when her hazel eyes meet mine.

"Um, hi," Claire says hesitantly as her posture straightens. She smooths a hand over her hair and adjusts the waistline of her fitted jumpsuit. It's far more modest than that purple cocktail dress, the lines of which have been burned into my memory. But I suppose that dress hadn't survived the night in one piece, much like me.

"Hi," I return, dragging my gaze away from her body. "It's good to see you."

"Is it?" she asks, her voice full of doubt.

I shove my hands in my pockets to keep myself from reaching out again. "Yeah. Unexpected, but good."

She shrugs. "Wasn't sure you'd remember me. That Benadryl buzz of yours was pretty strong."

"Not strong enough to forget you, Claire," I murmur. "I'm more surprised you remembered me."

"I don't get around *that* much," she says with a sardonic smile. "Plus, I was sort of expecting you to be here after recognizing you in my favorite work friend's family photos a couple weeks back."

My stomach bottoms out once she makes it clear she could have found me but didn't want to. "Maybe that's why I looked so familiar to you, then."

"I figured it contributed to that inexplicable trust on some subconscious level, at least."

"So you and Daisy taught together for a while?" I continue, trying to move past the ache in my chest.

"I was her mentor, actually," she explains, lifting a shoulder. "I got to show her the ropes."

Well, that makes two of us.

I clear my throat. "Then I suppose I owe you my gratitude for taking her under your wing."

"Your sister's a doll. You can't help but love her."

"Yeah, she's the best."

"And there are, what, nine of y'all?" Her eyes graze the crowd where some of my siblings and their families are gathered. I nod, my cheeks heating again as some of them take notice of our interaction.

"Growing up with so many brothers and sisters must have been amazing," Claire continues.

"It's certainly made life interesting," I say.

"For your parents, too," she adds wistfully. "Not many people would be open to having so many kids."

There's a twinge in my chest when I recognize that longing she mentioned before, the one we had in common, but I let my resentment override my remorse this time.

"Are you here alone?" I venture after an awkward silence.

She looks down at her feet as she speaks. "I don't have a date, if that's what you're asking."

"What about a husband?" My tone is rougher than I intend, but it's probably for the best since we have an audience.

"Officially my ex-husband," she confirms with an eye roll.

"Right," I say, clearing my throat and surveying the area again. One of my brothers and his wife are watching us more carefully now, as is my mother. "Well, you look nice," I add, but Claire ignores my compliment, probably because it didn't come out sounding as sincere as it should have.

"Did you bring a date?" she asks after a while.

"Nope, I'm all alone. The last of the nine LaFleurs without a spouse," I reply bitterly. "And no prospects of changing that any time soon."

She furrows her brow. "Why are you acting like this?"

"Like what? A stranger?" I ask, pointing to my chest.

"Like you're not the same guy who once insisted he was my soulmate and practically begged me for a second date," she says quietly.

"Yeah, well, you're the one who casually forgot to mention you were still married before you took me to bed, then made it clear you didn't want any kind of contact with me again. So you don't get to make judgments about what I'm like when you obviously don't care to know the real me."

"Wow." She blinks away her surprise. "Maybe you're right. I don't know you very well at all, because the guy I met before would never be this butthurt about anything, much less an arrangement he willingly entered."

I scoff. "Because you weren't honest from the jump. Not only did you let me think your divorce was already finalized, but you withheld the fact that you've been friends with my sister this whole time."

"That's not completely true. I didn't make the connection between you and Daisy until later," she whispers harshly.

"But you eventually figured it out," I fire back, even though my argument sounds weak now. "And you still didn't bother to reach out to me." She frowns, and my stomach churns with guilt.

"I couldn't find you on any kind of social media, so what was I supposed to do? Ask Daisy for your number, just in case you happened to be that random guy I almost hooked up with the other day? Scandalize your sister by telling her how we practically spent the night together despite barely knowing one another? That we were too busy exchanging bodily fluids to swap contact info?"

I sigh because she's right, even if she's being vulgar. And because a part of me still regrets passing up the rest of that exchange.

"A heads up before the wedding would have been nice," I say faintly, forcing those thoughts from my mind again. "You could have tracked me down without involving Daisy, especially since you know where I work."

"You could have found me just as easily. You knew I'd seen another doctor in your practice, so I'm sure you have access to my files."

"You've apparently changed your last name since then, and I'm pretty sure that would have been a HIPAA violation, anyway," I grumble, and she rolls her eyes again. "Besides, you only wanted me for one night. I had no choice but to respect your wishes."

"From what I remember, *you're* the one who walked out on *me*, and you're not exactly acting like you're happy to see me right now," she contends, crossing her arms.

She's right again. I'm making an ass of myself, but I don't understand why.

No, that's a lie. I know why I'm upset. But I can't exactly admit that I'm projecting my guilt without divulging some secrets of my own.

"I'm sorry," I say after a few seconds, softening my expression. "If it makes you feel any better, I don't like myself very much at the moment, either."

"Yeah, well, it wouldn't be the first time I brought out the worst in a man," she mumbles, her eyes looking shiny now.

"No, please don't ..." The urge to reach out and comfort her is so strong that it distracts me from my apology. I take a deep breath and fist my hands in my pockets before I start again. "I really am sorry, Claire. You deserve better. I'm just ... I guess I've been having a harder time dealing with all this change than I expected," I explain, nodding my head in the direction of the bride and groom. "But there's no excuse for the way I've behaved toward you."

She ducks her head as she runs a knuckle beneath her eyes to dry them. "I imagine today's been sort of bittersweet for you. And I get the part about not feeling like yourself as you're going through, you know, *changes*."

I cringe at the reminder that she's literally just been through a divorce. "I'm being insensitive again. I'm sorry."

"You're fine. It's not like I'm known for my tenderhearted disposition."

"Could have fooled me," I say, attempting a lighthearted tone.

"You should ask Daisy about the first time we met," she says with a sniffle. "I'm pretty sure she went home and cried about it."

"That makes two of us, then," I tell her.

"Yeah. Guess I left you with a horrible first impression and plenty of regrets, too."

"Oh, I have plenty of regrets about the night we met," I reply too quickly. "But not for the reasons you'd think."

She crosses her arms over her middle and looks away. "If you're anything like your sister, I can understand why it bothered you that my divorce wasn't final yet. You seem like a pretty upright bunch."

"We try, anyway," I murmur after I swallow the lump in my throat.

"Then I'm sorry, too. I didn't intend to mislead you. I'd honestly stopped thinking of myself as married a long time ago, but I should have been more transparent from the beginning."

Guilt gnaws at my stomach again. "I appreciate the apology, but I can't let you take all the blame. I probably shouldn't have gone up to your room in the first place when we barely knew one another, even if we had sort of trauma bonded before the end of the night."

"In hindsight, I can't imagine you being a one-night-stand kind of guy. I guess I shouldn't have invited you in," she pauses to smirk before she continues, "or suggested you take off your clothes."

I stifle a laugh as my insides get all warm at the memory. "I'm pretty sure that was a direct order."

"I was providing life-saving medical care," she retorts, swatting my arm playfully.

"By changing into your skimpiest pajamas and rubbing me down?" I ask with a raised brow.

"Those were *not* my skimpiest pajamas. And I was applying hydrocortisone cream, Benadryl Boy. It wasn't supposed to be sexy."

I grunt, purposefully brushing over the first half of her reply. "Neither was the part when you stabbed me with the EpiPen, but I wasn't lying when I said I'd risk anaphylaxis to have your hands on me like that again."

I don't mean to say it aloud, but there it is. I watch as her lips part in surprise and her eyelashes flutter, but it only takes a second for her to regain her composure.

"Oh, so now you like the idea of me getting down on my knees for you?" she demands, crossing her arms over her chest this time and regarding me skeptically.

I cringe and try my best to ignore the way she makes my stomach dip. "I'm acting like a jerk again, aren't I?"

"I guess that depends on your next move."

rowan

"CAN WE START OVER?"

Claire glares at me again. "Start over?"

I nod and shove my resentment aside. "Hi, Claire. I didn't expect to see you here tonight, but I'm actually very glad I ran into you."

"Oh, are you?"

"Yes. I've been hoping I'd get the chance to tell you how sorry I am about the way we left things before," I continue, because talking to her this way feels so much more natural than being as bitter as I was a minute ago. "And I wanted you to know that I haven't been able to stop thinking about you since the night we met."

She twists her lips to the side, as if she's considering whether she wants to trust me. "Maybe a small part of me has been looking forward to seeing you again, too," she admits shyly, and I can't help the smile that spreads across my face.

"It's actually pretty funny when you think about it, meeting again like this," I tell her.

"Yeah, I guess it is," she agrees, smiling back at me and making my heart speed up.

"Maybe a little more than coincidence?"

"You're not going to start with that star-crossed-soulmates crap again, are you?" she narrows her eyes.

"I did warn you about my fetish," I hear myself saying, though I'm not supposed to be flirting with her. And I probably shouldn't be reaching out to graze my fingers over her wrist, either, but it's a little too late for that now.

"Hmm," she hums, taking a step closer and hooking her little finger with mine. "You also told me you didn't do dirty talk, and we both know how that turned out."

I look away when I feel my face heat up, and she yanks on my hand.

"So, are you going to ask me to dance or what?" she poses just before we're interrupted.

"Hey, you two know each other?" Daisy asks when she and Landry approach.

My eyes widen in panic as I drop Claire's hand and take a step back, but she simply smirks at me before she turns to Daisy and says, "We've met before."

I clear my throat to disguise my relief. The last thing I need right now is my best friend and sister finding out that I'm just a big, fat, adulterous hypocrite. Because ...

Actually, now that I think about it, my love life is no one else's business but my own. I've only been so forthright about my celibate lifestyle to set a good example, but that ship has sailed now that the last of my siblings is sacramentally married to my best friend. Or it's scheduled to leave the harbor before the end of the night, at least.

Besides the blow to my pride when Claire inevitably denies having formed any real attachment to me, there's no need to worry about my family learning I'm not as perfect or pious as they all think I am. So I'm human; I'm not impervious to temptation. They love me in spite of my other faults, so this shouldn't be any different. They'll probably tease me if they ever find out I was moments away from losing my virginity to a stranger after waiting this long, but they're just as likely to encourage me to make better choices next time.

I'm also a grown man, and I don't have to answer to anyone but God at the end of the day.

I open my mouth to declare that Claire and I have done more

than meet before or at least imply that we've dated, but I'm overcome with another wave of panic and shame at the thought of Daisy and Landry realizing it happened while Claire was still another man's wife.

"She's a patient," I blurt out the half-truth instead. "Not mine, but … she's seen one of the other specialists."

Claire turns to glare at me. "HIPAA violation, huh?" she mutters under her breath, my chest tightening once I understand what I've just done.

"Oh." Daisy gives her a sad smile.

"Yeah, small world, I guess," Claire says quietly, but I see the pain in her eyes. And I hate that I'm the one causing it.

"Did Rowan tell you he's going to be working in Camellia now?" Daisy continues.

Claire's head swivels, and my pulse begins drumming in my ears as she stares me down. "He didn't. I guess he's just full of secrets tonight."

Daisy furrows her brow in confusion, but she goes on. "He's going to start seeing patients at Dr. Simms's clinic a couple of days per week."

"Looks like I'll have the pleasure of running into him more often outside of work," Claire says dryly, and my stomach turns at her word choice.

"Yeah," I rasp when I finally find my voice again. I want to say more, to dig myself out of this hole and make sure Claire understands how much I like the idea of seeing her on a regular basis. But I'm a coward, and I'm afraid Landry's on the verge of calling me out, if the way he's scrutinizing me is any indication.

"Why are you being so weird, man?" he asks me bluntly, and everyone sighs. Despite my sister's attempts to install a Landry filter, he still can't read a room.

He hisses when Daisy elbows him in the ribs. "What? It's true, I've never seen him like this before. He's hiding something," he says defensively.

Claire snorts and crosses her arms, daring me to prove Landry wrong, and I know this is the part when I'm supposed to come clean or at least make some charming allusion to a romantic connection between us.

But I open my mouth again, and nothing comes out.

"Maybe we interrupted an important discussion," Daisy volunteers, breaking the silence, but she's still studying me closely.

"Were you ... shooting your shot? With *Claire*?" Landry asks incredulously.

"I guess I should have prepared a better pickup line," I finally manage, forcing a smile.

"Funny, you didn't have any trouble charming the pants off me the last time we met," Claire retorts, and everyone laughs awkwardly.

"Eh, you might be out of your league this time, bro," Landry says, wincing when Daisy nudges him again. "Oh, come on."

And that's when it hits me—I'm not just worried about them finding out about what happened between Claire and me or that it nearly happened before her divorce was final. I'm embarrassed because Claire couldn't be further from my usual type, and I don't want them to say I've settled or given up on the kind of woman I've been holding out for. Not that Claire isn't amazing in her own right—I meant it when I said she was the most beautiful and interesting woman I'd ever met. But she is admittedly more worldly than the women I've dated before.

I glance over to find Claire's eyes looking misty, and my stomach lurches.

"You're right. I'd eat him alive," she affirms with a cold laugh.

"You don't think opposites attract?" Daisy poses to Landry.

He purses his lips thoughtfully before he speaks. "I think I'm the luckiest man in the world."

"Blessed," Daisy corrects him, and he nods in agreement before leaning in for a quick peck on the lips. "You haven't gotten lucky, yet, but I plan on changing that soon," she adds in a sultry tone.

I wrinkle my nose when Landry growls and shoots her a smoldering look, even though I'm grateful for the shift in conversation.

"There you are," my sister Magnolia says when she appears and reaches out to tug on Daisy's arm. "Come on, it's time to cut the cake."

Daisy whines. "Aren't we done with all that stuff?"

"Not even close. And what are *you* doing out here? You haven't even given your best man toast yet." Magnolia aims the second half of her reprimand at me as we're joined by another one of my sisters.

I groan, despite having prepared a nice speech. I'm just not a fan of Maggie's bossy tendencies.

"Ma-*ags*, you're not torturing the bride, are you?" chirps Marigold.

Magnolia crosses her arms and glares at her twin. "Someone has to keep things running smoothly."

Iris and Violet appear then, each of them toting a baby, and I blow out a frustrated breath when I notice Rosemary and my mother making their way over. I'm certain this impromptu meeting of the LaFleur women is just a guise for their investigation, but I suppose I was asking for it after having that heated conversation with a strange woman in front of everyone. I venture a glance at Claire and find her taking in the scene with interest.

"What's going on?" Violet demands. "Is Maggie trying to direct traffic again?"

Magnolia rolls her eyes. "Have none of you heard of wedding reception etiquette?"

Claire snorts quietly, and my lips twitch as I stifle a smile.

"I don't get the impression that the people of Camellia care any more for etiquette than we do, especially not after watching them balance those beers on their heads as they danced to that Mardi Gras song," Iris says sardonically and adjusts the infant in her arms.

"Regardless, it's Daisy's wedding," Mari says gently. "She and Landry will cut the cake on their own time, if they decide to have cake at all."

"Oh, I'm having cake tonight, one way or another," Daisy declares vehemently, and Claire lets out a loud chortle.

"Yeah, I think you'll like that cake better, anyway," Claire says, making both Landry and Daisy's cheeks darken, and I realize the rest of us must be missing the punchline of a dirty joke.

"What's so special about this cake?" Rosemary asks. "Or are we talking about the groom's cake?"

"Well, Landry's mom said she made that one herself, so I doubt it's gluten-free," Iris mumbles, triggering another fit of snickers from Daisy and Claire.

"Do I want to know?" I whisper to Landry, and he cringes as he shakes his head.

"From where I'm standing, it doesn't look like our Landry's been worried about gluten," my mom says, patting his backside affectionately.

"And I'm definitely looking forward to a piece of *that* groom's cake," Daisy barely manages to squeak out before she slaps a hand over her mouth to contain her giggles, and Landry surprises me again by smiling at her, seemingly amused.

Violet narrows her eyes at Claire, who's biting her lip and holding back tears at this point. "Wait a minute. You're talking about sex, aren't you?"

"Oh, but I'm the one who's bad at picking up on social cues?" Landry mutters, and Violet screws up her face at him. That does Claire in, and she chokes so hard on her laughter that it becomes contagious.

I shoot her a grin once everyone settles, hoping to convey my remorse after I left her hanging earlier. But her smile fades, and she doesn't hold my gaze.

"Right, and who are you again?" Magnolia asks Claire.

Claire's brow rises, but she doesn't bother waiting for me to introduce her. "Claire Bergeron, Daisy's work friend," she replies confidently.

"And an acquaintance of Rowan's," Daisy adds, lifting her chin and daring me to correct her.

My heart races as I struggle to form a response. "Yes. We have been ... acquainted before," I fumble awkwardly, and Claire huffs.

"You weren't at the bridal shower," Maggie says, a hint of accusation in her tone.

"I missed it. Something ... came up," Claire says, her eyes flashing to Daisy's, and I surmise that *something* was our acquaintanceship.

"Interesting tattoos," Iris remarks, eyeing her.

"Yes, very lovely." Rose leans forward to inspect Claire's arm while Claire simultaneously studies Rosemary's nun's habit, and I frown at the urge to protect them both from one another's scrutiny. But they both seem more curious than anything.

"And you know what? I think we're all here. I spy a marigold and a magnolia, an iris, a violet ... a daisy, a few roses ... oh, and a couple of camellias," Rose explains, pointing out each of the vibrant flowers in Claire's mural.

"Hmm, how 'bout that," I accidentally say aloud, and everyone turns to glare at me. But the only eyes I see are Claire's.

"There are others," Claire maintains. "Tulips, lilies, a sunflower."

"Orchids," I add, swallowing hard. Because even though I hadn't thought about exactly which *fleurs* grace Claire's arm, I could probably map out every inch of her tattoos with my eyes closed.

Claire shrugs and turns back to my sisters. "What can I say? I like pretty things."

I'm afraid I do, too.

"Assuming you meant to prioritize visual appeal over anatomical accuracy, it's actually quite nice, as far as tattoos go," Violet concurs, and I clamp my jaw shut before I blurt out something about Claire's agricultural background.

"It's beautiful," Marigold tells her with a warm smile. "As is the canvas."

"I agree, she is gorgeous," my mom says, moving in to wrap an arm around Claire's waist without warning. "And I'll be expecting you the next time Dr. and Mrs. Reed grace us with their presence at the homestead, Claire Bergeron."

Daisy grins, obviously pleased by their seal of approval, and Claire's expression softens as she relaxes into my mother's side. And

I'd be lying if I said it didn't cause my chest to tighten and a lump to form in my throat.

"Okay, now, time to get moving, people! I have a toast to deliver!" Loren calls out, clapping her hands as she joins us.

Landry's head lolls back, and he groans. "Do we have to?"

Loren scoffs and grabs me by the elbow. "Damn right, we do. Do you know how long I've been waiting for this?"

Daisy whimpers. "Have mercy, at least for my sake?" she begs Loren, who barely manages to stifle a smile.

"I'll see what I can do," Loren muses, casting a telling smirk in Claire's direction before she tugs me forward. "Come on, Dr. Athana-sius. Baby sis is ready to cut into that cake, from what I hear."

rowan

I SQUINT up at the street signs, but they're unreadable after having been peppered to death with a BB gun. Between the emotional rollercoaster of seeing Claire again and the cleanup efforts after the conclusion of Daisy and Landry's wedding reception, I'm utterly exhausted. And while rubbing my eyelids usually helps refresh my dry contact lenses, all it does is cloud my vision and make it even harder to see this time.

My right lens wrinkles, so I shift my truck into park and flip down the visor to get it straight. Blinding blue lights flash in the mirror, making me wince and scrape my eyeball. Then I flinch twice as hard a second later when an unexpected knock scares the heck out of me, and I accidentally dislodge the contact lens altogether.

" 'Scuse me, sir. I'm gonna need you to get down from ya truck, please," says a muffled voice with a strong accent.

"One second, I have to find my contact before it dries up!" I call out and lean down to search the floorboards, but I get an even more emphatic warning as the cop pounds against the driver's side door.

"I'm sorry," I say with my eyes closed, immediately raising my hands. "I just ... I got lost, and I can't see."

"Sir, step outta the vehicle," he demands.

I groan. "My contact lens fell out while I was driving, and if I don't get it now—"

"And I told you to get outta the damned truck, boy. Don't make me tell you again."

"Okay, okay. I'm coming out," I say as placatingly as possible and force my eyes open.

The deputy takes a step back when I open the door, his palm resting on the gun at his hip. Although I'm not sure how easy it would be for him to pull it out with the holster tucked under his gut that way. "Keep your hands up where I can see 'em, just like that."

I follow orders until he shines a flashlight directly into my already sensitive eyes, after which I stumble backward, bumping into the driver's side door and earning myself another warning. Pain pulses through my head when he scolds me again.

"You just don't listen, do ya?"

"I'm sorry. You're killing me with the lights," I retort angrily to my own surprise. While I'd normally pride myself on remaining compliant and respectful in a situation like this, this guy is catching me on a bad night. Or maybe I'm simply too tired, and my give a care is broken.

"Put ya hands back up," he scolds me, and I cringe as I obey. "You ain't from Camellia, are you, boy?"

"No, sir. I only came for my sister's wedding," I explain as calmly as I can.

"Wedding, huh? You kin to Coach Reed's people?"

"I am now."

He raises an eyebrow and spits on the ground at the hint of sarcasm in my reply. "Don't get sassy with me."

I let out a long exhale. "My sister, Daisy, married his son, Landry. In fact, I was trying to make my way to Coach Reed's house to stay for the night. I'm sure if I could call—"

"His boy, Landry, he's a doctor now, ain't he?" the deputy interrupts, still regarding me suspiciously.

"Yes, sir. We went to medical school together."

He stares at my pickup before he continues. "Well, Doc, whatcha doin' in that ol' Toyota with all that money you oughta have?"

I swallow hard. "My truck might be old, but it runs just fine. And I don't care much for fancy things."

As soon as I say the words, Claire pops into my head again. I bite my lip as I think about tracing the outline of her tattoos and wrapping her silky hair around my fingers. Then I clear my throat and shake my head, reminding myself that this isn't the time to fantasize about a woman I can't have. Not that there's ever a good time for *that*.

"Hmm. You been drinkin' tonight, son?" the officer asks.

"No, sir," I reply too quickly. "Well, technically, I had a small sip of champagne at the end of the wedding toast, but that's all. I don't really drink."

He narrows his eyes at me and steps in closer. "How 'bout a little sobriety test, then? Just to make sure you're fit to drive."

Is this thing on?

I blink at him. "But I'm *not* fit to drive. That's what I've been trying to tell you."

"So you're admitting to driving under the influence?"

"No, but I am currently blind in one eye, since I won't be able to unstick my contact lens from the floor mat by now," I say, unable to keep my annoyance from leaking into my tone again.

"Now, you listen here—"

"What's going on? Mr. Godchaux, is that you out there?" a female voice calls out.

"Who's dat?" the deputy asks, turning the beam of his flashlight to reveal the outline of a dark-haired woman a few yards away.

"Claire Bergeron, the ag teacher." I tilt my head back and let out another loud groan. "I welded that front grill onto your patrol car the other day, remember?" Claire adds when the deputy doesn't respond right away, I'm guessing because of the name change.

"Oh, hey, Claire. You all right?" he asks, glaring at me after my rude interruption.

"Yeah, fine," she answers, turning to face me. "Just came out to see who was blocking my driveway."

Of course *she's* going to witness my accidental DUI. What are the chances this would happen in front of her house? Wasn't it enough that I had to watch her interact with my family from afar all night after I butchered our reunion, then swallow my pride again when she so generously volunteered to stay behind and help us clean the reception hall?

My pulse quickens, and I scold myself for being more concerned with someone witnessing this whole fiasco than the possibility of actually going to jail. Because it can't just be the sound of Claire's voice making my heart go crazy right now, can it?

"Sorry 'bout that, sweetheart. But I'm in the middle of something right here, so I'm gonna need you to go back inside, for your own safety. At least until I can get this uncooperative drunk driver off the road for the night."

I roll my eyes and scoff, and Claire snorts out a laugh of her own. "This one might be uncooperative, but I don't think we have anything to worry about," she calls out with a tinge of amusement.

"You know this stranger?" Mr. Godchaux asks in surprise.

I close my right eye and attempt to make out Claire's expression in the dark. Yeah, she's definitely enjoying this.

"We've met," she replies cooly.

"*Mais ouai*, I guess you been at the Reed wedding, too," he says thoughtfully. "That little bride teaches wit' ya, doesn't she?"

"Yes, sir," Claire replies. "And she's a sweet girl. The whole family seems nice."

I sigh in relief when she takes pity on me. "Claire, please tell him I'm not drunk. I've never even been drunk in my life."

"I don't know about that last part, but I have seen him under the influence of allergy meds before. And he's a lot more fun when he's less sober," she says dryly. It seems like she might be moving closer, but it's still hard for me to tell. I squint again, and she pins me with a confused glare.

"What's wrong wit' you, boy? And why the hell you keep try'na wink at everyone?" the deputy asks, shining his light in my face again.

I wince. "Like I said, my eye hurts. And the way you keep blinding me isn't helping."

"Yeah, but there's something else," he insists. "You ain't from the city, are you?"

"Grew up on a farm," I mutter.

"Maybe it's because he was homeschooled," Claire chimes in, barely containing her laughter.

The cop shakes his head. "That ain't it, either. You on something else? Some of dem funny gummies?"

"Nah, he's too straight-laced for that. I think he's just weird," Claire says with her hands on her hips.

"Sure, because wearing contacts makes me the weirdo here," I grind out.

"Oh, I get it," the deputy says before turning to Claire and whispering, "He's gotta lil sugar in his tank."

Claire coughs as she stifles her laughter. "That would explain a lot."

A growl escapes my throat. "You really wanna know what's wrong with me? I'm exhausted, okay? I just married my baby sister off to my best friend, which leaves me all alone, the last of my nine siblings. And I am a *good* guy, all right? I definitely like women, for the record, and I respect them. Heck, I help women for a living. I never drink and drive. I love kids. I'm a really good uncle and a *Parrain* to a ton of my nieces and nephews. I go to church, I give to charity, and I pray the rosary, like, every day," I tell them, ticking my qualities off on my fingers. "I'm the kind of guy who walks across the parking lot to save his shopping buggy. Yet, there are eight examples of people with the same genes and upbringing as mine who were able to find true love—nine if you count the control group, AKA the grumpy asshole that's currently embarking on a honeymoon with my sister—and I can't even manage to avoid the emergency room or a sober DUI in front of the first woman I've liked in as long as I can remember!"

I hear Claire snort beside us, but I don't look her way. "So while the idea of drowning my sorrows with a few mood-stabilizing gummies and the rest of that champagne I passed on earlier sounds pretty damned good right now, I can honestly say I'm not high or drunk. I'm just pathetic and tired, and quite possibly blind in one eye. And I wanna go home, but I live two hours away. So my only option is to crash with Coach Reed, which probably speaks for itself."

Mr. Godchaux nods at that. "Yeah, Leslie Reed has always been an asshole," he offers, then flinches. "Sorry 'bout my language, sweetheart," he directs at Claire.

"I'm honestly more surprised to hear Dr. Green Flag knows how to cuss," she replies.

I shake my head and slump back against my truck. "Seriously, what do I have to do to get out of this? Can I call a lawyer? I've got one in Camellia who owes me a couple of favors."

The deputy clears his throat. "If I let you go now, how are you going to get to Coach Reed's?"

"I'll drive him," Claire answers for me.

"You will?" I ask hesitantly.

"Yeah." It looks like her arms are crossed again, but I still can't make out her expression. "You can leave your truck in my driveway and pick it up in the morning."

I gulp. "Thank you, Claire."

Deputy Godchaux looks back and forth between us a couple of times before he nods. "All right, then. I'll let you take it from here, sweetheart. If you're sure?"

"You heard the man. He's too down on his luck to give me any trouble," Claire says tauntingly. "Plus, I'm single now, and he sounds like quite the catch."

I stifle a smile, and the deputy chuckles one more time. "Y'all be careful. And you better show this young lady some gratitude, you hear?"

"Yes, sir. I'll be sure to repay her for her trouble," I reply, unable to hide my grin now.

He tips his head and goes back to his patrol car, leaving us alone in the dark.

"Thank you for that. I owe you one," I volunteer as she walks over. I open the door for her, and she smirks at me as she slides into the driver's seat.

"I'll add it to your tab, Dr. Green Flag."

claire

ROWAN RUBS his eyes again as he climbs into the passenger seat of my Bronco. "I think you're gonna want to take a left—"

"I know where Coach Reed's place is," I cut him off to say. "I may not have grown up in Camellia, but I've lived here long enough."

"Right," he replies and sighs wearily. He's quiet for a minute, allowing the tension to grow until I reach out to raise the volume on the nasally country song playing on the radio.

Rowan clears his throat. "This isn't exactly what I expected, but I should have guessed you were a restored-vehicle kind of girl."

"I can't believe you took me for a *girl* at all," I retort sarcastically.

"Sorry. I didn't take you as the kind of *lady* who would drive an old, jacked-up Bronco, but it suits you," he corrects himself, and the fact that he made it a point to call me a "lady" in lieu of a "woman" makes the corner of my mouth turn up.

"Yeah, well, I didn't peg you as the type to buck authority," I tell him.

He scrunches up his nose, looking sheepish. "I'm not. But it's been a long day. And like I said before, I haven't really been feeling like myself lately."

"So what's your excuse for driving a truck that's at least a decade old?" I ask after a while.

He shrugs. "I like my truck. It's reliable, and it gets me where I need to go. Why would I trade it in if it still serves its purpose?"

"Because you're a doctor and you can afford something nicer?"

"Seems like a waste when this one isn't even all that old. Toyotas are usually good for over three-hundred-thousand miles, you know," he says, frowning.

"Wouldn't you rather a newer model with more creature comforts?"

"Comfort is a gateway drug. Too much of it makes us lazy and entitled," he declares before he apparently thinks better of it and softens his tone. "Wouldn't you rather something new?"

"I added a few modern conveniences while I still had access to my ex's bank account," I explain, gesturing to the control panel.

"Didn't they start making Broncos again?"

"They did," I say, lifting a shoulder. "But this one was made for me."

"I can see that." He hums and runs a hand over the dashboard, and I could swear he was touching me instead.

"Are you attached to your truck?" I ask, my voice raspier than I intend.

"I'm grateful for it, but that's all."

I shake my head, reminding myself that he *is* Daisy LaFleur's brother, after all. "I bet you'd get more action in a brand-new truck or a fancy sports car," I pose and glance his way.

"I'm not into women who are more interested in men with money," he replies quietly. He's entirely too cute when he's shy.

"No, you wouldn't be," I confirm as I pull into Coach Reed's driveway. I'm still not sure how Loren and Landry's dad earned so much respect. By the time I started teaching at Camellia High, no one even dared to bother him with requirements like writing lesson plans or completing his online blood-borne pathogen training. He just flat-out refused to do anything but coach football, and I suppose the powers that be had no choice but to tolerate him until he retired. I wonder to myself whether I'll be that stubborn by the time I reach the thirty-year mark, but I guess managing teenage boys all day can do that to a person.

"Thanks again," Rowan says when I put my car in park, bringing me back from my thoughts. I watch him swallow hard before he turns to face me. "I'm sorry about earlier, too. You've been much nicer to me than I deserve."

I lift one shoulder in a shrug, suddenly feeling embarrassed. I probably shouldn't admit that I've been mostly motivated by guilt, and I certainly can't tell him about the part of me that genuinely missed him. "I wouldn't have wanted the bride and groom worrying about you today."

"Right," he says, looking surprisingly disappointed. "I'm glad my sister has friends like you looking out for her."

"It's easy to be a good friend to Daisy. She's the kind of person that makes you want to do better."

"Yeah, she is. Landry has his moments, too, I suppose," he adds with a smile.

"He's not so bad once you get past his bark," I agree, narrowing my eyes at him. Why are we talking about Landry again? Is he ... stalling?

Rowan nods. "I guess I should feel hopeful after all this, since there's apparently someone out there for everyone."

"Yeah, because if Landry Reed deserves to find his soulmate, shouldn't you?" I reply once I catch on to his thought process.

He cringes. "Gah, that sounds so much worse when you say it aloud."

"But you were thinking it," I point out, and his sigh is laced with regret.

"God forgive me, but I was," he admits.

"I get it," I reassure him. "And I'm sure your person is out there somewhere. Don't give up."

He rolls his lips in, as if he's considering what he wants to say next.

"You'd better get in there before Coach locks up for the night. He doesn't strike me as the kind to wait up for anyone," I add quickly to keep Rowan from turning my last claim into another deep conversation.

"Yeah, good night, Claire," he says, sounding even more disheartened. "I guess I'll see you in the morning?" He notices the confusion on my face and adds, "Once I work up the courage to ask Coach for a ride to pick up my truck."

"Oh, right. Don't worry about coming inside, though. You don't need to get my permission or anything."

He nods one more time and mumbles his thanks as he finally gets out of my car, and I let out a relieved exhale as I shift into reverse. But I can't bring myself to leave until I know for sure he's safe for the night. I watch with a restless foot on the brakes as Rowan knocks on the front door for the third time. Then I whimper to myself before rolling down my window.

"He's not answering, is he?"

"I'm sure he'll open up ... eventually," Rowan says, sounding less confident by the end of his claim.

"Have you met the man before?"

"You're right." He turns and leans back, his head hitting the door with a thud. "All I need is to slip inside long enough to grab the bag I left earlier, so I could have my glasses for the drive home. But this is just par for the course tonight."

I bite my lip, trying not to think about those glasses. Maybe I've been repressing some weird, girlish fantasy, because I can't recall another time when I thought glasses made a man sexy. But I'd be lying if I said my imagination hadn't been running away with the idea of a bespectacled Rowan since the night we met, especially once I realized I'd be seeing him again.

"Get back in the car, Rowan," I call out after a while, trying to hide the way my voice cracks.

He straightens his posture. "Are you sure?"

"Hurry the hell up before I change my mind." I stifle a smile when he shuffles down the front porch steps and climbs back into my Bronco.

He huffs into his hands as soon as he's inside, so I reach out to turn up the heat. The temperature has dropped a few degrees since our adventure began, and I'm already starting to regret not changing out of my cap-sleeved jumpsuit or at least grabbing a jacket before allowing those blue lights to lure me outside.

"Good thing I switched on the heater before I left home," I mumble to myself.

"Wish I could say the same for my truck. But I guess this is when you tell me remote start would come in handy, right?" He shoots me a grin as I pull out of the driveway.

I furrow my brow. "You don't have to fish for an invitation. I'm not heartless enough to make you sleep in your truck."

His eyes widen in what seems to be genuine surprise. "Oh, um, I wasn't ... I didn't think ..."

I scoff. "I don't know whether I should be more offended because you thought I'd really leave you out in the cold or because you're afraid I'll seduce you again if you come inside."

He's silent, and the fact that he doesn't bother refuting my claim makes me want to shrink back into myself.

"Don't worry, I get it. You can't help wondering what you missed out on, but you're not willing to stoop to my level again," I mutter after a while. "I'm done with trying to please men who think they're better than me, though, so you're in the clear. This is just another act of charity on your sister's behalf."

I'm determined not to give him the satisfaction of glancing his way as I drive up to my house and throw the car in park. But Rowan's hand encircles my wrist before I can make my escape, holding me in place.

"Claire," he begins, his voice pained, and I break. He waits until I turn to look at him before he continues. "I'm not going to act like your assumptions are completely unfounded, but I swear, they're wrong. I really am grateful for your kindness, and I'm sorry, again, for taking out my frustration on you. The truth is I am much more concerned about my own lack of self-control, since there's apparently something about you that makes me forget who I am. And I can't afford to push my luck right now."

"So that's why you seem so upset about getting stuck with me again? It's more complicated now that I'm Daisy's friend and not just some stranger?" I tug my arm back, and his frown deepens.

"It's definitely complicated, but not exactly for the reasons you'd think." He pauses and swallows hard before he starts again. "You're a beautiful woman, Claire, and you're easy to like. But as much as I wish our circumstances were different, you were right before. Ignoring the fact that we want totally different things wouldn't be fair to either of us. The problem is that I've never had so much trouble walking away from anyone before, especially when we weren't on the same page."

He lets out a tired exhale, hesitating as if he's unsure about what he wants to say next. "I thought I'd gotten pretty good at turning off that other part of my brain, too, but I don't know what to do with myself when I'm with you. And even though I appreciate it, it doesn't help when you keep rescuing me like this, reminding me of everything I can't have."

My jaw lowers in surprise, and a shiver runs through me. I've never been told I'm easy to like, much less that I'm a danger to someone's self-control, at least not in the way he means. And those feelings he's describing aren't one-sided.

If only he didn't seem so disappointed about liking me as much as he does, even to the point where he's afraid to acknowledge me in front of his friends and family.

"So what do you want from me, Rowan?" I choke out.

His eyes dart down to my mouth, and my whole body warms at the possibility of him leaning in to kiss me. I hold my breath when he licks his lips and brings his gaze up to mine.

"I don't know," he admits, his hand inching closer until his fingertips twist into my sleeve, holding me firmly in place. I watch as he extends his pinky to graze one of the red orchids of my tattoo, causing goosebumps to line my skin, and his eyelids lower when he senses the effect it has on me. But the boutonniere on his tuxedo jacket scrapes against my seat when he leans in, reminding me of the way he acted around me at his sister's wedding earlier.

"I need to hear you say it first," I mumble, testing him.

"*You*, Claire. I want you," he rasps, and I falter for a second before I tell myself that he's only toying with me.

It's hard to imagine Rowan as the kind of guy that uses women, though, especially when he's already turned down an offer for no-strings-attached sex. He wouldn't need to work this hard if that were all he was after, not when I keep making it so easy for him.

I lower my chin to tease him again, and he tilts his head to the side, waiting for my cue. He won't even kiss me if he doesn't think he deserves it. Because he's a true gentleman, like an old classic pickup on a highway full of trendy hybrid cars and push-button EVs. He's never going to indulge in a casual hookup with me because he's only looking for the real thing.

It's also why his attraction to me leaves him equally confused and irked. And while I can't deny how much I enjoy his attention, I can't risk losing myself to another man who'd only be settling with me.

"Are you sure I'm what you want?" I ask, pulling away the slightest bit, and he straightens in his seat when he finally senses my hesitation. "Because you're not all that convincing."

He lets go of me and turns away, clenching his jaw. And I wish it wasn't so sexy.

"Besides, you haven't really done anything to earn it yet," I add, unable to disguise my sarcasm.

"I'm sorry," he mutters after a while. "The exhaustion must be getting to me."

"Then we'd better get you to bed, since we both know your inhibitions are lowered when you're tired," I reply dryly before I get out of the car.

Rowan follows me to the front door, still seething, and I pretend I'm immune to the tension lingering between us while I sift through my purse for my house keys. I'm almost certain I've convinced him of my indifference when I remember I don't even have a damned house key. Turning my body slightly, I block his view of the keypad so I can punch the numbers in private. It's too bad I also seem to have forgotten the actual code.

The keypad turns red and scolds me with three loud beeps, and my face heats as I mumble some kind of excuse about changing the locks after my ex moved out. But Rowan has the good sense not to say anything, even when I have to use the app on my phone to unlock the door.

He reaches over my shoulder to push the door open, because the man is practically incapable of turning off his manners. Unfortunately, the thought of his arm muscles straining just inches away from my face makes my brain short circuit again, just long enough for us to get rushed by a pack of wild wiener dogs.

I cringe. "Sorry, I forgot to—"

"Hey, you guys must be Oscar and Frankie," Rowan says, his tone shifting as he squats down to greet the pair of overweight, long-haired dachshunds. How dare he remember my dogs' names from that time I mentioned them nearly a month ago?

I barely conceal an eye roll. "They can be a little bratty around strangers."

But Frankie contradicts me by flopping onto his back, and Rowan chuckles when Oscar follows his brother's lead and begs for his own tummy scratches.

"All right, time to go outside," I call out, but their favorite word barely even registers. Eventually, they roll onto their feet and waddle out the front door. "Little traitors," I mumble under my breath when they don't bother sparing a glance my way.

I turn back to Rowan to find a small smile lingering on his face, and I can't tell whether he's aiming it at me or the dogs. But I can't stop to dote on his all-around adorableness, so I busy myself with my evening routine.

"Make yourself at home. The tap water's gross, so you'll want to use the filter on the fridge. The spare bedroom and bathroom are down the hall on the right. I'll be on the left," I announce, waiting for Oscar and Frankie to march back inside.

"You're welcome to take a shower or whatever ..." I blink and shake my head to rid myself of *those* thoughts, and Rowan follows me into the kitchen where I top off their food and water bowls. "Give me a minute to change into my pajamas, and I'll find something for you to wear."

"Claire, wait," he says, grabbing my arm before I can scamper away.

"What?" I barely allow myself a glance in his direction and find a look of concern etched on his face.

"You're, um, you're not going to come out in the same kind of pajamas you wore last time, are you?"

I stifle a smile. "Would that bother you?"

"Yes, very much so," he admits without hesitation, and I tug my arm back before he can feel the goosebumps breaking out over my skin.

"I guess I'll look for something—"

He interrupts me with a growl. "No, I'm sorry. Forget I said anything, please. This is your house. You shouldn't have to go out of your way to make me feel comfortable."

I sigh. "No, you're right. This is already awkward enough. It's just that ..." I cross my arms and twist my lips to the side as I debate telling him this next part. "The clothes I wear for work are more functional than stylish, so I sort of overcompensate with my pajamas. Plus, it's probably a hormonal thing, but I run hot at night."

He gulps. "That makes sense."

"I like wearing something pretty to bed, even if it's only for myself. It's kind of like a little reward at the end of the day," I add quietly, realizing how dumb it sounds as I say it.

"I think it's great," he blurts out and cringes. "I mean, I love that you have such a healthy appreciation for your body, and it's nice that you've found a way to embrace your ... femininity." His throat works as he scratches the back of his head. "Kind of like your tattoos, right?"

I lift one shoulder in a shrug. "Single girl's gotta do something to feel good about herself, I guess."

His eyes run over me in a way that makes me feel lots of things until he reaches up to rub the side without a contact lens, and I realize he was probably just trying to focus each time I thought he was checking me out.

"Besides, you can't see me that well, anyway," I tack on self-consciously.

"I'm nearsighted, not blind," he declares, squinting one eye. "No chance you're getting a confidence boost from some of those house-coat-style nightgowns, though? Preferably the ones made out of flannel that come up to your neck but still drag the floor?"

I can't help but throw my head back in a loud cackle, because I know he's completely serious. "You're out of luck. It's laundry day, and all of my muumuus are still in the wash, along with my granny panties."

One side of his mouth curls up as he continues staring at me. "I missed your big laugh. I love it, you know, even when you're laughing at my expense."

I shake my head and turn to march toward my bedroom before he can see the way his compliment makes me melt. "Just for that, I'm coming out in something extra skimpy," I holler over my shoulder and smile to myself when he groans and stomps in protest.

claire

ULTIMATELY, I decide not to tease Rowan again, mostly for my own benefit. Instead, I wipe off my makeup and gather my hair into a messy bun before changing into a T-shirt and volleyball-style shorts. I grab another shirt and a pair of sweats for him, but I have to stop by the laundry room to get the last article of clothing directly from the dryer.

Rowan whimpers and lets his head loll back once I enter the kitchen.

I click my tongue. "I'm wearing shorts," I declare, setting his clothes down before lifting my shirt just enough to expose my hip. "See?"

He squints an eye as he refocuses on my bare legs. "Are you sure those are shorts?"

"Yep." I smirk.

"What have I done to deserve this?" he whines.

I huff. "Well, first of all, you—"

"I wasn't asking you. That question was for the man upstairs," he interrupts me to mumble, and I don't know whether to laugh or cry at the way he's still devouring me with his one good eye.

The clicking of claws over the floor keeps some of the tension at bay this time. "You're lucky I didn't make *you* wear the shorts," I tell him, gesturing toward the stack of clothes on the counter before I squat down to pet Frankie.

"Thanks." His brows draw in closer when he notices the boxer shorts sandwiched between the T-shirt and baggy sweatpants. "Are these ..."

"Yeah, they're yours," I confirm matter-of-factly as Oscar approaches.

He finally glances down at me, but his expression is unreadable. "You kept them?"

I shrug shyly, scratching Oscar behind his ears. "They were comfy. Seemed like a waste to throw them out."

"You've been wearing them?" he asks incredulously.

"Of course. I always save a token from my victims," I retort, looking up to narrow my eyes at him.

His expression softens, and he bites his lip as he stifles a smile. "Okay, I deserved that."

"Don't forget to moisturize—I mean, have a nice shower," I add in a sinister tone and tilt my head in the direction of the bathroom, and he chuckles as he finally takes off down the hall.

As soon as the door closes behind him, I give each of my pups one more affectionate squish and scurry over to the guest bedroom to tidy up. I'm fluffing an old pillow when Rowan waltzes into the open doorway a few minutes later, his hair a damp, tousled mess and the outline of his chest visible behind my threadbare T-shirt.

"Thanks, but you really shouldn't trouble yourself any more than you already have," he tells me, but I barely hear him over the sound of my desperation. Which reminds me, I should probably keep my mouth closed while I'm ogling him.

I force myself to look away. "I can't remember the last time anyone's stayed in here. Well, except for the nights when my ex couldn't stand sleeping in the same bed with me ..." I cringe as I trail off.

Why do I keep doing that? I haven't been able to talk about my failed marriage in front of anyone, yet I seem to contract verbal diarrhea every time I'm with Rowan. All he has to do is look at me, and everything just comes pouring out.

"We've already established that he was an idiot," Rowan offers with a soft smile.

"That's not exactly reassuring, especially coming from the last man to walk out on me," I mutter before I can think better of it.

Dammit, Claire.

Apparently, my involuntary confessions aren't only limited to the deep, dark secrets related to my divorce but also include the rest of the emotions I've spent a lifetime suppressing. I guess that's cool, though, even if I'd rather die than come off so needy and wounded.

His expression falls, and I'm tempted to reassure him that no one's as tired of my lack of a filter than I am. Instead, I do the next best thing and blurt out something offensive this time.

"But don't worry, I've washed the sheets since he moved out, so you should be fine." I clear my throat to disguise the wobble in my voice as I move to dart past Rowan.

"Hold on," he commands, side-stepping and blocking my escape.

I attempt to shove him out of the way, but he covers my hands with his own and flattens my palms against his chest. His heart pounds violently against his ribs, and I drag my gaze up to find his eyes looking more bloodshot than before.

"It's fine. Just let me go," I whisper.

"Not yet," he says firmly. It's unnerving, but not in the way I'd expect from a man holding me in place against my will.

"Please," I beg quietly.

He shakes his head and continues studying my face. "I really hurt you, didn't I?"

"I don't know what you're talking about," I lie.

"Claire." His authoritative tone makes my stomach dip again.

"Okay. Yeah, sure, my pride took a hit when you ran out of the room so fast that you forgot your drawers," I say, attempting a light-hearted tone. "But I was the one who insisted we keep it casual, so I wasn't dumb enough to take it personally when you left me in that hotel room, all alone ... and practically naked. Or when you didn't bother to call ... or when you looked so unhappy to see me at your sister's wedding earlier."

He frowns and moves one of his hands up to my face, using his thumb to swipe away a tear. Great, now I'm *crying*? Just when I thought I couldn't get any more pathetic ...

"I'm sorry," he breathes. "I mean it. I've been nothing but selfish and stupid this whole time. And I haven't been considering your feelings or treating you with the respect you deserve." He pauses to pull up on his shirt and dabs tenderly at my nose when I sniffle, turning me into a puddle all over again. "I should have known you'd be in a vulnerable place, especially with it being so close to your divorce hearing. But I panicked, and I didn't make the effort to look past my own feelings and consider how I might have hurt you by leaving that way."

I don't think I can manage to form a reply without letting out a sob, so I just shake my head.

"I'm afraid I was so enamored with you that night that I forgot how to think with the head on my shoulders," he continues with a self-deprecating smile. "I wasn't kidding before when I said there's never been anyone who makes me forget who I am and how to act before, but I've been making a mess of everything since the moment I met you."

"It's me. I'm the mess," I rasp, my voice cracking.

This time he pulls me in for a hug, and I don't think I've ever gotten this much pleasure from a simple embrace. The combination of strength and security, the warmth and comfort of being wrapped up in his arms, it's more satisfying than any form of physical touch. It's also terrifying, because I barely know this man, yet his presence makes me question how well I know myself.

"You're not a mess," he reassures me, his chin resting atop my head. "Well, no more of a mess than I am, anyway."

A soft laugh escapes before I can help myself. "That's not very promising, you know."

"No, I guess it isn't," he concedes. "But maybe that's why we keep finding one another. Maybe one of us is meant to help the other grow in some way."

I huff out another laugh. "Is that what you meant when you said we were soulmates?"

He loosens his hold on me and pulls away. "Eh, not exactly," he admits with a coy smile.

"Athanasius Rowan," I chide him playfully. "Are you telling me that was just a line you used to get me into bed?"

His face instantly flushes, and the implication of his guilt makes my stomach turn.

"I can promise you that wasn't the case," he mumbles shyly. "In fact, it was more like the other way around."

I take a step back as I let his statement settle. "So you thought I was just feeding you a sob story about my life being in shambles, all so you'd sleep with me out of pity?"

He groans. "Of course not. I only meant that I needed to know you felt a connection, too, or I wouldn't have had the courage to ...." But he shakes his head, as if he's unable to finish. "Look, Claire, there's a lot more I could say about that night. But I'm afraid I'm too tired for most of it to make sense right now. Think we can table this discussion for another time, when I'm less likely to keep putting my foot in my mouth? And less tempted to put my mouth on yours." He adds that last part quietly, and I can't decide whether I'm more pissed or turned on by it.

"I think we've both said more than enough," I mutter.

"No, we haven't. But can we please talk again in the morning?" He blinks lazily, his eyelids looking incredibly heavy, and I realize just how exhausted he must be.

"Good night, Rowan," is all I say.

"Good night, Claire. Thanks again."

Then he turns and practically staggers toward the bed, and I shut the door behind me.

claire

OSCAR AND FRANKIE take a few extra minutes to sniff the unfamiliar truck parked in my driveway when I let them out the next morning. I smirk to myself when they each lift a stubby leg to mark the driver's side tire. They come bounding in proudly after that, and I reward them with a few bits of bacon, their favorite treat.

"Who's Mama's good boy? Hmm? Is it you, Frankenstein? Frankfurter? Frankie-Panky?"

Frankie seems unbothered and simply chews his bacon while I cup my hands around his face and pepper him with ridiculous nicknames. His brother stands by, tail wagging as he waits obediently for his turn. "And you, too, Ozzy. My little grouchy boy, Oscar Meyer, Oscar Isaac, Oscar de la *Ren*-ta."

Oscar's ears twitch, and the little shit abandons me in the middle of our daily affirmations to join Frankie in welcoming the room's newest occupant. I roll my eyes when I hear Rowan greeting the dogs by name again in his husky morning voice and busy myself with pouring a cup of coffee.

Rowan clears his throat, presumably to get my attention, and I turn to find him standing there with a wiener dog draped over each of his forearms, grinning while they take turns licking his chin. It all seems wholly unfair, to be honest.

"Good morning," he says cheerfully.

"Morning," I reply flatly.

His eyes run over me before he seemingly thinks better of it, and he squints to focus on my face after that. "You're up early."

My brow lifts. "Did you take me for a late riser?"

"No, I guess not," he says, chuckling to himself as he sets the dogs down. "How did you sleep?"

"Fine." But I frown, because of course he's going to be polite and cute, despite having a shitty evening before. And now I'm a jerk if I don't engage with him, when I'd actually been hoping to find his truck missing by the time I'd gotten up.

"And you?" I ask after some hesitation.

"I slept surprisingly well," he says, smiling.

I nod and fidget uncomfortably, since I've apparently forgotten how to do this morning stuff after living solo for the better part of the past year.

"That coffee smells heavenly," Rowan volunteers.

"Uh, yeah. Help yourself," I blurt out and take a seat.

"Thanks." He smiles again and gestures in front of the cabinet, wordlessly asking for a mug after my awkward ass assumed he'd just drink it from the carafe.

"I don't have any creamer or anything, but there's sugar in that canister and milk in the fridge," I add begrudgingly.

He shakes his head as he pours. "You took your coffee black last time, so I wasn't exactly expecting a fancy peppermint mocha or a pumpkin spice latte."

Remembering how I like my coffee earns him another eye roll. "Let me guess, creamer is another one of those comfort drugs you try to avoid?"

"More or less," he says with a shrug and sits across from me. I notice he's holding a string of beads in his hand. "Do you always have your morning coffee in the kitchen?"

"Depends on the weather, I guess. Why do you ask?"

"Just pictured you drinking your first cup of the day outside as you watch the sun come up," he muses. "Or better yet, while you're tending to your chickens in the backyard."

I narrow my eyes, unsure of how I feel after his assessment. "I don't have enough room for a chicken coop out back. Besides, it's a little too chilly for that this morning."

"All the more reason for you to invest in flannel PJs, or at least a fuzzy robe," he drawls and takes a sip.

"Seems like a waste, since men don't usually mind my slutty pajamas," I retort, and his smile fades.

"Right," he says quietly, keeping his icy blue eyes trained on his mug after that.

"I guess you'll be needing a ride to Coach Reed's soon," I begin when I can't take the silence any longer.

"If it's not too much trouble." He sounds distracted as he moves his fingers over the next bead on that strand. It must be a rosary, like the ones I've seen Daisy and my Catholic great-grandmother use for prayer. I'm tempted to point out the predictability of his morning habits, but he'd only take it as a compliment.

"Anything else while we're at it?" I rise and tug down on my shirt self-consciously before I bring my mug to the sink. "Don't worry, I'll put on some pants before we go."

"Guess I could use another do-over and the ability to say the right thing around you for once," he mumbles before he crosses himself with the rosary beads and slips them into his pocket.

"You're fine. It's probably for the best if we weren't really friends, anyway," I say, my voice thick.

He huffs. "Is that why you needed to hear me say something insensitive again? So you could pretend you actually mean that?"

"It'll make things easier for both of us," I continue, ignoring him. "I'm going to get dressed. Be ready by the time I get back."

I dry my cheeks when I get to my bedroom and slip into some jeans and a Camellia High FFA Chapter hoodie. Rowan is waiting at the door by the time I return, rubbing his right eye again. Because he's still missing a contact lens. And now I feel even more foolish, since he probably couldn't see much of me in those shorts in the first place.

He bids the dogs goodbye while I turn to grab my keys and purse, and I click my tongue in annoyance when the keyring is missing from the hook where I left it.

"They're in the car," he calls out from the open door.

I glare at him and walk out to my Bronco, unable to hide my irritation when I discover it's already warm and toasty inside, courtesy of the chivalrous asshole in the passenger's seat. We're both quiet on the drive over to Landry's dad's house, and I take out my aggression on the shifter, jerking the car to a stop when I throw it into park.

Rowan lets out a loud exhale. "You're not going to drive off as soon as I step outside, are you?"

"I'm thinking about it."

"It's too bad I can't call Tiana for a ride," he says, a hint of a smile on his lips. "Then again, I don't think she'd approve of what we've become."

I snort. "There is no *we*, at least not in Camellia."

"Yeah," he says on another long sigh, as if he's not the one who made that point abundantly clear last night. "I'll be right back."

I distract myself with my phone as he goes to knock on the door. This time, Coach Reed appears to let him inside, and I send Daisy a text while I wait.

CLAIRE

Good morning, Mrs. Reed. How was that wedding cake? 😇

It takes a minute for her to reply, but a giggle bursts forth as soon as I read her message.

DAISY

Best. Cake. Ever.

I've already informed my husband that I'll be expecting a piece in bed every night. Luckily, he's assured me that it would be his pleasure to continue serving cake on a nightly basis. 😊

CLAIRE

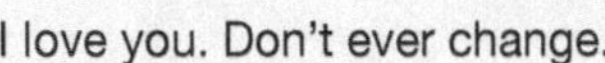

I love you. Don't ever change.

"Weren't you supposed to leave me stranded with Coach Sunshine?"

I wince at the sound of Rowan's voice, and he stares at me as he plops down onto the passenger seat.

"Yeah, well, I couldn't let you interrupt the newlyweds. From what I hear, your sister's waited long enough for this," I reply, though the bitterness in my tone is forced. He places the stack of borrowed clothes in the back seat, leaving a strong sense of dread and regret to settle in my stomach.

"Whatever the reason, I'm still grateful," he says quietly, his hand covering mine, and I finally glance up at him.

"Thank you, Claire," he adds. I swallow hard as I brace myself to withstand the warm, fuzzy feelings he's sure to stir up. Those glasses he's wearing and the light stubble on his jaw certainly aren't helping.

"It's nothing," I barely choke out once he interlaces our fingers.

"It means something to me," he says, his voice barely above a whisper, triggering a flashback from the night we met. "And so do you."

I stifle a whimper when he brings my hand up to his mouth for a kiss. "Rowan, please ... don't."

"I can't leave things on a bad note again," he tells me, then he flashes a rueful smile and loosens his grip.

I nod and tug my hand back before driving home on autopilot. Rowan thanks me again when he says goodbye, but I barely allow myself to acknowledge him. I wait until he drives away before I risk unbuckling my seat belt. And it isn't until I'm back inside the house and tossing the clothes I lent him into the washer that I find his boxer shorts tucked neatly between the T-shirt and sweatpants.

5:12 PM

ROWAN

Hey, Claire. It's Rowan.

CLAIRE

Who?

ROWAN

Daisy's brother?

CLAIRE

Daisy Reed? Funny. She never mentioned a brother. In fact, I thought she was an only child.

ROWAN

Ha ha.

Seriously, I hope it's okay that I'm texting you, but I sort of need your help …

CLAIRE

Deja vu, anyone?

ROWAN

I'm sorry. But you are kind of amazing.

And I have no one else to call.

CLAIRE

Tell me you didn't bother your sister for my
number? Not while she's off on her honeymoon
with your best friend …

ROWAN

Okay, that was a low blow.

CLAIRE

gif of "That's What She Said"

ROWAN

thumbs down react

I'm only asking for your help because I'm trying
to avoid interrupting the newlyweds.

I got your number from Loren Reed, if that's any
indication of my desperation right now.

CLAIRE

Oh, you mean Loren BOURGEOIS?

Wait a minute … is she the girl we talked about—
your best friend's sister, the one that got away?

Landry tried setting you up, but she was already
pregnant with Blake's twins, wasn't she?

AND THEN YOU HAD TO BE HER DOCTOR?

ROWAN

I never said she was the one that got away.

And I'm very happy for her and Blake.

CLAIRE

And Landry's not just your bestie—he's your
emergency contact.

Because you've lived with him before. Which
means …

YOU'VE SEEN IT, HAVEN'T YOU?

ROWAN

Are you done yet?

CLAIRE

Not until you pay the tax with an embarrassing confession of some sort.

Or you could either discredit or validate the rumors ... 🍆

ROWAN

Wasn't all of the above embarrassing enough?

And must you always be this crude?

CLAIRE

No.

And, yes, I must. It's who I am.

ROWAN

I'm afraid I can't participate in this conversation without disrespecting my brother-in-law's dignity. Believe it or not, even Landry Reed was created in the image and likeness of God.

CLAIRE

gif of little girl rolling her eyes

ROWAN

Besides, why are you bothering to ask me when it sounds like you've already gotten the answer you wanted from my sister?

CLAIRE

heart react

I know how much you like positive reinforcement.

ROWAN

Great, now that we've gotten that out of the way, can you please HELP ME?!

photo of busted water pipe under Daisy's house

CLAIRE

Well, shit.

That's not exactly the kind of gushing I normally respond to in a booty call, but I'll be over in a few.

rowan

"HEY, THANKS FOR COMING," I call over in Claire's direction when she steps out of her Bronco in a pair of chest waders, and I immediately know I'm in trouble.

"Were you able to shut off the water?" she inquires as she approaches, slipping a headlight onto her forehead. I'm impressed by her forethought, since it's only five in the afternoon and already getting darker by the minute.

"Uh, yeah. Once I finally found the water main, I realized there wasn't a key. So I struggled to turn that crusty old valve with a wrench from the emergency toolbox in my truck. But at least I got it done in time to avoid emasculating myself in front of you again."

Her eyes run over me, catching on the muddy spots on my dress slacks and the old hunting jacket I'd found in Landry's closet. "Hell, I'm honestly impressed you managed to get that far with those soft hands of yours, Doc," she replies, her voice tinged with amusement.

"Last I checked, you didn't mind that my hands were so soft," I say before I can catch myself, maybe because I'm relieved that she doesn't seem to be harboring a grudge after our last interaction. But it's hard to regret anything that inspires one of Claire's big laughs, anyway.

I stifle a grin and shove my fists into my pockets, trying not to think about the feeling of her smooth skin beneath my palms. "And I may not have any callouses now, but I did grow up mending fences and fixing pipes, in case you've forgotten."

"I could have suggested a better way to demonstrate your pipe-laying skills, farm boy," she muses as she saunters over and squats down to peer beneath the house. She flicks on the light over her head, and I lower myself to point out the source of the problem.

"I guess Landry hadn't expected the temps to drop this low while they were gone."

She snickers. "Wrapping these pipes wasn't on the agenda before he left. Trust me."

I roll my eyes. "Yeah, well, I noticed that busted pipe as soon as I drove up this afternoon."

"And you needed my help to fix that? It sounds like you know what you're doing."

"The thing is, Landry doesn't seem to have any spare PVC or glue lying around, and Camellia's only hardware store closed early today."

She clicks her tongue. "It's Mardi Gras weekend, so most of the businesses in town have already boarded up until next week. I'm actually surprised you're here. Isn't the clinic closed tomorrow?"

"I didn't know the streets were getting roped off so early, so I had the staff schedule a few patients in the morning," I say, barely hiding my annoyance.

She hums in understanding. "Well, lucky for you, I stopped by the ag shop on the way over and grabbed some supplies. My principal won't mind so long as we replace everything, especially since it's all for *Mrs. Daisy*," she explains, fluttering her eyelashes over my sister's name.

"Thank you," I tell her with a sigh of relief. "And I'll be happy to make a donation for anything else you might need in your shop." She bounces her eyebrows, letting me know she was banking on that offer.

"There's another reason I called, though," I add, cringing.

She glares at me. "You're too big to fit under the house, aren't you?"

I shoot her an apologetic smile. "Afraid so."

She groans as she rises to her feet. "I'm starting to wonder how you managed to survive the past thirty-something years without me."

"Funny, I've been thinking the same thing," I reply, my smile growing more genuine.

She rolls her eyes and shoves me before she walks to her Bronco, and I follow closely. After handing me a few pieces of pipe, she grabs a small handsaw and a tin of glue before returning to the job site.

"I guess I should have set out a tarp or something for you to lie on so you wouldn't get muddy," I remark as she prepares to slide beneath the house.

"Would have been nice," she mumbles, pulling her braid over her shoulder before leaning back and reaching for the broken pipe.

I watch as she uses the saw to cut out the cracked section, then she directs me to cut the new piece down to size while she applies glue and fittings at the ends. Once she's ready, I hand her the replacement pipe, and she glues it into place.

"That old PVC gets brittle over time. So I wouldn't be surprised if you find another crack when you turn the water back on," she tells me when she scoots out from the crawlspace and takes the hand I'm offering to pull her up. "But I wouldn't worry about wrapping the rest, since the temps won't be quite as low tonight."

"I guess we just need to let it cure for a while?"

"Yep," she confirms, gathering tools as if she's preparing to leave.

"Uh, let me grab you a towel. Don't go anywhere," I blurt out in a panic and dart into the house.

She's already packed up and drying herself off with a towel from her trunk by the time I make it back outside.

"Sorry, I should have been better prepared," I murmur, but she's still ignoring me.

"Well, good luck."

"Wait, you're leaving ... already?" I ask when she opens the driver's side door.

"With all your *pipe* experience, I didn't think you needed me to sit and watch the glue dry," she replies, her smirk confirming my suspicions that there's some kind of euphemism at work here.

"Well, no, but ... what if I find another problem when I turn on the water main, like you said?"

"Then I'll come back. I'm only about a mile down the road," she replies matter-of-factly.

"You don't want to come inside and wait? Maybe we can find something for dinner," I offer, and she narrows her eyes at me. Her hesitation is definitely justified, but I can't help that I want to keep her here a while longer. And I doubt she'd stay if I came right out and asked, especially if I told her how much I've been thinking about her and craving her company.

"We both know the Reeds can't cook, so that pantry is bound to be bare. Not to mention, the lack of running water would make food prep pretty inconvenient," she says, calling me out. "You're not looking for another invitation to my place, are you?"

"No, no," I say too quickly. "But I feel like I at least owe you dinner by now. Maybe we can find some takeout?"

She sighs as she stares me down. "Even if we had a fast-food option, it'd be closed by now."

I open my mouth with an offer to take her out of town for dinner, but I'm cut off by a loud hiss and a small geyser erupting from the water main behind me. Claire and I both curse and scramble over to the new water fountain I've inadvertently created in Daisy and Landry's front yard.

"I thought you said you shut off the valve!" she yells as we squat to inspect the source of the six-foot-tall waterspout that's currently raining down over us.

"I did, but the handle was rusty, so I wouldn't be surprised if it sprung a leak after I had to force it!"

"Oh, shit, the glue hasn't cured," she mumbles. "Grab the pliers from my toolbox in the back. I'm going to hold that pipe together."

I nod and run over to her Bronco as directed, casting a glance her way as she crawls under the house.

"Can you hurry the hell up?" she shouts, and I growl as I fight against the water pressure to clamp and adjust the pliers. It takes another minute and a few more embarrassingly loud grunts for me to shut the valve again.

"Got it closed. You okay?" I call out to Claire.

"Freaking peachy," she retorts. But when I turn and wipe the icy cold water out of my eyes, I realize my efforts were in vain.

My frustrated growl resounds as I approach the small swamp that formed beneath the house within the last minute.

Claire sputters and turns her head to spit on the ground. "Not only did our new pipe disconnect, but a few more followed suit," she explains, her voice tinged with annoyance. "This just became a much bigger job."

"In other words, we're not fixing it tonight."

"Not unless you plan to lift the house for me. And since it took you long enough to shut off a little old valve, I don't think that's possible." She rolls onto her belly and shimmies out from beneath the crawlspace, and cringe when her backside comes into view. She's soaked, which isn't surprising now that there's at least an inch of water on the ground.

"Claire, I'm so sorry," I begin, reaching out to offer her a hand.

"I thought you knew what you were doing," she grumbles, glowering at me as she takes my hand. But I slip when I shift my weight to one foot, and I perform one of those silly cartoon falls instead of pulling her up, my arms flailing as I teeter back and forth and eventually land flat on my butt beside her. She bites her lip and reaches up to swipe at some of the mud that splatters onto her face with my impact, and I cringe as I await her wrath.

"Okay, now I'm really, *really* sorry," I add with a whine, thinking she's going to throttle me any second now.

But this is Claire, so she simply flicks a handful of mud in my face before throwing her head back and cackling so loudly that it echoes throughout the yard. I can't help but join her, and we take turns smearing mud and playfully pulling one another back down a few times before I finally manage to get us both onto our feet. Claire sighs as our laughter dies down, and we use the cleaner water puddles to rinse off as much of the mud as possible.

"Maybe I was wrong about not wrapping the rest of the pipes, because it's getting c-colder by the m-minute," she declares when we finally make our way to the porch. "At least D-Daisy covered her plants."

"Yeah," I agree. The wind whips through, the cold permeating my wet clothes. "Sh-shoot," I barely get out with my teeth chattering.

"What?" she breathes, wrapping her arms around herself.

"We can't track all of this m-mud inside, because I won't be able to t-turn on the water to clean it up."

"Sh-shhit, you're right," she confirms. "We'll just have to ... leave our wet clothes out here."

I groan at the prospect of undressing in front of one another, especially since the cold will no doubt highlight certain body parts for her and cause others to shrivel for me.

She rolls her eyes and dances in place to stay warm. "You can be a gentleman and st-strip down f-first, then come back with a dry t-t-towel for me."

"F-fine. Just, turn around for a second, p-please."

"What f-f-for? I've s-seen it all already," she protests with a raised eyebrow.

I glare as I unzip my jacket and remove the first layer. It hits the wooden porch with a thud. "Why do you wanna s-see it again?"

"Be-be-cause I'm freezing," she retorts, as if the answer should be obvious.

I attempt to shrug as I unbutton my shirt, but the uncontrollable shivering makes both damn near impossible. "S-so am I."

She growls and steps forward to help me with the buttons. "Don't act like you d-don't know what I m-meant."

My stomach dips when the realization hits me, then it flips again when she opens my shirt and presses her cheek to my chest. Her popsicle hands slide around my midsection, and I flinch and hiss while she steals my last dregs of body heat. It doesn't stop the corner of my mouth from turning up, though, especially once she lets out a contented sigh.

"Is that really all it takes to get you all hot and b-bothered?" I ask, my heart rate and my core body temperature both spiking at the contact.

"Shut up," she breathes, her eyelids fluttering when she flips to the other cheek.

I chuckle under my breath and move to unbutton my slacks, no longer having to worry about the cold affecting me in a less-than-flattering manner. Claire steps back for me to toe off the boots I also swiped from Landry's closet, but she keeps her hands on my torso as I peel my wet pants from my legs.

"You're gonna have to let me go now," I tell her with a smile once I'm down to my underwear.

"Okay, but hurry up. And just drop a towel at the door. I don't need you watching me undress," she orders.

My smile fades. "Well, that's not fair."

"Neither is all this," she grumbles, gesturing over my midsection before she unhooks the shoulder straps of her chest waders.

"You say that like you're not walking around in the sexiest body I've ever seen," I mutter, secretly relieved I'm not getting the chance to see every tempting inch of her again. Ignoring her scoff, I dart into the house to grab a couple of clean towels from the dryer.

Claire snatches up my offering once I crack open the door and stick out my hand. She dances her way inside a few seconds later, tucking the tail end of the towel under her armpit.

I furrow my brow as I take in her bare ankles. "Um, where are your pants?"

"I was literally walking into the shower when you texted, so I barely had time to throw on a shirt and a pair of drawers before grabbing my waders on the way out the door," she replies defensively.

I shake my head. "You *would* walk around in chest waders and lingerie."

I wait for her spicy comeback while I adjust the towel around my waist, but she looks away and crosses her arms over her middle instead. "All right, grab your things so we can get out of here."

"Oh, no, I can't," I begin. "I mean, thank you, but I'll be fine."

"And how do you expect to clean yourself up without any water?"

I curse under my breath. She's right. I can't stay here tonight unless I want to show up to work in the morning with mud-crusted hair. I just hate that I keep inconveniencing her so much.

I'm also not fond of the idea of anyone finding out about our sleepovers and telling my sister, who would then tell my entire family, who would want to know the real story of how and when Claire and I first met.

On the other hand, I can't help wondering what kind of underwear she deemed appropriate on her way out earlier. Did she choose something she wanted me to see? And does that mean she was just standing out in the cold in nothing but her bra and panties a second ago while she waited for me to return with a towel? Better yet, was she secretly hoping I'd offer to warm her up myself?

I blow out a loud exhale in an attempt to clear my head. I've really got to get a handle on these thoughts, especially if my chance run-ins with Claire are going to become a regular thing.

"You, uh, really wouldn't mind?" I ask carefully.

"I mean, kind of. But I can't just leave you like this, either," she says, rolling her eyes.

"Like what? Cold, wet, naked, and lonely?" I offer, stifling a smile. "Some booty call you turned out to be."

I cringe when I hear myself. I only meant to lighten the mood, but I'm not doing anyone any favors by being overly suggestive like this. And I certainly shouldn't be leading her on or even implying I condone that kind of behavior for either of us.

Claire's eyes widen for a second before she collects herself, and I expect her to toss her head back and laugh any second. Instead, she looks away again and pulls the towel in tighter.

"You know, most guys wait until *after* we hook up to cue the self-loathing bit. It admittedly ruins the mood when you front load this much disgust at being attracted to me," she explains sarcastically.

My stomach lurches again, but not in a good way this time.

"Geez, Rowan. Stop looking at me like that. I can take a joke," she says after watching me struggle and fail to find my voice.

I clear my throat. "I'm sorry."

But that's all I can say, because she's not mistaken about the way I've been acting in front of her, even if she's made the wrong assumptions about why I'm having such a hard time dealing with my attraction.

She turns away, but I swear I hear her sniffling. "I'm going to crank up the heater in my car while you get your shit together," she chokes out.

"No, you're going to find yourself something to wear from my sister's room. I'll get the heater," I tell her, pushing my way through the front door before she can object.

rowan

THE COLD AIR nips at my bare back as I shuffle out to her car and over to mine, where I grab a set of clean clothes from my overnight bag. By the time I return from changing in the spare bedroom, she's sitting on the couch in one of Daisy's signature linen frocks.

"First of all, your sister is a freak for having a capsule wardrobe made exclusively of sundresses," she begins. "Secondly, she might just be the other kind of freak, too, because she and Landry are already sharing an underwear drawer."

I scrunch up my nose. "I'd sleep better tonight if we chalked that up to her doing his laundry. But then again, I'm probably not going to sleep at all until I give you a better apology and an explanation for why I keep acting like such a jerk around you."

She rolls her eyes at my transition and groans as she rises to her feet. "Or we could just go back to my place for a hot shower and a clean bed."

My brow nearly touches my hairline that time.

"Separate showers," she blurts out once she realizes her mistake. "And beds, of course."

I nod, willing my heart to slow down. "Right. I knew what you meant." I take a step forward before adding, "Besides, I was already thinking too hard about what kind of pajamas you're planning on wearing to catch that one right away."

She scoffs. "Don't patronize me."

"I'm not. I promise," I say with a sigh. "Is it wrong for me to admit that I find you equally terrifying and alluring?"

"Alluring?" she asks hesitantly.

I shrug shyly. "I was going to say *sexy*, but I don't want you to think I'm only drawn to you physically. I told you before, you're easy to like."

"It's just too bad I'm not the kind of girl you're looking for," she says dryly.

"What?"

She licks her lips and shifts her gaze to the floor. "Look, you don't owe me an explanation. In fact, I'd rather not do this with you at all."

"Do what, Claire? Talk about our feelings? Admit how much we like one another?" I reply a little too forcefully.

"Exactly."

"And what's so terrible about being honest and saying how you feel?" I demand.

"Besides spending the last decade without most of my feelings being reciprocated or even accepted? Being told I'm crazy or weird or stupid for having feelings in the first place, or worse for not being able to get a handle on them?" Her chest heaves when she's done, and I watch as a look of mortification crosses her features.

"Hey," I begin softly and take another step toward her. "Come here."

"No." Her voice cracks, and she turns away from me. "Dammit, Rowan. I told you I wasn't in the mood for this."

But I ignore her protests and reach out to rest my hand on her back. "I'm sorry I keep pushing you too far. But I swear it's only because I want to know everything about you. I think you're one of the most interesting people I've ever met, and your feelings matter to me. And if I seem like I'm upset with myself for flirting with you, it's only because I'm struggling to regulate my attraction."

"And if I'm so great, then why is being attracted to me such a bad thing?" she asks meekly.

"Because you've made it clear that you don't want to be pressured into anything serious, and I have to respect that," I tell her, ignoring my conscience when it prompts me to say more, to explain exactly why I need her to be open to the idea of marriage before I can risk getting any closer.

"Oh." Her expression falls, as if she's disappointed by my answer.

"Is that still what you want ... or don't want?"

She keeps her eyes lowered as she nods. "Yes."

I swallow hard before I continue. "Well, if you ever change your mind, I'd like to be the first to know."

"Why exactly is a relationship status such a big deal to you, anyway? I told you I wasn't looking for anything serious the night we met, and it didn't seem to be a problem for you then."

Guilt and embarrassment flood my chest. "You're right, and I'm sorry I downplayed it before, but I just can't handle anything physical outside of a committed relationship," I say quietly, understating it again.

"That's why you hate that you're so drawn to me, isn't it? Because I make you want to reconsider how far you're willing to go?" she asks, daring me to answer with her eyes.

"Gah, Claire, what do you want me to say?" I fire back. "Yes, okay, I'm confused. I've already admitted that the way I feel around you makes me forget what kind of man I'm supposed to be."

"And what kind of man is that?"

I throw my hands up in defeat. "I don't know. A good one? If nothing else, one who doesn't use women and discard them once he's taken what he wants."

"I suppose that makes me someone else's trash," she replies with a sardonic smirk.

A frustrated growl escapes. "That's not what I meant. Could you please quit putting words in my mouth?"

"Funny, you didn't seem to mind—"

"Would you just stop?!" I yell this time, and she takes a step back and blinks at me in disbelief. "I'm sorry. But if there's anything I hate, it's the way you assume I only want you for … *that*."

Her chin quivers and she crosses her arms. "I guess you're out of luck, then. Because I don't have much else to offer."

"Tell me you don't really believe that?" I demand in a softer tone.

She shakes her head and turns her face away from me, but she doesn't give me a real answer. And it's all my fault. Even though we didn't actually sleep together, not telling her about my beliefs and allowing her to go on thinking I only needed one night from her must have been enough to validate her insecurities.

I take a step forward. "I may not have known you for long, Claire, but I know that's not true. And I'm sorry for anything I've said or done to make you think I'm not interested in your company outside of the bedroom."

"Oh, you've made it crystal clear that our friendship only carries benefits of the emergency-contact and bail-posting variety," she says, though I can tell she's forcing the joke.

"Because you're knowledgeable and capable, and still charming enough to help me talk my way out of getting arrested. You also make me laugh when I need it the most."

Her smile softens into something more genuine. "I'm sorry," she says after a while. "I hate sounding so needy, and I've never been the type to fish for compliments. But maybe my divorce has left me a little more sensitive than I'm used to," she admits begrudgingly.

"I can't imagine it wouldn't. And I still wish you'd give yourself more grace."

She nods. "Yeah."

"I'm here if you ever need to talk about it, you know. You've got my number now," I remind her, making my voice as gentle as possible.

She nods again, but doesn't say more, and I get the sudden urge to tell her the whole truth, to earn her trust the right way.

"Claire, there's actually—"

"I appreciate the offer, but I'm actually sick of talking about my feelings. I've already overshared enough for one lifetime," she interrupts me to explain, and I have no choice but to honor her request since my confession is likely to garner an emotional response from both of us.

"There's no such thing as oversharing between soulmates," I hear myself saying, and she snorts.

"Okay, but you have to quit that mushy crap before I let you into my house again."

"Oh, so ... you don't like it when I flirt with you?" I ask hesitantly.

She purses her lips as she considers it. "I'm not saying we can't joke around, but stop making it so sappy. Flirt with me all you want, tell me I have a nice ass, just don't call me your soulmate."

I roll my eyes. "Only if you agree to quit cutting yourself down."

"Might as well prohibit any physical contact, too, for your sake," she mumbles as she sticks out a hand, and I reluctantly take it in mine, unsure whether I'm more relieved or disappointed by her suggestion.

"What if there's another medical emergency? Besides, it doesn't count if you were literally touching me while you said it," I reply smoothly, stroking the back of her hand with my thumb.

Disappointed, then—I'm definitely more disappointed.

"Fine," she concedes, yanking her hand back. "No kissing or touching of a sexual nature."

"What if one of us needs CPR?" I pose, narrowing my eyes at her.

"Good thing your brother-in-law is a doctor," she declares, and my groan elicits a smirk from her.

"And if I need someone to rub me down with hydrocortisone cream? You're not going to make me call Landry for that, will you?"

"I'll try not to enjoy it," she says on an exaggerated sigh.

I can't help but smile back at her now. "I should probably confirm that your house is peanut-free before I agree to all this."

She shrugs. "Can you really afford to say no?"

"I wouldn't want to, even if I could," I reply quietly, staring her down and watching her eyelashes flutter.

She clears her throat and collects herself after a moment, lifting her chin before she declares, "I'm going home. You can follow me there if you think you can manage to keep your pants on for the rest of the night."

Then she marches out the front door, and I scramble to lock up and chase her out.

claire

I PEER up at my rearview mirror to watch Rowan pulling in behind me. Then I switch to the side mirror when he gets out of his truck with his overnight bag and walks over to wait for me like an obedient puppy.

He lets out a measured exhale as he stands by patiently, shivering and looking adorably nervous, and I feel an ache deep inside my chest. I might have been able to convince myself that I didn't like him all that much before, back when I thought I'd never see him again, but I'm not fooling myself anymore.

Crushing on Rowan is also entirely too dangerous, especially since he has a knack for turning every conversation into a counseling session.

You're not doing this again, Claire. Get your shit together.

I huff and roll my shoulders back, preparing myself to step back into the role of the tough, emotionally closed-off divorcée. I can't keep letting him see Claire Bear, the soft, silly, self-conscious girl hiding behind the hard exterior.

"Are you really going to wait on me all night? You know I'm just messing with you now, don't you?" I call out from inside my car, trying to set the tone.

He smirks and steps forward to open my door, and I swallow hard, pretending I'm unaffected.

"I actually don't mind," he begins, offering his hand, "Especially since watching you talk to yourself in the mirror might just be the cutest thing I've ever seen." I gasp and reach out with my free hand to swat at him, but he absorbs the blow and laughs softly, refusing to loosen his grip on the hand he's holding. "Besides, what else am I going to do if not wait for you to let me in?"

I roll my eyes, trying not to dwell on the physical contact we're supposed to be avoiding or that he knows I needed to give myself a pep talk before facing him. But man is it hard not to squeal when he doesn't let go of my hand until I tug it back to unlock the door.

Shit, what's that code again?

"I can turn around if you don't want me to see the combination, but I'd like to think you can trust me by now," Rowan volunteers, stifling another laugh.

I click my tongue and punch in the numbers, grateful when I get it right on the first try this time. "I'm going to wash all this mud off," I tell him as I stoop to pet the dogs. "Mind letting Frankie and Oscar out before you shower?"

"Got it," he says, already crouching down to take my place. I toss my keys on the counter and move toward the hall, but he calls out and stops me. "Claire? Since we've agreed to be on our best behavior and all ..."

I groan. "Do my pajamas *really* bother you that much?"

He furrows his brow and nods. "I'm sorry. But, yeah, they really, *really* do."

A huge smile spreads across my face, despite my best efforts to conceal it. "I'll see what I can find."

I can't shake that stupid, silly shit-eating grin the whole time I'm in the shower, even though I nick the back of my knee shaving my legs. Like hell, I'm not coming out in something at least a *little* sexy.

After assessing the damage, I decide against a Band-Aid because I'd be giving myself away again. I gather my wet hair into a messy bun and make sure I don't have any leftover mascara lingering beneath my eyes before I venture out to put our muddy clothes washing.

Rowan stifles a whine when I enter the living room, but I'm afraid I'm the one whose breath stills at the sight of him. He's fresh from the shower in a T-shirt and gym shorts, looking good enough to eat. More importantly, he's wearing those gosh darn glasses as he reclines on my couch with both of my dogs in his lap.

I stop abruptly before I reach the sofa and cross my arms. "What do you think you're doing?"

A panicked look crosses his face, and he pushes the dogs aside to stand. "Um, I'm sorry. I guess I was making myself at home, but I shouldn't have assumed ... Should I not have let them on the furniture?"

He glances back at Frankie and Oscar, who continue staring up at me without a care in the world.

"No, um, they're fine," I say, clearing my throat awkwardly. "I meant ..." I let my explanation hang in the air and gesture over my face.

He furrows his brow and pushes his glasses up, most likely out of habit. Then I watch as the realization hits him, and he mirrors my pose, crossing his arms and tilting his head back as one side of his mouth turns up in a cocky smirk.

"Fair is fair, right," he declares, allowing his eyes to run over me. My skin prickles with his gaze.

"But I didn't even put on the slutty PJs this time," I say with a pout.

He blinks back in surprise. "These aren't the sexy ones?"

I scoff. "No, not really." The black ribbed-knit tank top and matching shorts aren't exactly modest, especially with the lettuce-edge curling the hem of the shorts up even higher, but it's certainly not the skimpiest set I own.

He looks me up and down again before grunting and squinting his eyes closed. "I was wrong. You definitely have an unfair advantage."

"Only because you're a gynecologist who's afraid of women," I mumble.

He groans louder and turns away, resettling himself on the couch. "I'm not even engaging with you on that one."

My pout returns. I'm slightly disappointed in my victory, maybe because I expected him to put up more of a fight.

"So, I don't know about you, but I'm starving," I venture quietly after a while.

His smile reappears when he glances up at me, keeping his eyes trained on my face this time. "I didn't want to be a needy guest, but I'm definitely aware that we skipped dinner."

"I'm sure I can throw something together that's kosher for you, but you should probably oversee it, just to be safe," I offer.

He nods and follows me into the kitchen, and we go about the business of sorting through the fridge before settling on grilled cheese sandwiches. It's endearing when he insists on helping.

"This is perfect for meat-free Fridays," he tells me while I plate our sandwiches. "My options are limited without peanuts, especially since I try to avoid the other likely suspects, like tree nuts, soy, and chickpeas, just in case."

I ladle some of the marinara sauce I made from scratch onto our plates, and he brings them around to the bar, where I've already set out a glass of lemonade for each of us. It feels very domestic, I realize as we sit beside one another, and I don't hate it.

Rowan surprises me by stopping to bow his head, presumably to say grace. I'm not sure whether I feel more relieved or slighted when he doesn't ask me to join him.

He smiles up at me once he's done making the Sign of the Cross, then reaches out to cover my hand with his. "Thanks for this. Not only would I have contracted hypothermia by now, but I'm sure I would have starved without your help tonight."

I swallow hard when he squeezes my hand. "No worries. Like I said before, I couldn't let you bother the newlyweds on their well-deserved honeymoon."

"Yeah," he agrees, his smile widening. "And I definitely didn't mind the company."

"Right, especially since I was small enough to fit in that crawl-space," I reply on a light laugh, attempting to free my hand. But he tightens his hold and keeps his gaze locked onto mine.

"Because you make everything more fun," he says, sounding almost breathless. "Even busted pipes and emergency room visits."

I lick my lips when his thumb begins stroking the side of my wrist. "Yeah. I've been having fun with you, too. Well, except for the parts when I end up crying, but I guess that's not completely your fault."

He smiles shyly. "I'd say I'm sorry, but I really do like learning everything there is to know about you." He pauses to swallow. "And speaking of confessions, there's something I feel like I should tell you. Something about me you probably need to know."

"You're not a serial killer, are you?" I ask, trying to lighten the mood.

But he brushes over my question, his expression hardening. "Remember how my family sort of teased me for talking to you at the wedding reception?"

"Yeah?" My heart is racing so fast that I can hardly hear him at this point.

"I ... well, in the past, I've mostly dated women who were ... religious ... like me."

I furrow my brow and manage to yank my hand back this time. "That's why you were embarrassed to be seen with me," I say flatly. "Because I'm divorced, and I don't go to church."

"But it's not that simple—"

"It's fine, Rowan," I interrupt him and shake my head. "You've already apologized. And I thought we weren't doing this anymore? We're supposed to be keeping it light ... and fun."

He blows out a breath and lets his head hang. "Yeah, I'm sorry. Forget I said anything."

"So, what are you going to do about your sister's house?" I ask after the silence stretches out too long.

"Know any decent plumbers I can call?" he quips as he picks a corner of grilled cheese and dips it into the sauce. Once I take the first bite, I realize I'm hungrier than I thought, and it doesn't take either of us long to devour our sandwiches.

I give him a rundown of our options for construction and maintenance services, and he continues asking questions about our small town while we finish dinner. Eventually, I go to the freezer to grab dessert. He turns down an ice cream sandwich after checking the label, but he accepts the frozen fruit bar I offer next. We sit together and slurp our popsicles as he listens to my rambling about the state of life in Camellia, his attention rapt.

"How did you even end up here?"

I wince at the question. "It's a long story, but I basically followed my ex. He's from the next town over, and we moved into this place after I started teaching at Camellia High."

"Were you close to his family?" he asks as he finishes his popsicle and stands to clear the table.

I shrug and follow him into the kitchen, where we drop the dishes into the sink. "Somewhat, but they all cut me out once Jeremy and I separated. I guess you could say I got the dogs and the house, while he got to keep all of our friends and family. Oh, and I got my Bronco."

"*All* of your friends?"

"Pretty much. I mean, I didn't really get to know your sister until a few months ago, but she's kind of it now."

He frowns and hands me a clean plate to rinse and dry. "You didn't really make her cry the day you met, did you?"

I huff out a laugh. "Our introduction happened only a few hours after I found out my ex was officially filing for a divorce. Unfortunately for Daisy, I wasn't in the right headspace for all that blonde hair and unbridled optimism. I'm pretty sure she went home and cried to Landry about her mean-girl mentor teacher. Although she did manage to keep it together in front of me, I'll give her that. She's tougher than she looks."

"Sounds like she bounced back just fine," he says, smiling.

"Yeah. I apologized the next time I saw her, and it turns out we'd both had a shitty day. And even though she probably doesn't need my friendship as much as I need hers, it's been nice having her in my corner. Whether she realizes it or not, her little sprinkling of sunshine has helped me through some of my worst days." I turn away, embarrassment coloring my face after that confession.

"I get it. She's my favorite for a reason," he adds, bumping my shoulder gently, and I can appreciate that he doesn't make me feel worse with some over-the-top sympathetic response.

"For the record, I've tried to pull my weight with a couple of cooking lessons," I tell him, attempting to hide my sniffle. "But I think that might be the only thing she's legitimately awful at."

He chuckles. "No kidding."

"You probably don't want to know about the other kind of lessons I've been giving her," I say with a more devious smile, and he groans.

"Right, because I needed one more reminder that my baby sister is now Mrs. Landry Reed and all it entails. Meanwhile, I'm starting to think I'll never ..." He turns and leans back against the kitchen counter, looking dejected.

"You'll find your soulmate one day. I'm sure she's out there, just waiting for you to come around and sweep her off her feet with all your sweet talking," I say with an involuntary pat on his chest.

He scoffs, and I yank my hand away. "Just *waiting* for me," he repeats mockingly, his eyes distant.

"Rowan?"

"Sorry," he says, shaking his head. "Thank you for that."

His reaction still seems out of character, but I'm afraid to dig any deeper, mostly because I don't think I'd be able to resist another advance from him tonight if he tried turning that whole soulmate thing around on me again.

I glance over at the clock on the wall. "We should probably go to bed. It's getting late."

"Right," he agrees, pushing himself away from the counter. Then he wraps me up in a hug without warning, and I can't help but melt into him after a few seconds.

"Thanks again for everything," he mumbles over the top of my head before he kisses it, and I sigh wistfully, my face still buried in his chest.

Dammit. I'm such a sucker for a good forehead kiss.

"I'm glad we've decided to be friends. Despite your allergies and your lack of pipe-laying skills, I might just keep you after all," I say once I find my voice.

He laughs, and I feel the vibrations in his chest. "I'm very grateful, because I'd really like to keep you, too."

I pull away after a while, since friends probably shouldn't hug alone in the kitchen for that long, but I immediately miss the safety and comfort of his arms.

"Good night, Rowan." My voice is thick.

"Good night, Claire," he replies, staring at me in a way that doesn't feel friendly at all. And I've never wished so hard for a man to lean in and plant one on me. I certainly wouldn't stop him if he tried to kiss me right now, even if that meant I owed him the girlfriend treatment for a while.

Instead, he respects my wishes like the good boy he is, gesturing for me to go first instead of pulling me back in.

"Wait," I hear him say just before his fingers wrap around my arm and keep me from moving forward. My stomach fills with butterflies at his touch, and I crane my neck to look at him.

"Yes?" I ask breathlessly.

"You're bleeding," he mumbles, crouching down to study the back of my leg. "What happened?"

"Oh, nothing." My face heats as I reach around to cover the evidence.

"Did you," he pauses to furrow his brow thoughtfully, "cut yourself shaving?"

I gulp. "I don't know. Maybe. I can't remember."

His eyes run over my calf, and he shoots me a playful grin. "You shaved your legs for me, didn't you?"

"No," I lie and kick him away. "I shave my legs every night." Another lie.

He laughs as he rises to his feet. "Of course you do. Where are your Band-Aids?"

"I don't have any," I retort, frowning. He crosses his arms and glares at me, calling my bluff. "Fine. They're in the master bathroom."

He steps forward and scoops me up into his arms without warning, making me squeal.

"This isn't a medical emergency, you know, which means it's a blatant violation of the no-touchy rule," I grumble as I drape my arms around his neck, my gaze already locked onto his mouth.

"I may have agreed to keep my lips to myself, but I also took an oath to do no harm. And I don't plan on breaking either of my promises, even if you are the most distractingly beautiful woman I've ever been tasked with healing," he replies confidently.

I scoff. "I can't believe I actually fell for this corny shit before," I protest instead of begging him to carry me to bed and feed me more of his cheesy lines all night.

After he takes off his shirt, of course.

"You can leave those glasses on, though," I accidentally say aloud.

Rowan lets out a quiet laugh as he turns and glides through my bedroom, stopping to set me down gently on the bathroom counter. "Medicine cabinet?" he asks, and I nod.

I lick my lips and watch his chest muscles flexing beneath his T-shirt as he reaches over me to retrieve a bandage. Then he wets a washcloth and props my leg on his shoulder to tenderly dab at the dried blood. It's all I can do not to whimper as he works with my calf resting against his neck.

If this is how he tends to all his patients, sign me up for the next pap smear.

I'm practically trembling with need by the time he presses the Band-Aid onto my skin, his eyes zeroing in on mine just to make sure I understand that he knows what he's doing to me. I swallow hard and flutter my eyelashes while I struggle to hide the way I'm clenching my thighs together and straining to keep my toes from curling.

"Be honest, Claire Bear. You like it corny, don't you?" he

mumbles as he straightens, the light scruff on his jaw scraping the inside of my ankle, and I gasp.

I furrow my brow as I stare up at him, trying to gauge how he'd react if I were to crook my leg around his neck and pull him down to me now. His control falters for a second, and I watch his eyes grow darker as he must be considering the same things I am.

"Rowan," I begin, barely able to get the warning out. But he clears his throat and lowers my leg after one more brush of his hands over my calf.

"Now, that should make it all better," he mutters, turning his eyes away and adjusting his glasses.

"Thank you," I breathe, white knuckling the counter to keep myself from reaching out for him.

"I'll get the dogs. Good night, Claire. Sleep well."

I accidentally let out an audible whimper. "Yeah, like that's happening now."

"Sorry. Maybe I am dangerous, just a little," he reminds me, stifling a smile as he saunters out.

He has no idea.

rowan

THE NEXT MORNING, I wake up earlier than usual with a surprising amount of energy, so I sneak into the laundry room to borrow a hoodie and put the coffee brewing before going out for a run. Retracing the route Claire and I took last night, I jog along the road to my sister's place. The crime scene we left behind looks even worse in the light of day.

I'll have to call one of the plumbers Claire recommended as soon as possible. At least Daisy's small garden seems to have survived the great flood, by the grace of God. I'm truly grateful, because I don't know if I could bear her disappointment had I ruined her precious flower beds.

She'll be even more dismayed if and when she finds out all the ways I've screwed things up with Claire, though.

What the heck am I even doing right now? Spending time with a woman I can't have, throwing myself at temptation, deceiving myself and everyone around me ... None of my actions have been in line with the life I'm striving for or the man I aim to be.

I let out a frustrated growl and reach for the string of rosary beads I keep in my pocket before turning to retrace my steps, but my mind continues to drift back to Claire as I recite the prayers that have become as natural as breathing for me. I've never felt any of this before, the inability to stop thinking about her, even to the point of distraction, the compulsive need to get closer to her, the undeniable connection we share—it has to mean *something*. I wish I understood whether I'm supposed to continue torturing myself and testing my restraint in the name of being a positive influence on Claire, or if I'm just fooling myself into thinking that.

The sight of her standing in the open doorway with a mug of coffee in her hand and her dogs playing at her feet squeezes the last of the oxygen from my lungs. I slow my pace as I reach her front yard, and the smirk she flashes me causes my heart to skyrocket. Who needs a cardio workout with a woman like this around?

"Good ... morning," I tell her when I stop to catch my breath.

"Morning," she returns and brings her mug up for a sip. I force my eyes to skim her tattoo sleeve in lieu of a full-body scan, but it's just as sexy as the rest of her.

"How are you today?" I ask with my hands on my hips.

"A little chilly. Seems my favorite hoodie's gone missing overnight," she muses, but she's taking me in as if she likes what she sees.

"Too bad you don't have a robe," I reply, laughing when she clicks her tongue in annoyance. "I hope you don't mind. Thought I'd go for a run this morning to check on Daisy's house," I add, gesturing over the hoodie.

"Don't tell me you swiped my favorite pair of boxers, too," she says, and my cheeks warm at the mention of my cheeky gesture of goodwill from our last sleepover.

I shake my head as I continue closing in the distance between us. "I wouldn't dare, not when I know how much you love wearing them."

She rolls her eyes playfully as she turns to go back into the house, and I follow her into the kitchen with the same enthusiasm as Oscar and Frankie looking for a scrap of bacon, though I tell myself it's the coffee I'm after. Once I've helped myself to the same mug I used last time, the one with the outline of a lamb and a four-leaf clover, I take off the hoodie and set it on the counter.

"Camellia High FFA, Agricultural Education," I read aloud as I study the logo.

"I don't suppose you homeschooled babies were members of the Future Farmers of America," she says, sitting with her mug.

"Not the LaFleur crew, anyway. We did join the 4-H Club, though." That earns me a smile of approval. "In fact, my brother mentioned his kids were interested in showing livestock this year. I'm guessing that's one of your specialties?"

"One of many," she replies coyly. "What do they want to show?"

"Lambs." I hold up the mug. "My parents were letting them pick from their spring flock, last I heard."

She nods. "They'd probably have the best luck with a late winter or early spring lambing."

I hum thoughtfully as I take a sip. "Were you a livestock show kid, too?"

"I was," she says wistfully. "My mom would have preferred a debutante or a cheerleader, but she got an ag girl instead. Showing sheep and goats helped me pay my own way through college, though."

"Wow, that's impressive. Although, I shouldn't be surprised at this point," I say, sighing.

"What's that supposed to mean?" she asks, though she seems amused.

I shrug. "Is there anything you can't do?"

Her expression falls, and I could kick myself for being so insensitive again.

"I'm sorry," I add softly.

She stands and moves to dump the rest of her coffee. "Speaking of FFA, I've got to get to work," she announces. "Don't forget your clean clothes in the laundry room. I'd ask if you needed anything else, but it seems you're capable of fending for yourself."

"Claire?" I call out.

She stops and lets out an exhale. "It's too early in the morning for a heart-to-heart about my infertility issues, Rowan. In fact, I'd rather not talk about them at all."

"I know. I ... I just wanted to thank you again for your hospitality," I fib.

"Don't mention it," she replies, crossing her arms.

"I'd love the chance to repay you for all your generosity, though. So if there's anything you ever need—not that I think you've only been helping me so I'd owe you in return," I ramble. "But just ... let me know if you come up with something ... please."

She snorts. "Okay, Doc. Why don't we start with a new stick welder for the Camellia High ag shop?"

I clear my throat awkwardly. "I'll get right on that."

"You should probably shower first, though," she says as she skirts by me on the way to her bedroom.

Frankie and Oscar whine when she shuts the door behind her, and I crouch down to console them. "Yeah, I get it, buddy," I tell Frankie after he lets out a woeful sigh.

After a quick shower, I dress in slacks, a button down, and a tie, and I run into Claire as I'm collecting my things from the laundry room. She's wearing a pair of jeans with another Camellia High sweatshirt, to my disappointment. I guess a part of me was looking forward to seeing her in her ag teacher uniform.

"Here," she says, placing a stack of clothes in my arms. "Don't forget to slip your sister's dress back into her closet."

"Right," I say on an exhale, my eyes still running over her. Now that I think about it, I should have been more excited to see her in one of Daisy's sundresses last night. But it's the sight of her in those chest waders I can't seem to get out of my mind.

"School's dismissing early for Mardi Gras break, so I'll be around this afternoon if you need me," she mumbles, and I gather that's the reason for her casual Friday wear.

"Yeah, thanks. I guess I'll try to find a plumber who's willing to meet me after lunch."

"Good luck with that," she says, gesturing for me to go.

I bid her another awkward goodbye and wish her a good day and a nice weekend and thank her one more time before she practically pushes me out the front door and gets into her Bronco. Then I relive every embarrassing moment on the way to the clinic where I've recently started working.

"Good morning, Dr. Cutie Pie," I hear as I'm greeted by one of the medical assistants.

"Good morning ... ah, Mackenzie, right?"

She nods, grinning proudly when I guess correctly. "Your patient has just arrived, so I'll get her set up in the ultrasound room whenever you're ready. But first, you've been summoned to Doc Simms's office. He and Nurse Tenley are waiting for you." She gestures toward the office of the practice's owner, and I furrow my brow.

"Oh, okay then. Thanks, Mackenzie," I reply, walking over to knock below the nameplate reading *Dr. Francis Simms, OB-GYN*. I step inside once the elderly doctor beckons me and exchange greetings with him and the nurse midwife who share ownership of the practice.

"I'm told you wanted to see me?" I ask hesitantly.

"Yes, have a seat, Rowan," Dr. Simms commands, and I settle into an old leather couch beside Tenley.

"Oh, yeah. This is definitely an ambush, in case you were wondering," she whispers, her playful smile at odds with her claim.

My brow lifts. "Well, all right."

Dr. Simms chuckles. "Less of an ambush and more of an offer," he amends. "But Tenley and I have been talking, and while you're still a relatively new addition to the family, we want you to know how much we all enjoy having you here at the clinic, staff and patients alike."

"Thank you," I say, a smile taking over my face. "I'm glad to be here, and the feeling is mutual."

"Good," he affirms. "I was hoping you'd say that."

I let out a soft laugh and shoot Tenley a silent plea to cut to the chase.

"You're scaring him, Doc," she says before turning back to me. "We want you here more often, Rowan. As often as you'd like." She grins as the offer sinks in.

"But ... I don't think you have enough high-risk patients to fill my schedule for more than one day per week," I remind them.

"We don't," Tenley confirms. "But with the new ultrasound machine we've acquired and the recent renovations to the hospital's L&D ward, we can't keep up with our caseload in general."

"I thought bringing Nurse Tenley on board would allow me to slow down and cruise into retirement, but we've become busier than ever," Dr. Simms jokes.

I nod, still trying to make sense of things.

"We'll have to stop accepting new patients if we don't find another OB-GYN," Tenley adds.

"So you want me to help recruit another doctor to take your place?" I ask Dr. Simms, and he and Tenley trade amused looks.

"I think we'd rather just skip the middleman and convince you to do it," Tenley tells me with a pat on the knee.

My posture straightens. "Oh, I see."

"We were thinking we could start incorporating a few regulars into your schedule, two or three days per week, whatever you're comfortable with. It would buy us some time while you decide whether you want to make it a permanent thing."

I swallow hard. "You want me to buy into the practice?"

"I'd prefer you just buy me out," Dr. Simms counters with a wide grin.

I glance back and forth between the two of them. "I mean, I'm totally flattered, but ... I don't know what to say. I haven't spent much time as a general OB-GYN. I'm not even sure I'd be prepared, even if I wanted to do it."

"Have you forgotten how to perform a C-section?" Tenley poses sarcastically.

"Well, no, but ..."

She shrugs. "I'll be here to remind you of the basics."

I open and close my mouth a few more times before I manage to form a reply. "I'm not sure I can give you a definitive answer right away, at least not the one you want. But I'll certainly think about it."

"That's all we ask. And know we're very amendable to whatever kind of arrangement you're looking for, even if you want a trial for now and decide it's not for you later," Dr. Simms reassures me.

I force a smile and rise to shake his hand and thank him for the opportunity, my mind still reeling as Tenley leads me out into the hallway.

She lets out a soft laugh as she regards the look of consternation I must be wearing. "I did warn you about the ambush."

I shake my head and huff out a laugh of my own. "This is certainly not how I saw my morning going, especially after the night I had."

She cocks an eyebrow. "Do tell."

"Just some trouble with the plumbing at my sister's house. She and Landry are still on their honeymoon, and I'm hoping to get everything fixed by the time they get back."

She crosses her arms and regards me skeptically. "Is that why the office gossip reported seeing your truck at a certain recently divorced ag teacher's house early this morning?"

My heart quickens, though I'm unsure whether it's because I've been caught with Claire or simply because she's back in the forefront of my mind. I clear my throat uncomfortably as Tenley purses her lips and dares me to deny the charges.

"I-I, um ..."

"Rowan," Tenley interrupts my stuttering and softens her expression. "I'm only teasing. You don't need to answer to me or anyone else here. Your love life is none of our business. Unless you're looking for advice, in which case I'd recommend confiding in anyone but Mackenzie."

I chuckle at that, and she pats me on the arm. "Seriously, though. I'm here if you need a listening ear."

"Thank you," I say, trying to convey my sincerity.

"What are business partners for, right?" She grins and bounces her eyebrows, and I narrow my eyes at her.

"I'm afraid it's going to take more than that to convince me to abandon my high-risk patients."

"No one said you'd be abandoning them altogether. You'd just be casting a broader net, which means you'd get to help more women overall. And there's something to be said for working in a small community, you know."

I sigh. "That sounds nice, but also a little counterintuitive."

"Doesn't make it untrue," she says with a shrug. "Besides, you might like being closer to your family."

"My family's in Baton Rouge," I remind her.

"Hmm. And I thought they were off making babies in some cabin in the mountains," she replies with a sly smirk, and I blow out a frustrated breath when I realize she's right.

I like Camellia so far, much more than I expected, and I'm going to have a hard time staying away once Daisy and Landry start having kids of their own. Not to mention the dark-haired, tattooed beauty down the road I can't seem to shake, even against my better judgment.

"Oh," Tenley blurts out, snapping her fingers. "Speaking of, I'm about to start a round of Natural Family Planning classes. You should pop in for a refresher, just in case you start seeing some of our regular patients. It'll be fun."

"Okay," I say, nodding. "That's actually a good idea. Thanks."

"I'll remind you when it gets closer. In the meantime, give that offer some thought, pray about it, run it by the important people in your life, whatever it takes to arrive at the decision that brings you the most peace," Tenley adds with a softer smile before she walks away.

monday

7:42 AM

CLAIRE

Wth. Did you send me a gift?

ROWAN

Well, good morning to you, too.

I'm doing great, thanks for asking.

How are you?

CLAIRE

Pissed af because some weirdo bought me a robe.

ROWAN

No need to send a thank you note.

CLAIRE

I realize you were homeschooled, but you get why this is completely inappropriate, don't you?

ROWAN

I think you may be reading too much into this. It's just a small token of gratitude for all the hospitality you've shown me.

CLAIRE

Rowan …

You don't send a woman lingerie unless you plan on helping her out of it.

ROWAN

Well, then. Maybe I have made a slight error in judgment.

I promise my intention was to keep you covered. In fact, this is probably the most selfish gift I've ever given.

CLAIRE

So you bought me a fancy designer robe to preserve my modesty? Because you want me to cover up in front of you?

ROWAN

I'm not hearing you say this in the right tone, am I?

CLAIRE

Kiss my ass, Athanasius.

ROWAN

Ah, gotcha.

So, um, sorry? I guess the robe was a miscalculation on my part. I honestly thought you'd take it as both a compliment and an inside joke, and I even pictured you opening it up and immediately having one of your big laughs.

CLAIRE

How in the hell did you expect me to interpret this as a compliment?

ROWAN

It was supposed to say, "I know I've been a screw up, and I'm banking on needing your help again," and "I can't be trusted to keep my eyes and my hands to myself around you."

I also know you like to wear pretty things to bed,
so I asked a saleswoman to help me find
something that was modest enough for drinking
coffee outside but still feminine and flattering.

And the design and the colors reminded me of
your tattoos.

CLAIRE

You went shopping in person and had this
delivered to my house?

ROWAN

Maybe.

CLAIRE

I didn't even think people did that anymore.

ROWAN

Okay, yeah ... I think I'm hearing how creepy this
whole thing sounds now.

I'm sorry. You're right, this was really
inappropriate. And you should probably just
throw it out, since you don't need another
reminder of my stupidity.

CLAIRE

It is a very lovely robe, though.

You didn't spend a fortune on it, did you?

ROWAN

It was a gift. All that matters is how it makes you
feel.

CLAIRE

Well, now that I'm wearing it, I have to say ... it
does make me feel pretty.

ROWAN

I'm glad. If the robe could talk, I'm sure it would
say the same.

CLAIRE

ROWAN

And just think, I considered gifting you a pack of my favorite boxers instead.

CLAIRE

Thank you. I guess this was actually a very thoughtful gift, albeit completely unnecessary.

ROWAN

You're welcome, Claire Bear.

CLAIRE

Who said you could call me that, anyway?

ROWAN

I'm pretty sure Tante Verna approves.

I hope you have an amazing week, and I'm counting down the days until we run into one another again.

CLAIRE

Yeah. You, too, you big weirdo.

claire

"THANK God my brother was here to turn off the water and call a plumber the next morning," Daisy tells me as she lets me into her house, her service dog trailing closely behind.

"Yeah, lucky," I agree, keeping my expression neutral. Part of me feels guilty for not volunteering my side of that story, but I guess Rowan has his reasons for omitting my role in his recount of the busted pipe fiasco a couple weeks back. "But other than that, the honeymoon was great, right?"

She bites her lip, and her cheeks flush as she plops down onto the couch. "Our cabin was *really* nice. And the view was amazing."

"I bet you got a good look at the ceiling," I say, laughing loudly as I make myself comfortable beside her.

"Sure did," she confirms, stifling a grin. "Sturdy headboard, too."

She earns another cackle and a nudge from me with that one. "So, um, speaking of your brother, what's his deal, anyway?" I begin once our laughter dies down.

Daisy's brow rises. "Were we talking about Rowan? I must have missed it."

"We both know you were just waiting for an opportunity to bring him up," I say, trying to downplay my interest after my transition wasn't as smooth as I'd hoped.

"So you can explain why you never mentioned the fact that you knew him before?"

Dammit. Withholding the truth has been hard enough, but I'm afraid this is going to require an actual lie.

"I didn't know he was your brother," I say with a shrug. "Besides, I was still married when I met him."

There. That wasn't technically untrue.

"And what do you want to know now that you're a single woman?" she asks as she tucks her feet beneath her. Juniper notices her position and takes it as a cue to relax.

"What's wrong with him? He's practically a walking green flag, yet he's still single," I point out.

She lets out a short laugh. "There's nothing wrong with him. If anything, it's probably the other way around," she mutters the last part to herself.

"Eh, I call bullshit," I say, pretending I'm not all that invested in her answer. "If he were perfect, he'd be married by now, wouldn't he?"

"I suppose Rowan isn't perfect, and maybe I'm a little biased, but he's pretty darn close," she muses.

I shake my head, not because I disagree with Daisy, but to rid my mind of the image of Rowan's nearly flawless body. "It's not possible," I tell her after a while. "You don't just stumble upon a hot doctor who's still available at his age, much less one that ... adorable."

Daisy grins. "I mean, I did."

I snort. "Yeah, but Landry was a take-home project. It took a little elbow grease to bring him around."

"All I did was dust him off and shine him up," she says with a wave of her hand and a mischievous glint in her eyes. "But I'd like to revisit your previous statement. Do you really think Rowan is adorable?"

Dead freaking sexy would be more accurate, I almost reply. But I figure I should spare her on this one, since it is her brother we're talking about here.

"Who wouldn't?" I retort instead. "Which brings me back to my original point—how is he still single?"

Daisy shakes her head and pulls her long hair over her shoulder. "I honestly don't know, but I imagine it has something to do with the high standards he holds for himself. Women must find it intimidating," she says thoughtfully as she twists her hair into a braid.

"What kind of standards?" I ask, my stomach clenching at the reminder.

She hesitates before answering. "Morals, I guess."

My brow furrows, and I think back to our last few conversations. "He's religious, like you."

"Yes, and, well, we were raised in a different environment. Our parents made it a point to protect us from the ways of the world, at least until we were mature and firm enough in our beliefs to make good decisions on our own. And even though Rowan acclimated pretty well in college, he's always been very strict on himself, probably more so than the rest of us."

"Oh." I think about his honesty on the night we met, how refreshing it was to interact with someone so genuine, and now that I consider it, a little naive for his age.

"Most of us assumed he'd become a priest after practically living like one for the past couple decades, but I know he wants a family so badly. It's a shame he can't seem to find anyone who appreciates his self-discipline," she explains wistfully. "I hate seeing him so lonely."

I blink at her a few times while I process what she's telling me. But something's not adding up here. "And when you say he lives like a priest, you mean ..."

"He hasn't taken a legitimate vow of poverty or celibacy as far as I know, but he likes to live more simply so he can give to charities and the less fortunate. And, you know ..." She lifts a shoulder in a shrug. But before I can fill in the blanks, the front door flies open.

Daisy immediately jumps to her feet and squeals with delight when Landry waltzes in. Leaving me on the couch, she bounds over to him with Juniper barking at her heels, and his shoulders relax as soon as he wraps her up in a hug.

"Miss me, Blondie?" he pulls back and asks with a smirk before he lifts her up onto his hips and kisses her, and my heart melts just a little.

Landry notices me after a while and leans around Daisy to shoot me a polite smile. "Hey, Claire," he greets me with much less enthusiasm.

"Hey," I return. "Long day, Doc?"

He sighs and sets Daisy back down onto her bare feet. "No, but I *was* looking forward to some alone time with my wife." She gasps and reaches up to swat at his chest, and he frowns, presumably because he didn't intend to sound so rude. I'm not offended, though. I'd probably be the same way if I found someone I liked coming home to.

"No worries. I'm on my way out," I say as I stand, freezing in place once I realize it wasn't my presence Landry was grumbling about.

"Hi," Rowan greets me from the open door, his expression unreadable. "I didn't expect to see you here."

"My car is in the driveway," I point out dumbly as Daisy and Landry exchange a look.

"The blue Bronco, right?"

I narrow my eyes at him. "Yeah. That's the one."

Rowan nods. "I'm seeing patients at the clinic in the morning," he explains, as if I wouldn't be able to surmise his reasons for being here. But the silence stretches after that, and it suddenly feels like I've worn out my welcome.

"Well, I was just leaving," I announce, scanning the floor for my boots. Of course, they're behind Rowan, so I gesture politely for him to move over. He stands firmly, though, his eyes running over me in a way that makes me feel warm and lightheaded.

"Is this your, ah, work uniform?" he asks carefully.

"Yeah," I say with a forced smile. "Just missing the steeled toes."

"Oh, sorry." Understanding finally dawns on him, and he shifts a duffle bag over his shoulder as he steps to the side.

"Wait, Claire, don't rush off," Daisy begins when I grab the first boot. "Why don't you stay for dinner?"

"What are we going to make her, an egg sandwich?" I hear Landry whisper harshly, then he grunts when Daisy presumably elbows him in the ribs. "I mean, don't go. We're, um, getting takeout … since Rowan's staying over."

My eyes dance around the room as I measure the sincerity of their invitation. Daisy looks as though she's bursting with excitement and plotting some kind of set up. Landry seems resolved but less than thrilled with the idea. And Rowan's expression is still uncharacteristically blank.

I panic and reach for my boot again. "Thanks, but I don't want to impose," I tell them before Rowan reaches out to stop me with a firm hand on my arm.

"Stay," he says levelly. "I'll make dinner for everyone."

I glance up to find him smiling softly. "Are you sure?" I ask hesitantly.

"Of course. I can't make any promises about what I can whip up with the ingredients they'll have, but I'm sure I'll think of something."

"Since when do you cook?" Landry crosses his arms and studies his friend carefully.

Rowan straightens his posture and shrugs. "Mom's been teaching me a few things. And I recently learned to make marinara sauce from scratch, which I've found useful for a lot of other recipes."

I roll my eyes, and I feel my face heating when everyone turns to look at me. I might have accidentally scoffed out loud.

"Sorry, ignore me," I say awkwardly.

"What, you don't think I can cook?" Rowan asks, his lips already curving up into a smile.

"If anything, I'm shocked you aren't a Michelin Star chef," I retort sarcastically.

He chuckles. "It's on my bucket list, but I haven't gotten around to it yet."

"Right," I confirm with a nod, trying to stifle my own smile. "You've still got to get your plumber's license and your CDL first."

His head lolls back as he groans playfully, and one of my obnoxious cackles breaks free before I can stop myself. These little inside jokes are becoming dangerous.

"And how do you two know each other again?" Landry chimes in.

"Oh, we both ..."

"Well, there was ..."

"He works with that doctor ..."

"And some mutual acquaintances ..."

Rowan and I talk over one another as we fumble through another purposefully ambiguous explanation of our chance meetings, though my mind insists on an inconvenient callback to lying in bed with him that first night, our legs tangled together and his chest vibrating beneath my cheek each time he laughs, him calling me his soulmate before he pulls me in for a slow, heated kiss—

"Yeah, because that makes sense," Landry says with a grunt. Daisy bites her lip from her place beside him, just itching to bring up our conversation from before.

I cross my arms over my middle and shift my weight to one foot, still trying to disguise my body's reaction to Rowan's current proximity. But it's impossible to keep my cool around him, mostly because he's so damned cute. And it's frankly a little annoying that he doesn't seem to be as bothered with our clandestine situationship as I am today.

"I think it's all downright *adorable*," Daisy declares after a second, batting her lashes at me, and I shoot her a warning glare.

"Well, I think they're hiding something," Landry continues. "And I'm shit at reading people, so I can't be the only one picking up on this vibe."

Rowan casts a terse glance my way, giving me the slightest bit of satisfaction before he clears his throat and steps forward. "And I think my sister has turned you into a romantic, Lan," he says, stopping to pat Landry on the shoulder on his way down the hall. "I'm going to put my bag up. Daisy, why don't you start digging through the pantry so I can see what we've got to work with?"

That traitor.

I curse Rowan under my breath when Daisy and Landry turn to

study me the second he's gone. I've got half a mind to blurt out something along the lines of *Oh, and by the way, I just happen to know Rowan's preferred brand of underwear and that sexy noise he makes when you kiss him on the—*

"Why do you look so guilty?" Daisy asks, narrowing her eyes at me. "Landry's right. You're hiding something."

I force a shrug. "I haven't done anything worth blabbing about ... lately."

Certainly not your brother, but not for a lack of trying.

"We may not have been friends for long, but I know you can't keep a secret." She wags a finger at me. "And don't think I'm not drawing conclusions after the conversation we left unfinished. You know, when we were talking about the same guy who seems to make you get all fidgety and nervous anytime you're in the same room together."

"I do *not* get fidgety and nervous around him."

Maybe just a little hot and bothered.

Daisy scoffs. "Okay, then why are you walking around with one boot? And why were you questioning me about Rowan's dating habits earlier?"

I look down to find that she's right and stifle another curse. "I wasn't fishing for you to set me up with your brother," I answer as I remove said boot. "I was only curious because I've been out of the dating game for so long that I honestly don't know how this works anymore. It was more like a case study."

Landry snorts. "Do you really think you could get away with asking her about Rowan and not be forced into at least one date after that?"

"You've all made it very clear that I'm not his type. And I don't think he's mine," I fib, mustering up as much faux confidence as I can.

"There it is again," Daisy points at me. "You keep doing this weird, blinky thing every time you talk about him."

"No, I don't." But I have to deliberately force my eyelids to stay open that time, and I'm pretty sure my cheeks are growing dark enough to make up for it.

"It's not her fault. The vibe is awkward because I asked her out a while back, and she turned me down. Happy now?" Rowan calls out from the hallway, barely glancing my way as he saunters into the small galley kitchen.

"At our wedding reception, you mean?" Landry asks, cocking his head to the side.

"Before that, when we first met," Rowan answers, to my surprise. "But I struck out that night, too."

"Really?" Landry stares thoughtfully in Rowan's direction, while Daisy keeps her gaze narrowed on me.

I force another noncommittal shrug and walk toward the kitchen, taking care not to blink this time. "Technically, I didn't turn him down. I told him my divorce was too fresh for anything serious. He's the one that decided we'd only be wasting one another's time."

Rowan's eyes flash to mine, and my shoulders droop when I see the disappointment hiding just below the surface.

"Can we get back to dinner?" he asks, his tone hinting at his annoyance before he shifts back into a more pleasant disposition. I'm starting to suspect I might be the only one who gets to see the other side of him, the tired, lonely, and slightly jaded thirty-something-year-old. It's another scary thought, since he's the only person who knows the more vulnerable, emotional half of me.

I clear my throat and walk over to join him. "Whatcha making, Chef Boyardee?" I inquire, and he smiles appreciatively before ducking his head into the freezer.

"I was honestly banking on using a bowl of my dad's famous duck gumbo as a starter, since I know my parents stocked the freezer while these two were on their honeymoon, but it looks like they've already raided the stash," he mumbles.

"I'll have you know that I'm getting better at cooking. I've practically perfected Mom's bread pudding recipe," Daisy yells defensively from across the room, and Landry grunts.

Rowan tosses a pack of smoked sausage onto the counter before moving toward the pantry, and my eyes immediately zero in on a red lid. I instinctively dart forward to snatch the peanut butter jar out of his reach.

"Probably ought to avoid this one," I say awkwardly, holding it up for them to see.

"Yeah, thanks," he replies with a grateful smile.

"Crap on a cracker!" Daisy squeaks. "I thought I'd thrown that out. Sorry, Rowan." She takes the jar and tosses it into the trash, but I can see the wheels turning in her mind before I turn to wash my hands at the sink.

Landry furrows his brow. "How'd you know—"

"Got any onions?" Rowan cuts him off. "I'm thinking I could throw some beans in with that sausage."

Landry clears his throat. "Uh, yeah. I think there's some in the back of the freezer. Want me to cook some rice?"

"That'll work," Rowan replies as he continues gathering ingredients. "Canned red beans and rice won't get me that Michelin Star, but it'll fill our bellies, right?" He glances my way, as if he's looking for my approval.

"Sounds fine to me, as long as you don't skimp on the sausage," I quip, earning a giggle from Daisy. Rowan presses his lips together, stifling a smile, and Landry nudges him when they cross paths.

"You heard that, man? She wants your—"

"Yeah, I got it, Lan," Rowan says dryly.

"You guys need to get your minds out of the gutter," I begin. "I wasn't referring to anyone's sausage, specifically ..."

But my argument falls flat when my eyes skim the pack of meat labeled as "Rowan's Deer Sausage" with a date from this past November. Of course he's a good hunter, too.

Rowan clears his throat. "I have a few more packs in the freezer back home. I'll bring some next time I'm in town."

"Yeah, sure. Call before you come," I mumble, making the others laugh, and my insides warm when Rowan and I lock eyes for a second.

CHAPTER TWENTY-THREE

claire

I DO my best to keep my facial expressions in check after that, and before long we're all seated at the table together. It's admittedly been a while since I've had dinner with friends like this, and although I felt a bit slighted by Rowan's evasiveness earlier, I'm not willing to risk ruining everyone's night by calling him out. Instead, I resolve to enjoy the company while I can, especially once the conversation shifts to Daisy and Rowan's huge family.

"And what's a consecrated sister again?" I ask in reference to their sister, Rosemary.

"One step away from a nun. It's basically like she's married to Jesus," Daisy replies in between bites of food. "Her vows weren't all that different from the ones a married couple or a priest takes."

"Oh," I say thoughtfully. "I never thought of it that way."

"Most people don't, but it's similar to a sacramental marriage, except their version of chastity means abstaining all together," she explains.

"So how is being a priest like being married?" I continue.

"A priest is married to the Church. He serves as a father to his congregation, which is one of the reasons behind the vow of celibacy. If he had a wife and children, then he'd naturally want to prioritize those responsibilities over his vocation as a priest."

"Interesting." I turn to Rowan. "And you've never thought about becoming a priest?"

He forces a smile. "Of course. I just never felt like it was the vocation God had in mind for me," he replies, mirroring what Daisy said earlier.

"What if you never get married? Can you just decide to be a priest then?" I ask, watching his reaction carefully.

He shrugs and lifts his glass, looking slightly uncomfortable. "Sure, but only if I hear that call later in life. It's not the kind of thing I'd do because I ran out of options."

"But what about the vows? What if it's too late for the whole celibacy thing?"

Rowan chokes and begins coughing loudly and slapping himself on the chest.

"You okay?" Daisy asks.

"Yeah, sorry," he wheezes before taking a drink and adding, "Went down wrong."

"That's not what you said last time," I mutter just low enough for him to hear. He glares at me before he yanks at his collar and coughs again, and I lean back in my chair with a smug smile, quite satisfied with the effect I'm having on him.

Until the very moment all of the pieces fall into place, that is.

I blink down at the table, feeling a flush crawl up my neck and face again as I think back on some of the things Rowan said to me that night.

"I don't usually talk like this, or act like this ... You said it's just sex, but it's still going to mean something to me ... I've never done this before ... You'll never understand what you took from me tonight ..."

"Is anyone going to answer my question?" I blurt out.

"Um, what was it again?" Daisy asks cautiously.

"Do you have to be a virgin to take a vow of celibacy and become a priest?" I demand.

"No," she answers, taken aback by my urgency. "Just like you don't have to be a virgin going into marriage, but you should at least be in a state of grace." I'm still silent, so she goes on. "A man who had been living an unchaste lifestyle could still enter the priesthood after receiving absolution in the sacrament of reconciliation."

Rowan stands abruptly and shoves his chair under the table, making it scratch the floor. "Sorry, I think I need some fresh air."

"I bet you do," I remark.

He stops in his tracks and turns his eyes back to mine, and I shiver. It's the same look he gave me before he walked out on me that first night.

"What's his problem?" Landry asks Daisy, then drops his fork. "Is it his allergies? I hope he's not coming down with something. What if he contaminated our food?"

Daisy smiles as she puts a hand over his and calmly reassures him that it's obviously not the food or a stomach bug that upset Rowan.

"Then what is it?" Landry asks, still confused.

"I think he might be uncomfortable with the current topic of discussion," she ventures. "Or the fact that we've started talking about him as if he isn't still in the room."

Rowan's chest heaves as he continues staring back at me. "Nothing's wrong. I'm fine," he mumbles and returns to his seat.

Landry's brows draw in closely as he mulls it over. "You're not embarrassed because Daisy just outed you as a virgin in front of Claire, are you? You've never been too *honte* to admit that before."

"Oh, I can name at least one time he failed to disclose that particular bit of information," I mutter quietly, and Daisy narrows her eyes at me.

"What are you implying?" she asks.

"Maybe you don't know your brother as well as you think you do," I retort a little too defensively, and Rowan sniffs beside me.

She rears back. "How can you say that when the two of you barely know one another at all?"

I bite my lip before I answer. "I've seen enough to know he's not perfect."

And I've seen just about every inch of him.

"Hold on, are we seriously fighting about whether or not

Rowan's still a virgin?" Landry interposes, his voice taking on a sharper tone.

"No," I say quickly. "It's just ..." I glance over at Rowan as I trail off, unsure of how much I should share.

I could be a Petty Betty and tell them exactly why I'm pissed, but then I'd have to admit that I threw myself at Rowan while I was still in my pre-divorced era. I'd also have to recount one of the lowest points in my life, when Rowan practically ran out of the room after I'd confided so much in him and he apparently couldn't be bothered to share anything this important with me.

But as much as it stings each time he equates becoming physically intimate with me to committing an unforgivable sin, it likely stems from the fact that I was still legally married the first time it happened. So I can't exactly hold that against him.

I sigh. "I'm sorry. Forget I said anything at all."

"Wait a minute," Landry begins again. "What if Rowan's upset that we're talking about this because he *hasn't* been celibate? And Claire's pissed because she didn't know he was supposed to be waiting until marriage ..."

I blink and look away as he continues, not even caring whether Daisy notices my nervous tick this time.

"But the only reason Claire even cares about this is because she and Rowan," Landry pauses to gesture in both directions, "Were not celibate *together*."

Daisy gasps, and my cheeks heat when Landry illustrates his point by intertwining his fingers. I glance over at Rowan again, but his eyes are still trained on the table.

"That's not exactly it," I mumble when I realize they're waiting on me to answer.

Daisy lets out another shocked gasp. "So he *did* ask you out after our wedding? Have you been sneaking around together?"

"Not ... exactly," I repeat, this time with even less certainty. Then I turn and pinch the back of Rowan's arm, making him wince. "You're not going to say anything?"

He frowns and rubs at the spot above his elbow after I knock him out of the spell he's been under. "It's not what it looks like," he directs at Daisy, his voice tinged with guilt.

She turns her glare back to me, and I figure I have to give them *something* now, even if it means letting them think we hooked up a couple of weeks ago to keep them from sleuthing out the whole story.

"The truth is Rowan has slept over at my house, but we didn't sleep *together*," I explain. "He needed a place to crash after your wedding, so I let him stay in my spare bedroom."

"So you didn't hook up?" Landry asks carefully. Rowan gulps audibly but is otherwise silent.

"Nothing happened that night," I say confidently. "And even if it had, I don't see why it would be any of your business. We're both single adults," I add, lifting my chin in indignation.

"But there were other nights?" Daisy asks. "Nights before you were both single?"

I cringe, regretting my decision to tell her that I was still married the first time Rowan and I met.

"Look, I don't have anything to hide," I declare, trying desperately to keep the panic from seeping into my voice. "Your brother's the one with a reputation to protect. So you might want to think twice before you ask another question, at least for his sake. You may just get an answer you don't like."

"Is it weird that I kind of want to ask even harder now?" Landry whispers, and Daisy nudges him in the side. "Hey, it's not so funny now that it's about *your* brother and not my sister, is it?"

She whines and pouts, and I can't help but feel slighted by her reaction. She's practically my only friend, not to mention notorious for seeing the best in everyone, and even she can't bear the idea of her brother with someone like me.

"All right, then," Landry says, bringing me back. "Since you said you have nothing to hide, go ahead and tell us. Have you and Rowan ever been ... intimate?"

"That depends on your definition of that term," I reply evenly, though my heart is pounding. Because the truth is that I've told Rowan things I've never told anyone else, and regardless of our physical involvement, he probably knows me more intimately than my ex-husband ever did.

"You know what I mean," Landry says with a sardonic smirk.

I clear my throat awkwardly as they continue staring me down. I'm also not sure how these things work, especially for devout Catholics like the LaFleurs. What exactly does and does not constitute sex?

"Claire's right. It's none of your business." Rowan finally speaks up.

Landry looks back and forth between us. "So you have slept together, then."

"No," Rowan says firmly.

"*Something* must have happened, though. You've kissed, haven't you?" Daisy demands, her question surprising me. It also triggers another one of those inconvenient flashbacks, one so steamy that it makes my mouth dry and forces me to lick my lips in lieu of forming an answer.

"Yes," Rowan admits begrudgingly. "We've kissed."

I resist the temptation to add, *a lot ... and not just on the mouth.*

"And when did you start ... dating?" Daisy asks.

"We're not dating, and we never were. Like Claire said before, she's not interested in me that way," he continues, and I nearly call him out for gaslighting me before remembering I'm the one who's been feeding him that lie.

"Now, are you satisfied?" Rowan turns to ask Landry, but he doesn't wait for an answer as he stands and begins collecting dishes. Landry sighs, looking slightly remorseful.

"It's getting late. We should probably clean up," Rowan adds on his way to the kitchen, and I realize I've missed my opportunity to escape once I see the look on Daisy's face.

"Did you really not know about the whole celibacy thing?" Daisy whispers, gesturing in Rowan's direction.

"No. And I already feel stupid enough for not figuring it out until tonight," I mumble.

"*That's* what you meant about Rowan not being perfect, then.

He lied to you." Landry states it as a fact, because he can't help but reiterate their findings.

I roll my eyes. "He definitely withheld some of the truth."

"Wow. And you couldn't tell?" Landry's brow lifts.

Daisy shoves him. "Seriously, Landry? That's what you're worried about? You don't think he's been beating himself up over whatever this is? You know Rowan. I'm sure the guilt has been eating away at him."

I click my tongue. "You're not making me feel any better, either, for the record."

She cringes. "Sorry, it's just that we're not used to watching Rowan make mistakes."

"Yeah. I can see that."

And I guess I'm his first and only mistake, I add in my mind. Because it's obvious they wouldn't find this whole thing so amusing or scandalous if I weren't the one responsible for ruining Rowan's reputation.

The sound of the front door nearly slamming makes all three of us flinch.

"So, uh ... who's going outside to talk to the slut?" Landry poses after a while.

"Not it," I say quickly, mostly because I'm afraid he'll turn this into another one of those times when I end up sharing too much about myself and getting overly emotional, and this one is about him.

"I love my brother, but I'm not sure I'm the right person to talk to him about *this*," Daisy retorts.

"Fine, I'll go," Landry says on an exhale. "But one of you will need to be on standby for when I inevitably say something that makes him feel worse."

"Didn't take Landry Reed for a heart-to-heart kind of guy, but he must really have a soft spot for you LaFleurs," I muse quietly once Daisy and I are left alone.

She frowns. "Claire, I'm sorry my brother wasn't honest with you. Regardless of what's happened between you, you deserve the truth from him." She pauses and purses her lips, as if she's debating whether or not to go on. "And I know it doesn't excuse his actions, but I'm sure he was just worried you'd judge him for this, like other women have in the past."

I scoff. "Or maybe he's just like every other man and was willing to say anything to get laid."

"No," she says, shaking her head. "Rowan's not like that, and this is such a big part of his identity, a core value for him."

My stomach churns. If Rowan really is a virgin, and this is truly one of his "core values," then that might make everything a million times worse. Because it would mean the emotional intimacy I was so certain we'd shared was all one-sided.

"Or maybe he's not the man either of us thought he was," I repeat.

"After the way you baited me into talking about my brother when you apparently know him much better than you've been letting on, I'm not sure you're the friend I thought you were, either," she replies, her expression pained, as if it hurts her to acknowledge it.

And that's when I break.

"You're right. I'm sorry, Daisy," I choke out, my chin trembling. "If it makes you feel any better, I've only been playing dumb for Rowan's sake, and it's been killing me not to tell you everything." I blow out a breath. "The truth is that he actually called me for help with the whole busted-pipe situation, and he ended up staying over at my place that night, too. But he's been sleeping in my guest bedroom, I swear."

Her eyelashes flutter as she digests the information. "I don't understand. You're both adults, and where you sleep is none of my business. But why go through so much trouble to hide the fact that you're friends?"

I whimper when I realize she's backed me into a corner again. And while a part of me wants to continue protecting Rowan, I can't keep lying to Daisy.

"Because he doesn't want you to find out about the night we met." She lifts a brow and gestures for me to continue. "I guess you could say we felt an instant connection, both emotionally and physically. And while he didn't go into much detail about his ... religious convictions, I wasn't entirely forthcoming about my marital status at the time."

Her eyes widen. "Does he know?"

"Yes. I ended up spelling it out before the end of the night, and he made it clear that being a few days away from a finalized divorce wasn't unmarried enough in his book."

"Oh."

"We parted ways on some pretty awkward terms after that, thinking we'd never run into one another again, much less share a common acquaintance. Yet, here we are," I explain, unable to keep the sarcasm from seeping into my tone.

"It's also why you didn't come to my bachelorette party, isn't it?" she asks quietly, and I nod.

"Sorry," I whisper. The situation with Rowan isn't the only reason I avoided most of her bridal festivities, but I'm not about to fess up to being jealous of her friendship with Loren or too cowardly to attend any kind of girls-only party in general.

"I guess I understand why neither of you was eager to volunteer the whole story," she says after a while. "But you're not married anymore, and there's obviously something left of that connection you mentioned. Now that you know the truth about Rowan, couldn't you just ... kiss and make up?"

I huff out a laugh. "Us not having a chance might be the only part we were both honest about. Your brother is definitely dating with intention, and I'm only fit for a good time."

"What makes you think that?" she demands, her tone shifting.

"He seems dead set on finding someone who shares those core values you mentioned, getting married, and starting a family. Which makes me an inconvenient distraction."

She clicks her tongue, and I'm worried I've upset her again. "He didn't actually say that last part, did he?"

I search my memory and come up short. "I'm paraphrasing. But it's my fault. I've told him a few times I'm not in a position to even consider the kind of relationship he's looking for. And that's why we settled on an awkward friendship, I guess."

"That son of a biscuit eater," she grumbles, making me smile. "He really is dumber than I thought."

I chuckle quietly. "In his defense, I wasn't exactly shy about what I wanted from him that first night. I can't fault him for paying attention to what kind of woman I am."

Her expression turns sour again. "And what kind of woman do you think you are? Because as far as I can tell, you're generous and loyal, you're intimidatingly beautiful, and you're constantly putting everyone else's feelings before your own. In fact, I can't rightly understand why the heck you've been so nice to Rowan at all, unless it's because you didn't want *me* to worry about him."

I look away when her words make my chest tighten and my eyes sting. "I think you're confusing me with someone else, but it's still really nice of you to say it."

"See? You're humble, too."

"And you have a knack for seeing the best in people," I say, standing and collecting the last of the dishes Rowan missed earlier.

"What I have is half a mind to kick my brother's ass right about now," she retorts, then claps a hand over her mouth once she hears her own language.

"I appreciate it, but I think I'm capable of handling him on my own," I fib once I'm done cackling at her. "I'll just be grateful if you don't disown me after all this."

"Claire," she whines, her eyes watering, and I can't help it when mine run over at the sight of her. She scurries around the table and wraps her arms around me, and I sniffle over her shoulder, an empty glass in each of my hands. "Of course we're still friends. In fact, Rowan can get in line. I saw you first."

I laugh through my tears. "You're still my favorite LaFleur. And the most adorable one, as far as I'm concerned."

"I'm a Reed now. So it's perfectly fine if my brother becomes your favorite LaFleur," she mumbles, squeezing me again before she loosens her grip and steps away. "You do know what all this means, though, right?"

I shake my head as I wipe my nose on my shoulder.

"You could become *my* favorite LaFleur," she declares with a grin.

I flash her a rueful smile. "I'm sorry, Daze. But I don't think I'll be changing my last name ever again."

She frowns. "But I've already let my imagination run away with the idea of you and Rowan getting married. So you and I could get pregnant at the same time and raise our babies as sibling-cousins, just like Loren and Tenley," she rambles.

"And how did you manage that when you only found out there was even a possibility of a Rowan and me within the last ten minutes?" I object.

"Oh, no, I've been plotting this since you told me you were getting divorced, and then again once I saw you two talking at my wedding reception," she replies cheerily, and I laugh again, even though my chest aches at her mention of having babies together.

"I really am sorry, but I'm afraid that's impossible. I love you for dreaming it up, though," I say, attempting to hide the sadness in my voice.

"I wouldn't rule it out if I were you," she continues, ignoring my protest and gesturing for me to follow her into the kitchen. "I've got a pretty long and influential list of intercessory prayer contacts."

rowan

I GROAN when I realize the footsteps on the porch are too heavy to be anyone's but Landry's.

"You really must have drawn the short stick," I remark, since I've never known him to initiate a conversation if there's even a chance of someone bringing up their feelings.

"Yeah. Claire's not your biggest fan at the moment, and I'm afraid Daisy's lost her hero," he says plainly, grunting as he makes himself comfortable beside me. "I'm the only one who finds this entertaining."

"And which vices are you out here to congratulate me on?" I ask mockingly.

"The fun ones?" His eyebrow quirks as he tries to keep his expression serious. "For the record, I don't mind that you're human. I might even like you a little better now," he adds when I don't respond right away.

"Wish I could say the same for myself," I mutter.

He sighs. "Come on, Rowan. Don't do this to yourself forever. Go to confession, work past it, do better next time. If anyone understands how God's mercy works, it's you, right?"

"I tried, but I don't know if I've ever been more disappointed in myself," I say, though I'm secretly impressed by Landry's maturity.

"So you slipped up, what, once in thirty-three years? And I get it, you feel bad about lying to her, but—"

"No, you don't get it," I interrupt him. "This wasn't an accident. I made the deliberate decision to sin, and I've been ignoring my conscience and throwing myself at temptation ever since. Not to mention all the lies of omission," I say, running a hand through my hair.

"So you and Claire really have been messing around?" he asks, sounding confused.

I open my mouth to say something else before I think better of it. "What exactly did she tell you after I walked out?"

His brow lifts in surprise. "I think I'd rather get your side of the story first."

"Not much, then."

"Enough to know she didn't actually turn you down the first time you asked her out."

"That bit was actually true. I asked to see her again, practically begged her to give me another shot, but she refused."

"And?"

I sigh. "And I was so lonely and desperate that I nearly slept with her anyway," I admit quietly.

He chokes on a laugh. "Nearly?"

"Why are you suddenly so interested in my love life?"

Landry shrugs. "I told you, it's reassuring."

"Yeah, well, you're not supposed to be celebrating my fall from grace," I grumble.

"I'd be lying if I said I didn't get some validation from knowing you're actually capable of something like this. But if I'm celebrating anything, it's that you finally found someone who makes you want to take a risk. I was honestly starting to worry you'd set your expectations too high. It's nice to see you giving one of us mere mortals a chance."

"I hate to disappoint you again, but Claire and I aren't dating," I correct him. "And we really haven't ..."

"Oh, so you *did* manage to preserve your virtue?" he asks, entirely too amused.

"Yes." I cringe. "Well, technically … I think."

"But you did more than kiss her."

I roll my eyes, but it's mostly to distract myself from my own thoughts. "More than enough to make a trip to the confessional pretty awkward."

"How do you confess that kind of thing, anyway?"

"I'm not even sure I used the right terminology, since I never had to before," I reply, scratching my head.

"Hmm," he hums thoughtfully. "Bet Daisy could tell you what to say."

Anger flares behind my eyes, and I instinctively punch him in the shoulder. But Landry only chuckles and rubs his arm. "Maybe I should've let your sister take this one after all."

"The last thing I want to do is look her in the eyes and admit that I'm a hypocrite for lecturing you guys about living together before you were sacramentally married. Meanwhile, I've been out here …" It's probably for the best if I leave things ambiguous.

"Call one of your brothers."

"They'll only make it worse," I say automatically. Heath and Cyprien are great guys, but Landry knows as well as I do that I've always felt like an outsider among my brothers, especially since they were so much closer in age. They were also lucky enough to get married in their early twenties, so they can't exactly relate to my challenges with dating. And I can already imagine the looks of pity on their faces.

"Your dad?"

I almost blurt out something about his disapproval of me pursuing someone outside of our faith, but if anything, my dad would be more likely to chastise me for that thought before saying anything bad about Claire.

"I'm not sure he'd understand this time," I reply instead.

"As much as it pains me to admit it, Blake and JD would probably be good at talking you through this kind of thing," Landry continues, surprising me again.

"You know, apart from the confessional, having to clarify exactly what Claire and I have and haven't done in bed is probably the second-to-last thing I want."

"All right, then. What *do* you want?"

I want Claire, and I want it to be okay for me to have her, I think.

"I want to do the right thing. But I'm tired of being lonely." It's not the whole truth, but it's close enough for now.

He purses his lips as he considers. "I guess you still want the same thing you've always wanted—a wife."

"Right, and this situation isn't helping."

"Isn't it?"

I turn to glare at him, not expecting something so deep to come out of this. "I don't know. I've been looking for a wife for the past two decades, and I've never been this reckless with anyone else."

"Because you like her," he says the words slowly, and my cheeks heat when I consider how naturally my body reacts to hers, how easily I fall under her spell, even when she's not trying to draw me in.

"I'm probably just confusing lust for something more. A good marriage should be based on love, honesty, and trust. The physical part isn't all that important ... right?"

"You might think that, but you've never made love to your soulmate and fallen asleep beside her, secure in knowing you get to keep her for the rest of your life," he replies with a smirk. "I'd say it's all pretty important."

"What the hell did Daisy do to you, man?" I ask incredulously.

His smile widens. "She insisted on loving me when I thought I was unlovable. She made me feel safe for the first time in my life and taught me how to manage my emotions. And then I taught her a few things about feeling good, too."

I roll my eyes. "I know I'm supposed to be happy for you since you're so *happy.* But it's still a strange combination of surreal and gross to hear you brag about your sex life when it includes my sister, even if you are married."

"And maybe it even hurts a little because you didn't think you'd be the last one left unmarried?" he asks hesitantly.

My chest tightens. I hate being jealous, and I hate even more that I'm not only envious of the people I love most, but that I can't stop myself from feeling so bitter about it all.

"You're getting pretty observant," I say after a while. "I'm not sure I like it."

"I'm just recycling some of my own crap that came up in therapy now," he admits. "Long story short, loneliness will make you say some petty shit before you even realize you're thinking it."

I grunt in response and return to staring at nothing and despising myself. I'm basically pre-Daisy Landry now.

"So?" He cocks an eyebrow expectantly.

"So what?" I grumble, still resentful of the way we've seemingly swapped roles in the past few months.

"Are you going to talk this out with Claire and admit how much you like her? Should I challenge her to a duel and force her to marry you, since she's already compromised your virtue?"

"Are you done?"

He tilts his head from side to side as he considers. "Almost. I was already saving a couple of digs after the way you looked at her earlier this afternoon, but it all makes sense now. You can't stop thinking about what's hiding under that Carhartt getup, can you?"

"She'd beat you in a duel, you know," I growl when he triggers an inconvenient mental image of Claire stepping out of her chest waders and leaving herself in her underwear on this very porch.

"I don't doubt it," he says with a light laugh. "Seriously, though, I know you well enough to fill in some of the blanks here. It's not like you'd just jump into bed with a stranger."

My eyes widen in panic as he continues. "You and Claire must know one another better than you're letting on, too, because there's no way you'd engage in anything physical unless you'd already formed an emotional connection with her."

I let out a relieved exhale when he gets at least one part wrong, though he's still better at this than I expected him to be.

"Yeah, okay, I admit there's more to the story, but it doesn't matter. You heard her—she's not looking for anything serious, and I'm not supposed to be wasting this much time and energy barking up the wrong tree."

"What makes her the wrong tree, though? Is it because she's afraid of getting into an actual relationship so soon after her divorce, because that doesn't seem unreasonable, and I'm sure you could wear her down after a while. Or is it because you don't want to admit that you've fallen for someone outside your normal wheelhouse?"

"Can't it be both?"

Landry leans back and regards me carefully. "*That's* what's eating you up, isn't it? You feel bad because you wouldn't have given in to temptation if she'd have been more like you. You thought this would be a throwaway try, a silly mistake you could forget about, because Claire isn't the type of woman you've been banking on marrying. She's already been divorced, and she doesn't follow your strict code of conduct, so you saw her as damaged goods. And now you feel guilty because you nearly used her in a way you didn't even think you were capable."

I frown at him after he hits the nail on the head this time. "Who are you?"

He shoots me a smug grin. "I'm an honorary LaFleur now, remember?"

I growl in frustration and rest my head in my hands. "Life was so much easier when you were the emotionally unavailable one."

"Hey, that was almost douchey. Maybe I do like you better uncorrupted."

"And I miss the days when you didn't use words unless you were yelling at someone, back before you developed a sense of humor," I retort, trying to stifle a smile.

"Come on, man, you know you love the new me. I mean, not as much as you love Claire, especially since she does that thing you like —" I shove him harder this time, and he guffaws loudly when he almost falls off the porch steps. "Fine, I'm done. For now, anyway," he says, settling down. "Should I send your girl out?"

"No," I say reluctantly. "Least I can do is man up and go to her to apologize." He pats me on the back encouragingly as we both rise to our feet.

Daisy and Claire are at the kitchen sink when we return, and I clear my throat to get their attention. "Ladies, I'm really sorry about the way I acted tonight," I say after a while. "I was rude to both of you, and I shouldn't have walked out like that. Most of all, I'm sorry for being dishonest."

My sister turns back to the sink. "Apology accepted ... strange man of loose morals. But you're still getting a piece of my mind later."

I struggle to keep a straight face as I stare at Claire, and I'm relieved to see her biting back a smile of her own. "Can we talk?" I ask quietly.

"Think that's code for something dirty?" Daisy whispers loudly as Landry comes up behind her to wrap his arms around her waist, and Juniper ambles her way closer.

"We should give them some privacy, just in case," he mumbles near her ear, and I cringe when she giggles and spins in his arms to face him. He kisses her for a second before he lifts her up to wrap her legs around his waist again. "We're going to bed," he calls out, and Juniper takes her cue to report to her kennel. "Good luck working all your shit out."

"He means that figuratively, by the way. That was not an invitation for you to fornicate in our spare bedroom," Daisy says from over his shoulder when they round the corner, and Claire stifles a laugh, drawing my attention back to her.

I heave out a loud sigh. "I'm tempted to ask Coach Reed if he's willing to rent out Landry's old bedroom."

She opens her mouth to speak, then thinks better of it and shakes her head. We're interrupted by a loud squeal from down the hall, and Claire can't keep herself from laughing when I scrunch up my nose in disgust. Even Juniper whines from her kennel.

"So ... you're not *really* a virgin, are you?" she asks after a while. "That's just something you've been telling your sister, right?"

I roll my lips in and lift my shoulders.

"Right?" she repeats, her voice cracking.

"To be fair, I didn't think I'd still be holding on to that title at my age, especially not longer than my baby sister, but here we are," I admit.

"How is that even possible?"

"It wasn't by accident, if that's what you're asking," I say dryly.

She furrows her brow. "Because you've been waiting for the right person?"

I shrug again. "Yes, but also the right time, preferably my wedding night."

"And you nearly let me ruin everything. Shit, Rowan, maybe I already have!" She adds another curse under her breath and looks away.

"You haven't *ruined* me. It's not like that."

I'm still thinking about that last statement and whether I believe it myself when she reaches out and shoves me in the chest. "You ass, you've been letting me make a fool of myself! When were you going to tell me? After the next time I threw myself at you?"

I cringe. "If it makes you feel any better, being celibate is the only thing keeping me from ..."

"It doesn't make me feel any better," she mumbles. "But I guess some of the stuff you've said and done makes a little more sense now."

"Exactly. All those times I've had to pull away were because I needed to and not because I wanted to," I tell her with a hopeful smile. But she doesn't smile in return.

"So what's your excuse for lying to me?"

She pierces my chest with that one, my guilt seeping from the open wound.

"I didn't intend to keep anything from you. It just ... happened. I mean, I tried to tell you, but I couldn't find the right time."

She clicks her tongue. "Funny how that works, since you've been encouraging me to open up to you and share so many personal ..." She shakes her head. "I've told you things I've never told anyone before. And all this time, you haven't been honest with me."

"Claire," I begin, willing my lungs to expand when my chest tightens again. "I'm sorry."

"Gah, I can't believe I was so stupid," she whines and covers her face with her hands.

"No, no, you haven't done anything stupid. I'm the one—"

"You're the one who's been pretending to care about me just long enough to get my help," she cuts me off.

"No," I repeat as I take an involuntary step closer to her. "I do care about you, I swear."

"All you care about is making sure everyone thinks you're a saint. But maybe if you spent more energy doing the right thing in the first place, you wouldn't be so afraid of people finding out who you really are."

I swallow hard. "I can't argue with that, at least not the second part." She frowns, probably not expecting me to agree with her. "I never meant to hurt you, though," I continue. "I may have been scared to tell you the whole truth, but I still hold all the things you've confided in me in my heart. Your feelings are very, very important to me."

Her chest heaves as she pins me with a dangerous glare. "Well, the jokes on you, then. I don't have any of those, remember?" she replies sarcastically, but the trembling in her voice betrays her. She growls in frustration and blinks back her tears as she turns to shove her feet into her boots, then she storms out, slamming the door behind her.

thursday
10:21 PM

ROWAN

📞 Missed Call - Rowan LaFleur

I really am sorry. Is there anything I can do to make it up to you?

Please talk to me, Claire. I'd do anything to make this right.

What if I told Landry and Daisy everything, so at least they'd know I've been in the wrong this whole time? Would that be okay with you?

📞 Missed Call - Rowan LaFleur

Okay, so interrupting my sister and my best friend in bed to tell them the story of the time I chickened out of losing my virginity might actually be the most humbling experience of my life, second only to the actual night itself.

Also, they both agree I'm the worst and approve of my plan to go over right now and grovel at your feet, if that's okay?

You don't have any guns in the house, do you?

📞 Missed Call – Rowan LaFleur

Claire, please open up. Oscar and Frankie are scratching and whining at the front door, so I know you can hear me knocking.

It's fine, I didn't need that porch light, anyway. I bought myself one of those fancy headlamps like yours. Figured it would come in handy one day.

CLAIRE

Go away, Rowan.

Don't make me call the deputy on you.

ROWAN

I can't. Not until you let me apologize.

And for the record, you're so much scarier than Deputy Godchaux.

CLAIRE

Aren't you worried someone might see your truck
here and assume the worst?

ROWAN

📞 Missed Call – Rowan LaFleur

I'll sleep outside if you don't let me in.

CLAIRE

Suit yourself. Comfort is a gateway drug, after all,
and I'd hate to contribute any more towards your
moral collapse.

ROWAN

Fair enough.

Good night, Claire. I'll see you in the morning.

claire

I TIGHTEN my robe around me and narrow my eyes at the faded pickup parked in my driveway. Frankie bounds excitedly down the front porch steps when he sees it, tripping over his own ears, and my smile widens when he trots over to pee on one of Rowan's tires.

"That's Mama's good boy," I coo and scratch his round *panse* when he returns, prompting Oscar to lift his own leg over the rim before returning to collect his belly-rub reward.

Rising onto my tiptoes, I lift my chin to peer into the truck cab. But I can barely see inside with all the ice coating the windshield. I have to pretend I'm checking on one of the plants Daisy gave me the other day to catch a glimpse of Rowan's bundled form. He looks like he's wearing the same jacket from the night the pipes busted, as well as an orange hunting beanie and a pair of camo gloves. He coughs a few times, and it's actually cold enough to see his breath in the air.

Oscar looks at me strangely when I let out a frustrated groan. I shouldn't be giving in so easily, I know. But I also hate staying mad at someone or letting them stay angry with me. And the sight of this man sleeping out in the cold just for the chance to apologize in person does funny things to my heart, especially since I wasn't on the receiving end of many apologies in my last relationship.

Okay, practically everything Rowan-related does funny things to my heart, but I'm choosing to ignore that at the moment.

Then again, I should just forgive Rowan and move on, because holding on to my anger would be tantamount to admitting I care enough to let him hurt me that deeply. If I let him plead his case now, I can pretend I wasn't devastated to learn that I've been baring my soul to a man who couldn't trust me with the truth, who held back on sharing the most basic elements of himself because he saw me as nothing more than a passing temptation. And I may not be the best human on the planet, but I know I deserve better than a hypocrite who only wants me when his pristine reputation isn't on the line.

It's just so hard to reconcile that guy with the one I thought I knew, the man who begged me for more than one night together, who couldn't deliver a pickup line without blushing, who gave me his underwear when my dress ripped, and who wouldn't kiss me until he was certain he'd earned it—the Rowan who wanted to take turns listening to me talk and making love to me all night because I was his soulmate.

But I knew he was too good to be true.

Despite being the only person who's ever made me feel safe and understood, Rowan LaFleur isn't the man I thought he was.

At least I figured it out early this time, before I let him talk me into molding my life around his for the next decade or so. Just in time to pull off the lie that none of this hurts me as much as it does.

I slip back inside and crack open the blinds before settling down with my cup of coffee and my phone. If I'm going to downplay this whole thing, I might as well have some fun while I'm at it.

CLAIRE

Okay, fine. I woke up in a charitable mood.

You have a thirty-second window in which I am willing to hear you out. And I'm only giving you one last chance because you're Daisy's brother.

The clock starts now, Benadryl Boy.

I watch closely as Rowan pops awake and searches for his phone. The way he bobbles it around for a second before taking off a glove induces another good laugh, as does the look on his face when he finally reads my message. Panic sets in, and from there he drops his phone, spends another moment looking for it, pauses to put on his glasses, checks his watch and curses—something I know he doesn't do often—and scrambles out of his truck and up the front steps.

I'm still snickering to myself when I calmly waltz over to open the front door.

"Sorry, time's up," I intone as I move to swing it closed, but Rowan steps forward and plants his foot in the opening.

"No," he begs, sounding out of breath. "Please?"

I roll my eyes and stifle a smile, letting him in and gesturing toward the coffee maker. He stops to remove the other glove so he can properly greet the dogs, and I hate that I love how sweet he is to them. Then he slips off his shoes before shuffling into the kitchen.

"You really are a saint, you know that?" he mumbles as he fills up a mug and inhales deeply, but I don't like the cough that follows.

"Tell me you didn't give yourself pneumonia, *tête dur*," I scold him as I go over and touch the back of my hand to his forehead, which feels a bit clammy for someone who spent the night out in the cold.

He gazes down at me and stifles another cough. "It'd be a poor penance, but I deserve it."

I roll my eyes again. "You can cut the shit, Rowan. I'm a high school teacher, remember? I'm immune to cute and sappy."

"That's all I've got right now," he says with a frown, reminding me of the Rowan I knew before. I turn away, because I've obviously never managed to build up a resistance to cuteness, or I'd never have lasted this long in the education field.

"Well, you're gonna have to do better than a few pity coughs," I lie as I pour myself a refill.

He sighs and puts his mug down to remove a layer, revealing a thick vest beneath his jacket. I realize he's wearing his work clothes beneath the insulation. Did he change in the car during the night, or did he actually come prepared to sleep in his truck?

"Any chance I can toss my shirt in the dryer while we talk? It's a little wrinkled." I nod, distracted by his hands as they work to peel away the vest. "I should probably just start wearing scrubs while I'm here," he muses to himself.

"So anyway, I spent the night thinking about what I could possibly say to make up for holding back and not telling you the full truth, and I figured I could start by fessing up to something else embarrassing," he continues, unbuttoning his shirt next.

"I'm listening," I say. But I'm not. The way his collarbones look peeking out of the collar of his white undershirt reminds me too much of one of our last close encounters, when I didn't hesitate to slide my hands over his chest to warm them up.

And warm me up, he did.

"... I basically ended up losing my lunch after the first live birth I attended in medical school," Rowan explains, and I notice a pink tinge to his cheeks when I finally drag my eyes up to his face. It's so cute that I want to blush, too, and I shuffle uncomfortably and tug on the ties of my robe again.

He holds up his dress shirt and gestures toward the laundry room, and I nod a little too quickly this time. "You should probably throw your pants in there, too," I call out after him, then cringe when I hear how thirsty it sounds. "I mean, they looked a bit frumpy, so you might as well."

He returns in his boxers and that T-shirt, and I take a big gulp of hot coffee, hoping it'll divert my attention.

"Anything else you want to know, I'm an open book," he says, grinning. "Like the time I was an altar server and almost took out the deacon with my overzealous thurible swinging. Or when I walked into an exam room to find my best friend's baby sister and the guy who was responsible for getting her pregnant."

I snort out a laugh that time. "Don't you hate it when you get invested with someone, only to find out they've been lying to you the whole time?"

He cringes. "Yes."

I blink at him, and he sighs, obviously not expecting me to interrupt his spiel. "I was planning on offering up a few more of my most mortifying moments before transitioning into my apology, but I think all the rest of them have happened in front of you."

"Let me guess, the worst one was having to admit to your sister that you almost had a one-night stand with her slutty work friend?"

"Claire." He says my name on an exhale, his expression falling. "Please don't talk about yourself that way."

"It's the truth, isn't it?" I ask sardonically.

Rowan shakes his head. "Not even close. If anything, I've been taking advantage of the fact that we don't share the same beliefs since the night we met. I convinced myself that giving into lust with you wasn't all that wrong if you were just going to find some other guy to hook up with anyway, which we both know you weren't going to do. And even if you had, I'm not in any position to judge you for it. I haven't done you any favors by letting you think you had to earn my affection by sleeping with me, either."

"But we didn't sleep together," I say quietly. "And you made sure no one suspects otherwise. You got what you wanted."

"I didn't want anyone to find out because ... Well, it's not that I'm embarrassed of *you* so much as what we ..." He stops and scratches the back of his head before he starts again. "Sorry. That's not ... Look, what I'm trying to say is that I don't usually care what anyone thinks of me. I haven't stayed chaste this long without earning some criticism or having to defend my choices, and a big part of my motivation thus far was to set a good example for my siblings. So it was more important for me to keep what happened between us quiet because I didn't want it to seem like I was condoning—Wait, that's not quite it, either."

I cross my arms over my middle. "What makes you so sure I wasn't just as embarrassed for people to find out about us? I made it clear from the beginning that a casual hookup was all I ever wanted from you."

He flinches, but I continue. "And I basically lied to my only friend on your behalf, so don't you dare act like telling Daisy the truth was a sacrifice for *you*."

"I know, I'm sorry. That came out all wrong."

"You say that a lot for someone so nice," I retort, though I'm already feeling guilty about my rant.

"I know," he repeats with a whimper. "It's just ... it's a poor excuse, but you always look so good in the mornings, and it's even harder not to notice when you're wearing that robe I got you. I shouldn't be thinking of you that way, especially since I'm already in so much trouble. But I mean it when I say you're distractingly beautiful. I actually worked on a speech all night, rehearsed it in my truck and everything, and my heart started racing and my head went blank as soon as I looked at you."

I twist my lips to the side, pretending to consider what he's saying. But the truth is that I enjoy unnerving him more than I should.

"You're right. That's the dumbest thing I've ever heard ... But go on."

His mouth turns up in a smirk, and I'm annoyed at the way his dimples make my stomach dip.

"I'm sorry. I'll start over." He takes a deep breath before he begins again. "Thank you for being willing to hear me out. I want to offer my sincerest, most contrite apology for failing to be honest with you from the beginning, as well as for not owning up to my actions so far. I've been a coward and a hypocrite, and that stops now."

"Hmm. You're getting warmer," I say with a shrug.

"And I ..." He trails off and looks down at his feet for a second. "I wasn't lying just now when I said that I lose my head around you, but that's not the only reason for my stupidity. I've been so absorbed with my own guilt that I let you take some of the blame for tempting me and highlighting my weaknesses. I've been acting like a resentful, self-righteous asshole, while you have been a caring, open-hearted, and compassionate friend in return."

He must have really done some deep self-reflection overnight, because that was pretty thorough. Luckily, he still hasn't poked at my biggest bruise.

But my lips part in a gasp when he surprises me again by kneeling down in front of me.

"I'm truly sorry, Claire, and I promise to do everything I can to make up for all the ways I've hurt you and to be a better friend from here on out," he says, gazing up at me.

He's in his underwear. This dude is literally on his freaking knees, in his *caleçons*, groveling and begging me for my forgiveness. Even with the dogs scampering around him, it's the hottest thing I've ever seen.

I cannot, under any circumstances, grab him by the face and kiss him ...

Can I?

His throat works as he awaits my reply, and I have to remind myself that he didn't intend for his apology to be so sexy.

"I know you thought you'd seem more sincere by getting down on your knees like this," I pause to clear my throat when I hear how breathy my voice sounds, "but it's not exactly eliciting the desired effect, especially since you're not wearing any pants."

"It's not?" he asks, frowning. "I figured it would just up the humility factor."

"Yeah, well, you're not the only one who's easily distracted," I mumble, and he struggles to hide his smile. "I'm not kidding. You'd better get your adorable ass up off the floor before I give you another reason to resent me."

He whimpers playfully and rises to his feet, and I take another sip of my coffee and force myself to look away.

"Can I assume you've forgiven me now that you think I'm adorable again?" he ventures after a while.

I heave out a loud sigh. "I appreciate all this, I do. But you sort of missed the point."

"I have?" he asks, his expression falling before he runs a hand over his face. "Of course I have."

Great. Now I have to hear him apologize again. I should have just left it at that.

"Look, Rowan, I'm not—"

"Wait," he interrupts me. "Last night, you weren't just upset because of the way I acted in front of Daisy and Landry. You were hurt because ... because I got you to let down your walls, but I hadn't taken mine down for you."

Butterflies swirl around inside my belly, but he seems too preoccupied with his remorse to notice he's hit a nerve this time. He blows out a dejected breath before he continues. "I can't even get an apology right, even after you told me exactly what I've been doing wrong. I'm sorry, Claire."

I swallow hard. "It's okay. I forgive you."

"No, it's not okay. I shouldn't have used this as an opportunity to clear my conscience; that's what the confessional is for. I'm supposed to be putting your feelings first."

"You've said enough, Rowan." I move to bring my mug to the sink, but he reaches out and grabs my arm. He stares at me, warming my insides, then he silently pulls me in and wraps his arms around me. His chest expands against my cheek, and he kisses the top of my head.

"We probably shouldn't be hugging while we're both pants-less," I say, but I don't move away, either.

"I've hugged you in less, though I suppose that's what got us into trouble in the first place," he murmurs, and I barely manage to hide the shiver that runs through me.

"Your breath is terrible," I lie, and he chuckles as he loosens his hold on me.

"Don't go anywhere," he blurts out before darting back into the laundry room and then sprinting over to the hall bathroom with his pants around his ankles. He emerges a few seconds later, swishing something around in his mouth while he struggles to zip his pants, and stops to spit what looks like mouthwash into the kitchen sink.

"You're not getting away that easily now," he says, smiling and fixing his eyes on mine.

I stick out my lip in a pout. "You could probably use a shower, too, if I'm being honest."

Which I'm not.

But he ignores my complaint and continues staring at me intently. "I'm sorry, Claire. I should have been more honest with you about the whole celibacy thing. You deserved to know exactly what you were getting into and how much that night would mean to me, and I was wrong to mislead you."

"You'll never understand what you took from me ..."

The memory of his pained expression crosses my mind, and I shake my head, mostly to call off my emotional response to all of this.

"Apology accepted. And I'm sorry if I made you feel like you couldn't tell me something so important to you from the beginning," I rasp.

"But it wasn't your fault. I've just been too afraid to tell you the truth. I've never really been embarrassed to own that part of myself before, but the news hasn't always gone over so well in the past. And I couldn't risk giving my conscience any reinforcement that first night, because I wanted you ... *so badly.*" He pauses, and I can tell he's being sincere by the way his throat works. "I was too scared you'd see me as broken and feel pressured to fix me, and I needed to know you really wanted me, too, that you felt the same connection, and that you weren't just going through with it out of pity."

I huff out a laugh at the irony of his confession. "And I was worried you were only stalling because you felt sorry for me," I say, lifting my shoulder. "That you were trying to talk yourself into doing a good deed and throwing the sad, divorced lady a bone."

He smiles and shakes his head. "Me, feel sorry for you, especially after you came out in those sexy pajamas?"

I snort in an attempt to hide the way his compliment makes me simper. "Weren't you betting on me being too desperate to notice or care that you didn't know what you were doing?"

He chuckles. "I *have* been studying the female anatomy in depth for the past decade or so. I mean, I mostly look at ultrasounds these days, but I'm still a gynecologist. I know where everything is."

"I suppose that's half the battle," I concede.

"My experience may be limited, but I'm probably not as sheltered as you'd think. Even my parents were pretty open and honest about that stuff when we were growing up. My family's not exactly … shy," he says, smiling.

"Oh. Have you talked to any of them about us and our situation?" I venture. "Besides Daisy, I mean."

He opens and closes his mouth awkwardly. "Well, I hadn't exactly planned on it. Not unless we'd have, you know …" I shake my head as he gestures with his hand. "I guess if we were actually dating, and they found out I've been staying over at your place, they might make some assumptions I'd want to correct. Especially since you've been married before."

I frown, thinking about how much I enjoyed meeting his mom and sisters at Daisy's wedding. But I imagine they'd be disappointed if their sweet angel brought home a tattooed jezebel like me.

"You claim you don't care what anyone thinks, but it sounds like their opinion of you is pretty important," I say after some hesitation.

"They're my family." He shrugs, as if he can't imagine the alternative.

"I guess that's another reason you usually date women with the same beliefs as you," I remark.

He smiles ruefully. "It makes it easier when we already share the same values and all, yeah."

I nod, reading between the lines. He's sorry he hurt me, but he's not willing to risk everything he holds dear for a chance to be with me. Not that I'd even want that, anyway.

"But I imagine it's going to be impossible for Daisy to keep all this to herself, at least among our siblings," he adds after a while. "So I should probably prepare myself for the worst."

"The worst," I repeat, looking away.

He groans. "Only because they'll tease me for being a hypocrite. But not because of *you*." Then he clicks his tongue before he starts again. "Okay, my brothers will probably make fun of me for going after someone so far out of my league, but that's not exactly your fault."

I roll my eyes. "Nice save."

He lifts his hands in surrender. "It wasn't a line. I'm being honest."

"Mm-hmm." I regard him skeptically.

"Claire?" he begins, smiling warmly at me.

"Yes?"

He straightens his posture and holds my gaze. "Thank you."

"For what?" I ask quietly.

"For everything—for holding me accountable and being patient with me when I wasn't my best self, for being so understanding and making me feel like I can trust you with anything, even when I hadn't extended the same courtesy. You really are a good friend."

It's the third time he's called me his friend in this conversation, though I'm not sure who the reminder is directed toward.

I nod and gulp down the emotion in my throat. "Yeah. You're welcome, I guess."

"Maybe we found one another at this point in our lives for a reason, you know?"

And even with my list of objections ready, the fact that he's the one who feels the need to keep clarifying that boundary stings just a little.

"You're sure it's not because we're destined to be friends with benefits?" I pose, pushing forward before I can dwell on those inconvenient feelings. "I bet there are a few more things I could teach you."

His eyes widen and he blinks away his shock, while I barely contain my laughter. "You're just messing with me again, aren't you?" he asks when my nostrils flare.

"Am I?" I shrug and look up at him from beneath my lashes, though I'm not sure what I hope to accomplish. Maybe I'm testing his reaction, and maybe I just want some reassurance.

He puffs up his cheeks and blows out a breath. "I think Landry was right before. You and I are not even in the same ballpark."

"I don't know. You were pretty convincing for a rookie," I say coyly, and he grins.

Then he catches me off guard by stepping in closer and backing me up against the counter. "Thanks for the offer, but I'm not interested in being a designated hitter. And I'm not just some pinch runner looking to steal home." He drops his gaze to my mouth, making my heart beat faster before he leans in to whisper beside my ear, "I'm holding out for a contract, a guaranteed spot in the starting lineup."

I choke back a whimper when he backs away. I've got to quit teasing the man when I know damned good and well he can back it up. Because despite his lack of experience and unassuming demeanor, Rowan LaFleur is easily the sexiest man I've ever had the pleasure of fraternizing with.

"Says the kid who got caught padding his stats," I manage to get out, and he snorts as he backs away.

"I guess I should let you get ready for work," he says, shyness seeping into his tone now that he's reeled his dangerous side back in.

"Yeah. You'll probably be needing your shirt, too," I remind him.

"Figured you collect additional souvenirs from your favorite victims," he replies smoothly on his way to the laundry room, and I heave out a sigh when I hear him coughing again.

If anyone's helpless around here, it's certainly me.

11:47 AM

CLAIRE

Wth is wrong with you?

ROWAN

Just the sniffles, from what I can tell.

Why? Did I get you sick?

CLAIRE

No.

Wait, you're sick?

ROWAN

Um ... is it too late to delete my last messages?

CLAIRE

I was talking about the brand-new stick welder that was delivered to my shop today. Do you really think you can buy me off with anonymous donations to the Camellia High ag program?

ROWAN

. . .

CLAIRE

Because you totally can.

photo of ag class with new welding machine

The kids said thank you, too. ♡

ROWAN

I will pass on your gratitude to the anonymous donor, if I find him. But I'm sure he'd just be happy you found it useful.

CLAIRE

Did you get sick after sleeping in your truck?

ROWAN

People don't catch colds from being cold.

But while you're possibly thinking about me in a favorable light or at least taking pity on me, can I ask you for another favor?

CLAIRE

WHAT NOW?

ROWAN

I told you about my brother's kids wanting to get into the livestock show circuit, right?

CLAIRE

Yes.

ROWAN

After I bragged about my friend Claire being a former champion, my niece Gertie has formally requested your consultant services in picking out a lamb.

CLAIRE

You've been talking about me in front of your family?

ROWAN

Of course I have. You're by far the coolest person I know.

My mother has also made her own demands. She insists that we feed you Sunday brunch before you're asked to help in the barn.

CLAIRE

Oh. Well, that's quite flattering.

ROWAN

Does that mean you're interested?

CLAIRE

Hell yeah, I am.

ROWAN

Great. Just name the Sunday, and I'll be there to pick you up.

CLAIRE

I can drive myself.

ROWAN

And upset my mama? Absolutely not.

CLAIRE

Fine. Weekend after next?

ROWAN

It's a date.

CLAIRE

It's not, though.

ROWAN

Nah, I'm just bringing you to the homestead to meet my parents. No big deal.

CLAIRE

That better be the fever talking, Benadryl Boy.

claire

"OH, hey, glad you could make it," I hear the instructor for my fertility awareness class say as I continue sifting through the folder of materials she handed out.

"Uh, yeah, thanks for the invitation," a familiar male voice replies, and my head pops up involuntarily. Rowan's eyes meet mine, and he swallows hard.

What on God's green earth is *he* doing here?

"Guys, this is Dr. LaFleur. He just started working with me at the clinic here in Camellia. He's here tonight to brush up on his charting skills," Tenley says to the rest of the class. "You already know Claire, right?" she directs at Rowan, a suspicious twinkle in her eyes.

Rowan glares at her, just the slightest, and the way she purses her lips in a challenge makes me wonder what kind of office gossip the two of them have been sharing.

"Right," he replies quietly after a while. "But, please, just call me Rowan."

"Have a seat, Doc." She gestures to the empty chair next to me, and he lets out a defeated exhale as he settles in.

"What are you doing here?" I whisper once Tenley turns to gather another set of materials for him.

"Exactly what Tenley said," he mumbles. "And before you ask, I didn't know you were taking this class."

I scoff. "Of course not."

Tenley turns back to hand Rowan a folder. "This is actually perfect. You guys won't mind partnering up for some of these activities, will you?"

"Actually, I'm not sure I'm comfortable sharing my charts with a stranger. It feels a little too personal." I turn to shoot Rowan a dirty look when he lets out an incredulous laugh beside me.

"No worries," Tenley replies, grinning. "We'll only be looking at the practice charts included in your workbook tonight. But if you're uncomfortable, by all means …"

I roll my eyes. "Fine."

"Great," she reaffirms and leaves us to finish setting up her presentation.

"So we're back to being strangers now?" Rowan asks under his breath.

"Not exactly. But we're not on our-cycles-have-synced terms, either," I grumble.

He snorts. "As someone who was moments away from being represented by a tiny heart on your actual chart, I beg to differ. Not to mention, you're my emergency medical contact now."

My brow lifts in surprise. "Oh, so we've gone from pretending we don't know one another to publicly acknowledging our hookup?"

"I haven't been going around bragging about it, but I'm told the good people of Camellia have noticed my truck in your driveway," he explains matter-of-factly.

"And what have you been telling them?" I ask in a harsh whisper.

He shrugs. "Nothing. I still think what has or hasn't happened between us isn't anyone else's business."

"Except to clarify for your sister and brother-in-law that you didn't actually go through with it," I mumble, and he frowns.

"I didn't exactly have a choice the other night. I wasn't even planning on confiding in Landry until he asked us point blank."

"Exactly," I say dryly.

He turns in his chair to face me now. "I thought we talked about this. What am I supposed to do, Claire? Tell people about our failed one-night stand? Keep it a secret and let you go on thinking I'm embarrassed to be seen with you?"

I open my mouth to answer before I realize he has a point. The problem is that no matter how indifferent I want to be about Rowan and our situation, I find myself caring entirely too much.

"I don't know, okay? I just hate the way all of it makes me feel," I blurt out, my face heating when my voice breaks.

His expression softens. "Now do you believe me when I say celibacy is easier?"

I sigh and offer him a rueful smile, but I'm interrupted by Tenley's loud throat clearing before I can say anything else.

"I guess you two aren't strangers after all," she says with a hint of sarcasm, and I look around to find the other couples watching us closely.

Rowan apologizes on our behalf and promises we'll be good students from now on, and Tenley starts the lesson, though she seems entirely too amused for my liking.

I do my best to pay attention to her descriptions of cervical positions and basal body temperature rises, but I'm admittedly distracted by my table mate's presence. My eyes drift to the side each time Tenley pauses to ask for Rowan's input and he enthusiastically chimes in with some connection between progesterone levels and breast tenderness, and it's ironically sexy when he defers to Tenley's expertise instead of trying to mansplain everything himself. In fact, the way his eyes crinkle as he processes each bit of new information is downright adorable, and I'm starting to understand what Tenley meant about ovulation symptoms as I watch him nod his head in agreement and jot down notes in his workbook.

I might have thought bad boys were my thing up until now, but I'll be damned if Rowan isn't proving to be more dangerous than any morally gray man I've ever met. Am I really melting over a thirty-three-year-old virgin who wears a scapular necklace and walks around with a rosary in his pocket?

Yes, yes I am.

Tenley mentions something about deciphering between arousal fluid and cervical mucus, making Rowan's neck turn red, and I let out an involuntary whimper at the thought of pressing my lips to his flushed skin.

"You okay?" he asks, turning to face me with concern.

My eyelashes flutter as I attempt to get my shit together. "Um, yeah, fine."

Then he leans in and smirks as he whispers, "I didn't think you'd get *honte* over this kind of stuff, but it's cute."

Gah, what is it about Rowan calling me cute that makes me want to believe him?

"Whatever. You're the one blushing every time she says the word 'intercourse,' " I argue, bumping his shoulder with mine.

"Not every time," he maintains before adding, "And it's only because you're around."

One of my loud cackles escapes before I can cover my mouth with both of my hands, and he snorts out a laugh of his own. Tenley shoots us a warning glare that looks suspiciously like an experienced teacher-look, silencing Rowan and I for a second. But we return to nudging one another and stifling our giggles as she introduces our first charting activity.

"What are we supposed to be doing now?" I whisper once Tenley walks away.

Rowan bites back another dimpled smile and shrugs. "I don't know. I missed most of the instructions because *someone* was distracting me."

"Me, distracting you?" I retort, and he shushes me. "You were the one flirting with me," I add more quietly.

His brow lifts in outrage before his expression softens. "Okay, yeah. I did call you cute first, didn't I?"

"Why are you even taking this class, anyway?" I ask, ignoring the urge to twirl the end of my braid around my finger.

He looks down, as if he was already busy skimming the directions in the book. "It's for work. They don't teach this stuff in medical school, believe it or not," he replies.

"But you're a MFM specialist. Why would you need to know about natural family planning if you're only tending to the babies that have already been made?"

"Maybe I'm hoping I'll need the information for personal reasons one day," he mumbles without meeting my eyes again.

"And you really didn't know I was going to be here?"

"No," he says on an exhale. "But I probably should have assumed Tenley had an ulterior motive when she practically begged me to come to this class in particular."

"Oh." I can't help sounding more disappointed than I'd like to let on.

He finally glances up. "Why are you here?"

The question catches me off guard. "Your sister's been on me to start tracking my symptoms, because she thinks it'll make it easier to manage my horrible periods once I understand what's going on with my body. And another doctor once said I could use fertility awareness charting to find the cause of my ... issues," I tell him, fumbling through my answer.

I watch his throat bob as he swallows hard. "But I thought you weren't interested in getting married again?"

"Maybe you didn't learn this in medical school, either, but you don't have to be married to make a baby," I tell him.

He looks away, rolling his eyes. "You know that's not what I'm asking you."

My stomach does another flip, but not in the same way as the last one. "I haven't ruled out the possibility of going at it alone."

It's not the full truth. I haven't ruled it out completely, but going through pregnancy, childbirth, and motherhood on my own certainly isn't my aim. Sure, I'd embrace the opportunity if my circumstances ever led me to become a single mom. But as badly as I want those experiences, I can't imagine purposefully trying to do it all without a supportive partner, at least in the beginning. Which is especially ironic considering my ex-husband wouldn't have been helpful.

"I may have been homeschooled, but I'm pretty sure they covered *that* in high school bio." Rowan's uncharacteristically bitter reply brings me back from my thoughts.

"Ever heard of a sperm bank?" I pose sarcastically, and he shakes his head in disappointment. "For the right price, donors aren't that hard to find."

"So once you resolve your infertility issues, you're just going to choose some stranger out of a catalog to father your children?" He picks up a pencil and begins scribbling in the workbook, but I can tell he's forcing himself to seem aloof.

"Unless I find someone the old-fashioned way, I suppose."

"You do realize how ridiculous that sounds when you've sworn off marriage, don't you? Especially since you'll be raising your kids alone and depriving them of a father figure."

"What's it to you, anyway?" I ask, ignoring the guilt his argument has already managed to lodge within my chest.

He slams the pencil down. "Forgive me for looking out for a friend and trying to preserve the sanctity of marriage and family life."

"Or maybe you're just jealous because your crazy religious rules are preventing you from doing the same," I lean in to say haughtily.

"Or maybe," he begins, staring me down, "this is your way of asking me whether I'd be willing to contribute to your cause."

My lips part in a gasp. "I'm not ... I didn't—"

"I want to help you, Claire," he interrupts me to declare, and I think I might be speechless for the first time in my life. "It's one of the reasons I'm here, so I could give you better advice."

I clear my throat. "You mean, you want to help me fix my infertility problems."

"I owe you a few favors, don't I?"

"Sure," I say, my mind still reeling from his last suggestion.

Then he inclines his head and lowers his voice before adding, "But, for the record, my crazy Catholic rules wouldn't keep me from making a charitable donation, especially if you'd be willing to collect it the old-fashioned way. In fact, that's actually encouraged."

"It is?" I choke out, and one side of his mouth curls up in a crooked smirk so sexy I'm tempted to rob him of a contribution on the spot.

"Yep. Didn't you hear Tenley? We're huge fans of that whole 'open to life' mentality for married couples," he drawls as he picks up the pencil and uses it to tap my left ring finger. He shifts his attention back to the charting activity after that, as if he hasn't just stunned me by extending both an indecent proposition and a marriage proposal in the last few seconds.

"Does anyone need more time?" Tenley asks while I struggle to form an appropriate response to Dangerous Rowan's first public appearance in Camellia.

But what in the hell am I supposed to say after that? I didn't even come here with the intention of learning about the family-planning side of things, yet here I am, shopping for a baby daddy and reconsidering my budget.

You cannot make him a counteroffer, I tell myself, especially since there's no guarantee I could make a baby at all. But I still give in to the urge to pretend it's possible, just for a second.

My gaze runs over the specimen beside me. Broad shoulders, crystal blue eyes, gorgeous blond hair, great teeth, and the most adorable set of dimples I've ever seen ... decent height, good muscle tone, amazing collar bones, not to mention the high IQ and the slutty little glasses he wears before bed ...

Maybe the imperfect vision should count against him, regardless of how good he looks in those glasses. But aside from the nearsightedness and the peanut allergy, Rowan is undeniably a genetic jackpot. I'd be insane not to take advantage of an offer from him, even if it meant going at it alone.

It's too bad I can't haggle him into making one of those contributions outside of a serious relationship or even marriage, and I'm not going to let him risk either with me, not with my poor track record. But even if he were willing to overlook my low customer reviews, Rowan would never forgo the chance to have a traditional family much less agree to waive his responsibilities as a father ... or a partner.

Dammit. That only makes him a million times more attractive.

"Claire, are you done?" I flinch when Tenley calls me back again.

"Yeah. Think I might need to add one of those little hearts to my chart after this, though," I mutter, making Rowan's lips twitch in amusement. It turns into a chuckle when I swat his arm.

"You're not allowed to flirt this hard," I grumble after another warning glare from Tenley.

"Why not?" he asks, that cocky smirk lingering on his face.

I pout. "Because ... well, because ..."

"Is it because I'm a virgin or because I manage to do it without objectifying you?" he poses, leaning back and crossing his arms.

"Because I've already asked you to cut the mushy crap," I retort.

He ignores me. "It's because I respect you too much to throw out a 'nice ass' and leave it at that. And that scares you, doesn't it?"

Lucky for me, Tenley calls everyone back to attention before I have to answer him. I'd still like to wipe the smug look off of Rowan's face by the time we get through the next part of the session, though.

"For this activity, you're going to brainstorm how you can make your spouse feel loved during those periods of abstinence. Abstaining can be very difficult for those of us who are wired to show or receive affection physically. It's important to find other ways to fill your part- ner's cup, or else you'll end up in the maternity ward or the confes- sional more often than you hoped," Tenley explains with a knowing smile.

Rowan glances my way, his confidence noticeably diminished. "I guess we should just fill in the chart for ourselves, since you're not going to want to talk it out with me now."

"What do you mean?" I ask carefully.

He lifts a shoulder. "I've already been pushing my luck all night. I don't want to make you uncomfortable again."

I narrow my eyes at him. "Or maybe you're the one who's scared to admit what he likes."

Okay, so passing up the opportunity to dodge this conversation was a dumb move on my part. But I can't help wanting to push his buttons after he's been practically slamming mine.

I can feel Tenley watching us as I tilt my chin up in a dare and Rowan's brow lifts in response.

"All right, then. How about we each propose what we'd do to satisfy one another's love languages?"

"Fine. I'm game," I affirm.

"I should warn you, though, I'm kind of an expert at not having sex," he counters, immediately biting his lip to keep himself from laughing. It doesn't stop me from letting out a cackle and earning an eye roll from one of the other couples.

"Guess humor isn't on her list, right?" Rowan muses. "But it's definitely on yours."

"So what? Are you taking me to watch a different stand-up comedian every month?"

He shakes his head. "Nah, just waiting until you least expect it to tell you that you have a nice butt. Or maybe I'll deliver a dirty joke with a straight face under the most inappropriate circumstances."

"And that's supposed to make me feel loved and appreciated?"

"I guess that's just for me, since I like earning one of your big laughs," he replies, and I roll my eyes this time. "But if I made it cheesy and sappy, then it would be for you. Because deny it all you want, you like my corny lines. You want to be wanted, and you desire *desire*. So even when I couldn't have you, I'd make sure you knew exactly how much I was looking forward to the next time. Even after being married for dozens of years, I'd constantly remind you that I couldn't live without you."

I look away when an unexpected surge of heat overtakes me. "Nice try. But that's more or less how you'd get me into bed, not how you'd keep me happy out of it," I fib.

He hums, seemingly unconvinced. "Okay, then. You take a turn."

I purse my lips as I try to imagine what would make a man like Rowan happy. But I haven't known many men like him, and it's been a long time since I've attempted to convey my affection without any physical advantages.

So what have I been doing or saying that keeps him coming back for more, even without having so much as a kiss since the night we met?

"Acts of service," I say coolly. "You appreciate being taken care of, which is why you've been looking for a sweet little trad wife."

His mouth turns down slightly. "Maybe."

"And you'd probably like it if I threw in some affirmations about how you're such a good boy every now and again," I add.

"Sure." He nods, but he still seems downcast, as if he's disappointed in my answer.

I sigh. "But if that stuff didn't work, we could always sit and talk about our feelings, I suppose."

His brow lifts in appreciation. "I might like something like that."

"Then again, you are a hugger and a hand holder," I continue, and his smile grows. "So you probably need some other lame, non-sexual physical reinforcement."

"Yeah, same goes for you," he says.

I scoff. "I don't think you can handle my brand of physical affection."

His gaze runs over me. "Then I guess we'd find ourselves in the kind of trouble Tenley mentioned, wouldn't we?"

Our instructor leans over and clears her throat, saving me again. "Maybe you two missed it, but class was dismissed a few minutes ago. And while I appreciate that you were both good sports, I'm kicking you out now."

Rowan cringes, and I worry for a second that he'll panic and leave me hanging again. But he stands and shoots me an apologetic smile, waiting for me to go first like the well-bred gentleman he is.

"Strangers my ass," Tenley mumbles as she grabs the rest of her things, and Rowan shares another secret look with me before he insists on carrying Tenley's bag out to her car.

"I recognize that look in your eyes," Tenley whispers when she catches me watching him too carefully. "You can probably go ahead and mark this down as peak day."

I glare at her, but she only laughs and thanks Rowan for his help in loading up her bags. We trade goodbyes with her, and Rowan comes around to open my door for me.

"Well, this was fun," he muses.

"I'm still not showing you my charts," I reply after I shut the door and roll down the window.

He reaches up to brace himself on the frame, leaning into the open window. "That's too bad, since I've already replaced Landry's name with yours on all those medical releases."

"Get out of here, you dork," I tell him.

He grins at me one more time. "Good night, Claire Bear. I'd ask you to text me and let me know when you make it home safely, but I know better."

"Good night, Benadryl Boy."

"Don't you want to know if I make it home all right?"

I roll my eyes. "That's not exactly my love language."

"What if I said you had a nice butt first? In a respectable way, of course."

"I'll see you around, Doc," I say, shaking my head as I roll up the window.

ROWAN

Hey, how's the charting going?

CLAIRE

I wish I had time to care.

ROWAN

Everything okay?

CLAIRE

Voice Note Transcript: Well, since Frankie ate something he wasn't supposed to this morning which made me late for work where I found out that the grant I was going to use to buy more supplies for my shop fell through right before I got an email from a parent accusing me of lying about her kid not turning in any of his work for the past few weeks which was just what I needed before my surprise observation which happened on the same day that I got home to a kennel full of dog puke, courtesy of Frankie.

Voice Note Transcript: Then I ended up spraying
myself in the face with a broken water hose
nozzle as I was attempting to clean out said
kennel right before I ran to the hardware store for
a new hose nozzle and ended up seeing the very
last person on earth I wanted to see.

So, no, it's not.

Also, have I mentioned my coffeemaker died this
morning?

ROWAN

Oof. I'm sorry …

Anything I can do to help?

CLAIRE

Unless you have an answer for the text I just got
from my mom asking me why I never go over to
visit anymore, no. I'm afraid there's nothing you
can do to make this day any better.

ROWAN

I guess I can't answer your mother, but what
about if I came by to clean out the dog kennel?

CLAIRE

It's already done.

ROWAN

I could bring you some takeout so you don't have
to worry about dinner. What's your favorite?

CLAIRE

I don't like food anymore.

I don't like anything or anyone anymore,
especially not myself.

ROWAN

Well, I still like you.

And you do have a nice butt.

CLAIRE

Don't patronize me.

ROWAN

I'm sorry. That one was poorly timed.

What's your favorite ice cream flavor?

Favorite candy?

Claire?

📞 Missed Call — Rowan LaFleur

Hey, I'm coming over, okay?

📞 Missed Call — Rowan LaFleur

Claire? Are you home?

I'm worried about you.

📞 Missed Call — Rowan LaFleur

I'm coming inside. Don't shoot me, okay?

claire

WITH MY FOREHEAD resting on my knees and my arms wrapped around my shins, I release another body-wracking sob.

Oscar whines as he waddles over to meet his brother and plops down beside the bathtub. But I can't offer him any reassurance right now, not while I'm still mad at Frankie for puking everywhere, and not while I suspect my uterus has taken over my brain.

Because everything is a mess. My whole life is one big, stinky dumpster fire.

I'm all alone, and I will be forever. I can't do anything right, like staying married, writing grant proposals, picking the right men, or even remembering to grab a clean towel before I get into the bathtub.

I'm an ugly, obnoxious, overweight, failure ... an altogether unlovable slob. Not to mention, I've been a bad influence lately and practically ruined my chances at a lasting friendship with some pretty great people.

It's no wonder someone like Rowan has had a hard time justifying his attachment when my own body can't help but betray me. I mean, of all the dumb, selfish, unfit women in the world who get pregnant on a daily basis, how come I could never manage to get it right?

Another loud wail pours out of me as I think about my ex-husband with his new family. Not that I was devastated to see him happy with someone new, because I honestly couldn't say I felt anything for the man anymore, one way or the other. But the tiny fissure in my heart feels more like a complete fracture after hearing the toddler in his arms call him "Daddy." Sure, he's not her biological father, but the fact that he was willing to fulfill that role cuts deep, especially since the only contributions he ever made toward my efforts to start a family were the occasional "deposits."

And it certainly doesn't help that I'm expecting my period any minute now.

The sound of claws skittering across the floor stirs me from my moping, and I lift my head to find I've been abandoned before I drop it again. Even Oscar and Frankie think I'm too pathetic to bother with at this point.

"Claire?"

I freeze, my heart leaping up into my throat when my name echoes down the hallway.

"Claire?"

This time I realize my intruder isn't approaching with malicious intent, not with that much concern lacing his tone. I wipe my eyes with the heels of my hands and blink to clear my vision, letting out a relieved exhale once I see Rowan and my dogs standing in the open doorway.

Then I panic again when I remember that I'm a naked, weepy, premenstrual bathtub goblin, sitting here in my most vulnerable state while my crush simply stares back at me.

"Hey, are you okay?" he asks, and I pull my knees in tightly to my chest.

"What are you doing here?" I reply, my voice still thick.

"I told you I was coming over to check on you, but you quit answering my texts. I knocked on the front door for a good five minutes."

"I've been busy," I reply stupidly. "How did you even get in here?"

He shrugs. "I remembered the code."

"So you thought you'd just let yourself into my house? What the hell were you thinking?"

His face flushes. "I was worried about you."

I sniffle. "Well, I'm fine, except now I have to add changing the locks again to my to-do list."

"You don't look fine," he mumbles then cringes. "I mean, you look like you've been crying."

"So what if I have?" I retort. "I'm entitled to a good cry after a shitty day."

He clears his throat and looks away. "I know. That's why I, um, brought you some supplies. And I thought maybe you could use the company."

"All I need is privacy," I say, pouting. "So I can finish crying in peace."

"Yeah, I'm sorry. I wasn't thinking again," he fumbles, reaching up to scratch the back of his head. "Is there anything I can get you before I go?"

My bleary eyes run over him. "Did you really drive all the way from Baton Rouge?" He shrugs again, and I sigh. "I can't exactly send you back home now, can I?"

"Don't worry about it. I'm getting used to the drive."

"Well, you might as well get me a towel from the closet while you're in here."

Rowan nods quickly and fulfills my request, setting a clean towel beside the bathtub. My chin trembles as I stare down at it.

"Actually, could you just ..." But my voice breaks off before I can finish, and he hurries to pick up the towel and spreads it open.

"Claire?"

I choke on another sob, unable to answer him.

"Come on, I've got you," he offers in a soothing tone.

"Promise you won't look at me?"

"My eyes are already closed," he declares, but I nod anyway.

He holds the towel out for me as I step out of the tub, then he wraps me up and immediately pulls me in for a hug.

My shoulders shake as I continue bawling my eyes out, but he only molds his body more closely to mine, alternating gentle shushes and whispering, "It's okay, I've got you." I fist his shirt in my hands as he strokes my back.

"I'm getting you all wet," I wail.

"Are you more worried about the tears or the bathwater? Because I couldn't care less about either," he muses, and I smile in spite of my mood. But he pulls back and narrows his eyes as he studies me with mock concern when I don't continue our banter with an even cruder joke.

"I know, I know. Missed opportunity," I say, making him laugh.

"Do you need me to get your clothes?" he ventures once my weeping finally evolves into sniffling.

"My robe is hanging behind the door."

He flashes me a dimpled smirk before he turns to pluck the robe from a hook, then squeezes his eyes shut again as he unwraps the towel and waits for me to dress.

"Thank you," I say with a sniff once I've tightened the belt around my waist, and he opens his eyes. "Wait for me in the living room?" I ask shyly, and he nods and leaves me in the bathroom, shutting the door behind him.

Once I take a few minutes to tend to my lady business and throw on some of my comfiest pajamas, because of course Aunt Flo has decided to make her grand entrance, I wrap myself up in the robe and venture out to find Rowan resting on the couch with Frankie and Oscar. I can't help the small tug on my lips.

"Hey," he greets me. "She lives."

"You know, every four-to-six weeks I have this day where nothing goes right, and I'm so depressed and disgusted with myself that I can't even fathom going on ... then my period arrives, and suddenly everything doesn't seem so bad. But I'm somehow taken completely by surprise when it happens again a month later," I explain, crossing my arms over my middle.

He stands, his smile growing wider. "Those hormones are tricky, from what I hear."

"Tell me about it."

"I wasn't sure what usually makes you feel better, so I kind of grabbed a little of everything," he says, gesturing toward the small grocery haul on the kitchen counter. He goes over to pull out a few different pints of ice cream, a tub of hot chocolate mix, and a wide selection of candy, some of which include peanuts. I swallow hard when he shows me a bag with a variety of tampons and pads next.

"I didn't tell you it was my period when we texted earlier."

"You didn't have to," he whispers conspiratorially.

I roll my eyes through a smile and select a pint of salted caramel ice cream while Rowan retrieves a pair of spoons from a drawer.

"You're having ice cream, too?" I ask.

"Figured you wouldn't want to eat alone."

I nod and turn to push myself up onto the countertop, and he hands me a spoon.

"You didn't have to do this, you know," I tell him after I dig in.

He shrugs and rests his hip against the counter before he opens up another pint of ice cream with a nut-free label. "This is the kind of stuff friends do for one another, right?"

"Yeah, I guess," I say thoughtfully. "I'm sorry about all that crap I said earlier, though. If I'd have known—"

"Don't be sorry," he cuts me off to say. Then he leans in to look me in the eyes as he adds, "I can handle you, you know."

I don't know if he's referring to the physical affection I joked about a while back or my hormonal mood swings, but I'm still left squirming and trying to hide the way his statement makes me shiver.

"Besides," he continues after a while. "I'm always looking for a good excuse to hang out with you."

I frown at that. "Are you working in Camellia tomorrow?"

"Yeah, so I'd have made the drive either way." He takes another bite before he goes on. "I'll actually be working out here more often from now on, at least a couple days per week."

"Oh."

"Tenley and Dr. Simms asked me to help by picking up a few extra maternity patients in addition to my high-risk cases," he explains shyly.

"That's great. I mean, if you're good with seeing their regular patients and all. I imagine you won't make as much money or get to pick and choose your caseload, though."

"That stuff doesn't bother me," he remarks, so I drop it. "Anything else new with you?"

I sigh. "I saw my ex today."

"Really?" he asks hesitantly. "Is that part of the reason ..."

"No ... and yes. It's not like I miss him or anything. But he had his stepdaughter with him, and well, you can probably figure out the rest."

He flashes me a rueful smile. "I'm sorry. That had to be hard for you."

"I guess it could have been worse. Doesn't look like his new girlfriend is pregnant yet," I say with a shrug.

He digs around in his ice cream for a while before he speaks again. "Did you ever find out why you couldn't conceive?"

"No," I say, shaking my head. "I had surgery to clean up some endometriosis about a year ago, but it didn't seem to help. And I couldn't convince Jeremy to run any tests on himself."

"Sometimes it just doesn't happen, even without a good explanation," he says softly, but it does nothing to temper my resentment.

"I never could understand how God could allow people who didn't want kids to keep having them and not give them to someone like me. I mean, I'm far from perfect, but how is this fair?" I demand, my tone bitter. "I'm sorry if you don't like the way that sounds."

"No, you're right. It isn't fair," he replies, his voice still even. "And I won't pretend to have some theological explanation for why God allows bad things to happen to good people. All we can do is trust that those who suffer in this life will be rewarded in the next."

I let out a shaky exhale. "Why would He want us to suffer, though?"

"I don't think God wants us to suffer, and I'm not even sure He's letting it happen for our own good. Maybe it's just the consequences of sin in the world in general, after thousands of years of free will. Like, the mistakes I make today might affect someone else in the future. I don't know. Maybe we're just not meant to understand."

"How can you do that, though? How do you just accept something you don't understand?"

He shrugs. "It's kind of the whole point of having faith, isn't it?

It seems rhetorical, so I silently scoop up another spoonful of ice cream in lieu of answering him.

"You don't believe in God?" he asks quietly.

"Not the version you believe in," I say. "My parents took me to a few different churches over the years and raised me to treat everyone the way I want to be treated. But we never really subscribed to organized religion, and I honestly can't see the appeal of it, especially if it doesn't even provide you with answers."

"That's fair," he concedes, to my surprise. "I once heard a priest say that it must be difficult to go through life and endure the trials and injustices of the world without at least believing in God and the afterlife. At least Christians have a purpose, right? After all, we can take comfort in knowing that our Creator loved us enough to send His only Son to redeem us and secure our place in heaven, regardless of the specifics. But everything changes once we begin imitating Christ by embracing our own crosses and offering up our suffering for the betterment of others, and we learn to appreciate the most difficult parts of life."

The melt-inducing smile he's wearing tells me he wholeheartedly believes in what he's saying, that he'd literally stake his life on it. I know I should be paying more attention to his justification, but I'm honestly too distracted by the way he says it.

"So the shittier the hand you get dealt in life, the easier it is to get to heaven?" I paraphrase once I get past the appeal of his confident side.

"More like, the better we imitate Jesus now, the easier it becomes to join Him in the next life," he corrects me, his smile growing wider.

I hum thoughtfully as I set down the pint of ice cream. "And how does that translate to following a ton of strict rules and not being allowed to have sex?"

He coughs through a laugh. "At the risk of oversimplifying things again, Catholics abide by all those rules and traditions because we need help to overcome sin and form holier habits instead. We basically look to the Church's teachings to guide us on the path to heaven."

"That's cool. But you didn't answer my question."

"Because you already know that I'm allowed to have sex, just not yet," he replies with a playful eye roll. "Remember when Daisy explained how chastity looks different for everyone?" I nod for him to continue. "Chastity is just another one of those virtues that keeps us in line. Every time we misuse or overindulge in good and holy things, we allow ourselves to become slaves to our selfish desires and eventually fall back on our vices."

"Comfort is a gateway drug," I say with a hint of mockery, and he laughs quietly.

"Yeah."

"Then why do most Christians avoid the topic of sex altogether and act like it's so dirty and sinful?" I ask without thinking.

He sighs. "Only because we made it that way. We took one of God's greatest gifts to mankind, a sacramental bond that was intended to give us so much pleasure and grace that it's the closest most of us get to experiencing heaven on earth, and we deliberately misused it. Once we stopped exercising temperance, we lost sight of the purpose of the act in itself. Now half the world claims sex should be a free-for-all, while the other half swears it's inherently evil, neither of which God intended."

I blink at him, unsure what to think. "You're awfully passionate about something you haven't fully experienced. What if you finally get married and realize it's not all you thought it was?"

He looks down and licks his lips. "That's kind of the point of faith, isn't it?" he repeats.

"In other words, if you're a good boy now, God will reward you with the perfect wife later."

"Not exactly," he returns with a frown, sounding much more uncertain about his answer this time. "I strive to do the right thing because I love God and want to serve Him well. I also believe chastity teaches us to curb our more selfish tendencies and helps us develop healthier relationships." He pauses for a while before he adds, "But I guess there's still a part of me that hopes I'll be rewarded for my good behavior, either in this life or the next."

"And you thought sleeping with me might cost you your future," I surmise.

He shakes his head, but he still doesn't meet my eyes. "Leaving you in that hotel room was the hardest thing I've ever done. And the fact that I regret walking out on you more than I regret giving into temptation has been eating me alive. For the first time in my life, I couldn't understand how something that felt so good and so right could be all that wrong. But look at what it's already done to us—we can't seem to stay away from one another, even though we can't make sense of it. And it's obvious we both feel *something* ... right?"

Well, this conversation has taken an unexpected turn.

My heart quickens when he finally looks up at me, and I struggle to form a response for a few seconds.

"I think you're getting too philosophical for me," I mumble as I move to hop down from the counter. But he plants his fists on both sides of my hips, boxing me in.

"Claire, can I ask you something?"

"Okay," I allow, though I'm sure I'll regret it in a moment.

"If I had told you the truth about myself that night, would you have let me stay? Would it have changed anything, or did you mean it when you said casual sex was all you ever wanted from me?"

My chest heaves as I try to formulate an answer. "I shouldn't have told you that. It wasn't a very nice thing to say."

"But did you mean it?" he asks again. He watches my expression carefully, standing between my legs as he awaits my answer.

"I think you're a great guy, Rowan, and any woman would be lucky to have you. But I'm not looking for the kind of relationship you've been holding out for." I pause to lick my lips when my throat goes dry. "After all, you've earned it."

"Maybe I was wrong. I'm not sure it's that simple, not anymore," he mumbles, his eyes fixed on my mouth.

"And maybe you're just confused because I was your first, in a way," I blurt out.

He straightens. "What?"

"It's natural to form an attachment after you're ... physically intimate with someone for the first time," I explain awkwardly. "And even though we didn't actually sleep together, I don't get the impression you've let anyone else ... do the things I did to you."

His jaw snaps shut, and he looks away. "No. I'd never let it get that far before."

"You've said you're more prone to lustful thoughts than usual around me," I continue while he slowly backs away. "Now that I understand what sex and intimacy mean to you, it all makes sense. You're confusing attraction with affection, probably since you've never had to differentiate the two before."

"Yeah. Makes sense," he says sardonically. "Thanks for clearing that up for me."

"Rowan," I begin on a sigh. "I didn't mean to hurt your feelings."

"And I didn't mean to fall for you, but ..."

"What?" I breathe, my heart behaving much like it did at the prospect of a home invasion earlier.

He shakes his head. "I'm sorry. I'm being sarcastic. I just ... I feel like an idiot for assuming you ... Forget I said anything, please?"

He gazes up at me with wide, watery eyes, and my chest tightens. "Can we just pretend this conversation never happened?" he begs.

"You don't usually let me off the hook that easily," I barely manage to say.

He huffs. "You're right. I don't."

"Lucky for you, I'm not into talking about feelings," I tell him before I push myself off the countertop and land on my feet. "And I'm also pretty grateful for the period mix, so I'll cut you some slack this time," I add, gesturing toward the grocery bags.

His expression softens. "Thanks."

"Are you, um, going to Daisy's? Or were you planning on crashing here?"

He scratches the back of his head. "I'm sure you'd like your space, right?"

Until he turned the question back to me, I hadn't realized I was counting on not having to spend the night completely alone. But I certainly can't admit that to him.

"I'd hate to keep you up past your bedtime with all the wailing and weeping I have left to do. It's my cycle day one tradition, you know," I say with a shrug.

"Yeah, can't think of a sound I'd hate more, even counting the things I hear over at *Maison* Reed," he replies dryly. "Good night, Claire. Call me if you need anything else."

"Good night. Thanks again for all this."

He nods and skips his usual practice of pulling me in for a hug in lieu of squatting down to pet Frankie and Oscar. And my chin trembles as I watch him walk out the front door.

rowan

"*MAIS, gardez donc.* If it isn't my long, lost brother," Daisy drawls when she opens the door for me.

I sigh. "Hey, Daze. Sorry for springing my presence on you at the last second."

She moves to let me into their small shotgun house, Juniper shadowing her as usual. "Did Claire kick you out or something?"

"Something like that," I mutter as I step inside and kiss her cheek. "Where's your husband?"

"Therapy. He's usually back by now, but he texted to say his appointment started late," she explains.

"I take it the therapy is working, then, since he didn't stomp out at the prospect of waiting," I say, and Daisy laughs.

"Yeah, it's been going pretty well," she agrees.

"I still can't believe you got Landry Reed to go to counseling in the first place. But if anyone can convince a guy like him to change, it's you."

She smiles. "Thanks, but it was actually his idea. Well, Loren probably planted the seed, but Landry's the one who wanted to go, so he could be prepared for fatherhood." She shrugs shyly when I cast a concerned glance her way.

"Are you ..."

"Not yet," she replies. "But we plan to start trying as soon as I get cleared by my neurologist."

My chest warms at the thought of my baby sister having a baby. It's followed by a familiar ache, but I ignore the feeling and pull her in for a hug. "That's great news. You and Landry are going to be amazing parents. And I'll be here for whatever you need."

"Thank you," she croaks over my shoulder. "That means a lot … to both of us."

"Of course. You know how much I love you guys," I reassure her, although my mind is already drifting back to Claire and how she might react to this news.

"I guess I've been a little worried we've been usurped," Daisy says with a light laugh and settles on the small couch, gesturing for me to join her as Juniper curls up at her feet. "And … well, you and I never really got the chance to talk about everything that's happened in the last few months."

I frown as I join her. "I guess we haven't. But you know I'm happy for you. And, not that you even needed my blessing, but I gave it to Landry months ago. If anything, I'm proud—"

"Rowan," she interrupts me. "That's not what I meant."

I shake my head in confusion, and she sighs.

"I know you *think* you're really happy for us, but you haven't been acting like yourself since you found out Landry and I were living together, and especially not since we told you about the Convalidation. It's okay to be upset with us, or even jealous in a way. But you've got to quit stuffing all those feelings down inside."

I blink back in surprise. "I don't … I'm not angry at either of you. How could I be?"

"Because your best friend went behind your back and married your baby sister—your favorite sister, at that!" she repeats incredulously. "Heck, I was ticked off when I found out about you and Claire, and it's not like you were *married*."

"Oh. I mean, sure, I was a little hurt when Landry told me you'd gotten legally married … especially since you'd kept it from me for so long. But it's only because you're both so important to me. I'd have liked the chance to help you with your health insurance problems and him with his anxiety or whatever, which I'd actually been trying to get him to open up about for, what, the better part of a decade, at least." I say that last part with a scoff, then immediately glance up to check Daisy's expression. But she only nods encouragingly, so I continue.

"I may not be as cute and bubbly as you, but I'd like to think I'm a supportive friend, and it really did take a lot of patience and understanding to put up with his grumpy, emotionally constipated ass all these years. Yet it only took *you* a few weeks to convince him that he needed therapy ... *and* Jesus."

"Okay, that's not a hundred-percent accurate, but I like the direction we're headed," Daisy says, gesturing with her hands. "Keep going."

"What did you bribe him with, anyway?" I ask as if she hadn't interrupted me, cursing under my breath a second later. "No, don't answer that. I don't wanna know."

She snorts. "I promise you, he'd never have taken me up on that kind of offer. I was the one pursuing him ... and ogling him every chance I got."

I frown. "I'm not sure that's any better."

"The point is, Landry looks up to you as much as I do. He was determined to do the right thing, even if it meant sacrificing his own happiness and mine, all because he couldn't bear to disappoint you," she explains.

"That's not what I'd have wanted for either of you, though."

"Of course not, but this is Landry we're talking about. He needed to hear you give us your blessing. The man is pretty literal," she says, smiling.

"I've noticed," I say on a short laugh. "But I still wish you'd have told me everything sooner. It made me feel like the two people I trusted most didn't ..."

I trail off and roll my lips in. "This isn't about you and Landry's secret marriage at all, is it?"

"Maybe a little," she replies with a shrug.

"Okay, fine," I concede. "I'm sorry I didn't tell you about all that stuff with Claire from the beginning. I was embarrassed of the way I'd acted and afraid of seeming like a hypocrite, especially in front of you."

She leans forward and boops my nose. "You're forgiven, silly. I want to know why you weren't honest with Claire, though. She's a lot like Landry, a hard egg to crack, but very fragile on the inside. Yet, you coaxed her into opening her heart to you without granting her the same courtesy. Can you imagine if I asked Lan to talk about his childhood trauma and refused to let him help me a minute later when I had a seizure?"

I let my head fall back with a groan. "You're right."

"Of course I am," she declares, lifting her chin proudly. "And you're never going to convince her to live happily ever after with you unless you manage to win back her trust."

"Even if I earn her trust again, she's not interested in the kind of relationship I want. And she's made it clear that there's nothing I can say or do to change her mind," I say defensively. But my heart's still a little sore from earlier.

"Or maybe you just don't want that happily ever after as badly as you think."

I furrow my brow. "What do you mean by that?"

"Well, first of all, you're not willing to compromise on what that looks like. You see only one formula and one answer, and you automatically mark all the other answers wrong," she explains.

"Right is right, and the truth is the truth," I reply, still confused. "I want to fall in love with someone who shares the same values as I do, to get married and have kids, to grow in holiness, and eventually spend eternity together. Is that not what I should be striving for?"

"But why does she have to agree with you on everything now for the rest of that to come true?" Daisy counters.

"Because I'd just be throwing myself at temptation," I argue.

"Rowan, you can't just opt out of falling in love if she doesn't check every box on your list, especially since it sounds like you're more worried about your pride than anything. Don't you see how shallow and judgmental you're being?"

I huff. "Is it so wrong to bypass a near occasion of sin and keep looking for someone who's eager to help me get to heaven?"

"It is when you insist that the help meets your unreasonably high expectations. Not everyone is fortunate enough to be born into families like ours, you know, where our faith was instilled early on, and you can't narrow your search to women who are already holier than you. You have to give everyone God puts in front of you a fair chance, to be patient and allow the Holy Spirit to work through you," my sister dictates.

"So, what, we're supposed to be missionaries in marriage, too?" I pose sarcastically, then wince at the way I sound.

"Maybe we've been called to grow in holiness as we bring others to God. And that requires an open heart, an open mind, and a willingness to meet people where they are ... as well as the strength to resist temptation."

I puff out my cheeks and blow out a breath, nodding in defeat. "When did you get so wise, Daisy?"

"I've always been wise. You're the one who seems to have grown so stubborn practically overnight," she replies matter-of-factly. But she gasps a second later, her hand flying up to her chest.

"What now?" I ask.

"It's not my marriage to Landry that's been bothering you, or even your guilty conscience after the night you and Claire met. You've already fallen for her, haven't you?" she ventures, her eyes round.

"I'm not sure I'd go that far," I begin, cringing when I remember what I'd let slip in front of Claire not even an hour ago.

Daisy glares at me shrewdly. "From what I hear, you've already gone quite far enough with her to contradict that claim."

I roll my eyes. "Okay, yeah. I do like her ... a lot. I mean, we have our differences, but we get along surprisingly well ... until we don't, I guess. Even when we argue, though, I can't tell whether we're fighting or flirting. It's probably the most fun I've ever had," I say with a short laugh. "Which I suppose means we have plenty of chemistry. And she's beautiful, obviously."

"Obviously," my sister agrees, biting back a smile.

"I don't know if I've ever found anyone more attractive, you know, physically," I continue, my cheeks heating. "But there's so much more to her than that. She's funny and kind, and she's open-minded. She's knowledgeable and good at so many things, but somehow still humble and selfless, despite everything she's been through. She has such a big heart, even though she tries to keep it tucked away. And, well, now that I think about it," I pause to swallow hard, "I've never liked anyone as much as I like Claire."

Daisy squeals this time. "And do you think it's possible God put her in front of you for a reason, apart from saving you from an allergic reaction?"

"Absolutely," I breathe.

Except I haven't exactly been fulfilling my role as the "good influence," I add in my head.

"Okay, so," she begins, turning to face me. "Could you see yourselves together, living out the kind of future you want?"

I lick my lips as I consider Daisy's suggestion. Even after our somewhat promising conversation during that NFP class, Claire doesn't seem like she's any closer to budging on the marriage front, as she was so quick to remind me earlier tonight.

"She doesn't like me nearly enough to consider a second marriage. And even if her feelings were anywhere close to mine, I'm afraid there are entirely too many obstacles. For all we know, she might need an annulment before she could have a sacramental wedding, and I wouldn't want to pressure her into anything like that."

Daisy's expression falls. "Are you sure? Maybe you can convince her—"

But she cuts herself off when the doorknob jiggles, and Landry swings the door open a few seconds later. Juniper rises to her feet, and I excuse Daisy from our conversation with a nod. She wastes no time in leaping from the couch and practically landing in her husband's arms.

"Hey, bro," he greets me after a kiss from Daisy.

"Hey, sorry to crash your evening, but ..." I shrug.

Landry smirks. "Don't worry. I can pretend you're not here."

Daisy rolls her eyes and shoves him playfully. "You never did tell me why you came over, anyway," she reminds me, even though she knows I went to see Claire earlier.

"Oh, I, um … I was going to drive straight to the clinic tomorrow, you know, to see how long it actually takes to get here with the morning traffic. But Claire mentioned she wasn't feeling well, so I ended up making the trip tonight. I dropped off some ice cream at her place on my way here."

Daisy looks thoughtful, but she doesn't say anything else right then. Landry excuses himself to go shower, and I pick up my bag to head to the guest bedroom.

"Rowan?" Daisy calls out.

"Yeah?" I ask.

"One more thing. I love you, but if you ever hurt my friend again, I'm going to have to get my frying pan on you," she warns, attempting an intimidating glare but coming up way, way short.

My lips twitch, but I manage to keep myself from laughing. "Yes, ma'am. I promise, all my intentions are pure."

"Pure?" Her brow lifts, and Juniper looks back and forth between us with interest.

"I said my intentions were pure. Don't ask me about my thoughts," I admit sheepishly, making my sister laugh.

wednesday

7:12 PM

ROWAN

How are you feeling today?

CLAIRE

A little better, thanks in part to the new coffeemaker that was randomly delivered to my house this morning.

ROWAN

How ever did that get there? Weird …

CLAIRE

Thank you, but I'm gonna need you to quit buying me all these gifts.

ROWAN

That one was actually for me. How else am I supposed to bum a cup of coffee this Sunday morning when I pick you up for our trip to the homestead?

(That was my way of asking you if you're still interested in helping Heath's kids pick out a lamb for the livestock show, by the way. Smooth, right?)

CLAIRE

I still have you penciled in for Sunday.

ROWAN

Looking forward to it.

Trying out that new coffeemaker, I mean.

CLAIRE

Unbelievably smooth. 😊

Anyway … what do you have planned on this fine evening?

ROWAN

Oh, you know, studying for my CDL, practicing my pipe-laying skills, the usual.

CLAIRE

Pics or it didn't happen.

ROWAN

shirtless bathroom selfie

CLAIRE

Um, excuse me, sir? WTAF?

I'm gonna need a warning before you send me a thirst trap like this!

ROWAN

What's a thirst trap again?

CLAIRE

It's what the kids call it when one purposefully poses or presents oneself in a way to appear more attractive and desirable.

And ugh. Could you be any more wholesome?

ROWAN

You say that like it's a bad thing.

CLAIRE

You could throw a beige flag in there sometimes, you know, just to make yourself look somewhat normal.

ROWAN

Funny. Feels like I've been raising plenty of red flags lately.

CLAIRE

You wouldn't know a red flag if someone waved it in your face.

I mean, obviously, since you're still friends with me.

ROWAN

So ... we're still friends, then?

I wasn't so sure after the way we left things last night.

CLAIRE

What else would you call the person who's willing to literally and metaphorically pick you up off the bathroom floor? Since I can't imagine you'd ever want to see me naked again after that, calling this a friendship seems fair.

ROWAN

That would be a fair assessment.

But it's still an incorrect one.

CLAIRE

Well, damn. I know I wasn't at my best, but I didn't think you'd unfriend me over a little PMS-inspired menty b.

(That's a mental breakdown, btw.)

ROWAN

I'm actually referring to the other half of your assumption. I wouldn't want you to go on thinking I hated seeing you naked, even though I tried really hard not to look.

CLAIRE

You're supposed to be a professional, you perv!

ROWAN

Is this like the time I sent you the robe? Because my intention was flattery.

I was homeschooled, remember?

CLAIRE

Fine. I'll take your pity compliments.

Especially since they're all I'll get for the foreseeable future.

ROWAN

It wasn't a pity compliment, which is why I probably shouldn't have said it at all.

And I'm sorry about the thirst trap. I'd just gotten back from a run and figured I'd snap a picture before jumping in the shower.

CLAIRE

NOT. HELPING.

ROWAN

You've seen me without a shirt before.

And I'm all gross and sweaty. I honestly didn't think anything of it.

CLAIRE

I hate you sometimes, you know that?

ROWAN

I'm sorry. I promise I won't send any more topless pics.

CLAIRE

Whoa, hold on, there … Let's not make any
promises I don't intend for you to keep.

ROWAN

Well, I assumed you were under a social
obligation to reciprocate with a selfie of your own,
and I didn't want you to think I expected a one-
for-one trade off.

But the aforementioned rules don't necessarily
apply to you, for the record. You're free to set
your own selfie guidelines.

Because I'm somewhat of a feminist.

CLAIRE

I just snorted so hard that my cramps came back.

But if you really want to make this equitable …

Selfie holding Oscar

ROWAN

That's one cute wiener.

CLAIRE

Fair is fair, right?

ROWAN

I'm afraid you've emasculated me now. I'll never
recover from this game.

CLAIRE

Oh, come on. It's just a little sausage pic.

ROWAN

Little?

CLAIRE

gif of Jennifer Lawrence cringing

My bad. Unfortunate word choice …

Besides, if either of us is subject to an unfair disadvantage, it's me. You're literally a professional lady part inspector.

ROWAN

And I've already admitted that I enjoy looking at your parts more than any others I've seen to date.

CLAIRE

bathroom selfie in a sports bra and boxer shorts

Okay, then. Have a look at this gorgeous period bloat belly.

. . .

image deleted

Oh-kay, then. Point taken.

I'm sorry for making you feel uncomfortable. I guess I took it too far.

Like I always do.

I'll leave you alone now. Have a good night, Rowan. Thanks for checking on me.

ROWAN

No, wait, I'm sorry.

I don't know how else to say this without being crude, but your selfie definitely made me uncomfortable. So much so that I had to take a cold shower, because I shouldn't be thinking those kinds of thoughts about you.

Better yet, I shouldn't be lusting after any woman like that.

I respect you, Claire, and I care about you. I also think you are a beautiful woman, and I find all of your parts to be very, very sexy. That's why I don't deserve to see you in such an intimate way, because I can't control where my mind goes.

Please don't think this is your fault. I started it when I made that first comment, and then when I sent you that pic, but I should have known better. I don't mean to come off so hot and cold all the time. It's just that I'm always getting in over my head with you.

Can you forgive me?

CLAIRE

A cold shower, you say?

ROWAN

You can take the amount of time it took for me to reply to you as an indication of how long I spent in a stream of frigid water before I could think of anything else.

CLAIRE

Pics or it didn't happen …

ROWAN

photo of frozen package labeled "Rowan's Deer Sausage"

rowan

"HI," Claire says when she opens the door, and I swallow hard when I take in the sight of her. The tank top she's wearing under her overalls showcases her tattoos and outlines her curves.

"Hi," I return in a breathy voice, adding an awkward wave and a hoarse throat clearing, because why not make my nerves and my unrequited feelings more obvious.

Frankie and Oscar scurry over for some attention, and Claire gestures for me to follow her inside after a minute. "I'm not quite ready, but the coffee is," she says, gathering her long hair over one shoulder.

I watch as she parts her locks into three sections and weaves them into a braid. It's not the neat French braid that she wears on weekdays, the one that begins at the crown of her head and integrates every strand of hair into a tight plait, but a more relaxed version that starts at the back of her neck and highlights the natural texture of her hair. Another wavy tendril falls free as she moves to secure the end with a hair tie, and I have to shove my fists into my pockets to keep myself from reaching out to capture it.

"Thanks," I reply, grounding myself with the rosary ring in my pocket. I amble into the kitchen and sift through the cabinet for the

4-H mug, the one with the lamb on it, since it feels more appropriate today.

"Oh, um ... Should I cover my arms?" she asks after a while, and the very idea that she wants to impress my parents stirs up the butterflies in my stomach.

I shake my head. "Absolutely not. My mom would be upset if she couldn't admire your tattoos."

And so would I.

"I can bring a jacket, just in case."

She smirks before she disappears down the hallway, leaving me to sip my coffee and start my morning rosary. I'm just finishing up the last decade when she returns, a light layer of makeup coloring her face now.

"You don't need to do that, you know," I say as I place my mug in the sink.

"Do what?"

"The makeup."

She sighs. "I know we're going to be outside, but—"

"No. I mean, like, ever. I don't know why you bother," I tell her.

She shrugs and slides her feet into her boots. "It's kind of like the frilly pajamas, I guess."

"The overalls and the chest waders look just as feminine on you."

She shoots me a side-eyed glare before she grabs a jacket from a hook. "You would say that," she mumbles and gestures for us to go, and I get another dirty look when I open the passenger door of my truck for her.

The first few minutes of the drive are quiet until she teases me for adhering to the speed limit. After that, she asks about my family and the farm, and I'm still rambling on about our life on the homestead as I pull into the driveway.

My parents are waiting to greet us in the kitchen, my mom pulling Claire into a hug with an insistence that we have some of the breakfast she's set out for us and my dad punctuating his embrace by complimenting Claire's tattoo sleeve. My brother and his family walk in a few minutes later, and I introduce Claire to Heath and his wife Naomi as we pile eggs, bacon, and biscuits onto our plates.

"I don't suppose you mind riding on one of these?" my dad asks Claire and gestures to the UTV parked out back, once we've eaten enough to satisfy my mom, of course.

She smirks at him and takes off walking, and I'm grateful when Heath helps his oldest two kids into the back seat, leaving Claire to fall in between my dad and me. Her lips are still turned up in a faint smile when my dad automatically reaches up to drape an arm over the seat behind her, though I'm admittedly a little jealous.

He takes the scenic route so he can play the tour guide, stopping every so often to elaborate on a feature of the small-scale farm and answering Claire's follow-up questions before giving her an affectionate pat on the shoulder and taking off again. We finally pull up in front of the massive barn that serves as a shelter for both the animals and their feed, as well as some of the smaller farm implements, and Claire turns another wide grin to me when I offer to help her out of the side-by-side. Her cheeks are rosy from the drive, and a few more wisps of her hair have worked their way loose. And she's so beautiful out here in her element that I forget how to breathe for a moment.

Dad leads us past the horse stalls as both Claire and Gertie reach out to stroke one of the older mares on the forehead before we make it to the sheep enclosure.

"Why don't you guys get some feed?" my dad suggests, and Heath shows Giles and Gertie where to find the barrel of grain. The ewes begin bleating and rushing in as soon as they hear someone approaching their feeders, their lambs skipping along behind them.

Claire gestures toward a nearby bale, and we add a few scoops of hay to the grains, watching as the mama ewes ruminate contentedly and the smaller lambs nurse.

"To find a show-quality sheep, you'll want to start by looking at the more active lambs, and then narrow it down by checking the more specific characteristics, like the coloration on their hooves and faces, their shape and muscle tone," Claire explains and brings Gertie around to have her point out some of the more promising lambs, providing feedback for each of Gertie's guesses.

Once the sheep have seemingly had their fill, Claire stoops down to pick up one of Gertie's favorites, quickly securing the squirming lamb by tucking its legs beneath her arm like a pro and bringing it to Gertie and Giles for a combination of petting and inspection.

They decide after a minute that this one, while adorable, wouldn't make the best choice for a show lamb because of its coarser pelt, and Claire aims a proud smile my way before she frees the lamb and picks up another. I can't help but flash her a grin of my own when I realize she'd purposefully grabbed that lamb specifically to create a teachable moment. I think I see a hint of blush on her cheeks before she turns away to snatch another lamb and repeat the process.

"All right, let's tag this little one's ear," my dad says to Giles once they find a suitable candidate.

"What about this one?" Gertie asks, tugging on Claire's overalls to bring her attention to another lamb, and after some inspection, Gertie gets the honors of tagging it.

Claire compliments the kids on their tagging skills and explains the next steps, how the show lambs can mingle with the others but will eventually need to be separated for special grooming and shearing as they grow.

"Thank you, Claire," Heath says, and I definitely see her cheeks darkening when Gertie wraps her arms around her waist in gratitude.

"I think *Grand-mère* has our lunch ready," my dad announces, and I automatically look to Claire.

"Oh, thank you, but I'm still full from breakfast," she remarks with a hand over her middle, looking concerned.

"Do you wanna hang out here for a while longer?" I offer, and she nods in relief.

My dad winks as he takes the others back to the UTV, leaving Claire and me alone in the barn. She shoots me a coy smile before she picks up a shovel and begins cleaning out the stalls. I join her, and we work in a comfortable silence for a few minutes.

"What?" she asks when she notices the way I'm staring at her.

"Nothing," I reply quietly.

"You're looking at me funny," she continues, narrowing her eyes.

"Well, you're pretty impressive. I know you think my crush is … immature. But you're not helping your case when you're out here …"

She snorts. "What, shoveling sheep shit with you?"

"Yeah," I say with a short laugh. "Exactly. I used to think my standards were high, but that was before I knew women like you existed. And I'm not sure you understand how much you've raised my expectations."

Her eyelashes flutter. "You don't have to shower me with gifts and compliments every time I do something nice for you. A simple thank you would suffice."

"I'm not …" I sigh and stick my shovel into the ground before I cross my arms over the handle. "I guess I'm just wishing things could be different."

Her dark brows draw in closer, but she doesn't say anything. I take her shovel and return them both to their place while she leans back against the wall and watches me.

"And I thought you were supposed to be holding out for Little Miss Prim and Proper," she says after a while, digging the already dingy toe of her boot into the dirt floor to make her point.

"Prim and proper are overrated. The more time I spend with you, the more obvious that becomes," I tell her, moving closer.

She tilts her head back and laughs, and I smile at the sound of it. "Now you want someone who's willing to have your babies *and* fix your busted pipes?"

"Is it too much to ask if she's also hot enough to rock overalls and a tattoo sleeve?"

"As long as she cleans up nice for church on Sunday mornings." Her sardonic smile causes mine to fade slightly.

"Maybe I am asking too much," I mutter.

"Don't worry. I'm sure the girl of your dreams is out there somewhere," she says, her tone softening.

"What about you?" I ask after a while.

She shrugs. "I'm not sure what the hell I want anymore."

I click my tongue in mock disappointment. "You're supposed to say you want a man in slutty little glasses who's willing to build you a barn with a sexy hay loft."

"I was hoping you'd forgotten about that," she says with a quiet laugh.

"I've been listening to every word. And I hear you when you say you're not looking to settle down, but I can't help thinking you'd be really good at marriage … with the right person," I force myself to say.

She looks away and blinks, and I know I'm pushing her boundaries, but something tells me I'm supposed to press on.

"Still think you'll never be ready to try again?" I ask carefully. "With anyone?"

She shakes her head. "I'm not sure I can see past the here and now."

"Have you ever tried envisioning your future? You know, just closing your eyes and picturing the first things that come to mind?"

"Not really."

"Wanna try it together?" I venture, leaning back and copying her pose.

She snorts. "You're such a dork."

"At least I'm not a chicken."

"Oh, so I'm chicken now?" she asks incredulously. "That's rich, coming from you."

"I'd like to think of myself as more careful than cowardly," I say with a laugh.

"And I've been called many things before, but a chicken isn't one of them," she retorts.

I hum, doing my best to play it cool although my heart feels like it's going to beat right out of my chest. "I think you're afraid of what you might see, that your subconscious wants something you're not willing to admit."

She scoffs. "Whatever."

"Prove me wrong, then," I say, smugly.

"Fine, I will." She scowls at me before closing her eyes and relaxing her face, and I smile before I do the same. "What am I supposed to be looking at, again?"

I gasp. "It's not that kind of fantasy, Claire Bear."

She elbows me, and I chuckle. "Think about a perfectly happy version of your life. Try to imagine it like a movie," I say, my tone more serious.

She inhales and exhales loudly. "All right."

My grin widens at the scene my mind immediately conjures. "Want me to go first?"

"Wait, you didn't say we'd be playing show and tell."

"How else do you plan to win this argument?

She grunts, and I crack an eye open and catch her staring back at me before I add, "Unless you're scared, that is."

She scowls and squeezes her eyes closed. "After you, dork."

"All right," I say, blowing out a breath. "I see … a house in the country with a huge barn in the back, where I'm cleaning out the stalls with my beautiful wife." She huffs again, but I continue. "And a whole slew of animals, because she's always taking in new ones."

"What about kids?" she asks, her voice sounding thick.

"Two, maybe three of them. They're playing outside with the dogs while we alternate working and flirting in the barn. They catch us making out, and they all cringe and say it's gross, but we tell them they're lucky to have parents who like each other as much as we do."

I pause and swallow hard before I go on. "We bring the kids inside to make dinner. And we say grace together as a family and thank God for all of it before we eat."

She lets out another shaky exhale. "I figured you'd have wanted at least a handful of kids."

"So did I," I reply thoughtfully. "But it's a little late to start on a brood as big as the one I grew up in."

"Your wife isn't younger than you?"

"No. She's not. She does have a nice butt and a really hot tattoo sleeve, though."

"But if you married someone younger, you could have more babies," she argues, brushing over my flirting.

"That's not how this game goes," I tell her with a short laugh. "The heart wants what it wants."

"Oh."

"What about your heart?" I ask after the silence stretches and peek at her again to check her expression. She's frowning, and her chin trembles lightly. "Claire?"

"I'm sorry," she whispers and sniffles. "I don't think ... I just can't."

I turn and pull her into my arms, and she seems reluctant, but she doesn't back away from my embrace. "No, I'm sorry. I shouldn't have asked you to do this. It was stupid."

"It's okay." Her voice cracks, contradicting her. "It's not your fault I'm a mess."

"It might be this time," I say, and she laughs softly, to my relief. "You're not a mess, though. You still have some healing to do, but that doesn't mean there's anything wrong with you."

"That's not what my heart says," she mumbles, and I lean back to look her in the eyes.

"Claire, you're not broken. You're one of the strongest people I know. And you have your whole life ahead of you, right?"

She sniffs as I bring up the hem of my shirt to dry her cheeks. "Even my imagination must know that stuff isn't possible for me anymore, since I can't see anything past the way things are now."

I furrow my brow, already feeling guilty for pushing her too far. "Of course it's possible. And maybe you don't see anyone else because your heart is telling you that you need to focus on loving yourself for now."

"I didn't say I was alone," she admits, and my pulse quickens.

"Oh. So there is someone with you?" I ask, barely able to get the words out.

"It doesn't matter. I can't see myself getting married ever again, which pretty much nullifies the rest," she mutters as she takes a step back, but I involuntarily reach for her arm.

"Claire, wait—"

"Can we please drop it?" she interrupts me before I can ask for more, and I let out a loud exhale.

"Yeah, sorry."

She sniffles again. "We should go inside before your mom starts to worry."

"Sure," I reply and lead her out.

rowan

CLAIRE and I are both silent as we lock up the barn and walk toward the house, waving to my dad when he acknowledges us from across the yard. The rest of my family is still gathered around the kitchen when we get there, and I gesture for Claire to use the sink first as my mom starts doling out slices of homemade king cake.

"Yes, but they aren't obligated to observe their Lenten penances on Sundays," my mother argues, and Heath exhales in defeat when she places a piece in front of each of his children.

"So," my brother begins once I'm done washing my hands. "I see why you weren't interested in that blind date we've been trying to set up for you."

My gaze darts over to Claire, who forces a smile and keeps her eyes locked onto the dish towel she's folding.

"I've been busy," is all I say.

My mom swats at my arm. "You'd better not be dating more than one woman at a time."

"Oh, no," Claire volunteers. "Rowan and I are just ... besties. He's free to date whomever he wants."

My stomach bottoms out, and the way she rolls her lips in as if the words taste sour is the only thing keeping me from breaking down in front of everyone. The sympathetic look my brother exchanges with his wife is nearly enough to do me in, though.

"Besties?" my mom asks with a fist on her hip. "Is that slang for one of those open relationships?"

"It means they're best friends and they tell each other everything," Gertie leans up to whisper to my mother, who feigns understanding.

"Oh, right," she confirms as she moves closer to Claire and wraps an arm around her waist. "Either way, we're glad to hear Rowan and Daisy have been keeping such lovely company, and we're grateful that they're willing to share you with us. You're welcome here any time, Claire, even if you don't plan on becoming a LaFleur officially."

My head falls back, and I let out a groan as the rest of my family laughs. "That's real helpful, Ma. Thanks."

"Well, someone has to propose to her, and you're not getting any younger, *cher*," my mom retorts, running a hand over Claire's braid before backing away.

Claire's cheeks pinken adorably, though I'm not sure whether it's due to my mother's overly affectionate disposition or the subject matter itself, and she clears her throat before she speaks.

"I mean, he *has* tried—you know what, never mind," she says, waving her hands apologetically. "Thanks for the open invitation."

I whimper and shovel king cake into my mouth, and Heath pats me on the back with a chuckle.

"Naomi's still willing to set you up with her church friend," he offers, sounding amused. My eyes flash to Claire's again as I force myself to chew, though I couldn't even name the flavor. And at this point, I wouldn't mind if it were peanut butter filled.

"So what's she like?" Claire leans over and directs her question at Heath. He furrows his brow, obviously not having expected her to call his bluff, but my sister-in-law speaks up.

"Her name is Cecelia. She's a cute little blonde who teaches at our Catholic elementary school. In fact, Rowan's probably seen her in Mass before. She wears a white mantilla and usually sits in the second pew on the left," Naomi explains as she wipes purple icing off the baby's chin.

"Yeah, I know exactly who she is," I remark with a short laugh.

I barely catch Claire's eye roll, but I perk up at the sight of it. At least I can always count on her face giving away what she isn't willing to admit out loud.

"*Mais ouai, ça c'est jolie*," my mom agrees, watching Claire's reaction almost as closely as I am. "Maggie's mentioned her before, too. I think they're in the same Bible study group together ... or maybe she's kin to her in-laws."

"Wow, she sounds perfect for you, Rowan," Claire says after a while, her smile obviously fake.

I smirk at her. "She does sound nice, but I'm not sure she's *perfect* for me."

"What makes you say that?" Naomi asks.

"Eh, I think I'm into brunettes these days," I muse, keeping my gaze locked onto Claire as her cheeks flush again.

I don't even bother explaining that I already know Cecelia isn't the one for me after Marigold insisted on setting us up over a year ago. Because it doesn't matter. I'm not interested in going out with anyone other than the woman in front of me.

"Besides, I'm not looking to start a relationship out here while I'm working in Camellia half of the time," I add after my mom's reproachful huff.

"Funny, that commute didn't seem to bother you when you went out with Landry's sister," Heath points out, and I elbow him gently in the side.

"Maybe he does have a thing for brunettes," Naomi says, smiling in Claire's direction. "Or tattoos."

Claire stops mid-bite and tosses her head back to laugh, and the sound of it warms my insides. "No, trust me. Your boy is still on the hunt for perfection," she says as her laughter dies down. "All I ever hear about is how badly he wants to find his *soulmate*."

The corners of my mouth droop at the way she says the word, as if she's invoking one of our inside jokes, only to make me the butt of it.

"I'm not looking for perfection, so long as she gives a shit about my feelings," I mumble as I turn and dump the rest of my king cake in the trash, just as my dad walks into the kitchen.

"Athanasius Rowan," my mom scolds me. "Language!" But it's the disappointment in my father's features that brings me the most shame.

"Sorry, everyone," I apologize on a sigh before turning to Claire. "It's been a long week. We'd better get on the road. Ready, *bestie*?"

She has the nerve to look remorseful as she sets down her half-eaten slice. "Yeah, we should get going. Thanks for breakfast and the king cake, and for the tour. I had a lot of fun today, and it was great to see all of you again."

I'm not surprised when my parents take turns pulling her in for a hug, but the sight of Claire stooping down to embrace my brother's kids is another one I'll be committing to memory. My chest tightens as she reminds Gertie how to care for their new lambs and promises to return soon for a shearing lesson. And I nearly growl in frustration when she offers to swap phone numbers with Naomi so they can "text her anytime" with their livestock show questions.

To think, I once worried my family might judge Claire for being divorced. But now that she's here, I should probably be more concerned about them adopting her and forgetting all about me.

My dad steps up to envelop me in a hug, and I welcome the distraction.

"Hey, I see you, son. Don't give up. Remember, love is patient," he says over my shoulder, and my breath catches in my throat.

I nod and force a sad smile for him when I pull away, and he slaps me heartily on the back, making me regret not asking for his advice sooner. My mother's embrace includes a warning about what will happen if I show up for Easter dinner without Claire or allow Daisy and Landry to starve out there in Camellia, as well as a kiss on the cheek and a reminder of how much she loves me.

Claire lets me lead her out to my truck and doesn't protest when I get the door for her this time.

"Thanks again for coming along today and being so willing to help Giles and Gertie," I say quietly once I reach the end of the driveway. "I'm sorry about my reaction and for making that last part so awkward. But my parents really meant it when they said they enjoyed having you over, and I ..." I pause to swallow hard, channeling that perseverance my dad alluded to, "I really enjoyed having you here with me."

Her eyes are watery by the time I work up the courage to glance her way.

"I'm the one who should be thanking you. And I'm sorry, too."

"For what?"

"It seemed like they'd gotten the wrong idea about us, so I thought I'd save you the trouble by correcting your mom's assumptions, that way you wouldn't have to worry about offending me when you set them straight. But I made things worse for you instead," she explains, her voice thick, and the rest of my anger melts away.

"It's okay," I reassure her. "Well, it's not okay that you thought I'd be more embarrassed to tell my family you were my girlfriend than to admit that you're not, but I guess that's my own fault for letting you believe it."

She sniffles and swipes at her cheeks. "I know how much their approval means to you."

"Nothing means more to me than your feelings do," I say, testing her reaction, but she doesn't reply.

I hold out my hand, palm up, and she hesitates before she laces her fingers through mine. An involuntary sigh escapes as I revel in the contact, and I consider bringing her hand up to my lips for a kiss.

"You should go, you know, on that date," she says after a while, popping my bubble.

"What?"

"That girl they mentioned, Cecelia? She sounds lovely. You deserve someone who can give you everything you pictured in your vision, and I bet she'd fit right in."

I squeeze Claire's hand. "You fit in pretty well with my family today."

"Your family's amazing. But that's not what I meant. You need someone who—"

"So you want me to just forget about the way you make me feel and force it with someone else because she sounds perfect for me on paper?" I blurt out.

Claire lets out a loud exhale and tugs her hand free. "Go on the date, Rowan. You owe it to yourself."

Why is it that the harder I try with her, the more I manage to screw things up?

I think back to some of the advice she's given me, when she said I've been too nice in my pursuits, but I'm not sure I've been nice enough to Claire in the first place. I suppose it couldn't hurt to try being a little more assertive, though.

"Won't you be jealous?" I force myself to ask.

She chokes on her reaction. "Why would I be ... jealous?" she replies in between coughs, and I bite back a smile.

"You've had me all to yourself for a while. But if either of us started dating other people, our relationship wouldn't be appropriate anymore. I definitely wouldn't be able to hang out at your place."

She lifts her chin indignantly. "Seems like a guy with your moral code would have considered coed sleepovers to be inappropriate from the jump. And what makes you so sure I haven't been waiting for you to start going out with other women so I wouldn't feel bad about getting back out there myself?"

I grunt. "I thought you said you couldn't see yourself getting married again."

"Who said anything about husband hunting?"

"So you plan on advertising that you're not interested in anything serious?" I blurt out before I can stop myself.

She snorts. "Why do you care?"

"I don't want you wasting your time on the kind of man who's willing to use you and leave you, especially since you're more sensitive about that stuff than you let on."

"Because that's so much worse than the guy who's always embarrassed to be seen with me, even though he knows better."

I clench my jaw tightly in lieu of answering her.

"Don't waste your energy worrying about me. I can handle myself. Besides, I could use a casual fling right about now, since I can't even remember the last time I've gotten laid," she says sarcastically.

"Yeah, well, you can't forbid me from worrying about you and say something like that in the same breath," I retort. "As your friend, I'm allowed to be concerned about your safety and your well-being. And your soul."

"Look who's back on his holier-than-thou bullshit," she grumbles, crossing her arms over her middle.

"I guess it's too bad you're stuck with me for the next couple of hours, *bestie*."

She growls, while my eyes instinctively graze the clock on my dash after I mention the time. I stifle a curse, and she winces at the sound of it.

"What now?" she asks defensively.

"I'm going to miss Mass this weekend," I say, gesturing to the time.

"How did you manage that?"

I shake my head. "I didn't go yesterday because I figured I'd make it back to Camellia before Sunday evening Mass. I guess I lost track of time, though."

"Oh," she says softly. "I'm sorry."

"It's not your fault. I've been slipping lately, in more ways than one," I reply, trying to curb my frustration. Regardless of our bickering a moment ago, I can't risk letting her think she shares any of the blame for my carelessness.

She clears her throat. "Just look for a church on the way home. I mean, if it's so important to you."

"I wouldn't want to put you out ..." I glance her way as I trail off.

She shrugs. "It's only, what, an hour?"

The tightness in my stomach begins to dissipate. "Don't your parents live around here? I could drop you off while I'm—"

"No, you'd have to backtrack. It's not worth the trouble," she cuts me off to say, and I make a mental note to bring it up later.

"Are you sure?" I ask and watch her expression carefully.

"It's not a big deal, Rowan. I'll just scroll on my phone while I wait in the car."

"Thanks," I say with a nod, but I'm already formulating a plan in my mind.

claire

"ACTUALLY, mind leaving the truck running while you're inside?" I ask when Rowan cuts off the engine.

"You're not coming in with me?" he gestures toward the church in front of us, and I can tell he's trying to pull one over on me by the way the corner of his mouth threatens to lift.

"Nice try," I tell him and hold out my palm, but he dangles the keys over my hand.

"Might have to crank it a few times to get the AC to stay on," he says, his dimples becoming more pronounced by the second. "Truck's getting old, you know."

"Are you really telling lies in the church parking lot now?"

"Of course not," he replies with exaggerated sincerity. "It's just that the air conditioner's been giving me trouble. I meant to get it fixed, but we've had such an abnormally cold winter that I haven't needed it lately."

"It doesn't matter. I can't go in there, especially not dressed like this," I protest, gesturing over my dirty overalls.

"Sure you can," he says, reaching over to tuck a stray hair behind my ear, and I hold my breath while his fingers graze the side of my neck. "You look ... beautiful. You always look beautiful."

I frown. "Lying *and* flirting? You're going to burst into flames the second you walk inside."

He bites his lip and stifles a smile. "Flirting isn't inherently sinful. And that's what the Holy Water is for, anyway, to wash away my venial sins."

"Which is exactly why I'm not going inside. I wouldn't have any idea what to do, and I'm going to look like a total idiot alongside all of the other perfect little Catholic girls with their pretty dresses and their modesty veils or whatever."

"You do realize you just described my sister, don't you?" he replies, and I growl in frustration, because he's right. Daisy is one of those perfect little Catholic girls, and she's still the best person I know, which makes me an ass right now.

"Seriously, though, we both know you've been to a Catholic church before and that you're well aware there will be plenty of women who won't be wearing dresses and veils," he says, his voice tinged with amusement. "And you don't even have to participate, but I'd be more than happy to show you what to do. In fact, it might even be the highlight of my life."

I pout. "Why do you want me to go with you so badly? You realize there won't be some miraculous conversion the minute I step inside, Holy Water or not."

"Maybe I just like having you around. And, sure, a miraculous conversion is unlikely, but I wouldn't rule it out completely," he muses and laughs when I let my head fall back with another groan.

"Please, Claire? Just this once ... *bestie*?" he adds, and he knows he has me up against the ropes after that.

"I can't believe I walked right into this," I grumble, grabbing my jacket from the back seat.

He beams at me before he hurries around to the other side and opens my door, and he seems completely undeterred by my side-eyed warning as he leads me forward with his hand on the small of my back. And I'm afraid this gesture means way more to him than I could have guessed.

I mime his actions when he dips a finger in Holy Water and

crosses himself, and again when he kneels before ushering me into the pew. I glance around, noticing all the variation in everyone's attire, and I honestly don't feel as out of place as predicted.

Rowan hands me an open missal to follow along and gives me a cue each time we transition from standing to kneeling or sitting, and I think I manage to blend in well enough.

There's plenty going on between the ringing bells and burning incense, especially with all the babies and children making themselves heard.

"So the kids stay the whole time?" I ask him at one point, and he nods and grins.

"Of course. Jesus is here—body, blood, soul, and divinity. We're all receiving grace from being in His presence," he replies, gesturing to the altar, and I make a mental list of additional questions to ask later.

Then Rowan leans over to whisper, "This is the best part," just before the priest lifts the host in the air and starts singing in Latin, and I can't help but smile at his all-around adorableness. And when he lingers a second too long after leaning in to kiss my cheek for the sign of peace, I have to bite my lip to keep myself from simpering like a silly teenage girl.

"What?" I ask when I catch him staring at me after he returns from communion.

"Nothing," he says, shaking his head and smirking, and I let out an exhale as I force my attention back to the gorgeous paintings in each section of the vaulted ceilings.

"Are you ... praying?" he whispers.

I scoff and elbow him. "You're not supposed to ask me something like that," I scold him, but he's still smiling. "But, no, I was just admiring the architecture."

He nods knowingly. "Sure you were."

I click my tongue, and he laughs softly.

"Were you praying for me by any chance?" he inclines his head to add quietly.

"No, but maybe I *should* pray for you ... to quit annoying me," I mumble.

"I pray for you, you know, every time I think of you. So, basically, all the time," he continues, and I swallow hard. I don't know why it makes my stomach dip, but it does.

"Aren't we supposed to be silent right now?" I return in a harsh whisper.

He grins. "Sorry. Do continue."

I roll my eyes again, and he stifles another laugh.

I'm starting to worry Rowan's face might crack by the time Mass ends and we make it back to his truck. And as much as I don't want to ruin this for him, I'm not sure I can take much more of his open adoration.

"Okay, what is your deal?" I demand after catching him staring for the umpteenth time today.

"Nothing," he repeats, and he continues gazing at me for a bit longer before he finally shakes his head and moves to crank the truck.

"Seriously, did I do something wrong back there?"

He shakes his head again. "No, it's just ... never mind."

"Now you have to tell me," I whine.

He releases a loud exhale before eying me carefully. "Fine. You were right before."

"About what?"

"I do like seeing you on your knees," he drawls, and my lips part in a gasp as a wave of heat runs through me.

"I can't believe you just said that!" I protest and shove him in the shoulder.

But that one-sided smirk makes another appearance. "I mean it. You're one of my favorite people, and I thoroughly enjoyed watching you participate in the Mass." He pauses to adjust his collar, and although the idea of him getting hot and bothered over something like this should be comical, it's admittedly having a similar effect on me.

"It might be one of the sexiest things I've ever seen, and that's saying a lot for you," he murmurs.

My jaw lowers again. "Isn't that sacrilegious?"

"Maybe if I were saying it to get into your pants, but that's not the case. I'm encouraging you to grow in holiness, because I care about your soul," he states with a more confident air. "It's not my fault that the incense and candlelight make everything seem more romantic."

I force another eye roll, but I can't help the way Self-Assured Rowan makes me squirm in my seat. "Sounds like you need to get laid more than I do."

His expression falls, but he doesn't say anything else once he redirects his attention onto the road.

"All right. Fine!" I blurt out after I can't take any more of his silence. "Maybe I didn't hate your precious Mass as much as I thought I would. And maybe I sort of get some of that redemptive suffering stuff you've been jabbering on about after hearing the part when Jesus offered up His body for all mankind or whatever."

He glances over at me, his face looking pained, and I watch his throat work as he swallows hard. "Are you *trying* to seduce me right now?" he asks after he seems to collect himself. "Because it's definitely working. Should I pull over?"

I groan and cover my face with my hands. "I used to think you were so different, but you're just as bad as all the other men, aren't you?"

"I do have the same programming," he replies with a laugh. "And the same hardware."

"You're like a MacBook. Your operating system is a little weird, you run a little cleaner, and you're less susceptible to viruses, but you're still just a slave to your hardwiring at the end of the day."

He shrugs. "I have been told I'm a dangerous man."

The look he gives me makes me shiver, and I reach out to mess with the AC vent, pretending to be cold when I'm actually burning up from the inside out.

"Yeah, well, you'd better watch yourself on that date. I'm not so easily bothered, but you're gonna scare Little Miss Perfect away. Wait a few weeks, you know, for your wedding night, before you spring all that dirty talk on her."

His shoulders droop, and guilt settles in my stomach again. The guy just said he spends the majority of his time thinking of me and praying for me, and I repay him by teasing him about his most deeply held convictions. But I'm not doing him any favors by encouraging him to flirt with me or letting him think that he can turn me into the woman he's been holding out for, either.

"Right," he says on an exhale. "It's probably bad luck to melt her panties on the first night."

The rest of our drive is too quiet, and I clear my throat to apologize again when I can't take the silent treatment any longer. "I'm sorry. I just don't want you to miss out on meeting your soulmate, especially not on my account."

"And once I find her, you won't stand in my way?" he asks as he pulls into my driveway.

My jaw lowers, and my head rears back. "Of course not."

He huffs out a sardonic laugh. "Do you promise?"

"I want you to be happy, Rowan," I say, scoffing. "I can't believe you think I'd do anything to keep you from ..."

But I don't bother finishing when I realize what he means, *the sneaky son of a—*

"Good to know," he drawls, interrupting my thoughts.

His laughter softens while I growl and struggle to unbuckle my seat belt, and he repays my scowl with a smile when he gets out to walk me to my door.

"Good night, Claire Bear. Thanks again for your services today."

"I did it for Gertie and Giles," I reply and unlock the front door, grunting after my dogs bypass me and run straight out to Rowan.

He ignores me and stoops down to pet them. "Pick you up early on Easter Sunday? Or should I just stay over that Saturday night so we can go to the vigil Mass together?"

"I can drive myself," I retort.

"And what will my mama think?" he poses, grinning.

I roll my eyes. "Go home, Rowan."

"Fine. I'll text you when I make it back. You know, in case the Holy Spirit moves you and you want to pray for my safety," he says with a wink.

rowan

MY BROTHER-IN-LAW SINKS ANOTHER PUTT, making Blake and JD groan in unison as he returns to save his club with a smug look on his face.

"Is this what playing football with me felt like for everyone else?" JD asks, patting his mid-section. "I mean, back when I was in better shape."

Blake snorts. "Pretty much."

Landry's cocky smirk grows wider. "That might be the most satisfying and vindicating thing I've ever heard," he begins, pausing before adding, "Coming from another man, anyway."

"We should hug it out," JD turns and takes a step in Landry's direction with outstretched arms, and Blake guffaws loudly when Landry picks up his club again.

"Touch me and I'll tee off on the nearest balls I can find, Golden Boy," Landry growls.

"Aw, and I thought you'd softened up since Daisy dusted off the old driver," JD muses, barely able to keep himself from laughing.

Landry shoots me an apologetic look before addressing JD again. "Not that soft."

"All right, all right, I'm sorry," JD says with his hands lifted. "I'm only kidding, but I'll cut you some slack in front of your brother-in-law."

"Oh, please, don't take it easy on him on my account. I've already been desensitized after staying over at their house so often. Now I'm just grateful my sister doesn't seem to mind keeping old Doc Reed in a good mood," I offer dryly.

JD and Blake laugh again, and Landry glares angrily in my direction this time. "Hey, you're supposed to take my side any time I'm up against a Bourgeois brother. That's the rule," Landry says, and I press my lips together to stifle a laugh at his serious tone. "Besides, you've been so far up Claire's ass when you come to town that I barely see you anymore."

He crosses his arms in satisfaction after making his point, and I frown at the Bourgeois brothers' chorus of "oohs."

"Now, girls. Remember, we're all friends here," Blake declares as he digs through his own bag to retrieve a putter.

"There's more space at Claire's house ... and less chance of walking in on someone making a baby," I grumble in my defense.

"And whose fault is that?" Landry retorts sarcastically.

The image of Claire in her pajamas flashes through my mind, and my frown transforms into a pout. "I don't say this often, but sometimes doing the right thing really, *really* freaking sucks."

"Ain't that the truth," Blake confirms before going over to his ball.

JD clicks his tongue. "A couple months of abstinence, and this kid thinks he's a saint."

"It was ten months, most of it spent living alongside the love of my life, also known as the sexiest woman alive, thank you," he replies and refocuses his efforts on his putt, cursing under his breath when he misses.

"Yeah, well, try thirty-three years," I mutter, and their heads swivel in my direction.

JD narrows his eyes at me. "Are you saying what I think you're saying?"

I sigh, figuring I might as well come clean now. "Yeah. Except I nearly ruined my streak a few months ago ... the night I met Claire."

Landry coughs over a laugh, and I shoot him an indignant glare of my own. "What? You're the one voluntarily spilling your guts to douchebag and douchebag junior," he reminds me.

"Hey, it's douchebag the *third*," JD corrects him with a smile. "And I'm not judging him either way. I'd already been celibate for a couple of years when Tenley and I got together, and we kept it that way until we tied the knot."

I lift my brow in surprise.

"Yeah, right. That's rich coming from the guy who's always cracking jokes about his sex life," Landry interjects.

"So my wife and I enjoy partaking in the sacraments, particularly the renewal of our marital vows," JD says with an unapologetic shrug. "There's nothing wrong with that."

"But what makes you think the rest of us want to hear about it, particularly your kid?" Landry fires back.

JD crosses his arms and stares Landry down. "First of all, you ought to know by now that we're all just competing to see who can get under your skin the fastest by oversharing."

Landry aims an incredulous look at Blake, and I barely manage to stifle a laugh. "Come on, man. That's Lo's thing, being purposefully crude in front of you," Blake adds matter-of-factly, and Landry lets out a defeated grunt.

"Second of all," JD picks up where he left off, "whether you believe me or not, one of the biggest reasons Ten and I chose to wait was to set a good example for Ethan. Despite feeling totally unequipped for the job most days, it's still my responsibility to teach him about sex and every other uncomfortable topic. Tenley and I want him to get the right message, but it's not easy with the rest of the world telling him he deserves instant gratification. The only way we can compete is by reinforcing the idea that it's better and more fulfilling within the right context. And I can't promote marital intimacy without bringing it up every so often."

I have to admire JD's confidence. He believes he's doing the right thing, regardless of his motivation, and he's less bothered by someone questioning his follow-through than his reasoning. I thought I shared the same convictions before, but maybe I've forgotten the point of all this ... *waiting*. Sure, avoiding sin is important, but I haven't exactly been treating sex the way JD's describing it, the way I explained it to Claire a while back.

I know the purpose is to offer myself to my spouse in the same way Christ did for mankind, freely and completely, but I haven't been *acting* like I know that. Instead, I've been afraid to grow, trying to bypass temptation instead of getting better at resisting it. Which means I've been holding back with Claire because I'm too much of a coward to face my attraction head on.

It's no wonder she can't bring herself to trust me with her heart when I've been too scared to give away my own.

"Plus, we've already learned not to take ourselves too seriously," JD adds. "I mean, Ethan's seventeen years old, and he obviously understands what's going on. So I might as well turn the awkward moments into either laughable or teachable ones."

"Yeah, well, what's your excuse?" Landry turns to Blake after stewing over JD's answer and probably realizing it makes too much sense.

"We all know my sense of humor rarely makes it out of the gutter. But also, my wife likes being reminded that she's irresistible, and she especially likes it when I declare that I'm happily detained in front of everyone else. And I like what she likes," Blake replies smoothly.

He's got a point, too. But the way I've been acting so hot and cold toward Claire while I'm struggling to overcome temptation has left her believing it's my attraction to her that bothers me and not my weakness in general.

"Listen, boys," Blake begins again when he sees us looking thoughtful. "Women need a lot of reinforcement. They don't compartmentalize shit the way we do. It's all connected for them, so they start to question how much we love them as soon as there's a small argument or we come home in a bad mood after a crappy day at work. It's important that we give them that reassurance, not only of our love and loyalty, but of our physical attraction to them. I tried going easy on that last part before, thinking I was being respectful. Turns out, it made Loren doubt how much I wanted her. You gotta find that balance, the sweet spot between 'I love you more than life itself' and 'I'm constantly thinking about you naked.' And make sure she knows there's nothing you wouldn't do to make her feel good."

JD clears his throat, and I laugh to myself when Blake adds, "As long as it's both unitive and procreative, of course."

"Sorry, I stopped listening when you mentioned thinking about my sister naked," Landry mutters under his breath.

"That's rich coming from the Big Bad Wolf himself," I reply, and Landry's eyes widen.

"How'd you know about that?" he asks quickly.

"There's a reason I run off to Claire's all the time. You have very thin walls, man," I say with a grimace. "And I don't even want to know why the shower's been covered in body hair lately."

"Whoa, whoa, whoa," Blake chimes in. "Have we just learned that Landry Reed is an undercover freak?"

"Unlike some of you, I don't feel the need to share the details of my love life with the class," Landry grinds out, his eyes narrowed at Blake. Meanwhile JD's face reddens with the effort it's taking him not to laugh.

"Bull," I call him out under the guise of a fake cough. Landry looks betrayed, but I continue, anyway. "You and Daisy both don't seem to mind rubbing your wedded bliss in my face. Not to mention, Claire's going to feel like crap when she hears about how you're trying to …"

I let the rest of that statement hang in the air once I realize what I've done.

"What do you mean by that?" Landry asks quietly.

I cringe and rub a hand over my face. "Forget it."

"We both know that doesn't work with me," he replies.

Even though I know he's right, I still hesitate to divulge the rest, especially in front of the others.

"Daisy already told me you were trying for a baby, but I'm

worried about how Claire's going to take the news. She's had some fertility-related issues in the past, so it's a sensitive topic for her. But it doesn't mean we're not happy for you guys or we won't be hoping and praying it goes well for you. It's just hard not to feel sorry for ourselves, I guess."

Landry nods. "I'm sorry, man."

"Don't be. You didn't know," I reassure him with a pat on the shoulder.

"Daisy must not know, either. I'll mention it to her, so we can be more mindful around Claire," he promises, and I can't be the only one impressed this time.

"You know what would make everyone feel better?" JD interrupts.

"You're not getting that hug, bro," Blake declares, and even Landry laughs.

"Hold on, though," Blake begins again. "You mentioned the *night you met* Claire earlier. Does that mean you just decided to hook up with a random stranger after all that time? Were you purposefully trying to lose your virginity?"

I look away and scratch my head. "I'd still been planning to stay celibate until marriage. But there were some circumstances that led me to believe we'd shared a special connection, despite being strangers."

"And you figured you wouldn't have to face your guilt, since you didn't think you'd ever see her again, right?"

"Except it turns out that the stranger was one of my sister's best friends, and now we're all ... *friends*," I confirm.

"Almost as awkward as that time we ran into one another in an exam room ..." Blake trails off and grins.

"Much, much worse," I say through my teeth.

"That's not even the best part." Landry surprises me by brushing over Blake's comment and nudging me to continue.

I heave out a sigh. "The only reason I didn't actually sleep with Claire that night was because I found out that her divorce hadn't been finalized yet."

"Oof," the other guys say in unison.

"Not that, the other stuff," Landry says.

"Oh, yeah. Thanks for the reminder," I add sarcastically. "I failed to tell her about my policies regarding physical intimacy at first, so I sort of made it hard for her to trust me again."

JD and Blake flinch at the same time. "I guess that's why you haven't upgraded to more than friends now that her divorce is over and done," JD remarks.

I lick my lips before I go over for my own turn to putt. "Pretty much. She claims she's not up for a serious relationship, even though I think she really does want marriage and kids. But I'll never convince her to give me a real chance, not after everything she's been through and all the ways I've screwed up."

They're quiet as I aim and tap the ball in. If only the rest of my life were this easy to control.

"So you're just giving up, then?" JD asks after a while.

"Am I supposed to keep begging her to love me back and hope she eventually changes her mind?" I grumble, but my dad's advice comes to mind.

"If *you* love her then, yeah. That's how it works," he replies, and Blake nods as well.

I look at Landry questioningly, and he sighs. "If you think there's a chance she's only holding out because she's unsure about whether she can trust you, then you just gotta hang in there and keep reminding her how you feel, like Blake said." He adds a shrug. "Daisy loved me enough to stick it out until I got over my shit, just like these guys did with their wives. Maybe Claire needs more time to see that you're willing to help her work through some stuff and that you're not giving up or going anywhere until she's ready. If that's what you want, I mean."

Is that what I want?

I'm certain God has His reasons for bringing us together. I'm also pretty sure I'm in love with Claire, and a large part of me believes we really could've been soulmates, if only I'd done a better job of showing her all that from the beginning.

But maybe this is how I make up for getting off to the wrong start and allowing my pride to get in the way for so long. Because now that I think about it, I can't imagine feeling this way with anyone else, and I don't even want to consider marriage or babies or any version of the future unless Claire is at the center of it all.

Landry stands by with his brow furrowed, looking deep in thought. "This might be insensitive, too, but I'm kind of a dick, so I'm just going to say it. You don't think Claire's afraid of letting you down?"

"What do you mean?" I ask.

"If she's struggled with infertility before, she's not going to let you take a chance on her, not when you've made it clear how badly you want kids," he explains.

My jaw lowers. "I mean, yeah, she knows I want a big family, but I've told her I'd be okay with ..."

Maybe I haven't said that to Claire explicitly, not in so many words.

"Being okay with something sounds like settling," Landry says. "And you never want to see the person you care about most settle for less than they deserve."

"Well, shit—I mean, shoot." I've really got to get a handle on my language these days.

JD raises his hand before he speaks again. "He makes a good point, even for a dick. This actually sounds a lot like the mental roadblock Tenley had to get over before she could admit she wanted a future together."

I narrow my eyes at JD, because I can't picture Tenley lacking the confidence to start a family. "Didn't she get pregnant right away, though?"

"She did, but it wasn't her ability to conceive that was in question. Ten's stuff was all related to what happens after the babies are born, ironically enough," JD explains with a shrug.

"Technically, Lo's insecurities were mostly my fault in the first place," Blake volunteers. "After all the times she shut me down in high school, I spent the next decade—well, we all know what I was doing," he admits, looking surprisingly sheepish. "Anyway, by the time I finally got her to give me a shot, I screwed it all up by doing things out of order and basically tapping into her biggest fear, which was becoming her mother. No offense, Lando."

Landry snorts. "Let's not get started with the ya-mama jokes."

Blake laughs quietly. "Mommy issues aside, I should have known better. And I deserved every minute of torture Loren put me through before I was finally able to earn her trust."

"Tell the truth. You like it when she makes you suffer." JD elbows his brother.

Blake hums. "Damn right, I do."

It reminds me of the night I met Claire, and then again when her face filled my mind the moment I wished for something like Blake and Loren have. I've already acknowledged that bickering with her is the most fun I've ever had. But I think I'd rather join Oscar and Frankie and follow her around like a lovesick puppy than chase after what I used to think I was supposed to have with someone else.

"Okay, so how do I fix it?" I blurt out. "I can't just tell her I'm in love with her without freaking her out. Every time I so much as hint around about my true feelings, she panics and reinforces our boundaries."

"You never know. She might surprise you and say all she needed was for you to tell her the truth and make her feel safe enough to do the same," Landry replies, and the others agree.

"Maybe that's it," I whisper to myself, recalling the ways I've hurt her by walking away or withholding the truth. "I haven't been honest enough with her. I keep leaving just enough room for her to doubt me."

"Yeah, well, until you convince her to change her last name again, don't forget to leave enough space for the Holy Spirit," JD leans over my shoulder to add, and I shove him away, unable to hold back my laughter. "For real, though. You could always try showing her what she's missing."

"What she's missing?" I repeat.

JD shrugs. "Make her see you'd be a better husband than the last guy. Show her all the ways you'd support her, how you'd make her life easier by lightening some of her burdens. Surprise her by doing the yard work or washing the dishes ... preferably without a shirt. Listen to her vent about work and take her side, even if she's in the wrong."

"Stop by unexpectedly with her favorite candy, especially if she's having a bad day," Blake adds. "And remind her that she's sexy when you know she's feeling her worst."

"Take care of something for her. It doesn't have to be anything big, just say, 'I'll handle it.' And then make sure it gets done," Landry offers.

JD snaps his fingers. "Oh, communicate with her," he says, as if it's the most genius thought he's ever had, and the others grunt in appreciation.

"But overdo it. Text her for no good reason at all. Pretend you're confirming plans, even if you remember. They go crazy for that shit," Blake affirms.

"He's right," Landry says on a sigh. "The more I talk about my feelings, the more I get to play Big Bad Wolf."

I roll my eyes. "Claire doesn't like talking about her feelings."

"Wrong," JD says, imitating a gameshow buzzer. "She's only holding out because she needs it to be a two-way conversation."

And to think I've been going around assuming I was ready for marriage all this time. I let out a long exhale and scratch the back of my head.

"I guess I've been doing some of those things, but obviously not well enough for her to take me seriously," I admit.

"Probably because you're afraid to let yourself fall for her completely, since you know it'll make it that much harder to resist her," Landry volunteers insightfully.

"And we have a winner," I say in my own gameshow host impression.

Blake hums. "How often have you been going to confession?"

I swallow hard. I'd gotten myself back to reconciliation a couple of times since that first night with Claire, but I hadn't been embracing the sacrament the way I used to.

"Not often enough," I mumble.

"Dirty truck?" Blake asks, nudging his brother.

"Dirty truck," JD agrees before he turns to face me. "So imagine you're driving down the road on the way back from washing your truck, and you see a huge mud puddle in the road. You're gonna swerve, right, because you want to keep your truck clean?"

He pauses for me to nod. "But let's say it's been raining all week, and your truck's already filthy. What's the use in dodging the mud, especially when you know it'll be more fun to drive through it?"

"Yeah." I purse my lips as I consider the metaphor. "I get it."

"It's a lot easier to keep your soul clean than it is to stop yourself from sliding back into the pit when you're already dirty," Blake confirms.

"Besides, we can't overcome sin on our own. Jesus didn't die on that cross so we could fool ourselves into thinking we're strong enough to withstand temptation or that He's not waiting for us to ask for His help," JD reminds us. "Even the little voice that pops up when we're in the middle of something we know damned well we shouldn't be doing isn't enough, because we're not meant to do it all on our own. He *wants* us to come to Him."

I blow out a breath as I consider how badly I've been failing at that last part in particular.

Landry grunts. "That's deep, Golden Boy, especially for you."

"Nice job, *Padre*. I think that was your best sermon yet," Blake confirms, smacking JD on the backside as if he'd just caught a touchdown pass instead.

"I think we've given you plenty to think about, right, Doc?" Blake directs the question at me.

"Yeah, thanks," I say, my mind still reeling. I may not have expected to get this much wisdom from what I'd have considered to be the smoking section, but that's what I get for counting these guys out, I suppose.

"Partake in the sacraments as often as you can, my guy. You're gonna need the extra grace," JD reminds me with a wink. "And in the meantime, if all else fails, you can always try making her jealous."

1:45 PM

CLAIRE

Hey, are you still coming over tonight so we can go to the homestead tomorrow?

ROWAN

I'm afraid I might not get there until later tonight. I'm sorry.

Can I pick you up in the morning?

CLAIRE

Is everything okay?

ROWAN

Yeah, great, it's just that I got set up at the last second. And you know how these things go … It's different with every woman. I don't want to mess up your evening if she ends up taking all night.

CLAIRE

Oh, well … nbd. I'll just be hanging out. And you know the code if you want to let yourself in after I go to bed.

ROWAN

Thanks, I'll see you later, then. Wish me luck!

CLAIRE

Yeah, of course, good luck!

So, how's the date going? Have you picked out your wedding invitations and baby names yet?

Have you kissed her? Are you making out rn?

You haven't replied, so I'm taking it as a good sign. I hope she's every bit as amazing as you are.

But just in case you need a confidence boost, allow me to remind you that you are a really, really good kisser. Don't second-guess yourself, dude. Close the deal.

And by close the deal, I don't mean ask her to marry you.

Okay, I'll leave you alone now. As long as you promise to wake me up when you get here and tell me all about it.

claire

I LEAP from the couch and bolt to the window the second I hear tires crunching over the gravel driveway.

"It's him," I announce to Oscar and Frankie when I see Rowan through the blinds. He's smiling to himself as he goes into the back seat for his overnight bag, and I feel my shoulders drooping. "I shouldn't be this sad because he had a good time, should I?" I turn to ask my dogs.

Oscar yips and wags his tail, and Frankie's tongue flops out as he pants and vibrates with excitement. I sigh, because the sight of Rowan makes me lose control of my tongue, too.

He makes it to the front door faster than I expect, and I scramble to fix the blinds and return to my place on the sofa when I hear him unlocking the door.

"Hey," he greets me warmly while I adjust my position and try to look aloof.

"Oh, hey. You're back," I say, keeping my tone even. I yawn and toss the remote away as if I've just been surfing through the channels. "I guess your date went well?"

He shrugs and crouches down to pet the dogs. "What makes you think that?"

"Well, you're smiling for starters. And you never checked any of my texts, so you must have been enjoying her company."

His lips lift higher on one side, making him look more smug than smitten. "Maybe I'm just amused because I caught you peeking at me through the blinds. It's almost as if you've been waiting for me to come home."

I ignore the way he's referring to my house as "home" in lieu of watching him take off his jacket.

"Are you wearing scrubs?" I blurt out. Because *holy shit* does he look hot.

"Yes, and I did read your texts, but I couldn't exactly make her wait on me while I stopped to answer you."

"Duh," I say, scoffing. "And that wasn't even me in the window, just so you know. It was Oscar," I lie, pointing to the disordered blinds.

He purses his lips. "So ... Oscar's the one who's jealous of my big date?"

I gulp and look away as he moves to sit next to me, tightening my robe over one of my more risqué pajama sets, a decision which feels pretty silly right now.

"Oh, yeah. Look at him. The poor little guy's been green with envy," I say. Oscar takes his cue to waddle over and push his paws into Rowan's shins.

"Those blinds seem pretty high for legs this stubby. Just sayin'," Rowan drawls while he gives Oscar another affectionate ear rub.

"Pointing out his flaws isn't going to make him feel any better. Especially since your date probably had better legs."

"If that were the case, he'd definitely be more envious of you."

I let out a defeated exhale and ignore his flirty tone. "Fine. I may have been a little anxious to hear from you. Not because I'm jealous or anything, though."

"Sure you're not," he replies, still smirking.

"So?" I ask after he doesn't say more. "Aren't you going to tell me how it went?"

He chuckles. "I don't know. I kind of like torturing you."

I shove him playfully. "Are you getting married next month or what?"

"Is that a proposal?" he asks, lifting an eyebrow. I growl and push at his chest again, and he laughs. "Nah, tell Oscar I'm his for a little longer."

An embarrassingly telling sense of relief floods my chest, and I bite my lip in an effort to keep my reaction neutral. "Oh, well, I'm sorry it didn't work out."

He shrugs, his expression still oddly buoyant.

"What happened?" I ask, pulling my knees up to wrap my arms around them and already feeling guilty for secretly hoping she wasn't the love of his life.

"Well, Tenley had introduced me to Gianna a few weeks ago—"

"Wait, I thought your date's name was Cecelia?" I furrow my brow in confusion.

He shakes his head. "I told you, I had no intentions of letting Heath set me up."

"But ... Cecelia's perfect for you," I protest.

"No, she's not," he says plainly.

"You don't know that unless you at least give her a shot."

Why am I defending this chick again?

He chuckles softly. "I *do* know that, because I *have* given her a shot before."

"Wait, what?"

"Cecelia and I went on a date about a year ago. She's Marigold's husband's cousin, and they insisted on setting us up. So I took her on a brunch date after Mass one Sunday, kissed her at the end of it and everything," he explains, still looking completely nonplussed.

"Oh." I may have joked about it earlier, but I'm too breathless at the thought of him kissing another woman to say anything else right away, especially since it all sounds so idyllic, so *Rowan*.

"Did it not go well?" I ask cautiously once I've gotten my shit together again.

"She was nice, but there wasn't ..." He shakes his head as he trails off. "It just wasn't there. I mean, we agreed that we were probably compatible enough to make do, but Cecelia was actually the one who said neither of us should be settling for *nice*."

"That makes sense," I reply when he looks at me as if he wants my reassurance.

"I left the date feeling disappointed, but she was right. The old me might have been perfectly satisfied with *nice*, had I never ..." He leaves his gaze locked onto mine as he lets me fill in the blanks, and my stomach dips.

"I never imagined chemistry would be so important to me until I actually felt it." He swallows hard, and my cheeks heat as I watch his throat work. "But now, I don't think I'll be able to settle for anything less."

"And ... what about Gianna?" I ask breathlessly.

A grin spreads across his face. "I didn't actually go out with Gianna, but I did meet a real beauty named Adele."

"What?" I practically shriek and throw a pillow at him. "Athanasius Rowan, how many girls are you stringing along at the same time?"

He tosses his head back and laughs, looking more like me this time, and Oscar and Frankie yip along with him.

"Adele is the baby girl I helped deliver tonight," he says, gesturing over his scrubs. "And Gianna is her mother. She and her husband Jonas wanted a VBAC, so Tenley asked me to be on standby in case she'd end up needing an emergency C-section. It's been a while since I attended a delivery, but thankfully, everything went well. I actually enjoyed it more than I expected."

"Oh," I say again. "That's great. But ... you didn't go on any actual dates tonight?"

He shakes his head, smiling ruefully. "No. I don't need to go out looking for what I've already found."

"But aren't you still worried about confusing lust with chemistry?" I barely manage to say. As much as I enjoy being wanted by him, I can't bear the thought of being the reason he passes up his best chance at getting the family he's been longing for.

He frowns. "I'd be lying if I said I was immune to lust, particularly when it comes to you. But I know the difference now."

So why is he still looking at me like he wants to do very, very lust-driven things together?

If I'm being honest, the line between wanting Rowan to fill the hole in my heart and the space in my bed has gotten pretty damned blurry for me, as well.

He sighs and taps on his smart watch when I don't reply right away, then flips his wrist to show me his resting heart rate. "See this? Normal, right?"

I nod hesitantly, and he switches to show a graph outlining the past few hours.

"No spikes, not even during that delivery," he tells me, as if he's proving his point.

"Okay, so your heart is healthy?"

This time he growls in frustration and scoots closer as he reaches out to grab my hand. "Here," he says, crushing my palm against his chest. "Feel that?"

His heart thumps within his solid chest, and my own pulse quickens from the contact. He turns his forearm to show me his BPM steadily climbing while mine follows suit.

"Now kiss me," he demands, and my eyes fly up to his.

"What?" I squeak.

"On the cheek. It doesn't matter. I just need to feel your lips on my skin."

But we don't need to continue with this demonstration to confirm his hypothesis. His breathing sounding more labored by the second, and I haven't even agreed to anything yet. My own chest rises and falls as I watch him get all worked up over the prospect of a cheek kiss from me, and it's so freaking hot that I couldn't stop myself from following through with it, even if I wanted to.

I lean up and shift my weight onto my knees, both of us keeping our eyes trained on his watch as I brush my lips over his cheekbone. There's a full-second delay before the numbers spike.

"See what I mean? If this is all it takes from you ..." he begins, his voice gravelly.

He's probably assuming I'll back away now that he's made his point. However, I'm already tracing a path over his jawline, watching his breathing grow more ragged as his short stubble scrapes my lips in the most delicious way.

He doesn't move to stop me as I continue down his neck. My nose grazes his pulse point before I place an open-mouthed kiss over the spot. The artery throbs beneath his skin and tickles my tongue, as does the moan reverberating from deep within his throat. I don't have to look at his watch to know what I'm doing to him now.

"Claire," he says my name on a gasp. "You're gonna give me a heart attack."

"Can you really get a heart attack from all your blood pooling in one extremity?" I ask with a short laugh.

"A stroke, then," he grunts in confirmation.

"Hmm, last I checked that's not exactly a fatal condition, Doc," I pose in a sultry tone.

He whimpers when I go back to kissing down his neck. "It certainly feels like I'm dying," he declares. "Although, I can think of worse ways to go."

I smile, and he tilts his head to give me better access as he brings his hand around to cradle my back, silently pleading for me to continue.

"There are a few life-saving measures I'd be willing to perform on you before it came to that. With your consent, of course," I mumble against his skin, and he groans. "I could put an end to our suffering right now. All you'd have to do is ask. Better yet, make it a direct order." I add a gentle nip at his jaw to make my intentions clear.

"You know we can't," he chokes out at the same time he fists his hand in the back of my shirt and pulls me in, guiding me as I climb into his lap. He may be saying no, but the way his body keeps betraying him speaks volumes.

"But if you didn't want this, why'd you make me kiss you? Why tease me and make me so jealous?" I ask, staring down at him.

He shakes his head. "I'm sorry, I didn't mean to ... to go this far."

I watch his throat work again as he struggles with himself, and it's a reminder that I care too much to coax him into doing something he'd regret. But my stupid ego requires me to crack at least one more inappropriate joke in order to bounce back from his rejection.

"You'd be less sorry if you took off your pants," I add to lighten the mood and smile when he snorts out a laugh.

He gazes up at me adoringly while he strokes my back, making me even more desperate to keep this going. "Were you really jealous?" he asks, surprising me with his forwardness.

I narrow my eyes and deliberately roll my hips over him as punishment for making me think about my feelings, and he whines again.

"Okay, okay," he concedes, squirming beneath me. "You win."

"Does that mean I get to name my prize?" This time I lean down so that my lips nearly graze over his, pulling back and smiling in satisfaction when he tips his chin up to meet me.

"Please don't tempt me, Claire," he rasps, melting away the resolve I'd just built up. "I'm so weak."

I sigh in defeat and rest my forehead against his. "So am I. And I kind of hate the idea of you kissing anyone else," I admit against my better judgment.

He straightens his posture as his brows draw in tightly. "You do?"

"Yes." I cringe.

"What are you going to do about it?" he asks, his expression still strained.

His dare sends a wave of heat through me, but I remind myself that he's just going to keep toying with me as long as I let him. He won't allow himself to make another move, no matter how badly he wants this.

"Whatever it is, I should probably make you beg for it," I reply coyly, testing his resolve.

Rowan licks his lips, bringing my attention back to his mouth. "I know I haven't earned it, but maybe just ... one kiss? To remind me what it's supposed to feel like ... *please*?"

claire

THE HOARSE *please* Rowan adds to his request nearly does me in, and I nod eagerly, not even caring how desperate I've become. I cup my palms around his jaw and kiss him so hard our teeth clink together. His right hand entangles within my hair as his tongue slips into my mouth, accidentally yanking a few strands free from my braid as he urges me closer with another hand on my lower back.

And I don't know how I've managed to resist him for this long, because kissing Rowan is even better than I remembered. I grasp desperately at his short hair, and then at his shirt, trying anything and everything I can to get closer to him.

Besides stretching that single kiss into a twenty-minute make-out session, we keep to our word, relishing in one another but never venturing beneath our clothes, despite how easy it would be with his scrubs and my practically indecent PJs.

He growls when we finally break apart, both of us breathing hard and struggling to keep ourselves from going in for more as he holds out his wrist.

"See … what you do … to me," he barely gets out and gestures to the wonky line graph. But I admittedly can't be bothered with anything else so long as his lips are still looking so irresistibly swollen.

"You *were* sort of asking for it," I reply with a giggle, pleased with my work. Truthfully, I can't remember kissing ever being this much fun, even when I was a teenager. Keeping my clothes on with Rowan is still infinitely hotter than actually having sex with anyone else.

I sigh when he nods and smiles at me, and it makes me feel like I'm floating. How is this all it takes from him to leave me in the same lazy, drunken state that I'd only have imagined was possible after a much more intimate act?

"Now do you believe me when I say I understand the difference between lust and love?" he muses, reaching up to push a strand of hair from my face.

The words are like a record scratch, popping my bubble and sending me plummeting back down to earth.

Even though he's agreeing with the point *I* made earlier, I find myself shrinking in. Hearing another reminder that he's only attracted to me against his better judgment hurts more than I expected, especially since I don't have much more to offer him.

"Yeah," I croak out, pushing off his chest to rise to my feet. "I guess you're capable of more than I thought."

He looks up at me with concern. "Did I ... have I said something wrong?"

I shake my head and point to his watch. "I just realized it's getting late. Your family's expecting us before lunch tomorrow, and you probably need to shower."

"Right," he says softly. "Sorry for keeping you up."

"It was fun while it lasted," I return dryly.

"I can, um, get the dogs if you want to turn in now." His eyelashes flutter, and I can see the mixture of regret and confusion in his expression.

"Thanks."

He sighs and runs a hand through his hair. "Good night, Claire."

"Good night. Sorry your evening turned out to be so ... disappointing," I mutter before ambling down the hallway to my bedroom.

I'd already been half-expecting to cry myself to sleep tonight, back when I was worried about Rowan meeting his actual soulmate, so I'm not surprised by the warm tears streaming down my face as I turn to shut the door behind me. I'd also predicted our connection would end up holding him back and keeping him from finding something real with anyone else, even before it happened. But the one thing I hadn't anticipated was the bruised heart I'd be nursing after hearing him confirm there was only ever lust and physical attraction between us after all.

A sob bubbles up from my chest, and I cover my mouth to quiet it. Why am I like this? What is wrong with me? Why can't I just admit how badly I want him?

Because I can't have him, that's why.

I growl in frustration and swipe at my cheeks, because I only have myself to blame. I can't keep playing this game with him, encouraging him one minute and pushing him away the next, then pulling him in deeper and deeper until he's become an irreplaceable fixture in my life. It's not fair to either of us, not when I know there's no future for us together.

A knock at the door startles me. "Claire?" Rowan calls out.

"Yeah?" I reply, trying to hide my sniffling.

"Are you sure everything's okay?" he asks.

I clear my throat. "I'm fine, really. Just tired."

The sound of shuffling and a soft thud emanate from the other side of the door. I turn and slide down to the floor, letting my head fall back with a thump of my own.

"I can tell when you're lying to me, you know," he says after a while.

My heart melts a little, and I can't help but smile. "Okay. I'm not fine."

"Wanna tell me why you're so upset?"

"Not really."

"Is it because I crossed a line when I asked you to participate in my demonstration?" he asks carefully.

"I don't know. Maybe."

"I'm sorry. I shouldn't have done that." He's quiet for a second before adding, "I was looking for a loophole, and it was selfish of me."

I scoff. "I'm just as much to blame for what happened tonight as you are. But yeah, I guess it could have messed with my head a little."

There I go again, being entirely too honest and vulnerable with him only seconds after resolving to reinforce my walls.

"Is it because of everything that happened the night we met? Because if so, you should know that I have no intention of leaving again. Not unless you ask me to, anyway."

"No. That's not it." But he's definitely getting warmer.

"Does it have anything to do with the part when I mentioned the L-word?"

I sigh. "Maybe. I guess it's just been so long since I had to navigate dating and friendships, and I hate not knowing what I'm doing."

"Are we still in the second category?" he ventures.

"Friends?"

"Yeah."

I shrug even though he can't see me. "Why wouldn't we be?"

"Because I'm lame and desperate, and I can't just kiss my best friend like that without hoping it means something more," he admits quietly, and I smile again.

I barely resist reassuring him that those feelings aren't one-sided, but only because it's for his own good. "Well, since nothing else has changed, it's probably best if we don't read too much into it and just forget it ever happened. Don't you think?"

"What if I respectfully disagree?"

My stomach flutters. "What do you mean?"

"What if I were willing to compromise on some of that long-term stuff, at least for now? Think you'd be able to meet me in the middle?"

"I'm not going to be the reason you don't get your happily ever after," I tell him, shaking my head.

There's another thud. "But what if you *are* my happily ever after?"

I bring my hand up again when my chin begins trembling. "I can't be."

"Can't ... or won't?"

"Both," I reply, my voice cracking.

"Claire, you know I don't care that you're not Catholic or that you've been married before, right? Of course, I'd love nothing more than to share my faith with you, but those things aren't dealbreakers for me."

"Maybe not in theory, but they're dealbreakers in practice," I say with a sniffle.

"Because I won't sleep with you?"

I squint against the stinging in my eyes. "You know that's not it."

He groans. "Then can we please talk about this face-to-face?"

"No," I say quickly. "If I let you in here, one of us is going to end up breaking some kind of deal."

"It's not helping your case when you're the one to point out it's safer if you don't let me into your bedroom."

"Or my heart," I accidentally say out loud, and he whimpers.

"It's too late for that. At least, it is for me."

"Come on, Rowan, you can't really believe God would lead you to someone like me, and I can't let you give up everything that's most important to you. Let's face it—if we were meant to be, this would all be easier."

"Maybe it would have been easy if we hadn't skipped all the important steps in the beginning and tried to go straight to the finish line," he grumbles.

What if he's right? What if our story had gone differently? What if I'd have just put him up in his own hotel room instead of bringing him back to mine? Would we have met up for coffee in the morning and started dating like a normal couple? Would we still have fallen for one another? Would he have even gone through the trouble of tracking me down later or approaching me at his sister's wedding?

No. He wouldn't have. Because I'm not what he's looking for.

It doesn't matter, anyway, because that's not how it went. And at the end of the day, I'm still a hot mess—broken, divorced, infertile— and I can't give him any of the things he's been working for his whole life.

At the same time, he may be all I have right now, and I'm just a little too selfish and much too lonely to let him go.

I cringe at the ache in my chest as soon as I consider a future completely devoid of him. I need Rowan in my life in some way, even if we have to settle for something platonic. So I'll just have to be on my best behavior from here on out.

"But at least this way we became friends, right?" I offer after a while.

"Yeah," he replies, his voice cracking suspiciously. "Friendship is still ... something."

"I'm sorry," I say softly.

"Me, too."

"I'll try to be better about respecting your boundaries. I promise." I sniffle as I wait for him to reply. "Rowan? You still there?"

"Yeah, I'm still here." But he sounds gutted.

"Would it make you feel any better if I admitted that I'm suspiciously close to peak day, so all of this was probably just a result of my raging hormones?" And there's my inappropriate and poorly timed, self-deprecating humor. I can't help myself.

He huffs out a laugh. "Not really. Then I'd just feel guilty for taking advantage of you while you're ovulating."

"You should know better. You're supposed to be a professional."

He grunts, and it sounds like he's standing up again. "Yeah. Speaking of, it's past time for me to get out of these dirty scrubs and wash off the day, like you said."

"Yeah, you probably should," I say, trying not to picture it.

"Thanks for letting me get that off my chest, at least."

I wince. "Thanks for being honest."

"Good night, Claire Bear."

"Good night."

9:01 AM

ROWAN

Good morning and Happy Easter!

Just checking in to make sure you're still up for our trip to the homestead today.

If you're not feeling well or something, let me know. I'm just used to seeing you up and moving by now.

Claire ... are you avoiding me?

CLAIRE

I'll be ready in a few.

ROWAN

I'm sorry again about making things awkward last night.

That's not completely true. I could never regret kissing you.

But I am sorry for putting so much pressure on you, and I'm grateful for your honesty about wanting to stay friends. It also means a lot to me that you respect my boundaries, you know, physically.

I hope I haven't ruined things by pushing my luck.

CLAIRE

No worries. We're fine.

Did you happen to make coffee?

ROWAN

Yes, would you like me to bring you a cup?

CLAIRE

I'll be out soon.

ROWAN

Can I ask you one more thing?

CLAIRE

ROWAN

I just want to know if I'm doing it again, being too nice?

Have I not been convincing enough? Do you need me to be more dangerous?

Or is that not the problem and you're just letting me down gently?

Because I can't help but feel like your "no" wasn't a hard one …

Also, I'm gonna need you to stop being so cute. I can hear you growling at me from here.

claire

ROWAN STANDS there with a mug in one hand and his phone in the other after I fling open my bedroom door. He offers me an apologetic smile to go along with my cup of coffee, and I can't tell which warms me more easily.

"I'm not getting an answer, am I?" he ventures after I take the first sip.

"No," I say firmly, and he frowns. "There. That one hard enough for you?"

He shakes his head as his smile returns. "And I thought I asked you to stop being this cute. You know I love it when you wear those overalls."

I roll my eyes at his crisp baby blue button down and the casual slacks that look like they were tailored to fit him. But then again, he's always appropriately dressed.

"Figured you'd inform me of some rule about women only being allowed to wear dresses since Jesus rose on the third day," I mumble, trying to ignore the way his shirt makes his eyes pop.

"Nah, I like this better, anyway. Especially since we both know you'll just end up in the barn with the kids," he leans in to add, making me scoff. I shove him out of my way after that, and he chuckles as he follows me to the kitchen.

Frankie's tail thumps against the floor when he sees me, so I set my coffee aside and stoop down to squish his furry face between my hands, already feeling guilty about leaving them all day. My chest tightens when he stares up at me with more love and adoration in his big, brown eyes than I could ever deserve. Oscar approaches a second later, and I try to hide my sniffling by greeting him in a silly voice. But when I glance at Rowan to see whether he's noticed my ridiculously emotional reaction to my dogs' everyday loyalty, I find him staring back at me with an expression that rivals Frankie's.

I clear my throat and dust my hands off on my thighs as I stand. "I'm not going anywhere with you if you don't quit looking at me like that."

"Like what?" he asks, casually taking a sip from the same mug he uses every time he comes over. And the fact that I let him pick out a favorite mug tells me I'm in more trouble than I thought.

"Like you're plotting against me or something," I reply with as much sass as I can muster.

He shrugs. "Do you ... want me against you?"

I narrow my eyes at him as he struggles to keep his expression blank. "Who's being cute now?"

"So you *do* think I'm cute." His brow and his lips lift on the same side, and it's downright freaking adorable. Not that I'm about to admit that to him, of course.

"What happened to not pushing your luck again and all that?" I fire back before I turn to slip on my work boots.

"We both know what seeing you first thing in the morning does to my brain," he says on a sigh. "Especially when you wake up in a salty mood."

I spin around, ready to deliver another smart-assed retort, only to find him mere inches away from me. My breath catches in my throat as his eyes run over me.

"I, um ... Maybe I should change after all," I pant, fluttering my eyelashes as if I'm fanning myself. But there's no cooling off once Rowan reaches out to hook a finger behind the bib of my overalls and tugs me closer.

"I meant what I said about these overalls. But if it bothers you that much, you could always take them off," he suggests, his voice gravelly, and my knees threaten to buckle when his fingertip grazes the clasp over my chest. "Or maybe you'd rather wait until we get to the barn for that?"

"Rowan, what are you doing?" I choke out.

"Looking for answers," he replies.

"What ... answers?"

His eyes lift to mine. "Is this what you want? For me to stop being so nice all the time?"

My lips part in a gasp. "Are you just messing with me right now?"

"You only seem to like me when I'm being dangerous, so I thought I'd test that theory."

His gaze zeroes in on my mouth, and I realize I'm twisting my fingers into his shirt, bracing for impact.

"Is that true, Claire?" he rasps.

"What?"

"Are you still only interested in me for one thing? Is it just lust for you?" he asks, furrowing his brow.

I should say yes, that ever since we met, I've only been interested in sleeping with him. I should tell him my attraction is merely physical, that I've never cared about anything below the surface or even wondered what it would be like to let myself fall for him completely. I should declare last night was a mistake, right before I add something about finding his religious principles almost as irritating as his belief in soulmates. And if he brings it up, I should deny how much fun we have together, how I crave being in his presence all the time, and how he's the only person who's ever made me feel special and safe enough to be myself.

I clear my throat. "No," I say instead, because I can't bring myself to lie this time. "But I'm still afraid that's all it is for you."

He shakes his head. "Claire, of the two L-words I used last night, you do know which one I'm leaning toward, right?" he asks with a different kind of desperation in his voice, making my stomach dip.

"Stop right there. Please," I tell him and reluctantly push away.

"Okay," he says, sighing and lifting his hands in surrender.

The silence stretches between us before I turn away. "Maybe I should just stay—"

"No, please," he begs me. "I'm sorry. I'll be good, I promise."

I eye him skeptically. I'm not sure that phrase means the same to both of us.

"And I already went to Mass earlier this morning, so you don't have to worry about walking into that trap again," he adds.

"Fine," I say, surprised by the hint of disappointment that last part brings. "But I'm only going for Daisy ... and your mom. And Gertie. Well, and your dad."

"Fair enough," he says with a sad smile.

"And I want to bring the boys," I blurt out, gesturing over to Frankie and Oscar. Oscar drops the toy in his mouth and bounds forward when he realizes he has our attention, tripping over his own ears and taking his brother down with him.

"All right," Rowan agrees, his smile growing more genuine before he waltzes over and scoops up the dogs. "Family road trip, it is."

I shoot another angry glare his way before I gulp down the rest of my coffee. Then I try to ignore him as he tells Frankie and Oscar about how much fun they're going to have on the homestead. And Rowan pretends he doesn't hear my frustrated growl after my plans to push him away backfire once again.

The tension fades on the drive, especially with the dogs to keep us preoccupied. In hindsight, stuffing two greedy pups into a back seat full of chocolate candy and boiled eggs probably wasn't the best idea. I barely keep Oscar from snacking on the chocolate bunnies Rowan packed for his godchildren, and Frankie manages to embezzle at least one dyed egg, as evidenced by the blue tongue he's sporting when we arrive at the homestead.

None of that stops the two of them from strolling in like they own the place, though, or the warm welcome they receive from the horde of children looking to get rid of the yolks from their *pâcqued* eggs.

To be fair, Rowan's parents greet me just as warmly. The embrace

I get from Mrs. LaFleur pokes at my guilty conscience after telling my own mom I wouldn't make it to dinner today, even more so once Daisy, Landry, and Juniper arrive and get the same treatment.

Daisy squeals with delight when she spots me and runs over to pull me in for a hug. "I'm so glad you're here," she says, making my eyes water just the slightest as she walks off to add a pan of bread pudding to the dessert table.

"Good to see you, Claire. Especially here, at the LaFleur homestead, spending Easter Sunday with your good pal Rowan and his family," Landry tells me with a knowing smile.

I cross my arms over my middle. "From what I understand, you were a regular around here long before Daisy ever caught your attention."

"Yeah. I wasn't always so keen on spending the weekends and holidays in Camellia. But my roommate couldn't stand leaving me behind, no matter how many times I swore I'd rather be alone."

"Sounds about right," I mumble with an eye roll. "Let me guess, Daisy was just as persistent?"

"Worse," he admits before leaning in to whisper, "I used to think they were sort of like a cult, but the good kind," and I snort out a laugh. "The kind that shows you what you're missing out on, and even makes you believe God could love you enough to let you have it all, too."

I blink up at him in disbelief after he adds that last part, though he only smiles encouragingly.

"Don't get any ideas. I'm just here for the free meal and the barn animals," I say faintly, gesturing over my overalls. "Nobody's getting me to drink the Kool-Aid."

"Did you say you were ready to go out to check on the lambs?" Gertie pops out from behind me and grabs my hand, tugging me onward and melting my heart.

"We'll go soon, I promise. But I'm pretty sure your parents will want you to finish your lunch first," I tell her with a laugh.

Gertie sighs and drops my hand. "You're right. *Grand-mére* is never going to let us go until we eat."

"Why don't you and your brother fix your plates, and I'll ask *Grand-pére* to take us on the side-by-side in a bit?"

"Yes!" she exclaims before she dashes off to grab Giles and inform him that "*Tante* Claire said she'll bring us to the barn after we eat."

"Sounds like you've already been sipping the sweet stuff, *Tante*," Landry muses as Rowan and Daisy return, and my cheeks flush.

"Can I get you something to eat?" Rowan asks, handing me a glass of iced tea before casually placing his hand on the small of my back. My eyelashes flutter as I attempt to keep my cool, and I look up to find Daisy batting her eyes mockingly.

"Thanks, but I can serve myself," I say flatly.

"You'd better move fast if you want a bite of that *couenne*, because I'm pretty sure my dad's been 'accidentally' dropping pieces of that pork roast for Frankie and Oscar since we got here," Rowan says with a smirk. We all turn our heads in time to catch Mr. LaFleur feeding Oscar a piece of the crispy pork belly from the Cajun microwave and chuckling to himself.

"I guess I could go for a plate, if you really don't mind," I concede. "Oh, and don't forget the rice dressing."

His smile grows, and he reassures me that he'll be back soon. I take a sip of the tea, cautiously raising my gaze to Daisy and Landry, who look even more pleased than Rowan.

"What?" I ask defensively. "I like meat."

"You should probably ask my brother for some of his sausage, then, since you seemed to enjoy it so much last time. I'm sure he'd be all too happy to share it with you," Daisy drawls, and I choke on my drink as an unexpected laugh bubbles out of me.

"Easy, Blondie. I'm starting to think you spend too much time with my sister," Landry says, stifling a grin.

She clicks her tongue. "Well, I have to hang out with someone, since my brother stole my other friend."

"Like you haven't been prioritizing hubby booty over bestie duty," I say with a snort, and Daisy frowns. "I'm only kidding, Daze. That's the way it should be."

"Babies don't just make themselves you know," she says softly, glancing back at Landry for support, and Juniper whines at her feet.

But I'm the one struggling not to crumble after I'm hit with the realization that I'm a shitty friend, just a half-second before my jealous side nails me with a gut punch.

"You're pregnant?" I ask quietly, my lips trembling with the effort it takes to keep the corners of my mouth up.

"Not yet, but we're hoping to be soon," she replies with a shy smile and a pink tint to her cheeks.

"That's great," I choke out, pausing to clear the emotion from my throat so I can hide my bitterness with some playful taunting. "I mean, how exciting? Especially for you, Lan."

"Yeah, thanks." Landry rewards my suggestive eyebrow wiggle with a short laugh, but I can tell he's not buying what I'm selling.

I've never been more grateful for Rowan's timing when he returns with my lunch. Daisy's still staring at me with what looks suspiciously like pity, but I ignore her and bite into a piece of roast.

"Gertie and Giles are waiting for me to take them to the barn," I mumble through a mouthful when Rowan regards me curiously.

"Better finish soon, then," he replies, gesturing to Gertie as she walks our way.

After some negotiation, Rowan's dad stays behind to keep Frankie and Oscar out of trouble, while another of Rowan's nieces joins the party, and Heath drives us out back on the UTV. We catch the tagged lambs from before and bring them into the barn for inspection and a refresher on their care, and I can't help beaming with pride when Gertie takes the lead and shows her cousin how to select another lamb with show potential.

"I knew you were an amazing teacher," Rowan leans down to whisper near my ear, and I swallow hard.

"Smart kids," I say. "Must run in the family."

He hums and hooks a finger through the side of my overalls again, tugging me closer and raising the thermostat out here. I'm already letting out a measured exhale when Gertie's gaze seems to settle on us.

"So, I know you have a lot of options, but I'd like to be considered when you pick a flower girl. You know, when you get married," she declares, stroking the lamb she's cradling in her arms.

Rowan and I both force an awkward laugh, and Heath swoops in to chide her.

Gertie rears her head back. "What do you mean, they don't know yet?"

"She doesn't have an engagement ring," her cousin points out, and Gertie frowns.

"*Tante* Daisy and *N'oncle* Lan decided to get married before she had a ring," Gertie argues.

Heath cringes. "*Tante* Daisy and *N'oncle* Lan sort of ... did things out of order."

I cross my arms over my middle at the reminder that my mere presence is enough to scandalize most of Rowan's family.

"They still did it the right way, though," Rowan adds. "Sometimes grownups get mixed-up. Even Saint Joseph and the Blessed Mother's marriage probably seemed a little crazy to some of their friends and family at first. But so long as we keep trying our best to listen to the Lord and to obey Him, and to love one another, of course, there's nothing that can't be unscrambled."

"Cool. So, can I be in your wedding, too?" Giles pipes up, and I stifle a whimper.

Heath smirks. "Come on, kids. Why don't we give these grownups some time to discern where the good Lord is currently leading them, and we can meet up inside later."

"Okay," Gertie concedes, though she's not happy about it. To be fair, neither am I.

I watch as Heath has to practically drag her away from the barn, already debating my next line of defense.

Should I pick a fight with Rowan? Make him think I'm absolutely disgusted with the idea of marrying him? Maybe I can get away with a few crude jokes about the barn loft and plant another seed of doubt.

My heart quickens as Rowan turns to face me. "Come on," he says softly, inclining his head. "I figure that's enough torture for one day."

"So you're giving me a free pass?" I ask, careful not to let him hear the regret in my tone.

"It's that or a proposal, and I figure you might kick me if I get down on one knee," he says, but he doesn't bother hiding his disappointment.

"I probably wouldn't complain if you got down on both knees, though," I mumble, and he snorts.

"You and your barn fantasy," he murmurs as he takes my hand, and he doesn't let it go until we reach his parents' house.

"I'll go around to get the dogs if you want to start saying goodbye," he tells me, so I nod and go in through the back door.

"What's he really doing with her, though? I mean, can she even get married in the church?"

I stop in my tracks when I hear the conversation coming from inside the kitchen.

"She might need an annulment."

"But if she's unbaptized, it wouldn't be a sacramental wedding."

My breath catches in my throat as I hear what sounds like Rowan's sisters debating our future.

"They could have a natural wedding, but she'd have to convert for it to become sacramental."

"Then again, if she's already been married, I'm sure his willpower has been put to the test."

One of them chuckles. "Are you kidding? Have you seen the way he looks at her? There's no way they haven't already—"

"Enough!" I wince when I recognize Daisy's voice. "Maybe she will need an annulment, maybe she won't. Maybe she's already been baptized, and for all I know, they've done a better job of remaining chaste than any of us. Well, except you, Rose. But, anyway, she's a lovely person, and one of my best friends. None of us knows exactly what she's been through or what her first marriage was like, and it's not our place to say what kind of future she and Rowan could have together, if she even wants that. Regardless, she deserves your respect and certainly not your judgment."

"Well, forgive me for worrying about my brother's heart and his virtue."

"I'm perfectly capable of minding those myself, Maggie, but thanks for your concern," Rowan's deep voice rumbles through the kitchen, and my stomach dips.

"We just don't want to see either of you get hurt," someone adds, maybe Heath's wife. "I can't imagine how hard it would be if you fell for one another and then found out it wasn't meant to be."

My eyes sting at the reminder that every person in the room doubts I'm good enough for him, Rowan included. It especially hurts when I stop to think that Daisy and Naomi wouldn't have felt the need to half-ass defend me if they didn't recognize that this is a mistake. And the fact that I didn't hear his mother chiming in on my behalf doesn't make me feel any better.

I fight against a sob as I attempt to silently slink out of the house, but Frankie yips and comes waddling over before I can make it to safety. I curse under my breath and blink back my tears before I venture into the kitchen.

"Claire," Daisy's hand flies up to her chest. "Have you been back there long?"

"Just walked in from the barn," I say, tugging on my overalls. "I hesitated to bring the outside in."

I avoid looking at Rowan, but I can feel his gaze on me. "The kids have Oscar in the living room, so whenever you're ready ..." he directs at me.

"Oh, no, you're not leaving already?" Mrs. LaFleur asks, walking across the kitchen. I suppose she could have been out of the room before, but I still can't imagine she wouldn't have sided with her daughters.

"Thanks again for having us. Happy Easter, everyone." I barely manage to say the words without my voice cracking. Rowan's mom shuffles over to give me a hug, and a tear accidentally slips out when she adds some affirmations about my return. But I don't even hear them, not really.

"See you later?" Daisy asks when I pass by and don't stop to embrace her.

"Mm-hmm," I agree and focus on dodging the rest of them on the way to Rowan's truck.

"How much of that did you hear?" he asks when we finally settle inside.

"Why? What did I miss?"

He sighs. "You're not a very good liar, Claire."

If he only knew. "Okay, fine. I walked in when someone was talking about your virtue. I assume that means your sisters finally arranged that intervention after they heard you'd gone off the deep end and started screwing around with a divorced heathen," I say nonchalantly, as if the offense disappears with a wave of my hand.

"You know that's not what they meant, right?"

"Yeah, I know," I retort. Because they meant worse. "But they're right."

He growls. "When are we going to get past this?"

"You tell me. Which one of us is more stubborn?"

"You might have a harder head, but I have more patience. So I guess we'll see which of us outlasts the other," he replies.

I roll my eyes and open my mouth to respond, but I'm cut off by the sound of my phone ringing. "Ugh. I was going to say the timing was perfect, except it's my mom."

"Then answer it," Rowan insists.

I scoff. "I'm not gonna—"

Then the son of a biscuit baker reaches over and accepts the call.

rowan

"WHAT AM I DOING? Well, I'm ..."

Claire glares angrily as she fumbles her way out of her mom's invitation to Easter dinner.

"Don't lie to her," I whisper, and she groans.

"I'm actually passing through Baton Rouge. But I'm on my way home."

Her mother's gasp comes through the phone. "Oh, that's perfect! You can still make it in time for supper."

"I would, but I have the dogs with me, and I know how you feel about animals in the house."

"And I've already told you that Frankie and Oscar are welcome here any time," Mrs. Bergeron replies.

"Thanks, Mom, but really—"

Claire drops off in the middle of her excuse when she realizes we've stopped moving. I shift my truck into park and look at her expectantly.

"What are you doing?" she demands.

"Waiting for you to tell me which direction we're going," I reply as if it's a silly question. "You know I don't have a navigation system in here."

"Sorry, Mom, can you hang on one second?" She hits the mute

button before her mother can answer. "We're going home," she tells me.

"Not when we're already so close to your parents' house. She's your mom. She misses you. And you miss her."

"I didn't say I missed her," she grumbles.

"You didn't have to." I flash her a warm smile. "Come on. You know you'd rather do this with me."

Her jaw lowers slightly, which I take to mean I'm right. "And have to explain our weird situationship to them? No, thanks."

"There's an easy fix for that," I drawl, and her breath hitches this time.

"Like you'd even agree to lie to my parents and pretend we were actually ..." She shakes her head.

"Who said anything about lying?" I reply evenly.

She opens her mouth, no doubt to shoot down my idea again, but she can't seem to get the words out. Each time I leave her speechless, she plants a little more hope within my chest. I think she's finally realizing that it's different now, that I can see how hard she's trying to stuff her feelings for me into a box, and I'm waiting patiently for her to give up and let them spill over.

"Claire? Are you still there?" her mother's voice calls out from the phone, and she unmutes it to speak.

"Yeah, uh, sorry." She pauses and swallows hard. "Would it be okay if I brought a friend over for dinner?"

Her eyes dart over to check my expression, so I do my best to look aloof and confident.

Nothing to see here, just my calm reaction to the love of my life bringing me home to meet her parents ...

"Of course, sweetheart. Any friend of yours is welcome here." Her mom's voice trills with excitement at Claire's tentative acceptance of her invitation. "It's not ... Jeremy, is it?" she adds hesitantly.

Claire coughs out a laugh. "No. Jeremy and I aren't exactly on speaking terms these days."

Her mom hums, and I can't tell whether she's disappointed or happy to hear that news. "Well, I guess we'll see you in a little bit, then. And don't worry about bringing anything other than your friend, and your fur babies, of course."

"Oh, um, one more thing. Can you please make sure everything is peanut-free? Rowan's allergic," Claire asks.

"Rowan? The cute doctor with the rash ... from Nana and Pop's anniversary party?"

She glances my way again, catching the smile that spreads across my face at her mom's recognition. "Yeah. It's kind of a long story."

Mrs. Bergeron lets out a soft chuckle. "No Reese's. Got it."

"Thanks. See you soon."

She hangs up the phone and silently gestures in the right direction, and I turn the truck around and head toward her childhood home.

"So, why exactly have you been avoiding your family again?" I ask after a while.

"I don't avoid them. I just ... give them lots of space."

"Fess up, Claire, or I'll make this super awkward," I warn her.

"It's already going to be ridiculously awkward!" she cries out.

"Don't think I won't ask your mom to see your baby pictures."

"Go ahead. I was a cute kid."

I shoot her a suspicious look before I turn a corner. "And I wonder what your mom will say when I tell her how many times you've been to the homestead lately."

She gasps. "You wouldn't."

I cock an eyebrow. "Well, since you wouldn't tell me the whole story, how was I to know that would upset her so much?"

She lets out a frustrated growl. "There's no story to tell. My parents just don't like me all that much, okay?"

"What?" I blurt out incredulously. "Of course they like you."

"I mean, they *love* me," she explains quietly. "It's not like they mistreat me or anything. It's just that I can tell I'm not their cup of tea."

"And what makes you think that?"

"I don't know," she shrugs. "The vibe, I guess. I'm an only child, and my mom wanted me to be her best friend, her little sidekick, but we never really meshed all that well. I didn't fit in with the other perfect, preppy girls in school, at ballet class, or on playdates with her friends' daughters ... I've always been too loud or too silly ... too rough, too muddy. My dad and I got along, but I think he felt guilty about letting me do all the outdoorsy stuff with him because my mom got left out. And even though she supported me when I picked livestock shows over pageants, I know she was disappointed."

I catch the wobble in her voice by the end of it, so I pull over again and turn to face her. "I'm sorry."

"For what, forcing me to pick at another one of my old emotional wounds until I cry again?" She sniffles as she tries to shrug it off.

I sigh and reach out to wipe a tear from her cheek. "Of course. But I'm mostly sorry that you've been going around thinking you aren't the most fun, the most beautiful, the most interesting, and the most compassionate girl in the room. Because you are, Claire. You're not too much *anything*. You're just the best and the most at *everything*."

Her chin trembles as she stares back at me, and Frankie and Oscar begin whining from the back seat once they sense her crying. "You have to say that because you're my friend. You just want me to feel better."

"No," I admit with a rueful smile. "The only lies I've ever told you were of the omission variety. I mean every word of that."

"Well, thank you," she says with a sniff. "It's too bad you weren't around ten years ago to talk me out of switching my college major and basically throwing my life away to follow Jeremy. Between moving to Camellia with him, not being able to get pregnant, and now my divorce, I haven't given my mom any reasons to see me in a better light. And I guess I could have been avoiding her because I don't want to hear her say 'I told you so.' "

I growl. "Don't do that, please. Everyone makes decisions they regret later for one reason or another, but you have to forgive yourself. And most of those things weren't your fault, anyway."

"Right," she nods and forces a smile before she turns to reassure the dogs that she's okay. I'm still suspicious about the pregnancy part, but I figure I shouldn't push her on it right now.

"For the record, as much as I hate how much you've had to endure, I'm a big, big fan of the woman it all helped you to become," I add, hoping she can sense my sincerity.

"Thank you," she says more shyly this time, but she keeps her eyes trained on Frankie. I watch her for a moment longer before I veer back onto the road.

"Oh boy," Claire calls out when we pull into the driveway a few minutes later, presumably because of the extra car parked there. I furrow my brow questioningly. "You remember my favorite feral great-aunt, don't you?"

I grin. "You mean sweet, old *Tante* Verna?"

"Better not call her that to her face," she mumbles.

"What, old?"

"No. *Sweet.*"

I chuckle as we walk Frankie and Oscar past the well-kept landscaping and the painted lawn ornaments to knock on the door of the Acadian-style home. Claire's mom swings the door open so quickly that the pastel-colored wreath rattles, and she apologizes as she scrambles to set it right.

"Happy Easter," Mrs. Bergeron greets us with a nervous smile, ushering us inside before stooping to pet the dogs and subsequently wiping her hands on her white slacks. She and Claire hesitate before they embrace, and I feel guilty when the hug I receive isn't as awkward.

We're led through the immaculately decorated home into the kitchen, where Claire's Aunt Verna awaits us. I peer around, noticing the somewhat dated but still sparkling clean counters and cabinets, as well as an attached formal dining room. The table is already set for eight, making me wonder if the room gets much use.

"Well, look what the Easter Bunny dragged in. How's that trail ride been, cowgirl?" Verna asks with a sly smirk.

Claire glares at her before she leans in to kiss her cheek. "I wouldn't know. Never did manage to get back on that horse."

"This ain't your stud?" Verna retorts before inviting me in for a hug. I stifle my reaction when she punctuates her embrace with a light tap on my backside, but I'm pretty sure Claire notices when my brow shoots up.

"Nope," Claire replies, trying not to laugh. "You can lead 'em to water, but sometimes you can't make 'em drink, no matter how thirsty."

"What a shame," Verna adds, leaning back to continue her perusal.

I clear my throat. "Well, maybe the horse is just worried about coming before the cart."

Claire's eyes widen in surprise, and her cheeks flush a shade darker.

"And maybe the cowgirl isn't looking to get saddled with anyone," she declares, crossing her arms over her middle.

"That's too bad, since this horse has been looking forward to giving bareback rides," I reply without hesitation, making myself blush this time. Claire and Verna both toss their heads back in laughter, while Mrs. Bergeron busies herself with her hosting duties, looking more scandalized than amused.

"Sounds like you'd better get your spurs and your whip ready, Claire Bear," Aunt Verna continues, and I can't help laughing, too.

Then Claire flashes me a grateful smile, warming me all over, and I know this is it—the relationship I've always wanted. The banter, the teasing, the inside jokes ... the sound of her big laugh each time I manage a particularly spicy contribution ... It wouldn't be the same with anyone else, but I could do this with her for the rest of my life. And from the way she's looking at me right now, I can tell she wants it, too.

Claire's dad walks into the kitchen a moment later, and she breaks eye contact to share a hug with him. I step forward to shake his hand, and we make small talk about our careers and the LSU baseball team's prospects of winning it all this year. He's warm and friendly, but it's obvious that Claire takes after her Aunt Verna more than anyone.

Mrs. Bergeron pulls a ham from the oven and encourages us to sit together around the dining table as she brings out the sides in separate serving dishes, sighing when she nearly trips over Frankie. Meanwhile, Oscar's already at my feet, begging for more food.

Claire still looks slightly uncomfortable as we open our fancy napkins and begin spooning potato salad onto fine china, though she seemed much more at ease throughout the casual buffet-style dinner at the homestead, even with so many people around. My family's informalities were mostly born out of necessity, but I've never appreciated them so much until now.

No one moves to say the blessing, so I bow my head for a moment, making sure to thank God not only for the life, death, and resurrection of His only Son, since it is Easter Sunday and all, but also for the other gifts I've been taking for granted lately, like my family, my career, and Claire.

All eyes are on me when I open mine again and finish making the Sign of the Cross over my chest.

"And he's Catholic, too," Verna drawls, leaning over to elbow Claire in the side. "Nana ought to love that."

"She certainly would approve," Mrs. Bergeron agrees, and I realize that her parents haven't even revealed their first names to me. "I suppose you'll think it's a good thing we had you baptized after all."

"Wait, you were baptized Catholic?" I ask, turning my head to face Claire so fast that I almost make myself dizzy.

She shrugs. "Not that I know of."

"My grandparents were very adamant about it," her mom says quietly, and I swallow hard and try to disguise the way my heart races.

"I don't ever remember going to Mass, though," Claire says thoughtfully.

"We felt like the nondenominational church was a better fit for us," Mrs. Bergeron clarifies with an apologetic smile.

"You may have been baptized by a priest, but I doubt there's a Catholic bone in your body," Mr. Bergeron says with a light chuckle.

Tante Verna huffs and shoots me a knowing smirk. "Hmm, I wouldn't be so sure of that one."

I clear my throat and scratch the back of my head nervously as Claire's eyes meet mine, but I can tell she's struggling not to laugh.

Claire's dad snorts, and her mom clicks her tongue. "Really, Verna? Do you always have to do that?"

Verna simply waves a bejeweled hand, making her bracelets jangle, but I can see the second Claire's posture straightens that she's not going to let this go. I reach beneath the table to place my hand on her lap, but she doesn't seem to notice.

"Do you always have to be such a prude?" Claire drops her fork and demands of her mother.

"Claire," her father calls her name gruffly.

Mrs. Bergeron lifts her chin indignantly but refuses to make eye contact with any of them. "There's nothing wrong with being modest and appropriate."

"There is when you'd rather offend your own family than risk saying something a stranger doesn't want to hear," Claire insists, and I give her knee a squeeze. She responds by sliding her hand over mine, so I flip it over and interlace our fingers.

"Don't you want your guest to feel comfortable?" Mrs. Bergeron gestures toward me this time. "I imagine he's important if he's still hanging around."

Claire tries to tug her hand back, but I don't let her. "What's that supposed to mean?" she asks.

"Well, to be honest, I'm worried. Rowan, you seem like such a great young man. But ..." Claire's mom trails off when her voice cracks. "I was hoping you'd give yourself a little more time before shacking up with someone else. I don't want to see you get your heart broken again so soon."

I tighten my grip on Claire's hand. "It's okay," she whispers to me. "It's not worth it, right?" And I can only imagine the restraint it's taking her to stay sitting in that chair.

"You'll understand one day, if you ever have kids of your own," her mother adds, and I watch the woman I love deflate before my eyes.

rowan

"TELL ME SHE DOESN'T KNOW?" I ask Claire quietly, and she shakes her head.

"And now that you've finally left Jeremy, I was looking forward to having you back again," Mrs. Bergeron continues and swipes a tear off her cheek. "We love you, and we miss you. That's all."

I clear my throat. "With all due respect, ma'am, I think you've said enough."

Everyone's eyes turn to me, and I realize it came out harsher than I intended.

"I don't doubt you love Claire, because it's impossible not to, but you don't understand the damage you're doing to her heart right now," I add by way of explanation.

"Maybe you're right," Mrs. Bergeron concedes. "Seems you know her better than we do, after all."

My thumb strokes Claire's wrist as she seethes, and the dogs whine at her feet.

"If there's something we don't know, it's because you won't let us in," Aunt Verna's voice breaks the silence after a while. Then she surprises us all by gasping and reaching out to backhand Claire's shoulder. "You little ... That's why you asked about Reg and me not having kids before, isn't it?"

She nods, keeping her eyes trained down on our intertwined hands.

"You never told us you couldn't have children," Verna holds. "You can't fault us for putting a foot in each cheek when you keep everything so damned secretive!"

Claire shrugs. "I never said anything because I wasn't sure why I couldn't get pregnant. And the last thing I needed was your pity."

"Of course you needed our pity, you stubborn-ass girl. That's what mamas and crazy old *tantes* are for, taking care of you, and giving you advice, and pissing you off and making you feel better at the same time!" Verna argues, her bangle bracelets tinkling enthusiastically.

Claire sniffles. "You're right, I'm a *tête dur*. So there's nothing any of you could have done to convince me not to move in with Jeremy, and you certainly couldn't have helped me with the infertility stuff."

"But I would have given anything for the chance to hold you while you cried about it," Claire's mom says, her eyes welling over with tears. "Even though I bet you were so tough and so strong that you never let anyone see you shed a tear over it."

Claire looks back at me, her bottom lip trembling. "That's only because I prefer to cry in the bathtub … like a lady."

Because of course her priority is lightening our spirits and making the rest of the room laugh, even in what must be one of the most difficult moments of her life.

I can't help myself when I bring her hand to my mouth for a kiss, and she flashes me another grateful smile before she reclaims her hand.

Mrs. Bergeron gets up and walks around the table to wrap her up in a hug, and not only does Claire let her, but she even gives her a good sob, the kind she only lets out the week before her period. And Aunt Verna shoots me a conspiratorial wink when I have to clear the emotion from my throat.

Once the ladies finally pull away, laughing and wiping their tears with their bunny-themed napkins, Claire accepts a hug from her dad and another from Aunt Verna.

"Now, you, Martha Ann, you're gonna simply roll your eyes and ignore the next crude joke you hear. And you, Daphne Claire, you're gonna mind your mama's sensitive constitution. See, was that so hard?"

"I'm sorry, hang on a minute," I say, interrupting Aunt Verna's speech. "Did you just call her *Daphne*?"

Claire crosses her arms. "So what if she did, *Athanasius*?"

My mouth tugs up on one side. "You do know what this means, right?"

"Jeepers, Fred, should I?" she retorts.

"Daphne shrubs make beautiful flowers," I drawl, grazing a finger over her tattoos and making her do that fluttery-eyelash thing I love so much.

"It's my great-grandmother's name, the one you met at the sixtieth anniversary party," she declares in a gravelly voice, pulling her arm out of my reach and lifting her chin.

She's probably thinking no one's noticed the way I affect her, but I know the truth. And I'm hoping that by helping Claire work out some of her issues with her family, I'll have finally earned her trust. So she might actually believe me once I work up the courage to tell her I love her.

Then again, I could be wrong.

The ride home is much too quiet. I'm not sure what I've done, but Claire's barely acknowledged me since we packed Frankie and Oscar into the truck. And although she doesn't seem angry with me, I can tell I've hit a nerve at some point tonight.

"Is everything okay?" I ask after a while.

"Fine," she says shortly, scrolling on her phone.

I sigh. "You're not fine. Can we please just cut to the chase so you can tell me what's really bothering you?"

"No," she replies. "I'd actually prefer not to leave you with the impression that you're the answer to all my problems."

"What's that supposed to mean?"

She growls and puts her phone down. "It means you need to butt out. You forced me into so many uncomfortable situations today that I lost count."

"Are you mad at me for convincing you to see your parents, even after you had that big breakthrough?" I ask incredulously.

She hesitates before she says, "I am. I'm also annoyed because you can't keep your hands to yourself every time we're around your family —or mine, for that matter. They all think we're some mushy, lovey-dovey couple, which also means they assume I've been seducing you and treating you like my sex slave."

I bite my lip to stifle a laugh, although the urge to tell her I'm not opposed to any of that is just as strong. "So you're upset because I like you."

"Yes, because I told you not to. And because you basically gave your niece 'the talk' and left her with the false hope of serving in our imaginary wedding." She has to pause for a minute and collect herself before she goes on. "Then you practically did the same thing at my parents' house, right before you helped them figure out that I can't have kids. You know Verna's never going to let me live any of this down."

My expression falls. "I'm sorry. Well, not about liking you or flirting with you, but I am sorry for the last part. I should have been more careful not to out you to your family, and I could have spoken more kindly to your mom. I guess I got a little too overprotective."

"But I'm not yours to protect!"

"That's not how I see things," I mumble.

She growls in frustration. "You're not getting it, Rowan. You can't keep wasting your time with me. For all we know, you're missing out on finding the girl you're supposed to marry because you're chasing a dead end."

"The time I spend with you is never wasted," I reply evenly, determined to show her how patient I can be.

"Your sisters were right, and you know it," she mutters.

"I don't know exactly what you overheard earlier, but my sisters don't know anything about us, and neither does your Great-Aunt Verna," I argue. "I'm here with you because I want to be near you, because I enjoy your company, not because I feel sorry for you or for myself, and not because I'm trying to trap you in a relationship with me. But I honestly think you like me, too, even if you're too afraid to admit it. And I don't know when you started caring so much about what people think, anyway."

She crosses her arms and stares out the window. "I'm sorry. I enjoy your company, too. But that's not enough, and I don't see the point in torturing ourselves when we both know how this ends."

I huff and shake my head as I turn into her driveway. "There you go again, putting words in my mouth because you want me to say something that will make you feel better about keeping your heart locked away."

"I don't want to hurt you. But I keep saying the same things, and you're not hearing me."

"No," I tell her with a sardonic laugh. "I'm listening, but I'm paying attention to more than just the words you're saying. And the way it feels every time we're together, the look in your eyes when you finally let down your walls for me, the way you kissed me last night— it all says the opposite. I think you're not hearing yourself."

"Then maybe we shouldn't hang out anymore," she says, cringing in the dark.

"No," I repeat. "You promised last night that we'd still be friends."

"You promised me you'd stop trying to ..."

"Trying to *what*? Prove that I can handle you? Convince you to let me love you?"

Her head whips around, and I see her eyelashes flutter as she blinks away her shock. It's not the first time I've used that word in the last few days, but you'd swear it's the first time she's ever heard it.

"Why do you want this so badly, anyway? All we ever do is argue and bicker," she replies, sounding breathless.

"We're not arguing. It's just that you're always making me beg, which I already told you I don't mind. And I honestly thought the bickering was your preferred method of flirting, since you outlawed the mushy crap," I say, pouting, and I could swear the corners of her mouth turn up.

"Fine. We can be friends, but that's it. I mean it this time," she concedes after a while.

"Okay," I agree, and we each grab a snoring wiener dog from the back seat.

"Are we still the kind of friends who send selfies and kiss from time to time?" I venture once I set Oscar down inside the house.

She snorts. "Only in case of emergency. So any selfies you send must include a 'guess this rash' caption or a wiener of the four-legged variety."

"Can we still bicker?"

"I guess," she says on an exhale.

"Family road trips?"

"Henceforth banned."

I grunt. "Sleepovers?"

"The minute I say no, you'll find yourself in some strange predicament, and I'll have to eat my words. So I'm putting sleepovers back on the in-case-of-emergency list, with a caveat for slutty PJs."

"What about slutty glasses?"

She growls. "Good night, Athanasius."

"Good night, Daphne," I say, grinning. "See you later this week. I'll make sure I pack my glasses."

She rolls her eyes and shoves me out the door, practically slamming it in my face. I turn around and lean against it, sighing to myself when her head thumps against it from the other side.

"I heard that, Claire Bear," I call out, and she pounds on the door with her fist this time.

2:31 PM

ROWAN

Hey, how's it going?

CLAIRE

It's the last stretch between spring break and the end of the school year, so you can just assume the answer is "wild."

ROWAN

I can imagine. Have Landry or Loren contacted you about Daisy's surprise birthday party next weekend?

CLAIRE

Yeah, I'll be there.

ROWAN

Great. So will I … obviously.

I'll also be in town tomorrow night. Think you'll be up for some company?

I can bring some of that sausage I've been promising you.

CLAIRE

You can't convince me that you don't hear
yourself.

ROWAN

Okay, that one was on purpose.

CLAIRE

I just remembered that the Reeds are in their
"trying" era, which is the only reason I won't force
you to stick it out over there. I may already be in
bed by the time you get here, but you know the
code.

ROWAN

Oh, Daisy told you?

(I'm purposefully not commenting on you being in
bed.)

CLAIRE

She did, but I'm assuming you already knew.

ROWAN

Yea. Not that it's any of my business, I suppose,
but it was nice of them to give me fair warning
since I'll need to monitor Daisy the whole time.

CLAIRE

You can use the word pregnancy in front of me.
I'm not going to fall apart every time.

ROWAN

Of course you won't.

But I might.

CLAIRE

Wow. How dangerous of you.

ROWAN

Need I remind you that this will be the child of my
baby sister and my best friend?

I'm allowed to cry this time. Charge it to my man card.

CLAIRE

I just cackled in class.

While we're on the subject, though, I also have something to tell you.

ROWAN

On the subject of Daisy and Landry making a baby or my man card?

CLAIRE

I have a date this week.

ROWAN

Oh … anyone I know?

CLAIRE

I doubt you guys run in the same circles.

ROWAN

I don't suppose a thirst-trap selfie would entice you to change your mind?

CLAIRE

Sorry. I've already gotten one of those today.

ROWAN

Ouch.

Well, good luck. I hope you have a nice time.

CLAIRE

Thanks. That's very gracious of you.

ROWAN

Promise you'll call me if you need saving?

CLAIRE

I promise.

claire

"HEY," Daisy greets me when we walk out of school at the same time.

"Hey." I force a smile, not because I'm unhappy to see her, but because I know I'm about to do something that will most likely ruin our friendship.

My pace quickens as we reach our cars in the parking lot, but she pauses before she reaches for the handle of her green Beetle. Juniper takes it as a sign to sit.

"How's it going? I feel like I never see you anymore, especially since I'm only here a couple days per week."

"Seems like you're a busy lady now that you're back on the road, making house plans, and hanging out with your in-laws, not to mention all the baby making," I remark.

Her shoulders droop, but she looks up at me through wide, green eyes. "There's always time for you, though."

Dammit. This is what I get for befriending an actual Disney Princess.

"I guess we are overdue for a girls' night," I tell her and watch as her face lights up.

"We definitely are," she agrees.

"Maybe we should plan something the next time your brother is in town, so he can keep your husband preoccupied," I suggest.

"Yeah, that's a good idea," she says, "except Rowan might get jealous."

I click my tongue. "He'll be fine. I'm not his only friend."

"No, but we both know he doesn't see you as only a friend," she reminds me. "And he's certainly never looked at any other woman the way he looks at you."

I drop my keys on the ground, hoping the move distracts her from the guilt written all over my face. "Then we should definitely plan to set him up with someone new. Put it on our girls' night agenda."

She sighs. "You're going to break his heart."

I cross my arms and stare down at my feet, unable to form a response.

"He deserves better, Claire."

My eyes begin to sting, and I struggle to swallow the emotion lodged in my throat. "I know he does. That's exactly what I've been trying to tell him, but he's not ..."

She furrows her brow. "I didn't mean better than you. I'm saying he deserves a chance *with* you. And you deserve to be loved by someone like him."

It takes me a moment to find my voice again after that. "As usual, you give me too much credit, and I think your brother is just as amazing as you are. But that doesn't make us right for each other. He's looking for something I couldn't give him, even if I wanted to. And I wish I knew how to spare his feelings, but he can't seem to accept that what we have now is all we can ever have."

"He's never going to accept that," she says with an incredulous laugh. "You're asking him to ignore a direct order from God."

I groan. Of course. I should have seen this sooner, but it makes sense that he'd be mistaking the need to fix me for actual romantic feelings.

"Well, I'd rather be alone than be his pity project ... or yours," I mutter and yank open the door of my Bronco.

"Claire, wait," Daisy calls after me. I stop, but I don't look her way.

"I understand what it feels like to be pitied, and it wasn't that long ago I prayed for you to like me enough to become my friend, in spite of feeling sorry for me," she explains, Juniper whining when her voice cracks. "I wouldn't be here asking you to give Rowan a chance if I so much as suspected he was motivated by pity. But you have to consider the way he's built. You said it yourself—there's no reason a guy like him is still single, unless he's looking for perfection. And now that he's found it, do you really think he'll be so easily discouraged?"

I let out a tired exhale. "If you really wanted to save your brother from disappointment, then you'd help him see that he's confused."

Daisy smirks and gestures for Juniper to get into the car. "I've already done that, silly. It's your turn."

And with that, she ducks into the front seat and slips on a pair of shades. She waves at me on her way out, her hand flying up to her mouth when she scrapes her rim on the curb, and I can't help but smile, even if she did just simultaneously poke at my guilty conscience and stomp all over my plans for the evening.

Daisy's intervention turns out to be at least a partial success, because by the time I get home, I'm not sure I can go through with the plot I concocted earlier this week. I've been thinking the only way to get Rowan to move on is to convince him that I have, so I took the plunge and responded to a DM I received a while back from one of Jeremy's old coworkers. As luck would have it, within seconds of extending a dinner invitation to Nick, I got a text from Rowan regarding my plans for the same night, setting up the perfect opportunity to at least make him believe I'm climbing back on that horse.

But I've been struggling to justify my plan since I made it. I know giving Rowan an out is the right thing to do, but this feels worse than a quick Band-Aid rip. I'd already been doubting whether I could follow through at the risk of hurting him and damaging our friendship, even before Daisy added another layer to the guilt settling in my gut.

I pull out my phone, thinking there's a way I can still accomplish my goal while mitigating the sting.

CLAIRE

> Hey, sorry to bail at the last second, but I don't think it's a good idea for you to come over after all. I'm not feeling well.

ROWAN

> Are you okay? Is there anything I can get you?

CLAIRE

> I'm fine, thanks. My stomach's just a little off.

ROWAN

> Call me if you need anything. I'll be right around the corner.

I groan, because of course he's going to be sweet while I'm preparing to drive a knife through his heart. Then again, this is exactly why I need to follow through with my plan. Rowan really does deserve better, and he needs to understand that he won't find the love of his life if he's too busy doting on me.

With a renewed sense of purpose and a slightly more humane plan on deck, I force myself to get ready for my date and ignore the way my stomach cramps and roils as I prepare dinner. It isn't long after I shove a pan of meat and vegetables into the oven that I hear the rumble of loud truck pipes.

Frankie and Oscar bark and circle my feet as I move to answer the door, but they don't bother hiding their displeasure when it swings open to reveal someone other than their favorite blond-haired, blue-eyed doctor.

"Hey," my date says with a crooked smile, his eyes immediately running over me.

He's handsome, I suppose, though his style seems identical to my ex's. His dark hair and beard match the tattoos peeking out from above his collar and past the hem of his tight shirt sleeves, and I suddenly find myself wondering how I ever thought the cowboy-gym-rat look was attractive in the first place.

"Hey, Nick. Come in," I reply, stifling a cough when his cologne wafts into the house before he does.

Frankie growls and snaps at Nick's boot-clad foot the second it crosses the threshold, forcing him to sidestep and trip over Oscar. He stumbles and grabs my arm to right himself, nearly spilling the open beer bottle he's already nursing.

"Sorry about that," I say, shrugging out of his grasp to catch the dogs by their collars. "They can be a little bratty around strangers."

Nick huffs out a laugh. "It's fine. Guess I'd be the same way if my gut dragged the floor."

"Yeah. Be right back." I blink away my annoyance and haul Frankie and Oscar to their kennels, frowning when they begin whimpering.

"I'm sorry, guys. But you kind of started it when you tried to bite my date."

Frankie howls in response, which translates to, *You started it when you brought that douche into the house.*

And I'm pretty sure Oscar yips out, *I'm telling Rowan about this.*

"This won't take long, I promise," I assure them before I shut the door behind me.

Then I clear my throat and adjust my boobs in preparation for my return to the kitchen, where I find Nick manspreading on one of the stools and twisting the cap off a fresh beer.

"Want one?" he offers as I walk past him to check on our food.

"I'm fine, thanks," I mumble, cringing at the prospect of his beer breath.

"So," he begins when I turn back from the oven. "What's for dinner?"

I open my mouth to answer him, but I'm interrupted by the lock beeping, and my heart leaps when the front door swings open.

"Hey, it's me," Rowan calls out. "You stopped answering my texts, so I got worried—"

He cuts himself off abruptly as his gaze lands on the extra occupant, and I clear my throat.

"Um, hey. This is Nick. Nick, this is Rowan," I say awkwardly.

Nick nods in Rowan's direction. " 'Sup, man."

"Good to meet you," Rowan says, his voice just low enough to contradict the sentiment. "I guess I didn't realize that date you mentioned was tonight," he adds in my direction.

I shrug, forcing as much nonchalance as I can muster. "It was sort of a last-minute thing."

"So ... you're roommates?" Nick asks hesitantly when the silence stretches too long.

"I live in Baton Rouge and only come to Camellia a couple of days a week for work," Rowan answers. "I usually stay at my sister's while I'm in town, but Claire lets me crash here sometimes."

"What he didn't say is that said sister just married his best friend, and he doesn't like to hang around while they're 'trying for a baby,' " I explain to Nick.

Nick forces a smile and draws an imaginary line in the air between Rowan and me. "And the two of you met ... how?"

Our eyes lock as we silently debate how to answer that question.

"His sister and I are coworkers," I finally manage to say.

"Right." Nick furrows his brow, probably trying to make the connection between "coworker's brother" and "guy friend who stays over on the regular."

Another uncomfortable silence ensues until Rowan speaks up. "Well, I can see why you weren't answering the phone, and it's not because you're sick, since you're obviously entertaining a guest. So I'll just leave this here and head over to Daisy and Landry's. Sorry about the interruption."

He steps forward to drop a grocery bag onto the counter, backing away just as quickly. And even though this was exactly the result I'd hoped for, I feel a flicker of disappointment when he doesn't put up a fight.

"You didn't have to ..." My voice gets caught in my throat when I realize he's brought me another PMS care package, this one with two pints of salted caramel ice cream, one of them bearing a peanut-free label. "Thank you," I croak out.

"Have a good night," Rowan says, shooting me an apologetic smile before he backs out of the house and shuts the door behind him.

I stare at the empty doorway for a second before I hear Nick huff out a laugh, and I turn to look at him questioningly.

"He had me worried for a second there," he says mockingly.

"What do you mean?"

Nick shrugs and takes a sip from his beer bottle. "Guy walks in like he owns the place, so I'm thinking he might be the competition. Then he apologizes, like he's the one encroaching on *my* territory." He chuckles to himself, and I frown.

"And what makes you so sure there's no competition?" I ask, my tone hardening.

He glares at me. "If anything were going on, he wouldn't have backed off so easily."

I lift my chin and ignore the stinging in my eyes. "Maybe he's just a nice guy."

"Either way, I'm good. Women like you don't do bad things with nice guys," he drawls, leering at me before he takes another sip.

"And exactly what kind of woman am I?" I demand, crossing my arms over my chest, but the door flies open again before I get my answer.

"Hey," Rowan says, sounding a little out of breath, and I can't help the thrill that runs through me.

"You're back?" I ask.

"Yeah. I was going to leave when—funny story—I realized you never said you didn't want me here," he replies carefully.

Nick scoffs and shoots me an amused look. "She's saying it now."

Rowan's eyes meet mine. "Are you?"

My breathing gets shallow as he continues staring at me, measuring my reaction. "I ... I'm on a date," I sputter.

"I know, and I'll leave as soon as you tell me to go," he continues, taking another step inside. "I just need to hear you say it."

"Come on, bruh, she obviously—"

"Nobody asked you, Nate." Rowan's gaze doesn't stray from mine.

"It's Nick," my date mumbles.

"Doesn't matter," Rowan says. "I'm talking to Claire."

A smile creeps across my face. "Then keep talking," I tell Rowan, and Nick grunts in protest.

Rowan smirks back at me and drops his overnight bag, letting it hit the floor with a deliberate thud.

"Maybe I'm tired of talking," he says as he strides across the room and stops in front of me. Then he cups his hand over my jaw and pauses to raise his brow, wordlessly asking for my consent.

My chest heaves as I nod, and he leans in to capture my lips with his. He hums when I yield to him and allow his tongue to slip inside, and I clutch at the collar of his shirt. Within seconds, I lose the ability to think about anything else but this, his firm chest beneath my hands, his fingers intertwining with my hair, the way he tastes like he's been sipping a cool glass of sweet tea in lieu of a room-temperature beer, and how amazing it would feel if I could just get closer. I *need* him closer, and preferably less clothed.

I'm still wondering how to get Rowan to lift me up and carry me to bed when he finally pulls away.

"Sorry, Nick," he begins, his voice gravelly and shiver-inducing. "But I think ..."

But his apology dies at the sound of the door slamming.

claire

"WELL, that worked even better than I hoped," Rowan says, sounding smug.

We must have been kissing for a while, judging by the rumble of Nick's truck as it leaves the driveway, although it wasn't long enough for me. My fingers are still twisted into the fabric of Rowan's shirt while my entire body continues humming with anticipation. But he doesn't move to kiss me again.

"Are you all right?" he asks, taking a step back to regard me carefully.

Dazed and drunk with desire, I blink and attempt to shake the fog from my head.

"Was he really that bad?" Rowan continues when I don't answer, his concern etched on his face.

That's when I realize he didn't come back to stake his claim. Rowan didn't march across the room and kiss the living daylights out of me because he was overwrought with jealousy. And he certainly isn't here to declare his attachment to me, since I've repeatedly told him that'll never happen. He simply thinks he's being a good wingman by rescuing me from a bad date. Meanwhile, I'm the dumbass getting all hot and bothered over what I mistakenly assumed was his possessive side.

"Um, no," I rasp. "Not that bad. It just wasn't there, you know?"

His expression softens, because he's relieved to hear that my date hasn't mistreated me. I don't think he even cares that the competition is out.

"They can't all be dedicated enough to risk anaphylactic shock for an excuse to hit on you, I guess," he teases.

I laugh, but it feels hollow. "Can't say I've found anyone else willing to go to the same lengths."

His face breaks out into a wide grin. "I'd say I'm sorry it didn't work out, but the truth is I'm grateful I don't have to go back to Daisy and Landry's tonight. I accidentally overheard her calling him the Big Bad Wolf again, and I may never be able to erase that imagery from my brain. Especially after he growled at her." He shivers in disgust.

"Hey, they've earned the right to let their freak flags fly," I say, trying to hide my disappointment.

"They definitely have," he concedes. "I'd just rather not be around while they're hoisting them up the pole."

I let out a more genuine laugh that time. "Fair enough."

He continues smiling and staring at me, making my insides feel all warm and mushy. "Are you sure you're okay? It seems like something's bothering you."

"I'm fine, really," I lie.

"Claire, if I overstepped just now—"

"No," I interrupt him. "I appreciate what you did."

I just wish you wouldn't have stopped doing it, my subconscious finishes for me.

"You know you can always call me if you need, right? Even if I'm not in town, any time a guy makes you feel uncomfortable or you just want to get away, I'll come to your rescue. I promise."

"I know," I say with a rueful smile. "Thank you." He reaches out to take my hand and gives it an affectionate squeeze, and my chest mimics the gesture with my heart.

Why am I so disappointed he's not making a move on me right now when I literally set this whole thing up to deter him?

I'm the one who keeps telling him I'm not looking for anything real or lasting, that I don't want any of the same things he does. And regardless of whether that's true, I can't give him what he wants. I've finally gotten him to see that I'm not only a danger to his virtue but a dead-end street.

So why am I standing here on the verge of tears at the very idea of him only seeing me as a friend?

Maybe his lack of jealousy is a blow to my ego. I guess a part of me expected a little more fire from his response after the way he's been chasing me lately. Although that kiss *was* pretty steamy, at least for me.

No, it's not my pride that's been wounded. I'm afraid the origins of this ache are closer to my heart.

I choke back the emotion lodged in my throat, but he drops my hand and turns away to sift through that bag of groceries before I can speak.

"So I guess you weren't really sick after all," he muses as he saves the ice cream in the freezer.

Maybe a little guilt-ridden and a touch lovesick ...

"My stomach's been sort of weird all day, but I don't think I'm contagious," I say dumbly.

"Hmm. Well, now that you're free and clear, what do you want to do tonight?" he asks.

Anything that involves your bare skin against mine, especially if we can talk and cuddle after.

"Nothing really," I say instead.

He sniffs the air as he walks by me with his bag, and I shamelessly run my eyes over him as I briefly consider the ethical implications of a not-so-accidental peanut exposure and a hydrocortisone cream massage. A little contact dermatitis wouldn't be all that bad, would it? Especially not when I'd promise to nurse him back to health ...

Holy crap. I'm actually losing it.

"Did your date request his steak well done?" Rowan poses with a laugh.

"Oh, shit," I curse before turning to the oven. "I almost forgot—"

But my voice breaks off when his hands cover my shoulders, and he steers me toward my bedroom.

"Why don't you run yourself a hot bath while I finish dinner? You look like you could use a little self-care moment."

"Okay," I squeak. My bottom lip trembles as I let him lead me on, and I worry I'm either going to start sobbing or yank him down to join me in that bath.

"You can even put on your spicy pajamas, and I promise I won't say a word."

I accidentally let out a whimper, and he stops once he realizes I'm trying not to cry.

"Claire," he begins, spinning me around. "What's going on?"

I shrug as the first tear slips down my cheek, and he reaches up to wipe it. But I can't answer him without defaulting to a full-blown ugly cry.

"Hey, you can tell me anything, remember?" he reassures me. I can't tell him what I don't understand, though, and everything suddenly seems so hopeless and overwhelming.

"I think … I just … I can't …" As predicted, a huge sob wracks my body before I can go on.

"Come here," he says in a soothing tone as he wraps his arms around me and pulls me into a hug. I bury my face in his chest, mortified, but he continues rubbing my back and crooning into my ear.

"It's all right, I've got you," he whispers, sending me on another emotional loop-de-loop.

No, that might actually be the ground falling out beneath me when Rowan lifts me up to cradle me within his arms. My stomach swoops and I cling to him as he takes a few steps forward, stopping to shut off the oven before he carries me to my bedroom. He yanks the covers back with one hand and gently lays me on the bed.

I clutch at his shirt when he tries to pull away. "No," I breathe. "Stay with me, please."

He frowns, but he nods and kicks off his shoes before he slides in beside me, and I curl into him before he can put any distance between us.

"I'm sorry," I rasp once I manage to stop crying, peering up at him through swollen eyes and undoubtedly looking like a snotty mess. "I don't know what's wrong with me."

He cocks an eyebrow. "Don't take this the wrong way, but I suspect it could be hormonal."

I sigh. He's right, of course. My period's due any day now. And here's to another month in which I let the infamous PMS-driven spiral into despair sneak up on me.

At least I can blame most of this on my shifty hormones, though.

"You'd think I'd have made the connection, especially with the stomach cramps," I say with a sad smile.

"Can I get you anything?" he asks, bracing himself to rise from the bed.

"No, thank you. Just ... don't leave me," I plead again.

"I'm not going anywhere," he reassures me. He continues stroking my back as he leans down to kiss my forehead, and I can't help it when the tears begin all over again.

"You're breaking my heart," he says quietly when I accidentally whimper loud enough for him to hear.

"I can't stop myself," I wail, and I'm grateful when he seems to assume I'm referring to my tears and not the way I keep hurting him. "It just feels like no matter what I do, I'm going to end up alone."

"You're not going to be alone. You can't get rid of me that easily. I'll always be here, overstaying my welcome until you force me out."

I shake my head, inadvertently wiping my snot onto his shirt. "No, you won't. I won't let you. You have to go out and find your perfect little Catholic girl, the one who realizes how lucky she'd be to cook and clean and pray for you all day. And she'll be as gorgeous and sweet and innocent as you are, and your family's going to love her. You'll have a beautiful church wedding and an amazing honeymoon, because you were smart enough not to waste yourself on me. And you'll probably knock her up the first time you have sex, and like, every time after that. So you'll have a shitload of babies, and they'll all be perfect, just like you. Because you deserve that, Rowan. You deserve everything you've ever wanted." It all comes out as a barely intelligible ramble from my place at his chest, but he's still listening intently.

He lets out a shaky exhale. "You deserve all that, too. And you're going to have it—a man who loves you for you and not only for what you can do for him, a man who lives to chase you and doesn't mind when you make him work for it. Someone who's willing to do anything to show you how much he wants you and needs you, because you're the most amazing woman he's ever known. He'll remind you every day that you're sexy and strong, and he'll tell you that he can't bear the idea of living without you, that one kiss was enough to scramble his brain chemistry and shift the way he sees the world forever ... that he could never go back to the man he was before you." He pauses and gulps loudly. "I'll make sure of it."

"But what if he doesn't exist?" I whine.

"He does. I promise." His voice cracks when he says it.

I shake my head. "I don't know. Maybe I'm just unlovable."

He pushes me away, and I panic for a second, thinking I've said too much. But he's only repositioning me so that he can gaze into my eyes when he says, "You are *not* unlovable—far from it. And I never want to hear you say that again."

"But if it weren't true, I'd be ..."

I can't finish when I read the look on his face, though. His brows are drawn together over his watery eyes, and the corners of his mouth are turned down.

"You'd already be in the arms of a man who loves you?" he whispers.

I have to force my lungs to keep working as he continues staring at me. "I know you care about me, but it's not the same," I venture and watch for his reaction.

"Only because you won't let me love you the way I want to."

My eyes are fixed on his lips as he waits for me to run with his confession. For once, I wish I could give him the response he's looking for. Instead, I make the dumbest move ever—or at least the most selfish—when I reach up and drag his face down to mine.

claire

ROWAN'S MUSCLES relax as he melts into the kiss, his lips moving against mine so slowly and deliberately that there's no mistaking his feelings for me. This isn't the way you kiss someone you only want to sleep with, or even someone you're trying to save from a bad date, and it's certainly not just a kiss between friends. He's savoring it, like he's been dying to kiss me, or he's worried it might be his last chance.

Despite all that, it doesn't take long for his careful, unhurried kisses to grow more demanding. His hands curl around my sides as he hauls me in closer, molding his body to mine and showing me how badly he wants me, to my relief. And the low moan that rumbles up from his chest in conjunction with me rolling my hips into his says he *needs* me.

Good, because I need you, too.

I must have accidentally articulated that thought aloud, because Rowan immediately tenses and pulls away, leaving me with my chest heaving as I struggle to catch my breath.

"I'm sorry. We can't," he rasps.

My chin quivers again as I twist my fingers into his shirt, clinging to him and forcing our bodies back together. He closes his eyes and inhales sharply when I press my lips to his throat.

"Please, Rowan," I coax, kissing my way up his neck.

"Don't ... tempt me," he barely gets out.

"But I need you to finish what we started the night we met," I mumble against his skin before nipping just below his ear. Then I reposition myself beneath him, arching my back and rolling my hips into his as I relish in his warmth.

He hisses and plants a knee between my thighs to stop me from doing it again. "It's not that I don't want to, believe me. But you know I can't," he repeats.

"Would it really be so bad if we gave in, just this once?" I ask, my desperation clear in my voice.

"Yes," he answers automatically, but I watch his throat muscles contract as he grapples with his conscience. "I mean, no, not now. It would be amazing now." He falters for a second and shifts his position over me again, crushing his hard body into mine. I seize the opportunity to hitch my leg over his hip and hold him there.

"But later ... we'd both feel sad ... and—and empty," he continues rambling as he presses himself into me in a way that both satisfies and intensifies that need at the same time.

I shake my head and clutch him tighter. "That's why I need you to fill me up," I reply in my most sultry tone and lean up to scrape my teeth over his bottom lip, earning a half-whimper, half-growl from him.

"I've never wanted anything more," he insists. "But I'm not sure I can give myself away until I don't have to worry about holding anything back."

"Then stop holding back," I tell him before I can think better of it.

He pants as he braces himself over me, his eyes searching mine. "Are you sure?"

"Yes," I nearly cry out, nodding vehemently.

And with that, he reaches to pull his shirt up over his head, and I scramble to help him out of it. He leans down to kiss me again as one of his hands drifts up my side, dragging the fabric and exposing me as he goes. The moment he presses his warm skin to mine, I realize he's not playing around anymore. This feels different than that first night. Even though he still has his reservations, there's a new sense of urgency. And knowing him makes it seem all the more reckless this time around.

Rowan's fingers work frantically as he unbuttons my jeans and slides them down my hips, his gaze catching on my bare legs, and I reach out to offer my assistance. But he gently averts my hands and sits back on his heels.

"I'm sorry," he says again, clearing the emotion from his throat. "I don't want to stop, but I have to make sure you understand what this means to me—what *you* mean to me."

I still myself in front of him when I finally hear the agony in his voice.

What the hell am I doing? Guilting him into having sex with me? Using him to make myself feel better? Taking away something so important and precious to him, all in the name of avoiding real intimacy?

This isn't fair to either of us. I shouldn't have to resort to seducing a man or coercing him to sleep with me, and regardless of our true feelings for one another, what I'm doing right now isn't coming from a place of love or affection. This is lust and pride and loneliness ... and probably a strong dose of hormones.

"Because you're afraid you might say something you don't mean in the heat of the moment?" I ask carefully.

"I'm more afraid of saying something I *do* mean," he admits with a rueful smile. "In fact, I want to say it, especially since I promised you the truth. But if you can't handle that, then ..."

My chest feels tight when I realize he's looking for a way out. He may be trying to soften the blow, knowing I wouldn't take his rejection very well, but he still can't bring himself to go through with it. And as much as I'd like to attribute the cold feet to his strict moral code and assume he's trying to avoid using me to satisfy his physical urges, with the way he keeps implying his feelings for me run even deeper than I thought, I suspect he's afraid *I'm* the one using *him*.

Which is exactly what I'm doing by not respecting his boundaries and taking advantage of his weakness for me. It's also why walking away from me in the beginning was the smartest thing he's ever done.

"No," I choke out. "You're right. We shouldn't ... not like this, anyway."

He looks equally disappointed and relieved. "I'm sorry I've ruined the moment again," he says softly.

"Don't apologize. If anyone should be sorry, it's me," I reply, frowning and reaching up to stroke his cheek. "There's nothing wrong with having standards or needing a different level of trust. And if I were a better friend, I wouldn't make you second guess yourself."

He sighs and holds my hand in place. "That's the thing—I do trust you, more than anyone, and I *want* to give you all of me. I want to make you feel good, to see that look on your face and know I put it there. I want to finish what we started, to follow through with my promise to make love to you over and over again, then lie awake and listen to you talk until the sun comes up."

I inhale sharply when his declaration sends a wave of heat through me, but he continues.

"But we're not meant to have that if you're only ever going to see me as a friend."

I tug my arm back. "Because you're supposed to be saving that stuff for the person you marry."

The intensity in his stare makes me shiver. "You know I can't take love and commitment out of the equation. It's all or nothing for me."

"And we both know I can't give you all the things you need," I add with a shrug.

"No," he replies, scoffing. "We don't know that at all. What makes you so sure you're not the person I've been saving myself for?"

I turn my eyes away when he reminds me of the claims Daisy made earlier this afternoon. "Come on. You've made it very clear that I'm not—"

"When have I ever implied that I only want you for sex?" His tone is deep and serious this time, and suddenly all of my worldly experience doesn't seem to matter.

"I ... well, you ..." I sound like the clumsy, young virgin with a crush, distracted by the way his jaw flexes as he waits for me to come up with an answer.

"You haven't exactly been shy about reminding me of how inconvenient your attraction is, since I don't meet your qualifications," I finally manage to articulate.

He shakes his head. "I'm sorry. It was stupid and naive of me to have so many expectations for the woman I should fall for, and I never should have let you doubt that you exceeded them in the first place. But I've been trying to tell you that I know better now, and the only thing I need *her* to be is *you*."

"You don't mean that," I squeak out in a small voice, because I don't know what else to say.

"Have you ever known me to be a liar?" he poses with a coy smile.

"Rowan ... I can't let you sacrifice everything you want most." He looks confused, so I continue. "I can't give you the family you dream about."

"None of that means anything to me if I can't have it with you."

"Don't say that," I whisper, my lip quivering at the realization that I've failed him.

"But it's the truth," he insists. "I love you, Claire."

"No," I whine. "You're confused. It's the chemistry messing with your head, and I made it worse when I—"

"I'm not the one who's confused. Not anymore."

"But you walked in on me with another man tonight, and you don't even seem to care," I practically wail.

"Of course I care. But you tried to convince me to date someone else first, and when that didn't work, you kept insisting you only liked me as a friend," he says with a shrug. "Even though I didn't actually believe you, how else was I supposed to prove you wrong without letting you figure it out for yourself?"

I feel myself pouting. "But you weren't even jealous."

His brow lifts in astonishment. "What the heck do you call that back there?"

"Helping a friend?" I offer.

"A better wingman would have found another way to get rid of

Nick that didn't involve kissing you in front of him," he admits as his mouth turns up in a dimpled smirk.

"But you ..." I can't even finish my next objection because the thought of him barging in and kissing me like that simply because he wanted to is enough to knock the wind from my lungs.

"I may not be much of a fighter, but I wasn't about to wait outside for you to reply to a check-in text after finding some other man's truck in the driveway. I'm nice, but I'm not *that* nice."

I bite my lip, unable to resist the urge to push his buttons. "Were you really jealous?"

He lets out a low growl. "Baby, I'm jealous of Oscar and Frankie as soon as you start giving belly rubs," he teases, making me simper.

He reaches out for my hand and begins playing with my fingers as he continues. "I'm resentful of my sister, because she gets to live so close to you and see you all the time. I'm pretty sure I've developed my first grudge, thanks to your ex. And I've never been envious of an inanimate object before, but I'd give anything to trade places with your chest waders. Hell, I'm still bitter because you won't let me help you with your charts," he divulges. "And you doubted I was ready to risk it all when I found out you were on a *date* tonight?"

"Wait, did you just say you're jealous of my midwife?" I ask, cocking an eyebrow.

He shrugs shyly. "To be fair, the chest-waders thing was much weirder."

"Is it weird that I like it?" I ask coyly.

He hums and pulls me in for a kiss instead of giving me a verbal answer, and it isn't long before we find ourselves in the same position as before.

"I meant what I said, Claire," he tells me between kisses. "You're all I ever think about, all I want. I'm so in love with you, and I need you to know that before anything else happens."

I clutch at his back in response, digging my nails into his muscles when he deepens the kiss again. This time I reach down to unbutton his pants, only to find them already undone. He backs away long enough to slide them down his legs, and I scramble to sit up and peel off my shirt.

His eyes devour me, and I swear I can feel the heat of his desire radiating off him. I lick my lips and take his hand in mine, bringing it up to flatten his palm against my chest.

"You're the only man who's ever made my heart race like this, you know," I admit, and his shoulders rise and fall. "I can't say I've been saving myself for you, and I can't even make any promises about what happens after tonight. But I already know it's going to be so different with you. You make me feel things I've never felt before, and we've barely even gotten started."

He groans and cradles my jaw as he moves in to kiss me, guiding me to lie back so he can hover over me again. But he stops abruptly, letting out a frustrated grunt when his scapular cord catches on my bra.

I stifle a giggle when he shifts his position to untangle us, but he doesn't laugh. Instead, he rolls onto his side and gazes at me with that tortured look on his face.

I sigh, unable to hide my disappointment. "I know. It's okay."

"I'm sorry," he says, his voice cracking.

"Don't be. I told you, this is a part of what makes you … *you*. Think you can forgive me for trying to molest you again?" I ask with a hopeful smile.

"There's nothing to forgive. I'd still eat a jar of peanut butter just to have your hands on me," he mumbles, his somber tone contradicting his favorite joke.

"So you're willing to risk your life for a night with me, just not your soul," I retort cheekily, trying to lighten the mood, but his frown deepens.

"It's not just my own soul I'm trying to protect," he replies, his expression finally softening, and I have to blink away the tears that immediately form again.

"Don't bother. I'm already a lost cause," I say quietly.

He heaves out a frustrated sigh. "There's no such thing. And even if there was, I'd argue that you're a better person than most, even on your worst days."

"Have you already forgotten the part when I lied to you and invited a strange man into my house? We both know he was only here for one thing, and it wasn't a spirited theological debate," I spit out, annoyed at myself for forgetting that I'm supposed to be pushing Rowan away. "So stop acting like all the reasons you judged me in the beginning don't exist anymore. We both know this could never work."

"What are you talking about?" he asks incredulously.

"You can't tell me it doesn't matter that I'm divorced, not when I know your church wouldn't even allow us to be together."

He props himself up on his elbow. "Who told you that?"

"You ... and your family," I admit, and he glares at me. "Even if I were to become Catholic for you, we can't get married in your church. I already had my suspicions, but I overheard your sisters talking about it at Easter."

He groans. "Contrary to what she may believe, Magnolia isn't always right."

"She's right this time, though, isn't she?"

"I love all of my siblings," he begins, as if he needs the reminder. "But none of them speak for me, not even Daisy, and they're certainly not ordained to represent the entire Holy Roman Catholic Church." He pauses to scrunch up his nose before adding, "Except maybe Rosemary. But that's beside the point, because—"

"Enough, Rowan," I blurt out, cutting him off. "Look, I can believe you'd get over the part about me already being ruined. But I can't understand why you keep stringing me along when you know damned well we can't actually be together! Why do you insist on torturing us both if you're just going to fall back on the rules again?"

My eyes sting and my face heats with embarrassment after my voice breaks off and makes that last part sound like a plea for mercy. But that's exactly what it is.

He gulps as he stares me down. "Is this why you won't let me love you, because you think it's not allowed?"

"It's not the only reason," I pause to sniffle, "but it's a pretty good one."

He bites his lip, and I want to knock the smile he's trying to hide off his face.

"For someone so good at so many things, you've done a very poor job of eavesdropping," he says in a patronizing tone.

"What the hell is your problem?" I demand, reaching out and shoving him in the chest. But he catches my hand and holds on to it.

"First of all, you're not ruined or damaged goods, and even though I disagree with most of your views on physical intimacy, none of that diminishes your value or dignity as a woman, and it's certainly never made me want you any less," he tells me without dropping my gaze. "Secondly, I'd never want you to convert *for me*. I'd love it if you decided you wanted to become a Catholic and share my love of God and the Church, more than anything, but I'd never want you to fake it on my behalf."

I sniff again, and he reaches up to swipe his thumb over my cheek as he continues. "And thirdly, if anyone's been ruined in this scenario, it's me. Regardless of whether I've been successful in upholding your virtue and mine, I don't need to have sex with you to know that I'll never want anyone else as long as I live."

I blink at him, unable to process what he's saying.

"I told you, Claire. One kiss from you was more than enough to alter my brain chemistry forever."

"But none of that matters," I repeat. "I can't—"

"Yes, you can. Well, most likely," he interrupts me to say with a shrug. "Your mom said you were baptized, right?"

I nod.

"I've already spoken to a priest and a canonical lawyer. If you ever wanted to have your first marriage annulled, there's a good chance it could easily and quickly be declared invalid due to a lack of form," he explains, trying not to grin.

I gasp and shove him again. "You spoke to a church lawyer about this without telling me or even asking my permission?"

He opens and closes his mouth a few times. "Okay, maybe I overstepped. But I didn't give out any personal details, I swear. It was one of those asking-for-a-friend conversations."

"Did you really ask a priest whether my first marriage was valid so you could walk around with this in your back pocket?"

"It's not like I did it just to win an argument," he replies, then he cringes. "Except, maybe this one."

"Ugh," I groan. "I can't stand you when you're right."

"And what about the rest of the time, since we both know I'm not right very often?" He smirks and tugs me closer.

I sigh and allow Rowan to drape my arms over his shoulders. I don't think anyone's ever looked at me with this much affection and adoration before. No human, anyway. And now that the possibility of a long-term future together seems slightly less implausible, I suppose I could risk dipping a toe into the bottomless pool of my feelings for him.

"The rest of the time, I think you're dangerous. And I like you so much that it scares me," I confess, because I feel like he deserves at least some of the truth, though it will take some time to come to terms with the rest of it myself.

He sucks in a breath, as if I've just delivered the greatest news he's ever heard. "Do you really?"

"I let you keep your boxers this time, didn't I?" I reply, and he grins so hard he barely manages to kiss me.

"Now, being that I'm so deeply in love with you, and you seem to be in such enthusiastic like with me, wouldn't that make us officially more than friends?" he asks once he pulls away.

"Unofficially, at least," I say, rolling my eyes and trying to stifle a smile.

"And by unofficially, do you mean we're not labeling it? Or is it unofficial because no one else can know?" He scratches the back of his head nervously as he awaits my answer.

"I guess that depends on how much you value your reputation," I mumble.

He flashes me another grin, this one more devious than the last. "Oh, but you're not getting off that easy anymore, Claire Bear. You can't just throw out one of those comments and not expect me to disprove it."

I groan. "You're totally going to do that whole love-bombing thing now, aren't you?"

"Absolutely," he confirms. "For, like, ever."

"Ugh, not the star-crossed soulmates crap again," I whine to hide the way I'm equal parts giddy and terrified at that prospect.

He hums and regards me carefully. "We both know how much you like it cheesy."

"That's not exactly what makes you dangerous," I tell him, my voice taking on a sultry tone.

He bites his lip and reaches over to trace a finger over my tattoos. "Well, then, it's a good thing at least one of us was paying attention in that NFP class. I'll need to remember some of those other methods for keeping your cup full, at least until I can convey the full extent of my affection physically."

My breath catches in my throat. "Maybe I should have gotten you out of those drawers while I still had the chance."

He shakes his head slowly. "I'm doing you a favor. If you think it's bad now, just wait until you hear me say I love you while I'm in the middle of proving it to you. There's no coming back from that, and you know it."

A whole new brand of desire overtakes me, one so strong it clouds my vision. I have to blink to regain my sense of sight, then remind myself how to breathe. Hell, I think my lady parts are applauding him for that one.

"You might be right," I concede, a chill running through me as I recall how close we were to that very scenario. "All the more reason to wait, I suppose."

"No sex until marriage?" He lets out an exaggerated sigh. "I mean, I guess, if it's *that* important to you."

My hand flies up to my mouth when a cackle threatens to escape, and he tugs it away, forcing the laugh out.

"You may have gotten me to admit that I like you and that it could never be just physical between us, but I'm still not sold on a second marriage. So I hope you realize you're setting yourself up for a long, torturous, and most likely fruitless wait," I tell him.

"I'm not worried," he replies cooly, taking my hand and bringing it to his lips. "In case you haven't noticed, I am a very," he pauses to brush a kiss over my knuckles, making my stomach dip, "*very*," he emphasizes and punctuates with another kiss, "very patient man, especially once I know what I want."

CHAPTER FORTY-ONE

claire

I'M PLEASANTLY surprised to awaken in Rowan's arms the next morning. He's usually up early, but today he skips the run and lingers in bed, sighing contentedly and pressing a kiss to the back of my neck. And I can't help the smile that spreads across my face as he tightens his hold around me.

"Not that I'm not enjoying this," I begin. "But I'm afraid I'm going to ruin the mood if I don't get to the bathroom in the next minute."

"Fine. Hurry back, though," he says with a playful tap on the butt as soon as he lets me go.

The second I roll over, I feel it—the dreaded gush announcing the start of my period. I groan and clench all of my core muscles as I waddle to the bathroom.

"Whatever you do, don't look at the sheets!" I call out when I get to the toilet and see that I've already bled through my clothes. I wouldn't have normally gone to bed without any protection so close to P-Day, but last night wasn't exactly routine. Thankfully, I keep clean underwear and a fancy robe in my bathroom for such an occasion.

By the time I make it back, Rowan has already stripped the sheets and is carrying the bundle out the door. He's also managed to retrieve his glasses, though he didn't bother getting dressed. Not that I'm complaining.

"What are you doing?" I ask, following him.

"Getting these in the wash before the stain sets in," he replies matter-of-factly.

I cross my arms over my middle. "Are you really taking care of my period sheets?"

The corner of his mouth lifts when he turns to glare at me. "Am I supposed to be afraid of a little menstrual blood?"

"Fair enough, Doc," I say with an eye roll.

He chuckles quietly as he ventures down the hallway in nothing but his boxers, and I pause to admire the view. Rowan might be right about this whole religion thing after all, because I certainly owe God my gratitude for creating the masterpiece in front of me.

As soon as I acknowledge the thought, an overwhelming sense of comfort and peace washes over me, as if I've been enveloped within a warm embrace.

My eyes water unexpectedly when I imagine it being God's reply to my silly, half-irreverent prayer. Then, an even crazier idea fills my mind, a flower blooming from the notion Daisy planted yesterday, and I find myself considering whether this man could have been *made for me*.

Is it possible Rowan isn't simply some random guy I rescued from an allergic reaction, but the person sent specifically to save *me*? He might even be a custom build, designed to meet my specifications long before I knew any better, and he's been aging to perfection until I could finally recognize him for what he is—exactly what I've always needed.

And if that were all true, wouldn't it mean I was also made just for him, flaws and all?

I let out an incredulous laugh and dry my eyes, resolving to keep those thoughts close to my heart for now.

Rowan returns as I'm retrieving a set of clean sheets from the linen closet and wordlessly falls in, helping me make the bed and smiling as he pulls the covers back and gestures for me to slide in first. My own grin widens when he slips in beside me and draws me into his arms again, as if he really meant it before when he said his time with me is never wasted.

"How are you feeling?" he asks, his lips finding my shoulder this time.

"Like I'd rather stay in bed all day," I reply, and he hums.

"Should I reschedule my patients and stick around to take care of you?"

I heave out a sigh. "While that sounds amazing, I'll just have to settle for a couple of Midol and something chocolatey from the vending machine later."

He growls and gathers my hair to expose more of my neck. "Are you sure you can't stay home and rest?"

My eyelashes flutter as he continues kissing his way across my shoulders. It feels ... heavenly. There's no other word for it. And it shouldn't—I remember hating the thought of my ex even breathing in my vicinity at certain points in my cycle. But I can't seem to get enough of Rowan's touch, and it makes me wonder if this is part of what he tried explaining before, about the purpose of physical intimacy within marriage.

"No, and I really should be getting ready by now," I say after a while.

"Okay," he intones and backs away. "I'll try to leave you alone."

"Go on, get outta here," I tell him, gesturing for him to get up first.

He narrows his eyes at me before scooting to the edge of the bed, and this time I'm the one who darts over to deliver a playful smack on his butt when he stands. It's a mistake, though, because he exacts his revenge by holding me down and tickling me senseless, which leads to me pulling him in for a short make-out session before we're interrupted by Frankie and Oscar's barking. And I can't fault them, since they haven't been let out since last night.

Rowan assures me he'll tend to the dogs while I get myself ready for work, and he hands me a cup of coffee when I walk into the kitchen about fifteen minutes later, after I give my boys the apologetic snuggles they're owed, of course.

"Since you won't let me stay home and pamper you, can I at least come back tonight and cook dinner?" he asks, filling me with equal parts panic and excitement. I'm also having a hard time getting over the way he looks in those scrubs he's started wearing.

"Don't you have to work in Baton Rouge tomorrow?"

He shrugs. "I'll get up early."

"Rowan," I begin on a sigh. "I don't know. This doesn't seem fair."

"What's unfair is making me beg you to stay when you know I'm in love with you and I can't stand being away," he replies, hooking a finger through one of my belt loops and tugging me closer. I swallow hard as I try to form a reply, but he pulls me in for a kiss before I can come up with a reasonable objection.

He rests his forehead against mine and sighs. "I'm smothering you, aren't I? I know it seems immature, but I can't help myself. Just don't be afraid to tell me when you need your space."

I cringe. "You're not smothering me. But I'm not sure it's a good idea for you to stay over anymore."

"Oh," he breathes, and I can tell he's trying to hide his disappointment.

"It's not that I didn't enjoy having you in my bed," I reassure him, and another wave of consolation fills me and gives me the courage to continue. "But I'm still new to this chastity thing. I want to respect your boundaries, but we can't keep pushing the limits, either. And I'm sure it's only a matter of time before one thing leads to another."

And if I have my say, another.

Okay, so the real Claire's still in there.

Rowan groans. "I know you're supposed to be warning me off right now, but all this talk of responsibility and chastity is just making me want you all the more. Your green flags are such a turn on."

"Get out of here, you dork," I say, trying not to simper at him.

He flashes me another grin before he leans in for one more quick kiss. "You know, there is a simple fix to all this," he mumbles before he grabs his keys and phone off the counter.

"Oh, is that the easy way out, then?" I repeat incredulously.

"I'd make marriage easy for you, Claire Bear. I promise," he says with a wink. And even though I roll my eyes and scoff at him, I can't help thinking it's the truth.

It's also a good thing I let him *cher-cher* me while I could, since my cramps are already flaring up by the time I get to homeroom. I manage to survive the first few hours of the day without bleeding through my clothes again, but I have to risk a copy run during my planning hour.

The machine is vacant when I get there, to my relief, and I greet Loren and the other teacher having lunch at the table before I get started.

"How come I never see you in the teachers' lounge?" Loren asks, and I turn to realize we're alone now.

"I'm usually too busy to hang out in here," I reply with a shrug, only offering her half of the story. If I were being honest, I'd tell her how I've always been afraid of being the odd girl out, so I either avoid situations where I might face rejection, like the gossip table in the teachers' lounge, or purposefully take myself out of contention with my off-putting humor.

But I'm certainly not going to admit all that to someone who girly girls as well as Loren does, who's pretty and dainty, yet still witty enough to snag a husband like Blake Bourgeois and tough enough to survive birthing two babies at a time, not to mention her history with Rowan.

How would *she* understand?

Loren narrows her dark eyes at me. "I always assumed you thought you were too cool for the rest of us." Then she pops a potato chip into her mouth and lifts a shoulder. "You kinda are, though."

I snort. "Bitchy doesn't equate to cool."

"You're bitchy? I never noticed. Guess I haven't spent enough time around you to tell," Loren continues with a satisfied smirk.

"You have been pretty sparse around here lately," I say with a smile of my own as I press the button on the copy machine and turn to lean against it.

Her brow lifts in acknowledgment. "Why aren't we friends again?"

I blow out a breath. "I'm not usually anyone's first choice for a girl friend."

"Funny, that's not what my guy Dr. LaFleur seems to think," she mumbles before taking a sip of her soda, and the way my posture straightens must be all too telling.

"You still talk to Rowan?" I ask before I can stop myself.

Her smile stretches. "We're practically family now."

"Right." I turn back to the copy machine to hide the flush crawling up my neck.

"He's pretty great. But I guess you already know that, since you're such good friends and all."

I swallow hard. "Yeah."

Think he's great now? You should see him in nothing but his boxers and his glasses.

I guess I'm still a work in progress, then.

"Just two single, attractive, heterosexual besties, with parts that are biologically geared to fit together ..." Loren crunches on another chip, seemingly oblivious to my inner monologue as she waits for me to fill in the blanks. "Besties that have sleepovers, from what I hear," she adds.

"Mm-hmm." I grab my copies and straighten the stack with a few taps on the machine, biting my lip to keep myself from blurting out something along the lines of, *Yeah, and I deserve a freaking trophy for not jumping his bones last night.*

"Claire?" Loren calls out, and I turn to face her. "Just so you know, if you ever needed someone to talk to about your relationship with Rowan, I'd be willing to listen. I imagine it feels awkward to discuss that sort of thing with Daisy. It was a little weird for us to make the transition from friends to in-laws, at least at first. Same with JD and me, too."

I let out a weighty exhale. "We're not really in a relationship, and there isn't much happening that I couldn't talk about with Daisy," I flat out lie, but I hate the way it sounds coming out.

Loren purses her lips and glares at me, calling my bluff. "That's not the impression Rowan's been giving me."

"What exactly has he told you?" I ask, my stomach fluttering with nerves.

"Oh, not much. But I've seen the way he looks at you, and it's a lot different than the way he looked at me," she teases.

I pull my braid over my shoulder and wrap the tail around my finger. "You think so?"

She stares at me for a second. "Can I ask you something personal?"

"You've been doing that for the better part of this conversation, haven't you?" I retort, and she rolls her eyes playfully.

"Has he kissed you?"

Not in the last few hours, sadly.

"Maybe. But we're adults. It doesn't mean anything." Again, my reaction must give me away, because Loren leans back in her chair with a satisfied grin.

"Oh, I beg to differ, and I married a man who kissed lots of women."

I look away, trying not to think about the fact that she and Rowan most likely shared a kiss in the past, as well. "Well, it's not like that with us."

"What's it like, then? Just for argument's sake."

The memory of his mouth devouring mine as I sit on the counter of the CVS self-checkout flashes in my mind, then the night we made out on the couch to test his heart rate, and the sweet, lazy kisses we shared in my bed this morning.

What's it like? It's enough to ruin me.

"Nothing particularly memorable," I lie again, though it's getting harder and harder to get the words out, especially when I can't even remember why I'm hiding it in the first place.

Am I avoiding the truth for Rowan's sake? Or am I just afraid to fess up to the way he makes me feel?

The clicking of a camera interrupts my thoughts, and Loren zooms in on the image of my reddened face before turning her phone around to show me.

"Liar, liar ... panties on fire," she drawls, and I cringe.

"It's ... not what ..." I stumble over an explanation, but she's not buying it, anyway.

"Claire," she begins, her tone softening. "For what it's worth, he never even tried to kiss me."

As stupid as it is, relief floods my chest. "He didn't?"

She shakes her head. "Nope."

"Oh," I breathe. Why does this small bit of information feel so significant?

"Sure you don't wanna tell me all about it, especially since you can hold it over my head?" she offers once more. "I promise, it'll be for my ears only."

I twirl the end of my braid around my finger as I consider it. She's right, I haven't really had the chance to dish about this to anyone. And I think I might want to.

Hell, who am I kidding? I'm *dying* to talk about Rowan.

"Why would you care? You're married to Blake the Snake. I'm sure you have much spicier stories to share," I reply, my lips twitching as I stifle another smirk.

Her eyebrows bounce suggestively as she pulls out the chair beside her and pats the open seat. "You're right. I might very well be married to the sexiest man alive," she muses with a dreamy sigh.

I give her a noncommittal shrug as I go around to plop myself down onto the chair. "You haven't seen much of Rowan, I presume."

Her eyes sparkle. "No, but I'd love to hear about it."

"He's absolutely gorgeous," I say with a groan, my eyelids feeling heavy at the mere thought of him. "And he wears glasses before bed."

Loren gasps. "Tell me they're of the chunky, plastic variety."

I shake my head. "The wire kind, the ones that can turn a perfectly nice man into a sexy paleontologist or an aging Scottish laird who isn't afraid to throw you over his shoulder," I explain, and she sighs again. "He's a great kisser, too, very attentive and eager to please."

She rears back, clutching her imaginary pearls. "Please, go on."

But I already feel guilty about the implications I'm making, less so for being crude than for only dishing about my physical attraction to Rowan.

"How much did he tell you about himself when you dated?"

"Not a whole lot, but I know those LaFleurs are a different breed," she replies. "And I mean that in the best way," she adds quickly.

"Right. So you probably know we haven't ..." But before I can even figure out how I want to finish my sentence, the door to the teacher's lounge swings open.

Loren's brother-in-law pauses a few steps into the room and glares at us. "Uh, hi."

"What the hell are you doing in here, JD?" she asks in a scolding tone.

"I work here," he retorts sarcastically before turning to me with a more polite expression. "Hey, Claire."

"Hey, Coach," I return.

"Well ... get out. We're having a girl-talk break," Loren demands as if she's not speaking to her boss.

"Technically, it's supposed to be your planning period. And I only came for a Gatorade," he says, gesturing toward the vending machine. "But now I might want to stay for the girl talk."

"Jay Dee-*hee*," Loren whines. "I'm finally making another work friend, and you're ruining it!"

He puts a dollar bill into the machine before mumbling, "I thought I was your work bestie," and adding a mocking face at the end.

"But you're a big, stinky boy. It's not the same. And I already know too much about your love life because you married my actual best friend."

JD snorts as he retrieves his drink. "I bet Daisy would be willing to tell you all about—"

"That's what I'm saying!" she interjects. "I'd really like to trade stories that don't involve one of my brothers by blood or by law for once!"

He leans back against the vending machine and crosses his arms. "I feel like Rowan pretty much fits into that category by now, anyway."

My stomach dips. "And what makes you so sure we're talking about Rowan?" I ask, mirroring Loren's tone from before.

"Come on, everyone knows he's been hanging around for you," he says before he gulps down half of his drink in one swig and lets out a burp. "Well, that's what my wife and I both think."

"Why do I find it hard to believe you and Tenley swap office gossip?" I reply in an attempt to take the heat off myself.

"He's actually kind of better at girl talk than Tenley is," Loren turns and admits quietly.

JD finishes off his sports drink and tosses the bottle into the trash can from across the room. "See, I can hang."

"Yeah, well, I'm pretty shitty when it comes to talking about real feelings. So all you're getting from me is crude humor, anyway."

Loren frowns. "Why not both?"

I blink and look away, unable to answer her.

"Yeah, why not both?" JD parrots, and Loren throws a chip at him, which he tries to catch in his mouth and misses.

"You're totally ruining this for me," she growls at him.

"I'm making it easier. It's called comedic relief," he says as he stuffs the chip crumbs into his mouth and walks over to steal another from Loren's bag. And I actually find myself laughing at him.

"This is totally weird. You guys know that, right?"

They glance at one another and shrug. "Families come in all shapes and sizes," JD declares as he pulls another bag of chips from his pocket and opens it up before placing it down on the table in front of Loren. She takes a chip without question, and the two of them stare at me expectantly as they crunch away. Truthfully, they're kind of adorable, and my heart aches at the notion of forming a familial bond like theirs.

"I mean, name a better duo," Loren continues, and JD squats down to press his cheek to hers as they pose with matching cheesy smiles, in spite of their comical size difference.

"Yeah, and on Wednesdays, we wear pink," JD declares.

A loud cackle bursts out of me, so I instinctively cover my mouth to muffle it. And maybe my heart's still a little too full from this morning, but I can't help thinking it's okay to be the girl with the big laugh and the loud feelings this time, at least with people who might actually care about me and like me for who I am. So I let myself laugh, and my friends join in.

claire

"I FORGOT what we were talking about in the first place," I say as my laughter dies down.

"I think we left off at what Rowan is like in bed," Loren reminds me, and my cheeks heat again.

JD lets out a whistle and rises to his feet. "Maybe you were right. This tea might be too hot for me."

I cock an eyebrow at him. "You talk a big game for a man who dips out at the first mention of a bed."

"I thought we were focusing on your feelings in this session," JD clarifies.

"You have to admit, it would be pretty awkward to have the details of everyone's sex lives in the back of your mind when you have to perform a classroom walk-through," I say with a grin, and Loren grunts and crosses her arms, presumably because JD's already traded stories with his brother.

"Then I'd better leave now, Ms. Claire, especially since you're on my walk-through list for next week," he replies with a silly face and an exaggerated tone.

I gulp. "What do you know?"

"Not much, other than there not being much to know. Besides

the night you met," he continues, clicking his tongue. "Now, the feelings part, I've gotten an earful on that front."

I shake my head in disbelief. "You, too? When the hell did you and Rowan become best friends?"

"Well, I figure I have the right to befriend my wife's work husband. But I thought you knew we were all golf buddies, now. Landry added him to our group chat and everything," he explains innocently, but I can tell he's growing more concerned with my reaction by the second.

"What exactly did he say?" I demand.

A crackly voice calls JD's name from the radio attached to his belt, but he reaches down to turn it off. He glances at Loren and swallows hard before he speaks again. "He told us a little about that first night, and how it shook him after he'd been so sure he was waiting for marriage. Then he talked about how well you get along despite not being on the same page about what you want in the future, all so he could get some advice."

I scoff. "Is that all?"

He cringes. "There was more, but I feel like you should hear the rest from him."

"Remind me not to trust you with any more of my secrets," Loren whispers to JD.

He clears his throat. "I'm sorry. I was honestly just looking for an excuse to bring up the chastity stuff and offer some encouragement. I mean, Lo probably has a more relatable speech on tap, but I wanted to reassure you that waiting for marriage is very rewarding and more common than you might think."

Loren jabs her elbow into his thigh, making him wince. "You could have just told her that part, you ass," she scolds him again, and he nods solemnly in agreement.

I sigh. "I'm not upset, I'm just shocked to hear that Rowan was willing to talk about what happened between us. I've sort of been thinking he's embarrassed of me."

JD rears back. "Uh, no. That's not the impression he gave me at all. Or Tenley, from what I'm told. And for the record, had he said anything to make me even think that, I'd have threatened to kick his ass."

"How bout I kick your ass?" Loren mutters, but it admittedly warms my chest to hear that JD would be so quick to defend my honor.

He rolls his eyes before he continues. "If he seemed embarrassed about anything, it's that he can't get a handle on his self-control and hasn't been able to convince you to take him seriously."

My heartbeat drums in my ears. "What do you mean, take him seriously?"

"I guess you could say he's hoping you'll actually consider something serious with him," JD replies carefully.

My cheeks heat again, and I open my mouth to speak, but I'm interrupted when the door swings open and a large bouquet of flowers appears. No, scratch that, a small shrub is being carried in by one of the secretaries.

"Is Ms. Claire in here by any chance?" she calls out blindly from behind the plant.

"Oh, she's right here!" Loren volunteers as she darts over and snatches the card from its stick. Ms. Sam hands me the flowers, while JD plucks the card away from Loren and holds it over her head until I can set the pot down and open it myself.

"You could at least read it out loud," she grumbles, stomping on JD's toe and making him curse under his breath. "After all, it's not like we don't know who it's from."

My eyes skim the handwritten note.

Dear Claire Bear,

Since the moment we met, you have filled every corner of my mind. Falling in love with you was the easiest thing I've ever done, and I promise to do everything I can to prove I'll be worth the wait. My heart beats for you and no one else. And my other parts only work for you, too.

Your soulmate,

Athanasius

P.S. Have I mentioned you have a really nice butt!

By the time I'm finished reading it aloud, I can barely make out the last few words with the tears blurring my eyes, so I hand the note over to Loren.

"Ugh, I just *knew* he'd be a Regency-romance level yearner," Loren declares and mimes a chef's kiss.

"Oh, and this came with it, too," Ms. Sam adds and drops a bag of salted caramel chocolates into my hands before she winks at me and scurries out.

JD lets out another whistle. "Wow. I think he likes you, Claire Bear."

"Yeah," I say, sniffling. "I guess he does."

"And how are you feeling about all those serious words?" he ventures hesitantly.

"I thought I said we weren't talking about feelings today?" I reply with a smirk.

JD lifts his hands in surrender. "Just sayin', a guy like Rowan LaFleur probably doesn't throw around the L-word or the butt-word unless he means it."

I nod. "Yeah. I'm afraid so."

Loren snatches the candy from me. "Good thing they're *soulmates*," she intones, helping herself to a chocolate. "What's up with the flower bush, though?"

"It's a daphne plant," I tell them. They drag out an *awww* in unison at the reference to my first name, which they only recognize because it's part of my school-based email address.

Loren gasps. "And Daphne is a flower, which means you were

always meant to be a *LaFleur*. Oh my gosh, the two of you are just perfection," she declares and adds another kiss to her fingertips.

I snort. "You mean, besides the part about one of us being divorced and the other being a virgin?"

"Eh, that kind of stuff all balances out in the end," JD declares, staring at me as if he's trying to convey something deeper. "You just have to be willing to look beyond the surface and think about the reasons God might have brought you together. He tends to have a sense of humor about these things."

"Yeah, I guess," I say, just as the bell rings, and I curse under my breath. "I've gotta go. Thanks for all this, though," I tell them, collecting my things.

"So do I," JD says, picking up the plant. "I'll bring this to your classroom in a minute," he reassures me, and I nod gratefully as he walks out.

"Wait, you're coming to Daisy's surprise party next weekend, aren't you?" Loren asks and walks around to help me.

"Yeah, of course. And I'm happy to help with anything."

"I was going to ask you to bring a finger food, but what about a soulmate instead?" she requests sweetly.

My eyes widen. "A what?"

"You and Rowan should totally soft launch your relationship," she says. "Daisy would love it."

"Oh, um, I don't know if we're ready for that," I choke out as soon as I think about his sisters watching from the sidelines.

"What do you mean? He's practically proposing to you in that note," she points out.

I swallow hard. "I know."

Her lips form a perfect oval as understanding dawns. "You're not sure you're ready to get remarried."

"Ever. And it's pretty important to him, as you may know," I confirm.

"Stop me if you've heard this one before, but I almost made the biggest mistake of my life and turned down Blake's proposal," she admits, cringing. "I was super knocked up, and the crazy baby-mama hormones had me convinced that he was only doing it because he felt obligated and not because he was a Regency-romance yearner."

"Seriously?" I ask, my brow raised.

"I was absolutely terrified to say yes. Insane, right?" She bugs her eyes, and I nod for her to continue. "But at some point, I realized I wasn't just keeping him from making a mistake. I was making myself the villain in his origin story instead of accepting the role of the princess in his love story. I had to learn to trust him when he said that I was *it* for him and that his parts worked for me and no one else."

She bounces her eyebrows suggestively, and I giggle.

"Finding one another at a weird time or through unlikely circumstances doesn't make your feelings any less true or real. If it signifies anything, it's that you'll have a better chance of making it through the hard stuff," Loren says, and I get another one of those warm, fuzzy feelings just from listening.

"And what if being with me requires him to give up one of his dreams?" I ask quietly. "How can I trust that he won't resent me for it later?"

"I guess there's no way to know that for sure, but I imagine a guy like Rowan wouldn't question God's will," she says with a shrug. "Then again, if he's anything like my husband, he wouldn't have any cause to resent you so long as you kept him happy and fulfilled and … *busy*."

I bite my lip when she emphasizes the last part. "I like the way you think, Mrs. B," I tell her and work up the courage to reach out and squeeze her arm. "Thank you, Lo."

She grins and returns the squeeze. "Anytime, Ms. Claire Bear."

"Oh, and don't forget," she calls out once I gather the rest of my things and turn to go. "On Wednesdays, we wear pink!"

rowan

"GOOD MORNING," Tenley says when we reach the back door of the clinic at the same time. "Someone's a little later than usual today."

I struggle to keep a straight face. "You sure you're not just early for once?"

"Since I know for a fact that I spent the past twenty minutes hooked up to a breast pump, just like I have every morning for the past six months, yes, I'm sure," she replies dryly.

"Oh, right," I say and gesture for her to go first.

"Don't you wanna give me an explanation before we walk inside? You know, in case you-know-who might be listening?"

I chuckle at her. "Why? I'm sure we'll both hear about my whereabouts from Mackenzie before I even know what's going on."

"Well, if you won't tell me, then perhaps Claire's charts will," Tenley purses her lips. "That was a joke, by the way. I'd never ..."

I let out another soft laugh. "I know you were only kidding, Ten. But for the record, you won't find any evidence of our relationship status in her charts."

Her brow lifts. "You have a relationship status?"

"Not officially," I admit. "But I *was* late because I stopped by the flower shop for a delivery your husband will no doubt hear of before the end of the day."

"Really?" she asks, a hint of excitement in her voice. "You know what? I think we need to talk." She glances around before she pulls me into her office and locks the door behind her.

"What's on your mind?" I ask hesitantly.

"So this is going to sound super corny, but I feel like you need to hear it." She pauses to sit on the edge of her desk and crosses her legs beneath herself. "When I first moved back to Camellia, I had no intention of staying here forever. But then I became Ethan's guardian and started falling for JD, and I realized pretty quickly that this is where God was calling me to be."

I furrow my brow. "Are you trying to use my crush on Claire to convince me to buy out Dr. Simms?"

"Maybe," she admits. "But more importantly, I want you to ask yourself where the Holy Spirit is leading you."

My expression softens. "I appreciate what you're trying to do, but I understand discernment. And I can't imagine God would want me to waste my time gaining all that specialized knowledge to work as a regular OB-GYN. No offense, but I was certain of His plan for me before, and I feel like I've been pretty obedient since then."

"And you don't think He could be calling you in a different direction now?" she asks, pausing before she adds, "You know He doesn't care about the same worldly constraints we do, right?"

I huff out a laugh. "Well, yeah, but ... I'm doing this to help people."

"Oh, so I'm not?" she replies with a taunting smile.

"You know that's not what I mean, Tenley."

"I once told myself I couldn't leave my patients behind in Texas because they needed me. Turns out, plenty of women have benefitted from my help in Camellia, and there were a few people *I* needed here, as well."

"Come on, I can't leave—"

"What are you really leaving behind, though? A medical practice with policies you don't always agree with? An empty townhouse and a lonely life? We both know you don't care about the money and the job title, and you still enjoy delivering babies."

I swallow hard and drop my eyes to the floor. "Things are finally leaning in the right direction. She'll panic and push me away if she hears I'm even considering something this big and permanent."

Tenley shrugs. "She might. But if she's the one, she'll get over it pretty quickly and want to make out with you as soon as she realizes what it signifies."

"I don't know," I say, scratching the back of my head.

"I know you won't get any closer by living two hours away," she continues. "Do me a favor, would you?"

"What's that?" I ask cautiously.

"Sometime later, I want you to imagine what your life would be like if you made the decision to stay. Then ask yourself which version of your future brings your heart a sense of consolation."

"I've already done that, and you're right, I could be perfectly happy taking over for Doc Simms. I enjoy working with you and the patients, I think the hospital's great, and I love the people in this town. But it's not my decision that makes all the difference in the end, and I can't risk scaring her off," I blurt out.

"I'm sorry," Tenley says softly, hopping down from the desk and placing a comforting hand on my shoulder. "I didn't mean to pressure you. Let's give it some time, hmm?"

I clench my jaw muscles and nod. "Thanks."

She pats my arm before she leaves me in the room, and my phone vibrates with a text message.

BLAKE

Just a head's up, but word around the courthouse is that someone's doing a title search for the plot of land on the other side of you, Lan.

LANDRY

Well, shit. Do you know who it is?

Actually, it doesn't matter who it is. Just help me put in an offer for the rest of it.

BLAKE

You'll be stuck with an assload of property taxes, man. Idk if it's worth it.

Maybe you should find someone else to buy it first …

JD

I know a guy who might be shopping for a place around here soon, especially if my wife has anything to say about it.

ROWAN

Nice try, guys.

But we all know Claire would murder me if I bought a medical practice and a parcel of land in the same day.

LANDRY

You're buying into the clinic? Why would you want to stay in Baton Rouge?

Oh, wait, I get it now. Ignore that.

So you're buying into the clinic here?

ROWAN

I guess it's okay for me to mention this if it stays between us, but Dr. Simms asked me to buy him out. Tenley and I would essentially become business partners and eventually look for a third partner to join the team.

LANDRY

So you'd be working as a regular OB-GYN?

ROWAN

Yes, but I'd still be seeing high-risk patients, too.

LANDRY

But that's dumb. You're already a specialist.

JD

It's not dumb if that's what he wants to do. That's like saying I'm stupid for coming home to coach high school football instead of playing in the NFL.

LANDRY

And that's not dumb?

BLAKE

Not when we have a family history of early onset Alzheimer's. I mean, those kids are probably rotting his brain faster than the CTE might have, but still. He wouldn't have been around to help Tenley get custody of Ethan if he'd have listened to me and became a free agent.

LANDRY

All right, fine.

Wait, is this the group with Ethan in it?

JD

Why? Are you scared he'll call you out, Doc?

LANDRY

Damn right I am.

But he'd also have made a decently objective third party for this debate.

JD

He'd probably vote for Rowan to stay if it means Tenley wouldn't have to worry about someone dependable taking Dr. Simms's place.

BLAKE

I guess I'm also biased. I'd certainly feel better about trying again if Dr. Red Flag was local.

LANDRY

Wait, what?

BLAKE

Calm your tits, Lando. It's a generalization.

LANDRY

You can't blame me for questioning you.

BLAKE

No, I guess I can't argue with that assumption.

In fact, I'm certain I'll be knocking up your sister again at some point.

It'll likely be planned next time, but still a relatively safe bet.

And you have to admit, she's awfully cute when she's pregnant.

JD

he says, though he can't remember the last time he slept more than four hours in one stretch

BLAKE

gif of "He's right You know"

I frown as I think about that last part—well, not the bit about Blake and Landry bickering, but that women like Loren and Daisy might be safer with a specialist close by.

ROWAN

Tell me more about the land.

I put my phone away for a while after that, though it buzzes every so often with a text from the group. I also get a message from Loren about the plans for Daisy's surprise birthday party this weekend, so I pause to answer her between seeing patients.

LOREN

So, just for headcount purposes, will you be bringing a plus one?

ROWAN

We both know this question isn't for planning purposes, because if I were, she'd already be on the guest list.

LOREN

Fair enough.

Is that your way of confirming the rumors?

ROWAN

Depends ... What exactly are the good people of Camellia saying about my love life?

LOREN

That you're practically shacking up with a sexy ag teacher ...

ROWAN

Sorry, cannot confirm.

LOREN

Can't deny, either?

I blow out a frustrated exhale, not because I'm concerned about people linking me to Claire, but because they're already making the wrong assumptions about us. But I guess the only way to fix that would be to give them the truth.

ROWAN

It's more like crushing really hard on the beautiful ag teacher and following her around like a puppy until she eventually caves and realizes we're meant to live happily ever after together ...

LOREN

Oh, I love it when we switch to his POV and he's already down bad! 😍

Is this your way of asking me to put in a good word for you?

ROWAN

I don't know exactly what that means, but I'm pretty sure I am in fact "down bad."

And, yes, please, I'll take all the help I can get.

LOREN

gif of man rubbing hands together

This time I can't help smiling when I slip my phone into my pocket and walk into my next appointment, nor can I stop myself from checking every so often and hoping for a text from Claire. Shortly after lunch, I get a message that makes my heart quicken.

CLAIRE

You're the worst.

ROWAN

Aw. I love you, too.

CLAIRE

Thank you for the flowers and candy.

ROWAN

You're welcome. How are you feeling?

CLAIRE

Crampy but less weepy, thanks to you.

Actually, scratch that, since you made me cry in the teachers' lounge today.

Are you planning on stopping by before you drive back to BR?

ROWAN

Are you ... asking me to stop by?

CLAIRE

I mean, Frankie and Oscar will probably be expecting you ...

(Don't tell them I said this, but I'm afraid they're a little obsessed with you.)

ROWAN

... and I haven't even gotten any wiener selfies lately.

CLAIRE

selfie with the daphne plant

Hope you don't mind unsolicited bush pics …

An obnoxious guffaw bursts out of me, one so loud that it prompts Tenley and one of the medical assistants to peek around the corner and investigate.

"Sorry," I say sheepishly. "I was just laughing at a funny text."

Tenley purses her lips shrewdly as Mackenzie flutters her eyelashes at me. "From your lady friend, Dr. Cutie Pie?" Mackenzie drawls.

I clear my throat. "Maybe."

"She looks good on you, Doc," Mackenzie declares, and my cheeks flush as I thank her.

By the time I leave the office later that afternoon, my entire body is humming with anticipation, just at the thought of seeing Claire. I'm afraid Tenley's right. There's nothing left for me in Baton Rouge, not so long as Claire is in Camellia. And maybe it's foolish of me to toss all my eggs into this basket, but I can't imagine this isn't where the Holy Spirit is leading me, especially not when a regular weekday fills me with the same joy and exhilaration I could only get from envisioning my future before.

I know the road isn't guaranteed to be an easy one, because if there's anything I've learned from the lives of the saints, it's that making the decision to trust in God and follow His will is only the beginning. But there's no doubt in my mind that this is what He's been preparing me for all this time.

My heart skips a beat when I pull up at Claire's house and see her standing in the doorway in her robe, watching as Frankie and Oscar scurry over to the driver's side and wait for me to step out of my truck.

"Hey, guys. Miss me?" I ask, reaching down to pet them both before I turn my gaze back to Claire. She's so beautiful that she literally takes my breath away, with her long, chestnut hair pulled back in a loose braid, her amber eyes framed by her dark lashes, and her robe falling open just enough for me to see my boxer shorts hugging her hips.

I can't look away from her as I close in the distance between us, and her lips tilt up when I trip over the dogs circling at my feet. By the time I stop a few inches in front of her, my chest is already heaving with the effort it takes to stabilize my heart. But it's all in vain, because the second she latches onto my shirt and drags me in for a kiss, I know this is the way I want to go out.

My hands curl around her jaw as I savor her warmth, her woodsy scent, her smooth skin beneath my palms. I don't think I could ever grow tired of this, but she pulls away much too soon.

I watch as she licks her swollen lips and twists the cord of my scapular around her finger. She smiles again when a growl rumbles within my chest.

"Hi," she breathes, still close enough for it to ghost over my face.

"Hi," I say on an exhale.

"I guess I missed you, too," she admits, prompting a silly grin.

"I missed you more," I say, blinking lazily and staring at her mouth.

"Rowan?"

"Hmm?" I'm not sure what she's going to ask of me, but whatever it is, the answer is going to be a resounding and enthusiastic *yes*.

"I think I might be in love with you."

My stomach dips low, and I struggle to regulate my heart again. "Hmm?"

A lovely flush spreads over her cheeks. "I said I love you," she repeats, tugging on the cord around my neck. I groan and move my hands to cup her backside, scooping her up and guiding her legs to wrap around my waist.

"And I love you more," I rasp before I stagger inside and wait for the dogs to follow before shutting the door behind us.

monday

5:58 AM

ROWAN

Good morning, beautiful.

CLAIRE

Good morning. How was your run?

Fine. It would have been better had it started and ended at your place …

CLAIRE

ROWAN

We both know you love it.

CLAIRE

Unfortunately, I do.

ROWAN

I miss you.

CLAIRE

Miss you more.

ROWAN

Heads up, but my sister thinks her surprise party is a regular dinner, and she wants me to invite you as my plus one.

CLAIRE

What did you say?

ROWAN

At first I told her I had plans that night, but she gave me her big-eyed, sad look.

CLAIRE

Of course she did.

Don't tell me you ruined the surprise …

ROWAN

I tried reminding her that you'd just gone out with another guy, but that didn't work, either. So I eventually admitted I'm just too chicken to ask you to be my date.

CLAIRE

She's going to hate me now!

ROWAN

I was trying to stick to the truth. And you know Daisy loves you … almost as much as I do.

CLAIRE

Nice save.

I still can't believe the news hasn't gotten back to her yet. I keep waiting for her to ask about your special delivery at work.

ROWAN

I think Loren's been telling everyone to keep it quiet until after the party. Daisy must have talked to her about trying to set us up.

CLAIRE

And I thought you'd quit all that lying and scheming …

ROWAN

But I'm only telling fibs of omission, and I'm doing it for a good reason.

CLAIRE

So you are actually afraid to ask me out?

ROWAN

Maybe … just a little.

CLAIRE

It's okay if you're not ready for everyone to see us together. I get it.

ROWAN

I'm worried you're not ready for that. And it's okay if you aren't. I promised we'd do this at a pace that's comfortable for you.

CLAIRE

Are you really prepared to face your family and everything they'll have to say about us?

ROWAN

I am very much looking forward to rubbing our official-adjacent relationship in everyone's faces.

CLAIRE

Then is this your way of asking me to be your date for the party?

ROWAN

No, hang on, you deserve better.

Daphne Claire Bergeron, would you do me the honor of being my date for my sister's surprise party this weekend?

(I'm on my knees right now, if it helps.)

CLAIRE

Hmm. Pics or it didn't happen …

claire

"IT'S JUST our friends and family, right?" Rowan reaches over the console of his truck to curl his hand around mine when I let out a weighty exhale.

I probably shouldn't be this nervous over the prospect of looking romantically involved with him when we've been behaving very romantically together, at least for the past few days. But I can't shake the voice in my head telling me I'm not the right woman for the job, even though my heart seems to think I am.

"You must not have heard everything your sisters said about me last time," I remark, intending it to be a joke. But I feel guilty as soon as his expression falls.

"I'm sorry again about that. I know it's not much of a consolation, but I don't think any of them meant it personally. They would have vetted any woman I brought home after thirty-plus years of being single," he reassures me, squeezing my hand.

"They weren't wrong, though," I mumble.

"Yes, they were," he insists. "And I'll prove it to you, as soon as you're ready."

"What do you mean?" I ask cautiously.

"I promised to keep my long-term plans on the back burner for now, but I am all set to crank the heat up as high as you can handle it. All I need is a green light."

My lips twitch with amusement at the same time my stomach flutters with anticipation. "I'm starting to rethink my decision to use the L-word. You're letting it go to your head."

He lifts my hand to his mouth for a kiss, ignoring my protest. "Admitting you were wrong will be the hardest part. After that, I'll make sure you never regret saying yes."

"I'm much more worried you'll be the one with the regrets," I mutter.

"That could never happen," he declares.

"And what about five or ten or even twenty years down the road, when you have to deliver the millionth baby that isn't yours?" I retort. "Are you sure you won't care what your family says then?"

"If I can't have children with you, then I'm not meant to have them," he says simply. "But I'm not worrying about something we haven't even tried."

I roll my eyes. "And we can't try until it's too late."

"Too late for what? Should I be looking into a prenup in case our wedding night isn't up to your standards?"

I groan and tug my hand back. "We're not even supposed to be talking about getting married."

"You brought it up first this time," he points out smugly. "But since we're on the subject, you should know that if and when I ask you to marry me, it'll be because I want to spend the rest of my life with you and not simply because I expect you to have my children."

I scoff. "This from the same guy who claims he wants marriage and family more than anything."

"And you haven't been pretending you don't want those things just as badly as I do because you're afraid of getting let down again?"

"No," I pout, because we both know he's at least partially right.

His brow lifts. "Are you sure?"

"I'm not afraid of getting let down."

"I love you, Claire," he begins softly, taking my hand again. "And if you can't tell by now, there's nothing I wouldn't give you. If babies don't come easy, we'll find another way."

My chin still trembles at the thought of disappointing him. "You don't understand how much it hurts to get your period month after month, to fail at something that comes so naturally to everyone else," I tell him, my voice small.

"No," he sighs. "I can't imagine how that feels, and I can't guarantee it won't happen this time around. But I can promise you'll never face anything alone again."

"It's too much. I can't expect you to console me every time I let you down," I whisper, surprised at myself for getting the words out. I cast a furtive glance his way and find him smiling.

"I would be the failure if I let you go on thinking that," he replies gently. "The only way you could let me down is by not letting me in, and you've already exceeded my expectations. I know it took a lot of courage for you to share all that, but I'm grateful you did. And I'm proud of you."

"Thank you for making me feel safe," I say with a shrug, stifling a smile of my own.

"You know, I'm beginning to think I've finally cracked the code. You don't seem to mind talking about your feelings as much after a few kisses and a dangerous line or two," he teases, referring to the twenty minutes we spent making out on the couch before we came here.

I click my tongue, even though my cheeks heat at the reminder. "I'm not that simple. But if you ever need my social security number or my blood type, you should probably start by trying some of those things you whispered in my ear earlier this afternoon."

"Thanks for the tip," he says, a wide grin splitting his face. "Should I ..."

"Only if you want *Tante* Verna's secret rum cake recipe," I mutter. But I can't stop myself from snickering, even as he leans in to press a kiss to my lips.

"Come on, Claire Bear," he says, resting his forehead against mine. "We've got a surprise party planned by Landry Reed to attend."

"Oh, Bingo!" I straighten and call out. "That square was right beside 'falling for a thirty-something-year-old virgin' on my card for this year."

He snorts and kisses me again before he comes around to get my door, and we hold hands as we amble down the road to Loren and Blake's house.

Rowan's parents are the first ones to greet us, and they don't seem scandalized or even surprised by our more intimate demeanor. His mom smiles knowingly when he pulls away from her embrace and immediately clasps my hand again, but she doesn't ask any questions.

The rest of the LaFleur clan seems more eager to speculate about our relationship status, though. Magnolia watches as I reach up to wipe some of the lipstick I smudged over Rowan's neck earlier, and he meets her scrutiny with an assertive gaze, staring her down until she turns away.

"What's that about?" I whisper.

"Nothing I can't handle," he replies cooly, and he's so incredibly sexy that I have to talk myself out of sneaking him into another room to reapply some of those lipstick stains.

Oh, hell. There's no reason I *can't* do that, is there?

I trail a finger down his chest. "Are you my bodyguard now?"

"Your bodyguard?" he asks, blinking.

"I need to find the ladies' room. Care to escort me, in case any mean girls try to corner me on the way?"

He smirks when he catches on and glances around the room for an escape route, but Loren finds us before we can slink off.

"Hey, you two. Glad you could make it ... *together*," Loren says, bouncing her eyebrows suggestively as she switches one of her twins to the other hip. "How's that soft launch going?"

"Trying to keep it soft," I mumble, and Rowan cocks an eyebrow, making Loren snort, and I suppress a smile as I continue. "I don't want to steal the birthday girl's thunder, but it seems like there's a spotlight on us."

"They'll get over it by the time Daisy arrives," she reassures me before she scurries off to her hostess duties.

Blake follows with the other twin in tow, stopping to shoot me a wink as he mumbles an aside that makes Rowan blush, and we earn an appreciative nod from JD and a 'that's what I thought' look from Tenley.

"Oh, they're here," one of Daisy's sisters shouts from near the window, and Loren pulls up the doorbell camera on the living room TV as everyone takes their places. Rowan moves in closer and grins at me before he looks up at the live feed of Daisy and Landry climbing down from his Jeep.

"You know what would make this an even better birthday dinner?" Daisy muses, her voice slightly muffled. Loren turns the volume higher so everyone can hear.

"What's that, Blondie?" Landry asks, their voices ringing out more clearly now that they're closer to the camera's microphone.

"If my stupid brother and my dumb-dumb friend would stop pretending they aren't in love and just admit how badly they want to be together, so they could have joined us tonight without it being awkward."

My stomach dips and Rowan stiffens beside me, but he doesn't say anything. And I don't dare bring my eyes up to see anyone's reaction.

Landry chuckles. "At least he's willing to admit he loves her, despite the way things started."

Daisy gasps and stops short. "Did he really say he's in love with her?"

"Yep." Landry urges her onward.

"Ugh, that makes it even worse! You can already cut the sexual tension with a knife every time they're in the same room. I guess it's a good thing they didn't actually sleep together the night they met, especially since she was still technically married, but I'm afraid Rowan's just torturing himself at this point," Daisy continues as she reaches the door. "How long can one man hold on to his virginity when he's actively throwing himself in the face of temptation?"

And, just like that, we've been outed in front of all our friends and his family.

I should probably ask Loren to turn off the camera feed, but my eyes dart over to check Rowan's expression instead. It's blank, and I watch his chest rise and fall as he continues staring up at the TV. I brace myself for the worst when I hear a few errant snickers and giggles in the background, but he doesn't move.

"Give him a break," Landry replies. "Forcing yourself to stay away from the woman you love takes a whole lot of willpower. Especially when she's actively trying to lure you into bed."

Daisy clicks her tongue and elbows him in the ribs, and my own face heats when Rowan's gaze flickers over to me. His shoulders relax, and he shoots me an apologetic smile, to my relief.

"You don't need to knock. Lo said we could let ourselves in," Daisy tells Landry when he lifts his knuckles to the door.

"It's so adorable how you trust my sister not to purposefully set us up to walk in on her and Blake the Snake getting freaky in the living room," he says, rolling his eyes and following through with the knock.

"We haven't exactly been any better in front of my brother," Daisy points out.

"Maybe that's why he's always running off to Claire's, then. He got tired of hearing us put in the work to make this little bean." Landry slips a hand over Daisy's belly and kisses her neck, and she grins proudly.

There's a chorus of gasps among the clatter of a remote hitting the ground when Loren drops it to clutch at her chest. It takes me a second to realize I'm doing the same, torn between the joy I feel for my friends and the ache of my own jealousy.

"She's *pregnant*?" Loren asks, directing the question at Rowan, and he shrugs and shakes his head in confusion. She looks to Tenley next, who bites her lip and sidesteps to hide behind her husband.

I reach out to intertwine my fingers within Rowan's, and he turns to smile at me again as he gives my hand a squeeze. But before either of us can say a word, Loren flings open the front door and screams, "YOU'RE HAVING A BABY?!"

A few seconds pass while Daisy stands there looking completely bewildered and Landry glares at his sister in annoyance, then everyone joins in with a disjointed chorus of "Surprise," "Congratulations," and "Happy Birthday."

Daisy's expression shifts as she takes it all in, and she beams up at Landry. "Did you do this?"

He smirks down at her. "Maybe."

"La-*aan*," she intones and throws her arms around his waist. "Best. Birthday. *Ever*!" she declares, pulling away abruptly when she hears her voice echoing over the video feed.

"What's that?" Landry asks gruffly.

"We were watching for you on the doorbell cam," Loren explains as Blake comes over to join her.

Daisy's face pales. "So you were all listening to our conversation just now?"

"If you mean the one where you said you're having a freaking baby, then yes!" Loren cries out.

"Crap on a cracker!" Daisy squeals before covering her mouth with both hands.

"Surprise, I guess," Landry adds sarcastically, and Loren wraps them both up in a hug as best as her small arms will allow.

Daisy leans down to whisper something to Loren, who glances our way before she swallows hard and nods.

"Oh, goodness," Daisy says hoarsely and mouths an "I'm sorry" in our general direction.

But I can't offer my congratulations or even acknowledge my friend's apology, not with her brother curling his arm around my back so possessively.

Daisy's eyes light up. "Wait, are you guys ..."

I expect Rowan to look somewhat anxious, but he's already grinning at me. "Unofficially?" he ventures, just loud enough for everyone to hear.

I shrug. "Might as well make it official-ish after that."

"Was that a proposal, Claire Bear?" he dips his head to murmur into my ear, and I snort and attempt to push him away. But he brushes his lips over my neck instead, making my cheeks heat and triggering a rumble of commentary across the room. At least most of the faces currently gawking at us are smiling ones, anyway.

I shoot Loren a look, and I'm grateful when she seems to understand my unspoken request.

"That's great and all," she calls out, gesturing in our direction before turning to Daisy, "But can we get back to the part when you said you were pregnant? Or better yet, when we were all forced to listen to your husband brag about your baby-making activities. *Blech*." She punctuates it with a nudge in Landry's side, and he rolls his eyes.

"We weren't going to say anything for a while longer, but ..." Daisy glances back at Landry, who's wearing a silly smile of his own now.

As if that's not enough to make my eyes water, Rowan tightens his grip around my waist as he sniffles beside me. I watch as he stares at Daisy and Landry, joy and admiration clear in his features. He closes his eyes, I assume to fend off the tears, but when his lips begin to move, I realize exactly what he's doing. I wait for him to finish before pinching his arm. He winces and looks down at me questioningly.

"I'm sorry," he mumbles, shaking his head and drying his eyes on his sleeve. "Charge it to my man card."

"Were you just praying for them?" I ask, ignoring the rest. He smiles sheepishly but doesn't deny it, and I lean up to press a kiss to his lips.

Rowan holds me there, but a light cough keeps me from going back for more. I pull away to find we've been surrounded by most of his sisters, as well as his sister-in-law, Naomi.

"Sorry to interrupt, but we need to borrow you for a second, Claire," Magnolia declares, her expression grave. I look to Rowan for reassurance, but he's already glaring at the lot of them.

"I'll go get us something to drink," he mumbles and gives my arm a squeeze before he saunters off, leaving me alone with them. And this time I don't have Daisy or Mrs. LaFleur to watch my blindside.

I cross my arms over my middle self-consciously. "Don't you need Rowan to stay for his own intervention?"

Maggie frowns, but Naomi smirks at me. "You missed that part, although Rowan was actually the interventionist," Naomi says, and I furrow my brow in confusion.

"We're here to apologize for the things we said at Easter," Maggie offers, somewhat reluctantly. Marigold coughs again and widens her eyes, and Maggie sighs before she adds, "And in the sister group chat."

"Oh." My shoulders droop at the realization that they've been talking as much crap about me as I feared.

"None of it was really about you, personally," Maggie continues, sounding eerily similar to Rowan earlier. "We can be overprotective of our family sometimes, and we were worried and even a bit curious after seeing how enamored Rowan seemed with you. But we were unkind and uncharitable all the same, and we hope you can forgive us and trust that we'll never gossip about you like that again."

I nod silently, willing my chin to stop trembling. What is it with all the crying lately? It's like Rowan broke the dam the night we met, and I haven't been able to corral my tears since then.

"For the record, no one said anything specifically offensive," Iris chimes in. "We only made some judgmental suppositions and assumptions, most of which Daisy immediately shot down and scolded us for saying in the first place."

"If anything, I think we've all developed a girl crush after seeing you rock a pair of overalls," Naomi affirms.

"Oh, and your beautiful tattoo sleeve," Mari adds enthusiastically. "You've actually inspired us! We're going to get a LaFleur-sister bouquet drawn up."

"They're going to let me and Cyprien's wife get one, too, don't worry," Naomi whispers.

"That's ... that's awesome," I choke out. "And thank you, for the compliments and for the apology. I'm very flattered by all of it."

Maggie sighs. "Maybe, if you like the way it turns out, you could consider adding our flowers to your mural one day."

"Yeah, I'll think about it." I bite my lip to steady it. "I mean, I'm sure I could find the space ..."

Maggie smiles, and we all relax after that, the conversation growing lighter by the time Rowan returns.

"Did you really stand up to Maggie for me?" I turn to whisper to him.

He hands me a bottle of water. "I told you I'd handle it, didn't I?"

"And I told you I don't need you to be the answer to all my problems," I say, and his shoulders droop.

He opens his mouth to apologize, but I continue before he has the chance.

"Although I must admit, I kind of like having a bodyguard, especially one so ... dangerous." I look up at him from beneath my lashes and move a little closer, and he lets out a relieved exhale when I add a "thank you."

"You know, I can still escort you to the ladies' room if you'd rather not go alone," he replies with a dimpled smirk, making me melt all over again.

claire

"UGH, MY FAVORITE," Loren moans as she takes a bite of a cookie. "Who made these?"

"They're from Caidence," Tenley replies, gesturing to her nephew and his girlfriend on the opposite end of the room. "A birthday treat for her favorite teacher, Mrs. Daisy," she adds with a conspiratorial wink.

"Hey," Loren and I both object. But Daisy beams at the compliment, just as she did when Rowan and I finally got to congratulate her and Landry on the baby a few minutes earlier. I smile at her as I pick up a cookie and take a huge bite.

"Hmm. Not bad," I observe as I chew.

"You know these have peanut butter in them, right?" Loren warns me. I cringe and hand over the rest of the uneaten cookie, and she's all too eager to accept it.

"Why does that feel illegal now?" I muse, dusting my hands off on my hips.

"Because you're in *loooove*," Daisy croons.

I nudge her, my face heating. "I guess I'd rather keep him alive, at least."

"You must like him more than that, since your peanut butter

habits only matter if you're planning on playing tonsil hockey with him later," Loren mumbles through another mouthful of cookie.

"He does get contact dermatitis, too," I quip, after which Tenley chuckles, Loren chokes on her cookie, and Daisy turns her widened eyes to mine.

"I'm kidding, Daze," I reassure her, but it doesn't help that Rowan's scratching his neck when we all glance his way.

"So Rowan has a peanut allergy?" Tenley asks.

"Yes," Daisy, Loren, and I all answer at the same time. I clear my throat and add, "a pretty severe one."

"Hmm. He's never mentioned it. I'm glad you said something," Tenley continues.

I shrug. "He's careful."

"Still, we can make the clinic safer for him. We want to keep him alive, too, since his name's going on the building and all," she explains, smiling.

I pause before taking a sip. "What?"

Tenley's eyes bug out, and she curses under her breath.

"His name is going on the building?" Daisy squeaks. "Here, in Camellia?"

"Mm-hmm," Tenley confirms, biting her lip.

"Is that why Blake mentioned helping him with some paper-work?" Loren asks.

"Um, probably," Tenley answers hesitantly.

"Wait, I thought that was about the land?" By the time Daisy adds her own question, I think I've forgotten how to breathe.

"What land?" I grind out.

"The empty plot on the other side of ours, the one that's still for sale," Daisy replies. "You know, for the little family neighborhood we're building. Landry was worried about a stranger buying it up, and he mentioned that Rowan ... But, um, you don't know about any of this, do you?"

I shake my head, my gaze already fixed on Rowan. He offers a faint smile once he notices the way we're all staring at him from across the room.

"Hold my beer," I tell Daisy and shove the bottle of water at her before I march over and snatch Rowan's hand.

"Are we going somewhere?" he asks as he lets me drag him toward the door.

"Apparently we're staying here, indefinitely," I growl and yank him outside.

It takes me a few seconds to catch my breath before I can speak. "Are you, like, moving to Camellia?"

His brow rises, and he swallows hard before he regains his nerve.

"What's it to you?" he replies, an annoying smirk playing at his lips.

I roll my eyes. "I'm not kidding, Rowan."

His expression turns serious. "Okay, then. Yes, I've decided to move here."

"Mind telling me why, since you casually forgot to mention it?"

"Because I feel like this is where I need to be." But his answer lacks the same confidence as before.

"I hope you don't think you're moving in with me."

"Wouldn't dream of it," he retorts.

"And what about your job?" I demand.

"I have a job, remember?"

I shake my head, and he sighs.

"Dr. Simms is retiring, and he and Tenley have asked me to buy him out of the practice. I'll be working as a general OB most of the time, but I don't mind. And I'll still get to see my high-risk patients in between."

My head is swimming with all this new information. "So, you're sticking around for a demotion?"

"I'm sticking around because I want to be here," he repeats.

"For me?" I ask in a small voice.

"Your presence in Camellia definitely carried the bulk of the weight in my decision, but you're not the only person I care about here."

I glower at him. "Tell me you didn't uproot your life to be closer to me, Rowan. Not this soon, and not without talking to me about it first."

He growls. "Look, I didn't exactly plan for it to happen this way, but everything started falling into place right around the same time you finally softened up to the idea of us. And I was already looking for a way out of my life in Baton Rouge, if I'm being honest. What was I supposed to do, turn down that offer in case you might feel pressured to spend more time with me?"

"Well, no, but—"

"And you're the one who told me to stop being so nice. You said you wanted a man who wasn't afraid to make you feel desired." He takes a step closer and spreads his arms, but I see his pulse throbbing in his neck. "Well, here I am. I want you, Claire. I can't live without you. And I'm not backing down."

My chest heaves. "But ... but this isn't fair!"

He turns his eyes up as he pretends to consider my claim. "Why, because I actually listened and followed your advice? Or because I'm not giving you a chance to hide from your feelings this time?"

I open my mouth to protest, then snap it shut once I realize I have no argument. He raises his brow and gestures for me to offer a rebuttal, but all I can do is cross my own arms and pout.

"Come here," he begins, reaching out to tug on my elbow. I let out a shaky exhale as he unwraps my arms and pulls me in. "I'm sorry I haven't told you about this sooner. I swear, I wanted to include you in this decision, but I was more afraid of overwhelming you or making you feel like you owed me some level of commitment you weren't ready for. And the opportunity was too good to pass up."

"And you really didn't expect your decision to change anything between us?"

"Of course not. All my hopes and dreams are pretty much riding on you taking it as a romantic gesture," he tells me with a self-deprecating smile.

"I guess this is what you meant about having all those plans on the back burner," I say dryly.

"Mostly," he admits. "I actually tried weaving it into our conversation earlier, but the longer we talked, the clearer it became that you needed to understand exactly how I feel about you first."

"You see why I've had to be so careful?" I grumble from within his arms. "This is exactly what I was afraid you'd do."

He's still smiling, though, as if he's already won. "What, call your bluff and make you consider a future with me?"

"Rowan," I begin, hesitating before I continue. "It's not that I couldn't picture us together this whole time. I just hated how much you'd have to sacrifice to make it happen."

He furrows his brow at my confession. "A career shift and an address change are nothing if it means I never have to spend my days without you."

"You would say that," I roll my eyes as I stifle a smile.

"I mean it." He takes my hand and places it on his chest before he covers it with his own, and that mixture of contentment and reassurance washes over me again. "No one has ever made me feel the way you do. You know that, right?"

My eyes flutter and I barely manage a nod.

"I'm so grateful for the past few months we've had together. You've become my best friend, my favorite person, and I don't think I could ever go back to a life without you in it," he swallows the emotion lodged in his throat. "And I realize I'm asking you to take a huge risk, but I promise it'll be different this time. I'm so in love with you, Claire, and I know this is where I'm meant to be. Here, with you."

I pull my hand back, and that inner solace disappears. "Rowan ..."

"Don't think. Just tell me what your heart is saying."

I shrug. "It says I love you, too. But—"

"Then I don't care how we got started or what it's going to take to make this work. I just know I need you in every way. I don't want anything unless I can have it with you." His eyes search mine desperately as he says it.

"I'm afraid I'm not as easy to love as you think I am," I reply, reaching up to stroke his face.

"I fell for you within the first hour I met you. By the end of that night, I knew you were my soulmate. My heart beats for you and no one else, and it always will," he tells me, putting my hand on his chest again. "I could understand if you didn't feel the same way about me, but I don't think that's what's holding you back."

I close my eyes and inhale deeply. "Of course I feel the same."

"Then why are we wasting time apart?"

"Because ... because I'm the opposite of what you need," I say, grasping at straws. But I know it's all in vain. He knows it, too.

"You are *all* I need," he corrects me, his smile growing when I let out a defeated groan. He invites me back into his arms, and I give up.

"I'd like to tell you I love you and need you, too. But I'm afraid you'll pull a ring out of your pocket or something," I mumble.

"What if I promise to get down on both knees, just the way you like it?" he returns before he dips his head and kisses me, making me hum contentedly.

"You don't really have a ring, do you?" I ask in between kisses.

"Don't make me answer that," he replies, just inches away from my mouth, and I whimper. "You're not going to hold out on me forever, are you?"

I shake my head. "Oh, no, baby. I put out, remember?"

He throws his head back in a loud guffaw, reminding me more of one of my crazy cackles than anything, and I can't help but join him.

Rowan rests his forehead against mine when our laughter dies down, and I inhale deeply, reveling in his admiration.

"Claire?"

"Hmm?"

"Don't be mad, but I also bought the plot of land beside Landry and Daisy. It doesn't have to be *ours*, necessarily. It's more of an insurance policy, just in case you'd be willing to let me fulfill your barn fantasy one day."

My lips curl up into a smile. "I guess Frankie and Oscar are going to need to get their asses in shape with all that space to roam."

He growls before he cups his hand around my jaw and brings me in for another kiss.

"Is that your EpiPen in your pocket, or are you thinking about that barn loft, too?" I ask breathlessly after we finally break apart.

He crooks an eyebrow. "Only one way to find out."

This time I'm the one who cackles.

We slip back inside the house a few minutes later, and I look at Rowan in confusion when we're greeted by cheers and applause. He smirks and hitches his thumb at the TV, which must have been broadcasting our conversation.

He opens his mouth to comment, but his expression immediately shifts, and my embarrassment is instantly forgotten once I recognize the look of fear in his eyes.

"Hey, are you okay?" I ask, stepping forward to take his hand.

He shakes his head, and his chest heaves. "No, I don't think so."

My eyes dart around the room and find everyone's attention rapt as Rowan begins hyperventilating. My pulse throbs in my ears as I brace myself for the worst again, but he doesn't make a move to run out. He simply stands there, panic-stricken, reminding me of the times he hesitated to claim me in public before.

"Are you upset?" I venture carefully.

"You ... you kissed me," he rasps, gesturing with his hands. "After ... after you ..."

"I'm sorry. I didn't know they were watching." My eyes water as he shakes his head more vehemently.

"My ... pen," he croaks, and I'm pretty sure I hear a scandalized gasp in the background when Rowan grabs my hand and shoves it down into his pocket. But understanding finally dawns on me when my fingers find the EpiPen.

"Oh, no," I mumble the second I realize I'm literally going to be the death of him. He's reacting to the peanut butter cookie I'd forgotten I'd tasted just minutes before going outside to kiss him like my life depended on it. Well, I guess *his* life is kind of depending on it now.

My instincts kick in, and I drop to my knees to uncap the syringe and jam the needle into his thigh, his gaze locking onto mine as our breathing synchronizes and eventually slows.

"Hey, I'm here," I hear Landry say from over my shoulder. Someone must have called for his help earlier.

"I'm ... okay," Rowan replies, sounding as if he has sandpaper in his throat, but his eyes never leave my face. Out of all the people in this room, including his parents, his siblings, and even his former roommate-slash-doctor-slash-emergency contact, he trusts me. He chose *me*.

He smirks down at me and strokes my cheek as if I'm the only other person in the world, as if he's the one consoling me, and I'm overwhelmed with gratitude. I shiver when Rowan brushes his thumb over my bottom lip.

"There are easier ways to get me to pray for you, you know," I mutter, and Rowan coughs out a laugh as he helps me back up to my feet.

He wraps his arms around me and presses a kiss just below my ear, and I let out a sigh of equal parts satisfaction and relief.

"Maybe," he leans in again to whisper, "but it was still worth it."

EIGHT MONTHS LATER

ROWAN

"I'M NOT SAYING NO, but we could stand to brush our teeth first," my wife murmurs when my lips find her bare shoulder. She hums contentedly as I continue pressing kisses to her skin.

"You didn't seem to mind my morning breath for the first round," I say, snaking a hand around her waist and dragging her closer so I can mold my body around hers.

"That was before I knew you had such a dirty mouth," she says in a sultry tone and arches her back in front of me.

I choke out a half-whimper, half-laugh. She claims I'm dangerous, but I'm no match for her.

"You're never gonna get me out of bed like this," I mumble and press myself against her again, and I see the way she clamps her teeth down over her lip, stifling a moan. She's self-conscious, I realize. It's her own dental hygiene she's worrying about.

"And I couldn't care less about morning breath, anyway, not when I have all this to distract me," I continue, my hands sliding down and around her thighs.

She acknowledges my reassurance with a sigh, her head lolling back onto my shoulder as she shifts her position in front of me. It's an unspoken declaration that she's no longer concerned with such worldly tasks, not when we have this small taste of heaven at our fingertips.

It hasn't even been two weeks since our wedding, but my memories of life before this are already shrouded by a fog. Seriously, what did I do with my time? What was I thinking about when it wasn't Claire? I don't know how I managed so long without her, without *this*, being able to give myself away, freely and completely, and receive the same gift in return, then lie beside her, content in the knowledge that I get to keep her forever.

I thought I'd figured out everything there was to know about Claire in the months leading up to our marriage, but I honestly think I could study her forever and never get enough. At the same time, I finally understand what it means to find my other half, to know someone better than I know myself.

Today I discovered that my wife has a favorite position. Well, not *that* kind of position, although I've definitely noticed which of those seem more advantageous for her. But she also has a default cuddle position.

Okay, so it's her *naked* cuddle position, but it's still adorable.

She turns to her side and scoots closer, then I automatically gather her hair and fan it out behind her as she nestles in beneath my arm. Her head rests on my shoulder, and her palm covers my chest, right above my racing heart. And I reach around to trace a finger over her tattoos without hesitation. It reminds me of the night we met each time.

"Can I ask you something weird?" she ventures after a few seconds.

"Always," I reply.

"Do you ever wonder what it was like for me before ... with anyone else?" she asks, her voice small.

I keep my breathing even and continue stroking her arm as usual, though I'm sure my heart betrays me. "Not while we're in the middle of it," I say, and she snorts. "But my thoughts have drifted over it a couple of times, even if I know it's dumb."

"I'm sorry you have to live with that," she whispers, curling the cord of my scapular around her finger.

"Don't be," I tell her.

She exhales before she goes on. "Do you want to hear the truth?"

"Always," I say again, and I try not to brace myself.

She tilts her face up to look at me. "It was never like this, not even close."

My chest expands with my relief, and I can't help but smile. "Not even once?"

She grins and shakes her head. "Not a single time."

"Thank you for telling me that, even though you didn't have to," I say, and she nods. "Is it my turn now?"

"Go for it," she says with a more serious expression.

"Are you afraid that I'll be upset or disappointed if you turn me down?"

Her eyelashes flutter in a way that gives me my answer before she articulates it aloud. "A little."

I frown. "I'd never get angry with you if you weren't in the mood, you know, for whatever reason."

"I know. But I understand what it feels like to be rejected, and I'd never want to make you feel that way, either. Especially after you waited so long."

"And how many times have you pushed through it so far?" I ask carefully.

She purses her lips as she thinks. "I guess that depends on what you mean by 'not in the mood.' "

"Oh." I can't help the way my frown deepens.

"There have been at least two times when you tried to initiate something while I was busy or my mind was elsewhere, but that just means I wasn't thinking of starting it first. There have been exactly *zero* times in which I was not a very willing participant by the time you planted the idea in my head," she says with a grin, and a smile immediately takes over my face. "How many times have you gone along with it for my sake?"

I pretend to consider it. "Let's see, there was that one time ..." I glance down at her as I trail off, unable to keep my lips from twitching. She huffs and pinches me in the side.

"I am *always* in the mood for you. The only thing that can knock me out of it is when you aren't feeling it for whatever reason. If you're into it, I'm into it. Every time."

"What if I made you mad first?" she poses.

"Then I'd lose an argument real fast."

"What if I got sick?"

"I'd offer you a dose of my own special brand of penicillin."

She giggles and raises her arm to sniff her armpit. "What if I hadn't showered in a day or two?"

"Didn't I just tell you twenty minutes ago that you could never turn me off?" I remind her. "I don't care if you have morning breath, hairy legs, and musty armpits. If anything, I'm a sucker for your natural pheromone smell, especially in combination with the barn hay."

She rolls her eyes and stifles a smile. "Okay, what if I had tummy troubles?"

"We both know you could literally let one rip, and I'd still be into it."

"That was a bad example, especially since you're the one who tooted on our first date," she admits.

"Look, I'd like to think of myself as a pretty hygienic guy, but I'm still a guy. Not to mention, I'm a doctor. You have no idea what it would take to gross me out."

She scoffs. "You say that now, but you haven't had to stare down the barrel of period sex yet."

We both fall silent at that, I imagine because we're thinking the same thing but afraid to say it out loud.

Hopefully we won't have to cross that bridge for a while.

I stare down at her as I graze my finger over her arm again. "I'm not afraid of a little menstrual blood, you know," I remind her after a minute, hoping she hears the double meaning behind it.

"That makes one of us," she says softly, and I reach down to tilt her chin up for a kiss, morning breath be damned.

"Is it selfish of me to say that I almost wouldn't mind a little more time to ourselves?" I confess when I pull away.

It's not something I'd have divulged outside of this context, but it's the truth. Sure, I'd been looking forward to all this physical intimacy, but it turns out that I enjoy it even more than I expected. And although a baby would be the cherry on top of an already amazing whirlwind romance, the thought has occurred to me that I could very easily make the best of things if we didn't get pregnant immediately.

She lifts one shoulder in a shrug, and I add, "Technically, we're still within our honeymoon window. And we have some lost time to make up for, right?"

"You're such a MacBook," she mutters, though she's smirking.

"Well, you know what they say, once you go Apple ..." I tease as I pull her on top of me. One of her signature laughs escapes, and I stare up at her in complete awe of the fact that I managed to make this woman my wife. I run my hands over her sides, checking again to make sure she's real.

"There's nothing I could have done to deserve you, you know."

Her smile softens. "I thought it's what you didn't do that earned all this for us."

I shake my head. "Can I say something weird?"

"Always," she declares.

"When I look at you like this, I can't imagine everything we're supposed to believe about God isn't true."

She glances down at herself, then narrows her eyes at me. "And I thought you were an ass man."

I chuckle. "I'm talking about the way I botched things up so badly for us in the beginning, yet you're still here with me right now, even though you shouldn't be. Not only did He send me the perfect wife, my soulmate, undeserving as I am, but He sent her to me at the right time, in the right place, so she'd make me a better man. Even though I'm a sinner, I've been blessed beyond my wildest dreams, and all I had to do was let God lead me. Well, He may have had to drag me at some points, but He still brought me here, to you."

She leans down and kisses me after that. "Yeah," she says, sniffling when she pulls away. "Ditto. I mean, amen, or whatever."

I laugh and wipe an errant tear from her cheek, and she leans forward to rest her head on my collarbone. But she pops up a second later to remind me that we're supposed to be getting ready for Mass by now.

"It's either get up now or skip the coffee," she says, pushing off my chest as she moves to swing her leg over me.

"Who needs coffee?" I grunt, grabbing her and holding her in place.

She smirks at me. "Coffee first, then shower."

My brow lifts when I realize it's an invitation, and I finally let her go.

I slip on my boxers and my glasses, and Oscar and Frankie are waiting to greet me when I shuffle into the kitchen. After starting the coffeemaker, I let them outside and reward their successful business venture with some of the bacon we keep on the counter for them. Then I return to our bedroom with two mugs of fresh coffee.

"We may have to chug these. I'm afraid it's later than I realized ..." But I trail off when I walk into the bathroom and see my wife crying from her place on the toilet.

"Claire?" I breathe, my heart stopping.

Her chin trembles and she shrugs, unable to meet my eyes at first.

"Claire," I repeat, softer, though I know exactly what she's going to say.

She finally looks up at me and shakes her head solemnly, and I set the hot coffee down to kneel before her.

"I'm sorry, my love," I tell her.

She inhales shakily and adjusts her robe. "Me, too."

"You have nothing to be sorry for," I insist.

"I guess it caught me off guard," she says meekly. "I hadn't expected to start so soon. I mean, my temperature only rose nine or ten days ago."

I frown. "Maybe we should check your progesterone again. That's a short luteal phase."

"I don't get it, though. I mean, my temperature actually went up a few more tenths of a degree. It usually drops the day my period starts," she laments with a sniffle, and I sit back on my heels and furrow my brow.

"I was feeling a little crampy the last day or so, but I honestly thought I was just sore … you know, from all of this," she gestures between us, and even though I shouldn't be allowing a cocky smirk to take over my face at a time like this, I can't exactly help myself. She rolls her eyes and allows it, though.

"Can I see your chart?" I ask her.

"My phone's still on the nightstand," she replies, looking confused.

"Bleeding or spotting?"

"Uh, spotting, for now."

I hum thoughtfully then move to dig around beneath the sink for a pregnancy test. "Think you've got enough left in the tank?"

She frowns. "Rowan, don't …"

"I'm serious. Trust me," I tell her, and she swallows hard and nods before she takes the box from my hands.

I return with her phone a few seconds later, just as she's setting the test strip onto the counter, and I pull up the charting app she's been using since the NFP class we accidentally took together less than a year ago.

"You're about nine days past ovulation, according to your peak day. Since we started with the little hearts a few days before that, there's a chance this is implantation bleeding. It would also coincide with this secondary temp rise," I point out, goosebumps lining my arms when I realize I could be right.

She bites her lip and stares down at the chart. "I don't want to get our hopes up, just to be disappointed."

"I know, I know. And the odds of it happening so quickly are pretty crazy. But then again, everything you've done, all the bloodwork and the hormones, it's all come out normal, right?"

She shrugs only one shoulder again, as if she's afraid to confirm what we already know to be true. "Mostly, yeah."

"It's not impossible," I add.

She gulps and reaches out for me, and I pull her down to sit in my lap on the bathroom floor. "I guess ... maybe it's time for me to learn to let go of what I can't control, to let God lead me to what He wants for us," she ventures, and I nod and kiss the top of her head.

"Don't be too discouraged if we don't get a positive result right now. It's still pretty early for an hCG spike," I say. Before I can finish the statement, though, she's already craning her neck to peer up at the test on the counter.

"Might as well wait another minute," I say with a chuckle.

But her gaze is still zeroed in on that test strip, and I watch as her face pales.

"Claire?"

Her chest rises and falls with heavy breaths, and her throat works as she continues staring.

"I ... I see it," she chokes out, making my stomach dip.

"What?"

She licks her lips. "I see the second line from here."

My eyes dart over to the counter, and I immediately know she's right. She clutches one of my hands in her own as she slowly rises and leans over the test. Sucking in a sharp breath, she grabs the test and sinks down into my lap again, and we stare at it together as I whisper a prayer of gratitude.

"Is this what they mean by God having a sense of humor?" she asks, torn between laughing and crying.

"Because He literally answered your prayers within the same minute you handed over the reins?" I say through a sniffle.

"Well, yeah. But also because ... after all these years of thinking the answer was no, He was only asking me to wait until He could knock them all out at once."

My heart skips a beat, and her bottom lip trembles as she lifts her chin for a kiss.

"Never could have guessed a virgin with a peanut allergy would be the answer to all of my prayers, either," she adds with a laugh, and I kiss her again.

We sit there so long holding one another and drying our tears that our coffee gets cold. By the time we're able to move, we barely have enough time to shower and dress before Mass.

I promise Claire that we can stop by the clinic on the way home to run a blood test, mentioning that Tenley would be glad to check her charts as well, but she says, "Not yet. It's just for us right now." Then she turns to stroke my cheek as she adds, "And not just because I'm afraid it's too good to be true, but because you're my soulmate." I can't help but agree with that and tack on a few reminders of how much I love her.

I do pull the doctor card on her, though, and require that she at least sneak in to check her progesterone levels tomorrow, just in case. She also insists on taking another at-home test before we go, a digital one this time, but we get the same result. It seems to satisfy her and make her a jittery mess at the same time.

"Guess I should shop for a new truck now," I think aloud as I open the passenger door for her.

Claire clicks her tongue. "Oh, now he wants to be comfortable."

"Aren't you going to—"

"Touch my Bronco and find out," she interrupts me to say. "Community property, my ass."

I snort out a laugh and reach over to hold her hand on the way.

"You know you'll never be able to keep this a secret, right?" I say as we drive up at church and spot Landry's Jeep in the parking lot.

"Of course I can." Her eyelashes flutter wildly, and she glares at me when I point it out. "You're the one with the silly grin. I'm sure you're just itching to announce that you're going to be a daddy in a certain golf-buddies group chat," she argues, shoving me playfully, but her cheeks flush with the prettiest shade of pink when I bring her hand up to my mouth for a kiss.

"Never been more proud or excited, even if you count that time I needed an epinephrine shot right after everyone saw *you* eating a peanut butter cookie," I drawl, pressing my lips to her knuckles and making her simper.

"You're amazing, you know, the answer to all of my prayers, and then some. I couldn't have asked for anyone more perfect for me," I remind her after a while.

"Are you saying that because I'm pregnant, or because I did that thing you like this morning ... twice?" she muses.

I heave out a sigh, not even caring about the silly look on my face anymore. "Well, that, too. But mostly because you're my soulmate."

"I've already used that one today," she replies. "But you haven't said anything about my butt yet."

"You didn't let me finish," I protest. "You see, I used to have this one really, really spicy fantasy about bumping into my soulmate in the most unlikely circumstances, then marrying her and making her the mother of my children—"

And that's when she cuts me off and drags me in for a kiss.

---

acknowledgments

This novel was written with the intention of bringing glory to God and highlighting His greatest gifts—His infinite love and mercy. Let us remember to ask for His grace and to treasure the sacraments on our own paths to holiness, as well as to invoke the power of prayer and the intercession of the Blessed Mother and all the Saints.

To my husband—I could never put into words how proud I am to call you my soulmate. I love you. Thank you for everything you do to support me as a writer, but most of all, for helping me grow in holiness.

To my amazing children and grandchild, especially my beautiful daughter, E, who holds it down for me and is truly the real MVP, my parents/biggest cheerleaders, especially mom, L, and my sister, A, who are always willing to help and support me, and the rest of my extended family—thank you for your patience and your encouragement. You are my greatest blessings, and your support means the world to me. I love you all so much.

To my awesome cover designer and author bestie, Cindy R—I'm so grateful for this journey, especially because it brought me your friendship. I keep saying this, but I couldn't have gotten through this plot without you. I love you.

To bfff Kait—Jeepers, Fred! Thank you for coming in clutch, as always. The editing was top notch on this one. I could go on and on, but I seriously would never have published a single book without you. You are truly cultured celery powder, and I love cake. Also, remember when you won first place at that book trivia game at TN LitCon?

To my friends, family, and coworkers—especially Kate L, Emily C, RG, ST, Maci, Kim M, and Allie M, as well as Claire M and the

'Fettes, thank you for your input and your support. I am so grateful to you all for your guidance, your friendship, and your prayers.

To my alpha and beta readers—especially Amber (my favorite part-time Author Event PA/Beta Reader/Lady Ag Teacher Consultant), Julie D (my unofficial Spiritual Director for this novel), KL Hester, Audrey C, India & Grayson (my author friends), Joanna, Laura N, Shannon, Krissi, and anyone else I may have missed—I can't tell you how much I appreciate your input. From offering livestock show tips to redemption arc interventions and theological realignments, you have all made this story so much better than I could have hoped for.

And to all my readers, especially my Camellia Crewe, Book Launch Team, ARC readers, all my supporters from back home, and the Bookstagram/BookTok Community—thank you *so very much* for your time and energy. I am truly grateful for your support and reviews. I hope you each get something from this, at least a few laughs and a character crush, but especially a reminder that God loves you and is always waiting to embrace you with open arms.

about the author

A former high school literature teacher from South Louisiana, Marie Veillon is still learning to balance her ridiculous accent, Cajun-French—inspired vocabulary, and horrible speaking syntax with writing humorous stories and creating characters and situations relatable enough to make readers forget they aren't real. She enjoys reading books about her Catholic faith and rom coms with guaranteed HEAs, watching football, fangirling, and spending time with her amazing family.

Thank you for reading and reviewing!
marievwrites.com
@marievwrites

instagram.com/marievwrites

threads.com/@marievwrites

marievwrites.substack.com

facebook.com/marievwrites

tiktok.com/@marievwrites

bookbub.com/authors/marie-veillon

goodreads.com/marie_veillon

amazon.com/author/marieveillon

lagniappe
...A LITTLE SOMETHING EXTRA

Sign up for my newsletter and join the Camellia Crewe Facebook group to receive updates and announcements, including free content and the latest news regarding the next installments in the Camellia Rom-Com Series!

Need more Claire + Rowan?
Get a Bonus Epilogue, a Cajun Glossary,
NFP Resources, and more at
marievwrites.com